CW00410211

THE WITCH'S S...
By
CEANE O'HANLON-LINCOLN

A Sleuth Sisters Mystery
Book seven in the bewitching series

A Magick Wand Production
"Thoughts are magick wands powerful enough to make anything happen– anything we choose!"

This book is lovingly dedicated to time-travelers everywhere ~
And to my husband, Phillip R. Lincoln, who bought me my ticket.

Warm gratitude and blessings bright and beautiful to:
My husband Phillip,

And to my muses Beth Adams; Carrie Bartley; Janet Barvincak;
William Colvin; Ron Enos; Glen Gallentine;
Renowned High Priestesses Joyce Henderson and
Kelly M. Kelleher;
Kathy Lincoln; Marie Lorah; Jean Minnick; Robin Moore;
Madeleine Stephenson;
And songstress, poet and author extraordinaire,
Rowena of the Glen~

For all the reasons they each know so well.

A special, heartfelt thank-you to Rowena of the Glen/
Rowena Whaling
For the permission to use the lyrics to "Pagan Lover"
From her magickal album *Book of Shadows*

And in loving memory of my dear friend, Sandra Leigh Bolish,
One of the most interesting people I've ever known.

THE WITCH'S SECRET
By
Ceane O'Hanlon-Lincoln

A Sleuth Sisters Mystery

The Sleuth Sisters Mystery Series:
~By Ceane O'Hanlon-Lincoln~

In this paranormal-mystery series, Raine and Maggie McDonough and Aisling McDonough-Gwynn, first cousins, are the celebrated Sleuth Sisters from the rustically beautiful Pennsylvania town of Haleigh's Hamlet. With their magickal Time-Key, these winning white witches are able to unlock the door that will whisk them through yesteryear, but who knows what skeletons and dangers dangle in the closets their Key will open? One thing is certain– magick, adventure, and surprise await them at the creak of every opening door and page-turn.

Ceane crafts each of her *Sleuth Sisters Mysteries* to stand alone, though for the most surprises, it is always nice to read a series in order:
The Witches' Time-Key, book one
Fire Burn and Cauldron Bubble, book two
The Witch's Silent Scream, book three
Which Witch is Which? book four
Witch-Way, book five
The Witch Tree, book six
The Witch's Secret, book seven of the *Sleuth Sisters Mysteries*: When the Sleuth Sisters travel to the "Witch City" of Salem, Massachusetts for their cousin Emerald's handfasting ceremony, their Great-Aunt Merry, the McDonough *grande dame*, gifts them an enchanted locket– infused with the most powerful magick they have ever encountered. The locket proves its worth when the Sisters return home to Haleigh's Hamlet, Pennsylvania and discover their local college campus immersed in mystery, mayhem and murder!

Careful What You Witch For, **book eight in the bewitching**

series– coming soon!
Amazon Books / www.amazon.com/amazon books
~~~

v

Also by Ceane O'Hanlon-Lincoln:

In the mood for something different– something perhaps from another time and place?
Autumn Song is a harmonious medley of short stories threaded by their romantic destiny themes and autumnal settings.

Voodoo, ghostly lovers, Native American spiritualism, and figures from the past– all interwoven in a collection of tales that will haunt you forever.

Read the stories in the order the author presents them in the book for the most surprises. *And this author hopes you like surprises!*

Each tale in this compelling anthology evokes its own special ambiance and sensory impressions. *Autumn Song is a keeper you will re-visit often, as you do an old and cherished friend.*

O'Hanlon-Lincoln never judges her characters, several of whom resurface from tale to tale. These are honest portrayals, with meticulously researched historic backdrops, intrigue, *magick*, surprise endings– and thought-provoking twists.

For instance, in "A Matter of Time," on which side of the door is the main character when the story concludes?

From the first page of *Autumn Song*, the reader will take an active role in these fascinating stories, discovering all the electrifying threads that connect them.

How many will *you* find?

Available at Amazon Books / www.amazon.com/amazon books

~~~

Ceane O'Hanlon-Lincoln's award-winning history series:
"If you haven't read this author's *County Chronicles*, then you haven't discovered how *thrilling* history can be! With meticulous research and her "state-of-the-heart" storytelling, Ceane O'Hanlon-Lincoln breathes life into historical figures and events with language that flows and captivates the senses." ~ Mechling Books

"I write history like a story, because that's what history is, a story– or rather, *layered* stories of the most significant events that ever unfolded. Each volume of my *County Chronicles* is a spellbinding collection of *true* stories from Pennsylvania's exciting past." ~Ceane O'Hanlon-Lincoln

The Witch's Secret
~ Cast of Characters ~

Raine and Maggie McDonough, PhDs– Sexy, savvy Sisters of the Craft, who *are* more like sisters than cousins. With sorcery in their glittering emerald eyes, these bewitching Pennsylvania history and archeology professors draw on their keen innate powers, making use of all their skills, experience, and magickal tools to sort out the mystery, mayhem and murder riddling Haleigh College's Valentine Fest.
Will these mystery magnets be able to clear the cobwebs of their current mystery *and* the secrets from the past connected to it?

Aisling McDonough-Gwynn– The blonde with the wand is the senior Sister in the magickal trio known, in Haleigh's Hamlet and beyond, as the "Sleuth Sisters." Aisling and her husband **Ian**, former police detectives, are partners in their successful Black Cat Detective Agency.
The Gwynns have a preteen daughter, **Meredith (Merry) Fay**, who mirrors her magickal mother. Merry was named for the McDonough *grande dame*, who resides in the "Witch City" of Salem, Massachusetts.

Aisling Tully McDonough– The Sleuth Sisters' beloved **"Granny"** was the grand mistress of Tara, the Victorian mansion where Raine and Maggie came of age, and where they yet reside. Born in Ireland, the departed Granny McDonough left her female heirs a very special gift– and at Tara, with its magickal mirrors, Granny is but a glance away.

The Myrrdyn/ Merlin Cats/ Panthèra, Black Jade and Black Jack O'Lantern– Descendants of Granny McDonough's magickal feline Myrrdyn (the Celtic for Merlin), these devoted "Watchers" are the Sisters' closest companions. Wholly *familiar* with the Sleuth Sisters' powers, desires and needs, the Myrrdyn/ Merlin cats faithfully offer moral support, special knowledge delivered with timely messages– and protection.

Cara– The ancient spirit in the Sleuth Sisters' poppet continually proves– as the witched little doll's name suggests– to be a great *friend* to Raine, Maggie, and Aisling. But will Cara's magick prove strong enough against such a multi-faceted enigma?

Thaddeus Weatherby, PhD– This absent-minded professor and head of Haleigh College's history department has an Einstein mind coupled with an uncontrollable childish curiosity that has been known to cause unadulterated mischief for the Sleuth Sisters. Thaddeus and Maggie are lovers and reunited kindred spirits.

Dr. Beau Goodwin– Raine's dashing **Beau**, soul mate, and next-door neighbor is a superior veterinarian with an extraordinary sixth sense. After all, his patients can't tell him what's wrong. Like Raine, this Starseed, too, is an empath and Old Soul. To be sure, each half of this remarkable couple creates magick in a singular way, together enkindling an utterly magickal *Raine-Beau.*

Hugh Goodwin– Beau's semi-retired veterinary father– whose acute sixth sense matches his son's– has an avid appetite for mystery novels and an astonishing aptitude for solving them that the Sleuth Sisters find absolutely "wizard."

Betty Donovan– A retired librarian, Hugh's attractive companion shares his intense love of mysteries and is fast becoming his equal in solving them.

Great-Aunt Meredith/ "Grantie Merry" McDonough– A celebrated Salem witch and the McDonough *grande dame* whose awesome magickal gifts prove invaluable to the Sisters. Grantie's magick is wholly benign.

Hannah Gilbert– The Sleuth Sisters' loyal, protective housekeeper is a fountain of homespun wisdom. Her quirky purple sneakers and garish muumuus are indicative of her colorful personality; and like many snoopy servants before her, she continues to supply information that abets and serves the Sleuth Sisters in their quests.

Eva Novak– The Gypsy Tearoom proprietress' own special brew of "Tea-Time-Will-Tell" is not the *only* sustenance this charismatic woman delivers to the Sleuth Sisters.

Kathy Wise– Distinguished throughout Haleigh's Hamlet as "Savvy Kathy," this receptionist at the Hamlet's Auto Doctor has been known to set the Sisters rolling on the path to discovery.

Sophie Miller– The owner of the delightful Sal-San-Tries café-deli. Her scrumptious **sal**ads, **san**dwiches, and pas**tries** often fit the bill for the swamped, short-of-time Sleuth Sisters.

Dr. Elizabeth Yore, PhD– This Margaret Mead figure, with her long, signature cape and tall, forked staff, can only be described as something betwixt and between an impish witch and a stern schoolmarm. As joint head of Haleigh College's archaeology and anthropology departments, Yore is forever posing questions. In any case, the haunting questions begging here are: "Who is behind Cupid's menacing arrows and the naughty cherub's poison?" And "Are the campus murders connected to a love-scorned witch's curse?"

Dr. Benjamin Wight– Braddock County's supercilious coroner unconsciously finds himself faced once again with the supernatural!

Professor Karel Hass– This mannish, gravelly-voiced, never-a-good-word-for-anyone English professor has harbored a myriad of jealousies throughout her sixty-odd years. Most of her cohorts would suggest that the "H" on her surname is silent.

Professor Ken Longbough– "Old Bull's-Eye" or "Longbow," as he is commonly known on campus, Haleigh College's longtime archery coach holds a pointed hatred for Professor Karel Hass and a quivering abhorrence of anything that smacks of Valentine traditions. Is negative baggage inciting him to target the college's Valentine Fest with heart-felt resolve and– dead-on aim?

Ron Moon– The owner and bartender of The Man In The Moon, Haleigh Hamlet's English-style pub, tips off the sleuthing Sisters when the telling refrain "That Old Black Magic" capsizes his memory bank, sending Raine and Maggie into a spin back in time to WWII England.

Jo Nosh– This café owner dishes up a heaping serving of recollections that plops the cherry on top the Sisters' harvested clues.

Dr. Rex Lear, PhD– A stickler for perfection, the imaginative head of Haleigh College's theatre department is striving to make his Valentine production of *Romeo and Juliet* the most convincing play ever staged on campus.

Professor Annabel Lee– During the college's romantic Valentine Fest, this ethereal, starry-eyed English professor is thrilled to receive a proposal of marriage from the man she adores.

Dr. Barron Whitman, PhD– The patrician head of Haleigh College's English department hails from Boston, a son of one of that city's elite families. Whitman has won several accolades that have made his family proud; however, his engagement to Professor Lee has sent his mother rushing on a chilling wind from their "kingdom by the sea" to visit the enamored couple in Haleigh's Hamlet. Will this flurry prove to be a *killing* wind for Annabel Lee?

Mildred Whitman– Barron's mother. This "Nurse Ratched" revamped to high-society dowager is determined to put a stop to her son's "unacceptable" engagement. The question begging *here* is: *How far is this overbearing mother willing to go to do that?*

Trixie Fox– A sexy vixen whose merry-go-round life is all about her graduate thesis; but for all her scholarship, this go-getting young woman has been dangerously ignoring an important life's lesson– "What goes around comes around."

Liza Berk, Sylvia Blair, and Tiffany Browne– These insolent, cheating students meet their match when they tangle with the Sleuth Sisters, and now, the "Bitchy Bees" are out for blood!

x

Gillian Shipton– This progeny of a long line of powerful Scottish and English witches is believed to have invoked a curse on the American lover who "abandoned" her in WWII England, as well as on his male descendants. Is the curse real or imaginary?

Major Tristan Lear, US 8AAF– The fighter ace who was Gillian's dashing American flyer during his stint in WWII England.

William Lear– Tristan's great-grandson has a lot to sort out.

Jill Holroyd– Gillian's descendant is in for a *reverberating* surprise.

Chief Fitzpatrick– The Chief of Police of Haleigh's Hamlet is ever amazed by the Sleuth Sisters' uncanny ability to solve a mystery.

"I don't think you really want to know if I am a good witch
or a bad witch.
I'm not *just* a witch– I'm a storm with skin!"
~ Dr. Raine McDonough, PhD

"Evil comes to all us men of imagination,
wearing as its mask all the virtues."
~ W.B. Yeats

"Careful! Careful what you *witch* for!"
~ Author Ceane O'Hanlon-Lincoln

"For all you know,
a witch might be living next door to you right now."
~ Roald Dahl

"I do believe in magick.
My heart is a thousand years old. I am not like other people."
~ Author Ceane O'Hanlon-Lincoln

"Any time women come together with a collective intention,
it's a powerful thing …
when women come together with a collective intention–
magick happens."
~ Phylicia Rashad

"We all have our own life to pursue,
Our own kind of dream to be weaving,
And we all have the power to make wishes come true,
As long as we keep believing."
~ Louisa May Alcott

~ Prologue ~

Known far and wide as the "Sleuth Sisters," raven-haired Raine and redheaded Maggie McDonough, cousins who shared the same surname, residence, and occupation, as well as a few other things in what could only be termed their *magickal* lives, were preparing to leave for the "Witch City" of Salem, Massachusetts. It was a cold, snowy day in mid-February. As they tucked a few last-minute things into their suitcases, their thoughts were on *mystery*, for they could keenly sense that another astonishing adventure was about to unfold in their extraordinary lives.

Last fall, in a neighboring town, they saved an ancient oak, known as the Witch Tree, from destruction. Moreover, they were successful in untangling the dark web of mystery and murder that had unfortunately attached itself to the historic tree's story, proving yet again their merit as super-sleuths.

In her woodsy-themed bedroom with its large, green-marble fireplace, Raine popped a compact, the gold lid a lion face, into the large shoulder bag she used for travel. The compact had belonged to Granny McDonough, and it was chockfull of protective energies. Twisting partway round, she checked her reflection in the tall cheval glass, turning to view herself from all angles. *I'll stop wearing black when they invent a darker color.* She smiled. *Black is my **power** color. It creates an air of mystery, is elegant, dramatic, sexy, and it crafts a barrier between me and the outside world, protecting my emotions, sensitivities, insecurities … secrets.*

The raven-haired Sister often donned Gothic attire, the style suiting her to the proverbial "T." Her Beau called her witchy chic "Raine gear."

Witches have always known that wearing black– like showering something, or someone, with water– neutralizes negative energies. Black draws in all natural energies, enhancing the strength of the witch's personal power and connection to nature.

"One with the night," the Sister chanted to her reflection in the mirror. "One with the day. One with the earth– this is the witches' way!"

Raine's trim figure was sheathed in a black body suit, topped with a vintage, black highwayman's coat that she accented with a ruffled, white flounce at the throat. The Goth gal loved witchy shoes and boots, and the ankle-high boots she chose today possessed all the witchy-woman wow she fancied. She grinned at the thought: *Women who wear black lead colorful lives.*

To complete the outfit, she fastened to a lapel the diamond magick-wand brooch that was her signature piece of jewelry, imbued with the credo "Thoughts are magick wands, powerful enough to make anything happen– anything we choose."

Down the hall, Maggie was concluding *her* final travel preparations. Stepping back from the bureau's swivel-mirror, she checked her overall appearance. Taller than Raine and fuller-figured, Maggie, like her cousin and sister of the moon, enjoyed donning vintage clothing. But unlike Raine, this vibrant redhead loved color– bright colors concordant with her passionate Scorpio nature. The green, wool, Fifties-style suit she chose for today was at once warm and attractive. Seeking the vivid purple scarf she'd set out earlier, her eyes scanned the room.

As spacious as Raine's bedchamber, this Sister's room, too, was enhanced with a substantial fireplace, though the marble here was dark red, the high-ceilinged room's palette the fiery tones of garnet and gold. Fall was Maggie's favorite time of year, and in her boudoir, it was forever autumn. "I was born in October," she liked to say, "and it is imprinted on my bones, for they ache, in the best way possible, for all things multi-hued, misty– and *mysterious*."

Maggie was busy arranging the scarf in a chunky cowl round the turtleneck of her suit's black sweater, when Raine sailed gaily into the room, carrying her suitcase and a purse slung over her shoulder.

The brunette Sister flopped down on Maggie's bed. "I hate to leave town during our college's Valentine Fest, but *no way* can we miss Cousin Emerald's handfasting ceremony."

"Not to mention that we're both in a haze of excitement over the prospect of seeing Grantie again … and receiving her promised surprises." The redheaded Sister used their affectionate title for their great-aunt, bestowed in gratitude for generosity. "With focus, the dear lady told us, on an antique, bejeweled locket that holds the *strongest* magick she ever encountered."

"I keep trying to envision it, but the protective shield around the piece must be ultra-strong. I can't image it. Remember, she said the locket's magick would be *my* special talent, as Athena, our crystal ball's, is *yours*, Mags. What's more, Grantie mentioned she also wanted to gift us with something for astral projection, since that's one of *Aisling's* fortés," she pronounced, referring to their slightly older cousin, the senior Sleuth Sister.

Raine meditated for a moment on the college's Valentine Fest. "It's such jolly fun to dress in costumes reminiscent of love and romance, while the campus is bustling with all the vendors and planned Valentine activities. This is one of the best ideas the Student Union has ever come up with, and I enthusiastically hope, with all of us pitching in, we raise a goodly sum toward the restoration of our beloved Old Main. The building's well over a hundred years old. It's time for a major facelift." She grinned, deepening the dimple in her left cheek. "I plan to dress as the Queen of Hearts. I rented the outfit from Enchantments costume shop yesterday, so I'd have it ready to wear for next week's campus fun."

"At least we won't be missing the Valentine's Dance. It was moved to the final day of the Fest, which is supposed to run to the end of the month. The Student Union will need the whole of February to reach their goal, and the fund-raising activities will culminate with the dance." Maggie glanced at her lapel watch. "We've time yet. Wait for me. I have only a few more things to toss into my bag. Thank the great Goddess that our teaching duties were confined to morning classes today." She slipped a makeup kit into her shoulder bag and began rolling a couple extra pairs of pantyhose into a lavender-scented nightie.

"I keep thinking about that errant arrow that grazed one of our students last night. A boy and girl, strolling hand-in-hand across campus at twilight, and the girl is hit with an arrow." Raine looked thoughtful. "Probably just a careless Cupid, and the student is afraid to come forward for fear of being put on probation or expelled. I *hope* it was an accident and nothing more sinister."

Maggie looked up from her chore. "Let's not program anything negative for ourselves or anyone else. Only toy bow and arrows are permitted with Cupid costumes. I can't see how anyone got a real weapon past campus security." The attractive redhead pursed her lips. "Unless ..." The rest of the thought went unspoken when Raine interposed.

"Great Merlin's beard! I dread that meeting in the Dean's office Monday morning with those troublesome students. I don't believe for one second this is their first time cheating, or even their first time getting caught. You and I both collared them in the act, independently, yet they tried to convince us that each offense was their first and to give them a chance to retake the exams. It's *obvious* they're lying. And that Liza Berk! No respect for anyone or anything. The classic spoiled brat. I don't believe I've ever encountered such an ill-bred young woman."

"Liza's the worst of the lot; that's for certain," Maggie asserted dryly. "She's a *clever* girl, though not at her books– perhaps *cunning* is a better word choice, *devilishly* cunning– with a perpetual sarcastic way of speaking. A controlling sort, or more pithily put, a *bully*, who enjoys, I think, stirring others to anger. And she seems to have Sylvia Blair and Tiffany Browne under some sort of evil spell, doesn't she? Now, where's my turquoise dress? Ah!" She placed the rolled garment in the open valise.

"The evil she casts is really quite simple," Raine replied. "Her game is to coerce her two cohorts to do something they shouldn't, after which she holds the sword of Damocles over their stupid heads. I'd wager that's been her MO with fellow students since kindergarten … no *pre*school."

"Doubtless spot-on. I've noticed that Liza's all for the boys, though boys don't appear to be at all for her. Likely that's another … what would you call it? *Fixation* she's held since kindergarten. Could be it's the reason she hangs out with the eye-catching Sylvia and Tiffany, but enough about Berk, Blair, and Browne. We'll deal with the Bitchy Bees, as you call 'em, on Monday, and *firmly*. For now, let's not allow them to ruin what we've programmed to be a perfect weekend." Again Maggie checked her watch. "Almost ready with time to spare."

"What smashing good luck for us that Latrobe Airport added a trial flight direct to Boston, and just in time for our trip!" Raine's eyes, green as any cat's, danced with mirth. "I have a witchy suspicion that our little airport's Boston route will catch on. Most convenient when we want to travel to Salem."

"One of Aisling's best ideas, and a powerful spell it was. Saves us driving to Pittsburgh," Maggie returned. "We'll all fit easily in Hugh's Suburban. It seats nine."

"Let's see," Raine began, counting off on her fingers, "Beau and I, you and Thaddeus, Aisling, Ian and Merry Fay, Hugh and Betty… yep, there're nine of us. Oh, incidentally, I booked Besom Limo again. They were good to us last trip. The driver will pick us up at Logan International and drive us the scenic, seaside route from Boston to Salem. Besom will carry us to the rehearsal dinner this evening at the Avalon's Secret Garden, and again to the hall's Camelot Room tomorrow for the handfasting ceremony. Cousin Sean will pick us up in his rental on Sunday morning to visit with Grantie before we have to leave for the airport. She made it clear that, and I quote, she wants '... only the Sleuth Sisters at the cottage for a confidential audience.'" The Goth gal brought her graceful, little hands together. "I can't wait to speak with Grantie privately; I'm so excited about the forthcoming surprises!"

Maggie responded with a brisk nod. "My witch's inner voice is telling me that soon we'll be needing the strongest makickal tools we can muster."

"I know, Mags. I've an unsettled feeling, based on nothing I can put my finger on, just those butterflies Granny used to talk about. But we won't stress it; we'll handle whatever's coming. People don't call us the 'Sleuth Sisters' for nothing."

The three Sisters were often the topic of discussion in Haleigh's Hamlet. Indeed, there was something about the phrase "the three Sisters" that conjured all sorts of witchy images, the words themselves *magickal.*

When tackling a new mystery, it was the Sisters' custom to throw themselves into spirit-boosting pep talks, for it quite bolstered their confidence. "In keeping with the Great Secret," Raine touted, touching her signature brooch, "the *real* magick is believing in oneself."

"I just hope," Maggie twirled a strand of dark-red hair in a vague, pensive gesture, "there won't be any–"

"Uh, UH," Raine cut in swiftly, lifting her hands in the signal for interference, "we'll handle whatever comes."

"And *I'll* handle tings here!" a tiny little voice with a big bravado enthused nearby.

The Sisters turned their heads to see their poppet materialized on Maggie's bed. The feisty Cara was bestowed on the Sleuth Sisters by a former Hamlet enigma, an eighteenth-century hermit and fellow sister of the moon, whose violent murder the Sisters solved when they time-trekked to the perilous eighteenth-century Pennsylvania frontier.

Approximately eleven inches tall, the doll's head bore a mop of what used to be, over two centuries earlier, bright-red wool yarn for hair, faded now to a pale orangey hue. The rag-stuffed head and body were fashioned of a coarse, age-darkened muslin. Two faded, but still faintly visible, black ink dots represented the eyes; and the mouth, smeared undoubtedly by countless childish kisses over the tumbled years, was crooked, giving the evident impression of a *mischievous* grin.

As it were, the poppet Cara was inhabited with the ancient spirit of a formidable Irish sister of the moon, an entity whose powers the good Sisters were grateful to have on their side.

A green vest, the design in the cambric long claimed by Time, was pinched in at the doll's waist by a narrow, rope-like cord. The uneven skirt was pinked and somewhat tattered, the purple-ish color nearly gone the way of history; and though the poppet sported no shoes, the ink-blackened feet were shaped as though it did, the soles turning up at the toes and evoking the notion of a leprechaun.

"Merry Meet," the Sisters voiced.

"Merry Meet," came the reedy reply.

Raine blew the haunted ragdoll a kiss. "We'd like for you to house-and-cat sit while we're in Salem, Cara, if you please. Hannah and her hubby Jim will be staying here whilst we're gone, and it'll be your job to keep the cats in line. I especially don't want them darting out an opened door. Hannah wants to get a jump-start on the spring cleaning, and Jim will see to the stable and the horses."

"Iffin I kin git a wor-rd in, sure 'n I'll watch over tings, puss," the ragdoll retorted to Raine, its manner seeming to heighten the wily grin. The witched little doll's speech was a lilting Irish brogue with shades of the Pennsylvania frontier whence she came. "By the bye, lass, will Aisling be goin' t' Salem wit ya?"

"She will," Maggie answered, turning to the dresser to apply protection balm on her wrists. All three Sisters wore magickal balms and oils of their own creation in lieu of commercial perfumes.

Raine stood to dip into Maggie's defense balm, touching it to pulse points. "Aisling's always busy with clients, but *no way* would she miss Emerald's handfasting, especially since we've been personally summoned by Grantie Merry." Raine's pouty lips curved upward. "And when we're away, see you keep out of mischief, poppet." She truly loved Cara and occasionally fretted over losing her. "But you're a wizard guardian; I'll say that for you. Wiz— zard!"

Before Cara could respond, Maggie, with head cocked in wistful attitude, replied, "When you utter your pet expletive, it never fails to remind me of our *Hamlet's* shadowy Wizard." Scrappy remembrances wafted across her mind. *I wonder if we'll ever discover who the mystifying advisor to our dear sisters, the Keystone Coven, really is?*

A kittenish moue manifested on Raine's face, as she looked up from checking the contents of her purse. "Now *there's* a mystery!" the Sister exclaimed, having seized her cousin and sister of the moon's thought. "The *Coven* doesn't even know who he is. Increasingly, it appears that might be the one puzzle we *never* crack. Sometimes I think it's Thaddeus, other times Hugh, and then," her voice dropped, "there are *fervent* times, I'm convinced the Wizard is my Beau."

Maggie came back with "Well, darlin', in my opinion, Beau, Hugh, and Thaddeus are each suspect. You know what finely honed sixth senses Beau and Hugh possess, the pair of them. It's why they're excellent veterinarians. After all, their patients can't tell them what's wrong. As for Thaddeus," a Mona Lisa smile transformed her cheery expression to mysterious, "well now, he's a *recurrent* wizard. Every little thing he does creates magick ... *magick with unbridled passion.* To quote Grandpa McDonough, 'Genius is talent set aflame.'"

"All we and the Coven are certain of is that their advisor resides in our Hamlet. The Keystone sisters don't even know if the Wizard's a man or a woman, never having met their mentor in person. Over the years, the Coven has referred to this enigmatic advice-giver as the 'Wizard,' but, like we've said before, it could well be a *sister* of the Craft, a solitary witch who prefers anonymity."

"Indeed it could." Maggie tucked a pair of heels into the suitcase. "I've entertained the thought that the joint head of our college's archaeology and anthropology departments is a good candidate for the Coven's covert guru. With her long, signature cape and tall, forked staff, Dr. Yore– wise crone that she is– is betwixt and between an impish witch and a stern schoolmarm. No one could teach her curriculum and not believe that real magick *does* exist. And as we've both reasoned," Maggie said abruptly, "just because the Coven sisters refer to this unknown entity as their *senior* advisor, due to the steady stream of wisdom he or she imparts, it doesn't necessarily mean the so-called Wizard is a person of golden years. Why, for all we know–"

Raine opened her mouth to interject something when *both* Sisters were sharply silenced.

"Whist!" the ragdoll shrieked, throwing her little muslin arms into the air. "Iffin' I tole y' once-st, I done tole ya a hundred times– some tings aire meant t' be a mystery. Save yer sleuthin' f'r whaire it's needed."

Raine swooped Cara up, holding the doll out in front of her. "If Granny were here, she'd say in her own sweet brogue that you, my wee friend, are a corker."

"Granny *is* here, me darlin's!" The words issued with sudden force from the cheval glass in a corner of the bedchamber.

The Sisters and Cara whirled about to find the familiar image in the tall mirror. "Granny," they echoed in unison and with energy, though not with much surprise, "in peace and love we welcome you."

Granny– the cloud of soft white hair in its loose bun, adorned today by an aurora borealis crystal snood; the unlined, pink-and-white face; the venerable demeanor– so angelic and profoundly loved by the two young women poised before the looking glass with their poppet.

Gazing at the shimmering image, the Sisters noted that Granny was wearing Elder's attire, the long gown and cape dazzling white and sparkling with stardust of silver and gold. They remained quiet, for they knew the *grande dame* could be called away any second to the important Celestial conference in the offing.

"I'm here 'n gone in a tick, so let me have yer full attention. Short 'n to th' mark: Enjoy y'rselves at Salem, f'r whin y' return, you'll have a heap o' trouble t' sort out."

As was often their habit, Raine and Maggie responded in sync, "We're not surprised. Mystery and mayhem again, will it be?"

"Indaid. I sensed you already knew, but sure 'n I wanted t' alert you that a new challenge is on the horizon, to which, I am sor-ry t' say, I must add *murder* to th' mix. A double-barreled mystery, as yer grandda' wud say."

The Sisters' faces reflected dismay.

"You know b' now," Granny hurried on, "you can do whativer ya set yer minds to. *Together* you can, and you will. *Tré neart le chéile– together strong!* Now heed me wor-rds. Whin y' return home, keep yer eyes 'n ears open. T' nip a phrase I larned fr'm one iv our new messengers– just got his wings; former military lad–

'Keep yer head on swivel!'" Granny tilted her head and shook a finger at the Sisters. "Make use of ivery protection I taught ya, and I taught you well. As our dear Mr. Yeats once cautioned: 'A pity beyond all tellin' is hid in the heart of love.'"

When a baffled Raine opened her mouth, Granny lifted the pointing finger for continued silence. "I'll answer the question you'll be askin' me in th' near future, in case I'm in conference whin ye raise it later. Will it be an abuse of the Time-Key t' draw on it f'r a reason that differs from its use in th' past? The answer will sing out in yer own hearts, though I'll address it now. You will *need* to make use of th' Key to save an innocent from the fate of his fathers."

With that, Granny vanished from the mirror, after blowing a kiss, that reached Raine, Maggie, and Cara in the sparkling form of gold and silver glitter that spun round and round them, making them feel all warm and fuzzy– *and loved.*

"Bless my besom, Mags, we really are *mystery magnets.* Grab your things and let's go downstairs. We might have just enough time for a bracing cup of tea before everyone gets here, and we have to leave for the airport." Raine stood, slinging her shoulder bag over an arm and picking up her single suitcase. Turning, she hurriedly plopped Cara on Maggie's bed, against the pillows, giving the faded yarn head a little pat, which brought a champagne giggle from the poppet.

The Sisters always traveled as light as possible, each limiting herself to a large purse and one small valise that would easily fit in an overhead compartment. They never liked to check their baggage, for most of their things were cast with strong magick.

Seizing her bags, Maggie followed her cousin and sister of the moon to the stair landing.

Starting down the steps, the Goth gal repeated thrice, more to the universe than to Maggie, "We've bested evil before. We can do it again, and that's for sure!"

Raine was referring to their vanquishing of the ancient *Macbeth* curse from Whispering Shades, the Hamlet's "little theatre in the woods," that resulted in the most terrifying of battles. Besides ousting a bane of evil from their town and popular theatre, they managed, in the bargain, to soothe Whispering Shades' resident ghost.

As the pair swept down the ornately carved staircase, they passed the framed oil painting, mounted on the stairwell wall, that Maggie had done of the famous Irish dolmen Poulnabrone, the prehistoric set of huge stones resembling a portal to the netherworld. A gifted photographer and artist, Maggie executed the oil painting from a photograph in which she'd captured the setting sun just as it flashed, star-like and centered, beneath the horizontal slab of the great standing stones.

Several years prior, Raine and Maggie made the most significant journey of their lives– a trip to mystical Ireland, where they happened upon more than they had bargained for. There, they sought and found answers to the haunting questions connected to a very special quest of their own– and to a series of murders and legendary lost jewels at Barry Hall, a noble, old estate in County Clare. It was in Ireland where, after years of research, the pair ferreted out the magickal Time-Key, which, when properly activated, whisked them through the Tunnel of Time to yesteryear– to *any* year that they encoded.

Maggie's eyes drifted to the stair landing's tall stained-glass window that depicted the McDonough coat-of-arms with its fierce wild boar and lions *en passant*. *Witches are like stained-glass windows,* she happened to think. *They sparkle and shine when the sun is out, but when darkness sets in, their true beauty is revealed only if there is a light from within.* Lingering briefly on the landing, she peered out a clear pane of the huge window to the magnificent woods that shown with a sparkle of their own in new-fallen snow. "Winter in our Hamlet is utterly enchanting."

An enchanting place *any* time, Haleigh's Hamlet was a picturesque village– a historic southwestern Pennsylvania town that conferred countless glimpses of the past– with a charming cluster of Victorian, castle-like homes, replete with gingerbread and old money, all built during an era when help was cheap and plentiful, and the owners, coal and railroad barons (the life's blood of the village during its heyday), could well afford a bevy of servants.

To folks who lived elsewhere, the Hamlet's kingly mansions, each occupying a triple-sized wooded lot, were ever mysterious, bringing to mind secret rooms revealed with a touch to a certain "book" on a shelf and hidden staircases exposed by the twist of a latch disguised as a wall sconce. There was never any danger of anyone undesirable moving into one of the Hamlet's manors. The cost and upkeep prohibited that problem.

A stately, turreted Queen Anne, Tara was Raine and Maggie's nineteenth-century Victorian home, located in the quaint, storied Hamlet, on the edge of Haleigh's Wood. Anyone who visited Tara inevitably went away thinking that it was the right setting, the *perfect* setting, for the Sisters' personalities. Perfectionists by nature, they liked the atmosphere in and about their home to be flawless– and it was.

The winter sun spilled rainbows through the Queen Anne's jewel-like stained-glass windows, splashing a cornucopia of color on the already vibrant collection of curious things the old mansion nestled within its sturdy walls, whilst the windowsills sparkled with rows of vari-colored crystals– each charged with strong magick.

Among them were amber for vanquishing negativity, disease and dis-ease; amethyst for healing and inducing pleasant dreams; aquamarine for calming the nerves and lifting the spirits; citrine for cleansing; moonstone, "wolf's eye," for new beginnings and intuition; peridot for release from guilt; rose quartz for unconditional love and retaining youthfulness and beauty; tiger's eye and falcon's eye for protection; sapphire for insight and truth; emerald for bliss, loyalty, and wealth; and ruby for passion, energy and vigor.

The Sisters comprehended that many worlds exist and that holding special stones, crystals, or seashells, opens doors to those other realms.

On the center sill of the dining room's trilogy of castle-themed stained-glass windows, a small smoky-glass bowl held Apache tears. To the Ancient Ones, these were frozen tears lost in the sands of time, the magickal stones proffering grounding, good luck and defense, as well as the ridding of negativity that hindered realized dreams. Like amethyst and tiger's eye, Apache tears shielded the Sisters against psychic attack– also known as the "Evil Eye."

Here too the Sisters kept a large Herkimer Diamond, which, despite the name, was not really a diamond at all but a powerful clear crystal. The Sisters understood that "Herkies," perfect conduits of the Universal Life Force, were exceptional healing crystals– the high-energy seekers of the crystal world that amplify the influence of other gemstones. Like candles, crystals and gemstones were essential and effective in the magickal lives of witches.

In Tara's east windows hung hollow glass balls called "Witch Balls" to protect home and ward from detriment. Dating back to the eighteenth century, legend has it that evil spirits, attracted to these orbs, were pulled inside and trapped. It's told yet today that fishermen of old used these colorful balls in their nets to fend off evil on the high seas.

When the Sisters entered Tara's kitchen, the blue opalesque stained glass in the tall cabinet doors was shimmering with sunlight. It was a happy-feeling kitchen, and Maggie hummed merrily as she and Raine busied themselves with the proper brewing of a small pot of tea. Introduced to them years before by their beloved Granny McDonough, teatime was something these steeped-in tradition ladies enjoyed whenever and wherever they could.

The spacious kitchen's focal point was the pretty, sky-blue, hooded stove, restored to its Victorian splendor, which had been their granny's pride and joy. The old house held most of the modern conveniences, but in the kitchen especially, Raine and Maggie preferred the Old Ways– trusted, tried and true.

Above them, bunches of dried herbs and flowers dangled from the dark, massive ceiling beams of abiding English oak. A small herb garden thrived year-round in the kitchen's bay window, and affixed to the brick chimney, a broom-riding Kitchen Witch thwarted the bad and invited the good.

A besom-riding witch topped Tara's highest gable too. Celts have always been superstitious, as well as deeply spiritual. The tradition of the witch weather vane, imbued with Irish and Scottish folktales of enchanted old women flying over castle and field, casting spells and weaving magick, dates all the way back to the 1300s– or even earlier. Legend has it that if a passing witch saw such an effigy, she knew she could rest on the chimney top and consequently would cast no mischief upon the household.

Whilst the majestic manse's waterspouts channeled rainwater from Tara's slate roof and rust-colored brick walls, these conduits also served as watchful gargoyles, their mouths open in the silent shrieks that staved off evil.

Protective holly grew by every one of Tara's entrances and close to the rear gate leading into the garden, where, upon a faerie mound, spell-cast items were recharged under the full moon's energizing glow. Here, a garden plaque was engraved with a J.M. Wonderland quote: "The sun watches what I do, but the moon knows my secrets." And at Tara's front entrance, a small, decorative sign near the holly bush read: *Magickal Black Cats Guard This Home.*

Like a bubbling cauldron, Tara– a grand old house, one of the Hamlet's great houses– *overflowed* with magick, casting its spell over anyone who set eyes upon it. Invisible to non-magick people, powerful energies encircled and safeguarded the house and its occupants. In all honesty, it was not the most beautiful residence in the district but, unquestionably, it was the most unique– *as were its mistresses.*

Surrounded by a black, wrought-iron fence with fleur-de-lys finials, the turreted 1890s home was crowded with antiques, the cousins' vintage clothing, and a collection of *very special* jewelry, all of it enchanted, most of it heirloom and quite old.

The "McDonough Girls," as the Hamlet called them, had a charismatic flair, each for her own brand of fashion, each possessing the gift to *feel* the sensations cached away in their collected treasures, "As if," they were inclined to say, "we are living history."

A long line of McDonough women possessed the gift for sensing, through proximity and touch, the layered stories and energies of those who previously owned the antique articles they acquired. Attired in their vintage clothing, these women were all gossamer and lace; but make no mistake, they bore spines of cloaked steel.

Plainly put, the McDonoughs ran to women of passionate personalities generation after generation. For the most part, they ignored convention, were headstrong and willful– with every intention of staying that way.

The family was an old one, full of tradition, mystique, and fire that dated back to the *Ard Ri* of Tara– the High Kings of Ireland.

The grand lady who named the house for Ireland's sacred Hill came, decades before, from County Meath, bequeathing her female heirs a special gift– and a great deal of magick.

McDonough women could make magick just by walking into a room. They had ages of it behind them, following in their wake like the long, fiery tail of a comet. *Samhain*– Hallowe'en– was their favorite holiday.

And then there were the cats, known in the world of the Craft as "Watchers," though some might say "Familiars," five at the moment, three of which, Black Jade and Black Jack O'Lantern, along with the more elusive Panthèra, were descended from Granny McDonough's unforgettable tom, Myrrdyn, the Celtic name for Merlin. After all, it was a commodious old house, and it literally *purred* with love.

Back in the day, when Granny McDonough floated grandly into a room, the theatre, a shop, restaurant, or hall, whispers abruptly broke out like little hissing fires throughout the space. The villagers used to babble that Granny McDonough's "big ole black cat" assisted her with black magick. Black cats do that to some people, the un-magick anyway, rendering them shivery and illogical, while conjuring up all sorts of dark-night superstitions.

"Psychological poppycock! I have *no* patience with that sort of talk," Granny used to cite, Granny whose magick was forever white. Her advice on the subject: "If a black cat crosses your path– **pet it.**"

In response to those harsh muggle critics of the Craft who would say, "Magick is magick, and there is no such thing as "*white* magick," Granny would smile sweetly and reply, "There is no good or bad magick, only good and bad people. It all depends on *intent*, my dear. Magick is intended change, and *intention* creates th' change." Her granddaughters would add: "Every intentional act is a magickal act."

Anyroad, tittle-tattle never bothered "The McDonough," as, in Irish custom, Granny was sometimes called. Mostly, she laughed it off, advocating, "Sure 'n ya might as well get th' benefit of it– gossip liberates you from convention."

But that's the way of any small town. People talked, and they always would; their tongues were never idle. Not to say that the folks of Haleigh's Hamlet didn't like the McDonoughs. They very much did, some even going so far as to flaunt pride for this longstanding Hamlet clan. Despite the whisperings of the town folk, many were the times someone of them came knocking at the back door, under the veil of darkness, for a secret potion or a charm.

As a result of the Hamlet grapevine, Maggie and Raine never forgot the advice they overheard Granny give to one overwrought woman: "*Pshaw*, fools' blather! Mark me, lass, the greatest burden– to wit *fear*– in th' world is the opinion of others. But the moment you aire unafraid of th' pack, you aire no longer a sheep. You become a *lion*," she enthused. "A great r-r-roar rises in yer heart– and that, my dear, is the roar of *freedom!*"

Over the long years, the McDonough family home gathered within its stout brick walls its fair share of arcane, esoteric, and cloak-and-dagger mysteries. Without the least bit of puffery or purple prose, Tara could be summarized as a house that embodied a host of veiled secrets, old and new.

The greatest secrets are hidden; the most significant, influential things in the universe unseen; and those who do not believe in *magick* will never experience it– will never uncover its mysteries. As Granny always said, paraphrasing her oft-read Mr. Yeats: "The world is full of magick, patiently waitin' f'r our senses t' grow sharper."

No less than three generations of the Hamlet's women found themselves drawn to Granny McDonough, wanting to confess *their* secrets to her in the shadows of Tara's porch, where the sweet-smelling wisteria still grew thick in spring and summer, gracing the lattices with cascading, grape-like, pink and purple blooms.

And the Hamlet men, though they might scoff at such things, believed secretly, then and now, that on occasion a beautiful, young Aisling Tully McDonough, before she became known as "Granny," visited their dreams, igniting their carnal desires or whispering to them ways in which they might succeed in their careers.

The Hamlet learned that they could trust Granny McDonough with their secrets, and she conscientiously passed that torch on to her trinity of granddaughters– to her namesake Aisling, to Maggie, and to Raine.

A solitary, eclectic witch, Granny entrusted her accumulated knowledge and wisdom to her granddaughters, teaching them well. Of course, The McDonough didn't confuse the two– knowledge and wisdom, that is. "Never mistake knowledge for wisdom," she instructed. "One helps you make a livin'; the other helps you make a life."

Forthright and candid, Granny had always looked straight into the eyes of anyone with whom she spoke. She was never one to sit on the fence or pussyfoot around, leaving "… that to the neighborhood cats, sugar-coatin' to th' baker, and elegance to th' tailor."

It was quoted far afield that Granny McDonough was a wise woman and a healer of a great many things. "Witch and famous," mouthed the Hamlet folks. They had feared her, yet they sought her out, over time coming to love her, even going so far as to believe that if her long, black cloak brushed against them, as she passed on the street, its mere touch brought them good fortune for the remainder of their days.

Suffice to say the Celtic history of healing is a rich and powerful one, and *Celt* is synonymous with "free spirit." Never was a McDonough born who was not a free spirit.

Once when Raine was sent home from school for soundly thrashing a fellow student, a boy much bigger than she, who had relentlessly teased her for being a witch, Granny sat her down and said, with a twinkle in her eyes, "Sure 'n didn't ya lar-rn Grandpa McDonough's KO punch better 'n Aisling or Maggie put t'gether!" (It had been the widowed Granny who'd taken the girls in hand, when they were pre-teens, to coach them on how to defend themselves.)

"Now lar-rn this," Granny chided: "Be yerself, *a leanbh*, child," she reinforced in Gaelic. "*The world will adjust.* An *original* is always better than a copy. When you dance to yer own rhythm, people might not understand you. They might not even like you–"

"I don't think they do like me, Granny," Raine had sobbed.

"*Whist,* let me finish! They might not understand or like you, but by the Goddess, they'll wish they had the courage to *be* you. And remember, you not only have th' *right* to be an individual, as a *McDonough* you have an *obligation* to be one."

When Raine, drying her tears, remarked that all she wanted was to be "normal," Granny drew herself up to full height to expound, with high-flying Irish temper: "Me darlin' gurl, if y' feel like y' don't fit in, in this world, it's because you aire here t' help create a new one– a *better* one. I'll tell ya true, here 'n now, that bein' 'normal,' as you call it, is wholly ordinary … *commonplace, dull 'n utterly unimaginative.* And I'll tell ya flat out, lass, it rather denotes a lack iv courage!"

That's all it took. The willful, ofttimes hoydenish Raine was cured forever of wanting a "normal" life. Ever after, she delighted in quoting her adopted maxim: "Why be normal when you can be– *magickal?*"

When Raine was older, Granny advised, "Give yer heart to th' soul who loves you to madness 'n who loves yer 'madness,' who sees beauty in th' wildness of yer spirit– *not* the eejit who tries to force you to be 'normal.' And never f'rgit that whin people are intimidated by yer strength 'n happiness, they'll try t' tear ya down, break yer spirit. Remember, that sort iv behavior is a reflection of *their* weakness and *not* a reflection of *you.* You owe *no one* an explanation f'r bein' *who you are.* Let the *amadáns* figure out yer mystery."

Of the Sisters, Raine, especially, took that advice, never letting the muggles get her down. Anyone who tried was usually thumped with the phrase, "Go smudge yourself!"

After Grandpa McDonough passed on, Granny, who spoke to the end of her life with a brogue as thick as her good Irish stew, never wore anything but what the Hamlet referred to as her "widow's weeds."

With her shadowy cape billowing out behind her, she often walked her big, black tom, Myrrdyn, on a leash after supper in the magickal owl light of evening. To the amazement of the villagers, the cat pranced– tail held high to form a question mark, neither twisting nor turning in any effort whatsoever to escape– at the end of a black velvet lead that was fastened to a fancy, jewel-studded collar around his neck, the other end wrapped several times round Granny's bejeweled hand. As self-important as you please, proudly and demurely did that tom swagger, with attitude and countenance that clearly avowed, "I am Granny McD's cat if you please– or if you don't please."

Granny fathomed what most here in the New World of America did not– that gently stroking a black cat nine times, from head to tail, brought good fortune and luck in love (that went triple for *Samhain/* Hallowe'en). Treating cats kindly, with the respect they deserve, and warmly sharing one's home with cats of any color brought a multitude of blessings from the great Goddess.

"You will always be lucky if y' know how to make friends with cats," advocated The McDonough with all the sagacity of a wise woman. "Cats possess charms a-plenty, and annyone who has iver owned a cat, if indaid one *can* own a cat, has fallen under Bastet's endurin' spell. Cats aire th' only bein's that can enter or leave a magick circle without breakin' th' energy field. Many aire totems, spirit guides, or have come into yer life as magickal familiars."

Granny taught her granddaughters many useful things about cats, including the fact that they love to curl up and nap within a circle. Indeed, they will intentionally stay put inside a circle for long periods, sitting almost trancelike.

As one might expect, Granny McDonough's love of cats stayed with her all her life, just as the musical lilt of Ireland remained on her tongue, and given that she raised Raine and Maggie, some of Granny's expressions and patterns of speech carried over and became part of them.

Cat tales abound in the McDonough and Tully clans, and Raine especially enjoyed spinning the colorful yarns– complete with Granny's brogue.

One year, for instance, when Mrs. Jenkins' brown tabby gave birth to kittens, that everyone *knew* Myrrdyn had sired (when he darted out the door one brisk autumn night under the bewitching glow of the Hunter's Moon), it surprised the kibble out of a suddenly-younger-acting Gypsy and her owner. That tabby had thirteen years on her, if a day, and well past her kitten-bearing time was she. "The old fool!" Mrs. Jenkins had complained to anyone who would listen.

But there were kittens all right– *and what kittens!* The villagers took to calling them "faerie cats," and to be sure, there was something *magickal* about those glossy kittens, black as midnight each one, and shiny as patent leather, with bright pumpkin-colored eyes that bored clean through whomever they fixed with their mystical regard. Every child in town had fussed for one, and all these years later, Myrrdyn's charmed progeny still inhabit a few of the Hamlet's quaint old mansions. It's funny how things can stick in the mind over the mumbo jumbo of so many years– but that story has real sticking power.

Closer to the moment, Raine and Maggie were sitting at table– a heavy, round, claw-footed affair that matched its oak, pressed-back chairs– in Tara's kitchen, where the former lit a thick, red candle-in-a-jar labeled "Witches' Brew" that smelled suspiciously like cinnamon spice.

There was *magick* in candlelight. Its soft glow not only converted a room into an entrancing space, its illumination raised psychic awareness, and most significantly– a lit candle released energies. Raine had just pulled the new candle from its box, and she wanted to light it straightaway, for Granny imparted that it was unlucky to keep a candle in the house that had never been lit.

Granny instilled many, what some might call, "flights of fantasy" or "old wives' tales" into her granddaughters, such as a toppled chair upon standing was a bad omen. Spilled salt was too, unless you promptly tossed a pinch of it over your left shoulder to stave off the bad luck. Needless to add, if you built a house over a faerie fort, you'd have infinite ill fortune.

Remembering Granny, as she always did when she made tea, Maggie poured herself and Raine each a fragrant cup of the special brew they ordered from Ireland. Nary a tea bag ever found its sorry way into Tara's traditional door. As was their habit, the pair used the eggshell-thin cups their granny had carefully carried, years before, from the "Old Country." At Tara, tea was never taken from a mug, or as Granny used to call it, a "beaker."

Raine sighed wistfully, looking across the room to the Boston rocker, where The McDonough had often sat by the kitchen window to read her arcane books. *We miss you, Granny.*

Following Raine's gaze, Maggie gave a knowing nod. Her eyes shone brilliant green as she lifted the cup to her lips, her rings catching a beam from the sun that sparked a rainbow off a stained-glass window.

Through the window, the redheaded Sister could see Tara's small, cupola-crowned stable, home to their horses, Raine's ebony gelding, Tara's Pride, and Maggie's cherry chestnut mare, Isis. The stable's antique weathervane, a broom-riding witch, identical to the one atop Tara itself, told her there was a stiff wind out of the west.

Maggie looked absorbed, reaching up to flick back the wave of fiery hair that frequently dipped over one eye. "It's too bad our parents can't attend Emerald's handfasting, but no way can they leave the South Pacific whilst they're knee-deep in fieldwork. Archeology's in their blood. Now that they're retired from the Smithsonian, I'm glad they can indulge their yen for travel to all the remote, exotic, magick-carpet destinations in the world. They've at long last the time to compile their field studies into books, and my keen witch's instinct is that their completed series is destined to receive international acclaim." Maggie's eyes met Raine's. "They'll be sorely missed at Salem. Nonetheless, it'll be wonderful to see kith and kin again."

"It will." Raine sipped her tea. "Ahhh, tea is so restorative. Hmm, meant to tell you: Aunt Kate and Uncle Ronan arrived in Salem last night," she said of Aisling's parents. "They're staying at the Hawthorne too, but they won't be riding with us in the limo to and from the handfasting events, because they've rented a car. Aisling said they plan to do some sightseeing and shopping while they're in the Boston area. No one's staying at Grantie's this trip, because Grantie's friend and caregiver, Witch Hazel, lives with her now, and the cottage only has two bedrooms."

The Goth gal tilted her head, force of habit to pick up her sister of the moon's thought. "I know what you're thinking. And I think Emerald's changed for the better too," Raine remarked. She rested her chin in her palms, elbows on the table, with the air of one who is recapitulating. "I daresay, I *hope* she has, if she wants the marriage to work."

"*Quite.*" Maggie dabbed at the corners of her mouth with a paper napkin. "Since Emerald and her beloved were wed this morning in a judge's chambers, the judge being a close friend of the groom's father, her nuptials are *legally* binding, in accordance with Massachusetts' law."

"*I* would've opted for the traditional year and a day handfasting, with an *out* on that day, if not *blissed* out, but," Raine lifted her cup in a toasting gesture, "bright blessings upon them!"

Maggie raised her cup. "Love and Light and all that is Merry and Bright. May their lives be filled with magick!" After a long sip of tea, the redheaded Sister said in a musing manner, "Emerald finally settled on Valentine's Day for her handfasting, because that was the day she and Jack Quin met. I'll always remember her face when she Skyped us to say how they chanced upon one another in a Salem coffee shop, when both were standing at the counter, waiting for their orders. He took one look at her and, thunderstruck by Cupid's arrow, beseeched, 'Will you be my Valentine?'"

"Jack has certainly stood by Emerald through thick and thin. He seems to adore her. At any rate, I guess the whole family thought Emerald had settled on Yule for the handfasting; but she'll still have the winter wedding she wanted. Salem will be a snow-white wonderland this time o' year." Raine paused. "Just think, Mags, one day Grantie's 300-year-old, seaside cottage will be ours, with Aisling; and we'll have a second home in the 'Witch City' of Salem. I still can't believe Grantie's leaving the historic cottage to *us*, along with so many of her magickal possessions. *Bless her.*"

"Though the dear lady turned a hundred and one last April, I hope that day is a long way off."

Raine raised her teacup again. "Hear, hear!"

Maggie stood, carrying the tea things to the sink. "Let's get moving, Hugh will be pulling in at any moment now. You know him; he's never late."

"I was just thinking that it's always exciting to be embarking on a new mystery. This time especially, because we don't even know what this one's about."

As the Sisters began washing up, they chanted softly, "Still around the corner a new road doth wait. Just around the corner– another secret gate!"

✳✳✳

The pair set their bags at the front door to pull their black wool capes over their shoulders.

"Granny continually reinforces," Maggie was saying, "that it's our destiny to solve crimes, come to the aid of innocents, and put things as right as we can."

Raine made a kittenish face, wordless.

Wordless, however, was a rare condition for the verbose, brunette Sister. Often effusive, at all times bold and ever more-than-ready for a new adventure, Raine was a sexy, somewhat naughty pixie who was destined to keep her looks and her youthful appearance. Pixies, after all, are enduring as well as endearing.

Whimsical Fate had ordained that Maggie, too, be blessed with a forever-youthful mien. In addition, the redheaded Sister was most enchantingly– *sensual*. Perchance it was her wittiness and vibrant sense of fun that helped retain her beauty and allure. Maggie loved to laugh, and she did so often. Her voice was soft, almost musical, and she had an especially attractive, lilting expression of amusement.

The short laugh, however, she'd just pitched Raine, carried a trace of trepidation. "God and Goddess grant we don't encounter anything as risky as our last shock of quests. Stuff and nonsense,"

Maggie rapidly amended. "We won't let our imaginations run away from us with the bit between the teeth. We'll program our way."

A hint of alarm flickered in Raine's gut, but she quickly blew it off, not allowing it to flame.

Their ability to read each other's minds bonded Maggie and Raine; and though they sniped at one another on occasion, they were close– much more like sisters than first cousins.

For one thing, the magickal trio– Raine, Maggie, and Aisling– had identical eyes, arresting to anyone who looked upon them. The "McDonough eyes" the villagers called them– tip-tilted and vivid green, the color of Ireland itself, fringed with long, inky lashes and blazing with insatiable life.

"God's fingers waire sooty whin He put in th' eyes of me lovely Irish granddaughters," Granny used to say.

Like their blonde cousin Aisling, raven-haired Raine and redheaded Maggie accentuated their eyes with intense makeup, too theatrical for most– dramatically stunning and signature sexy for the Sleuth Sisters. And like their granny before them, the McDonough lasses had beautiful complexions– rich cream, glowing and flawless.

Granny recognized, from birth, how extraordinary each of her granddaughters was– even for a Tully or a McDonough– predicting that they would be able to see what others, including their own kind, could not.

And from the moment the McDonough girls entered puberty, it was like bees to honey! Boys suddenly couldn't keep away from them. Just looking at them left most males so giddy, they acted like they'd had too much of old Buck Taylor's 'lectricfyin' applejack. Would-be suitors followed the McDonough gals home from high school and college, tied up their phones evenings, and fought over who would escort them to dances and such.

"You don't find yer worth in a man," Granny schooled her granddaughters when they reached adolescence. "You find yer worth within yerself, and then find a man who's worthy of you. There's no greater power than that of the sun, the moon– and a woman who knows her worth. *Remember that.*"

Perhaps it was Granny's special olive-oil soap the threesome used that made their skin so luminous and turned their auras so bright that people– well, those who believed in magick, anyway– virtually saw them in dazzling, sparkly radiance, like the beautiful leaders of splendor and light they actually were. Or maybe it was simply the self-confidence Granny instilled in her granddaughters that made them shine so. Poise has an enchanting way of doing that. Granny unerringly quipped that "Sex appeal was fifty percent of what you've got, and fifty percent of what people think you've got." Whatever the reason, the McDonough lasses radiated something that was impossible to ignore.

Their theatre friends summed them up by saying, "Raine, Maggie, and Aisling have that intangible *je ne sais quoi* that makes them unforgettable."

No one ever forgot a McDonough woman.

In all fairness, they did not collect hearts as one collects seashells or butterflies, and yet …

A few seconds ago, Raine, who was usually fearless about plunging into tomorrow, felt that fantastic McDonough confidence and optimism slip a notch. *Mystery, mayhem, and murder– again!* The harrowing thought, delivered on Granny's caveat, skimmed along her spine like cold, bony fingers, the disquiet making itself evident on her face. *Granny took time from an important Celestial conference to pop in on us, so that makes me think our upcoming challenge will be fraught with …*

Instinctively her hand flew to the antique talisman suspended on a thick silver chain around her neck. She brushed her ringed fingers across the large emerald embedded in the center of the amulet's broad silver-and-black-enameled surface. A bright sprinkling of tiny, pinhead-size gems of moonstone, garnet, emerald, ruby, sapphire, amethyst, citrine, and various hues of quartz and topaz glittered in the treasured heirloom.

For a spun-out suspension in time, Raine regarded the inspiring piece, as Granny's words zoomed back to rouse her: *The enemy is Fear. We think it is Hate, but it is Fear. Everything you want is on the other side of Fear.*

Looking to Maggie, Raine remarked, "Beau always ribs me that the mere mention of a mystery quickens my pulse. I love a good mystery," she shrugged. "Guess my uneasy feeling is due, this time, to the unknown."

Maggie declined to respond, except to comment that the Merlin cats– Black Jade and Black Jack O'Lantern, with Panthèra– perfectly aligned, were out of the blue sitting before them in the foyer, their combined steady *purrrrrr* growing louder.

Raine scrutinized their Watchers for a charmed moment. "They're warning us that this upcoming mystery will be especially tangled and troublesome." The Sister cocked her head, hoping to pick up more information telepathically. It was one of her special powers, the ability to communicate with animals. She made it a point to pay close attention when she saw her familiars stare– for magick was most definitely near.

Maggie answered with a nod, picking up Raine's train of thought, as the latter's mind sped on. From under her clothing, she extracted the talisman she habitually wore on a strong silver chain around her neck.

Understandably, Maggie's heirloom piece matched Raine's, save that the big center stone was a blood-red ruby. Tracing a finger over the amulet's bejeweled Triquetra surface– or more precisely, her talisman's *third* of the Triquetra design– she said, imaging their accomplished Leo cousin Aisling, whose talisman hosted the focal stone of sapphire, "There's indeed something to be said for the magick Power of Three.

"We'll prove ourselves yet again," Maggie managed to insert with quiet Scorpio force. "As Granny reminds us, it's our destiny, and she left us more than just this house and a great trust fund. We've been blessed with many gifts, but with those gifts have come accountability. We worked hard to earn the Key to a mystical portal, a gateway that unveils a world of ancient mysteries and hidden knowledge. Among our utmost responsibilities is to guard the Time-Key's secret– and to use it for good."

A surge of witchy-woman power fired Raine's Aries *chutzpah*, and she flashed her cousin and sister of the moon an appreciative grin. *Woman In Total Control of Herself … that's what it means to be a witch. And what a **delicious** word it is!* "At a time like this, I can't help but be reminded of what Granny liked to quote from Abraham Lincoln, whom she believed was rather a mystic: "The best way to predict the future is to create it."

"That's our MO."

"It's our credo … or one of them."

There in the entrance hall, Raine reached down and scooped up a black cat that on silent paws had shadowed her to Tara's front door, where just the day before she'd hung a nice set of antique, brass Witch Bells. Extending a hand, she flicked them, their jingle causing the cat's ears to twitch. Like their familiars, the bells, on each of Tara's exit doors, helped to keep negativity and evil at bay.

Gazing into the depths of Black Jack O'Lantern's mesmerizing pumpkin-colored eyes, the Sister recited her favorite tale, "Once upon a time, there were two pioneering college professors and one former police detective turned private eye– young but possessed of very old souls– from an unheard-of little hamlet in the backwoods of Pennsylvania. Nevertheless, the good works of this magickal trinity were widely noted, winning them the well-earned soubriquet the 'Sleuth Sisters.'"

"All we've got to do," Maggie added with emphasis, "is keep to our path. That's how we ferreted out the Time-Key. It's how we crafted our dissertation on time-travel so that it was accepted by our fellow colleagues of letters, and how we defended it successfully to gain our doctorates. In addition, we've solved a run of wicked murders in the past few years. And we did it *all* by keeping to the path of the Great Secret."

Tilting her dark head, Raine's fair cheeks took on a rosy tint. She ran her ringed fingers through her short, sassy asymmetric hair– as black and lustrous as their cats– the point-cut bangs dipping seductively over one eye. "Likewise, we've safeguarded the secret of the Time-Key through, I might add, *six* nerve-jangling time-travel missions."

Raine's phone sounded with the enchanting music of Rowena of the Glen's *Book of Shadows*.

"Dr. McDonough," her deep voice rumbled. After listening for a beat, she uttered into the phone, "Yes, we're ready." Disconnecting, Raine related to Maggie, "They're on their way."

The Goodwin property was just through the connecting woods, so Hugh would be pulling into Tara's circular driveway any second. While she waited for the sound of his SUV, the raven-haired Sister strode past the life-size knight-in-armor in the foyer to the pillared entry that led into Tara's parlor with its massive Victorian furniture, green velvet drapes, and wall of books, the shelves crammed with leather-bound tomes spilling over with arcane esoteric knowledge. Instantly her eyes locked with the pair, so like her own, of her grandmother whose fascinating portrait hung above the ornate fireplace.

The oil painting by Charles Dana Gibson captured Aisling Tully McDonough at the height of her beauty, the soft cloud of red hair, upswept in the famed Gibson-Girl coiffure of the era, graced the flawless oval of the face, the low-cut, off-the-shoulder, shimmering green gown accentuating the hour-glass figure. Streaming down over one white shoulder, a long tendril of fiery red hair formed a perfect question mark. Gibson had entitled the captivating image *The Eternal Question*, and thus read the neat, brass plate at the base of the portrait.

There Raine lingered for a solemn moment, deftly voicing her thought aloud: "Granny, it's *empowering* to know, from our past endeavors, that we can travel down the Tunnel of Time, at will, to unlock the door that'll whisk us through the thrills and chills of yesteryear. It's easy to get carried away. We need and welcome your continued guidance in making prudent choices."

The eyes in the portrait seemed to kindle, and a little-cat smile lifted the corners of Raine's candy-apple-red mouth. "I can't help my feeling that with each new adventure, Aisling, Maggie, and I advance to a whole new level of skill and achievement."

She dressed her normally husky voice with a thick coat of drama, "And as I always say– who knows what skeletons and dangers dangle in the closets our Time-Key will open? Along with those secreted perils– magick, adventure and surprise await us at the creak of every opening door." In her saucy manner, she finished with an eerie laugh.

Entering the room, Maggie said, "If and when we run into a snag, we'll make good and proper use of *all* our magickal tools, including our Time-Key. With it *and* the powerful gifts bestowed on us by Granny and Grantie Merry, we should be able to solve virtually *any* mystery that History has cloaked in shadow. One thing's certain– our lives are never boring. Again, we've some exciting days ahead."

"Peril and risk? Absolutely, but remember what both *grandes dames* drilled into us: 'To be forewarned is to be forearmed.'"

"Right," Maggie put in, "and a word to the wise should suffice."

Raine shifted her gaze from the portrait to the redhead beside her, as her voice took on an even stronger element of anticipation, and her heart gave a leap. "Let's go. Hugh just pulled in."

Maggie concurred with a gentle nod, her eyes lifting to the riveting canvas. "Guide and guard us, Granny Angel."

"So mote it be," Raine quickly ordained.

As the Sisters hurried out the door, Maggie, with her fiery witch's passion, repeated the time-honored phrase, "So mote it be!"

Manifesting in a front window, the poppet Cara, watching the Sisters hasten down the driveway, their black capes fluttering out behind them, fortified the magickal mix with her own invocation.
"With the Power of Three– so mote it be!"

"Upon this day, our hands we bind, a symbol of our hearts entwined."

Chapter One

Besom Limo was as pleasant as everyone remembered from their last visit to Salem. Raine asked for the same driver; but since Ron was booked, the service sent his twin brother, who also drove for Besom. Everyone pitched in for the stretch limo, champagne, and light hors d'oeuvres to enjoy on the picturesque sea route from Boston's Logan International. Though the famed "Witch City" is only about sixteen miles north of Boston, it took Chauffeur Don Karr about forty-five minutes, due to traffic, to navigate the journey from the airport to Salem.

Ensconced in luxury, the Sleuth Sisters and their party were reminiscing on the past, their conversation as bubbly as the drinks.

"I love family stories," Aisling laughed, taking another sip of champagne, "and our clan's sure got some good ones."

The senior Sleuth Sister, Aisling McDonough-Gwynn was, concisely put, the classic tall, cool blonde. Aisling was cool in the sense that she kept her head in even the most dangerous situations; however, she had as warm a heart as any good witch who ever waved a wand. A bang-on Leo, Granny McDonough's namesake was a versatile woman, skilled in many aspects of the Craft. This was the Sister most likely to take control of a situation, and she was usually the first to take the initiative to help an innocent.

Aisling's husband, Ian, a burly ex-police detective, possessed a mellow Leo personality that harmonized well with his wife's feline persona; and though he could be fanciful at times, like Aisling, he had no wishbone where a backbone ought to be. Indeed, he liked to emphasize that, "To succeed in life, you need three things– a backbone, a wishbone, and a funny bone." There *were* times when Ian roared, though never at his wife or young daughter, who each had a talent for making him purr. Lions, on balance, are more than just roar.

Ian's coloring was entirely red-gold. Thick, wavy reddish-gold hair covered his leonine head, whilst his hazel eyes flashed bright gold glints. Even his weathered skin gleamed golden, though it could instantly flame red with stirred emotion.

Aisling and Ian met on the Pittsburgh police force, several years prior, where they'd worked together as detectives, the springboard to their current career. The Gwynns' Black Cat Detective Agency was a successful operation; and all in all, these master sleuths were a well-matched, lionhearted couple. Aisling often said that she and Ian were true soul mates, and anyone seeing them together recognized the bond and the love they shared with one another, as well as with their precocious Fay of a daughter.

The blonde, preteen Merry Fay mirrored her magickal mother– in more than just her charming looks.

"I like these stories too, Mom. One day, you guys should put them in a book. A big book with the McDonough women on the cover. I could be in the center."

Her comment induced Maggie to whisper to Aisling, "Witches know from a young age they're special."

The youngest McDonough witch was enjoying a Shirley Temple, which Karr thought to garnish with a pretty swirl of orange peel, lending, as he jested, "*Appeal de la sophistiquée.*"

"I love to read," Merry was saying. "I open a book and scoot inside, where," she dimpled with a giggle, "no one can find me."

"I'd find you," Raine broke into a laugh, pushing her pointer finger into the mini-charmer's belly. "You were born to light up the world, Merry Fay." She took a moment to consider the child's idea about the family stories, and her lips curved in her familiar kitty-cat smile. "We might just do that," she said, popping a seasoned cracker with sharp cheddar into her mouth. "Compile our … *bewitching* family vignettes into a book one day … when we're crones. Names would be changed to protect the innocent, and we could entitle it *No Rest For The Wiccan.*"

"It's a clever title and certainly tells the tale that we're the busiest witches alive, but," the exacting Aisling refuted, "we're not Wiccan. The McDonough witches are all eclectic witches, though mostly Celtic." Aisling cocked her head in a thinking gesture. "How about *Sisterhood of the Traveling Witches? We'll* know, for all intents and purposes, it's fundamentally *Time-Traveling.*"

"Or," Maggie interjected, "perhaps *Witches' Brew* ... or *A Savory Witches' Brew. Savory* would embrace the salty, sweet, and," she raised her expressive brows, "*spicy.*"

Raine made a little moue. "If ever we decide to compile our family stories, we've plenty of time to think up a title, Sisters. I sort of fancy *A Witch in Time.*"

"When you make that kittenish face, you remind me of our Emerald," Maggie declared.

"These prawns are great," Thaddeus said. "Try one." Dipping it into the spicy cocktail sauce, he slipped a jumbo shrimp into Maggie's mouth, remarking her expression. "What did I tell you?"

As the esteemed head of Haleigh College's history department, Dr. Thaddeus Weatherby had been the perfect advisor to Raine and Maggie when they were working toward their doctorates in history. His mentorship bonded him with the McDonoughs and aroused his fervent love for Maggie. As the Sisters came to discover, the inimitable Dr. Weatherby was well-versed in a wide range of subjects, and he possessed a colorful spectrum of talents. Not to intimate that he was a jack of all trades, but he most assuredly was a master of many.

Moreover, and to the point, Dr. Thaddeus Weatherby, PhD, was the textbook absent-minded professor with a brain like a steel trap. To put it another way, the highly respected Dr. Weatherby was a bona fide genius, and like most intellects, he was distinguished by his quirks. For instance, he occasionally displayed a childlike nature, or more precisely what, owing to his passionate curiosity, colleagues *mistook* for a childlike nature that, at times, drove his fellows in the history department, to use *his* word, "bats." But then, as those of the Craft know well, the secret of genius is to carry the riddle of the child into old age.

Children see magick because they look for it.

"I am happy to report that my inner child is still ageless," he informed his colleagues at their last departmental meeting. Another of the things Dr. Weatherby was fond of saying was, "You're never too old to enjoy a happy childhood. Take time *every* day to do something amusing. Play is the highest form of research." Thaddeus Weatherby was not one to flout his own advice. From his teen years, he stepped out of bed each morning with the affirmation, "And so the adventure begins!"

One of the most special characteristics– *and there were several–* about the professor was that he possessed extraordinarily accurate and vivid recall, both visual and audial, an "eidetic memory" some might call it. The amazing man's sharp Scorpio wit and courage, or as Hemingway penned it, "grace under pressure," served the Sleuth Sisters well on more than one close-call circumstance in the past. Dr. Weatherby held that "The brave may not live forever, but the cautious don't live at all," a stance in spot-on sync with the Sisters. "Because, in the end," Thaddeus told his close associates, "you won't remember the time you spent working those extra hours, cleaning or repairing the house, or mowing the lawn. Climb that goddamn mountain!"

As one might suspect, Dr. Weatherby was an exceptional teacher because while teaching others, he continually remained the student. This was one bit of wisdom he didn't have to convey to the Dr. McDonoughs. Raine and Maggie already lived it.

A wiry and surprisingly muscular, middle-age man, Thaddeus' dark-grey hair, thanks to Maggie's influence, was no longer reminiscent of Einstein's; rather, it was professionally and becomingly styled. "It doesn't look as if you comb your hair with firecrackers anymore," Raine teased when first she'd seen Thaddeus' new look.

His once careless manner of dress was now "country gentry," Irish tweeds replacing the rumpled, mismatched "Weatherby wear," about which, once upon a time, his students did genially jest. However, he retained, regardless of what he was wearing, his signature, cherry-red bowtie. It was as much a part of his personality as his quick wit and old-world charm. Due to his significant other's sway, nowadays the professor sported a neat van dyke mustache and beard, and though he wore his contacts more often than he used to, this afternoon his bright blue eyes peered from behind his workaday Harry Potter spectacles that adjusted to light.

"This hummus is tasty," Beau commented, as he dunked a piece of pita bread into the savory dip he'd spooned onto his plate. "Raine says it's the satisfying snack that's actually good for you."

Tall and powerfully built with wide shoulders, trim waist, and the muscular legs that do proper justice to a kilt, Beau Goodwin was blessed with the thick, jet-black hair and scorching blue eyes of a long line of Scottish and Scotch-Irish ancestors. In his thirties, his body was all lean muscle– muscle that moved with the kind of intensity and power that comes to men who get plenty of exercise a good deal of the time outdoors. His relentless farm calls afforded him continuous bodybuilding workouts; and like Raine, Beau enjoyed spending his free time, the turning wheel of the seasons, in Nature's rejuvenating company.

Like his Celtic father, Hugh, Beau hyped the Natural World: "Place your hands in the soil or walk barefoot on sand or earth to feel grounded. Wade in stream, river, or ocean to feel emotionally cleansed and healed. Fill your lungs with fresh air to feel mentally clear. Raise your face to the sun and connect to that energy to feel your *own* immense power. It's like wishing upon a star. Doesn't matter who you are– it's free and accessible to all."

But Raine's favorite dissemination gained from the Goodwin doctors was this: "The best medicine for humans or animals is love. If a patient asks, 'What if it doesn't work?' The answer's simple– 'Increase the dose.'"

There was something, simply put, *extraordinary* about Dr. Beau Goodwin that people– and above all, animals– noticed straightaway. Perhaps it was that *special something* that peered from his eyes, a soulful softness that revealed a good and pure heart. Animals reap a "knowing" when a human possesses empathy and kindness through the vibrations the human emits, and this provides the "fur, fin, and feather people" with an instinct of safety in the company of that human. On the wall in the Goodwin veterinary clinic was a plaque that displayed a Buddha dictum: *Be kind to all creatures.* **This** *is the true religion.*

If his patients could talk, they would say that Beau was a born healer with the perfect bedside manner; and like the Sisters, he was an Old Soul and an empath. (Most empaths *are* Old Souls.) Raine knew, from Granny's teachings, to treasure what the McDonough clan called "Soul Clickers," "… people who walk into your life and straight off click with you– for these are souls known before."

"The voice of the Goddess calls to Beau and me from another time and place," Raine believed. Often did she experience a keen Celtic knowing, just as he frequently did of her, that Beau had come from somewhere else– somewhere not of this earth. At times, each felt homesick for a place they weren't even sure existed. "For that elusive, faraway star," Raine alleged, "where my heart is full, my body loved, and my soul understood."

Beau understood. More and more, it seemed to Raine, Beau understood her needs, her desires, and her dreams. To be sure, each half of this remarkable couple created magick in a singular way, and together these two Star Children enkindled an utterly magickal *Raine-Beau.*

Like all Starseeds, who are intrinsically programmed to find others like themselves, both preferred to work in fields that allowed them to use their innate but heightened talents– healing, imparting knowledge and truth– and searching for their own truths. "Truths beyond the ken of men," Beau was wont to philosophize on the infrequent occasion when he could relax with a tall glass of the Scottish ale he favored.

Raine had a saying of her own regarding their relationship. "It's said some lives are linked across time, connected by an ancient calling that echoes down the ages. We're like magnets, Beau and I, with each incarnation, reaching out and leaping through space to reunite. We cross oceans of time to find one another."

Magick calls to magick.

The couple *shared* several common denominators as well as *untold memories of their hearts, these the love letters of past lives*; and though there had been others in each of their current lives, this was *why*, after so many years, Raine and Beau still were mutually enchanted.

Only a few things triggered Dr. Beau Goodwin's temper, causing him to lose his Leo chivalry– animal cruelty (he did *not* tolerate animal cruelty in the least) and, at times, Raine's too-daring, impetuous Aries disposition, along with her unwavering outlook on the woes of marriage, conventional muggle marriage, at any rate.

As the long, black Besom Limo, with silver logo of a broom-riding witch on the driver's door, rolled toward Salem, the Sleuth Sisters and their party continued to enjoy themselves.

Betty flashed Hugh a smile, prompting the couple to blurt at nearly the same time, "Everything's delicious!" It was apparent they were beginning to read each other's thoughts.

Betty Donovan and Hugh Goodwin became enamored with one another almost from the moment they met, opening their hearts again to love. They just seemed so right for one another: both widowed, both animal lovers, and the pair of them ardent mystery buffs. When Betty posed the question, how much was due to Raine's magickal finagling, the latter answered, "Oh, it was magick all right! Who's to say what love is?"

Within a short time, Betty's frisky Irish setter, Boru, nicknamed Barkus Boru– practically impossible for her to manage after her husband passed away a few years earlier– heeled perfectly when they walked with Hugh and his two shepherds, Nero and Wolfe. And more significantly, Betty and Hugh both slept better nights after companionable sessions of reading aloud followed by lively discussion of whatever whodunit they were currently sorting out.

Betty quickly became a believer in the maxim "It might take a year; it might take a day; but what's meant to be, will always find its way."

A retired librarian, Betty was an attractive woman with short, casual, salt-and-pepper hair and eyes like polished turquoise. She indulged a taste for Southwestern fashions and bold silver-and-turquoise jewelry that suited both her coloring and her adventurous Sagittarian personality. Like many of her sun sign, Betty's enthusiasm knew no bounds, and she possessed an intense optimism and perception that the Sisters– and Hugh especially– found captivating.

Tall and robust like his son and their Highlander forebears, the senior Dr. Goodwin's once-ebony hair was now an ennobling silver, as was his full, what-used-to-be-called "cavalry mustache." Indeed, the dear man habitually carried himself in a smart, soldierly manner, and he was known, by family and friends, to soldier on when the going got tough.

Beneath his wiry, expressive brows, the vivid blue of Hugh's eyes had faded some with age, but the years did not diminish his zest for life, not perceivably anyway. In truth, Time had been gracious to Hugh Goodwin; and there were those ladies in Haleigh's Hamlet who considered him handsomer now than when he was young, and they'd all vied for his attention. But women have always been attracted to men with cavalry mustaches and soulful "bedroom eyes."

A virile, inventive Aquarius, Hugh was a good, upright man, a lover of life and all living things. If he had a fault, it was that he sometimes spoke gruffly, but he was never deliberately unkind, and his words carried truth. Those spells, when he'd huff salty words into his mustache with the fire of his fierce Highlander ancestors, Raine swore she could see the mystical symbols of Celtic warriors, in blue woad war paint, on Hugh's face and body.

"I hope these hors d'oeuvres don't spoil our appetite for the rehearsal dinner," Betty remarked.

"I doubt that will happen," Hugh answered. "I'd wager we won't be sitting down to eat till eight-thirty or nine. It's not quite six now."

"That reminds me. We won't be able to dawdle at the Hawthorne," Raine said. "No sooner will we get checked in, than we'll have to leave for the Avalon. The hall's not too far, a couple of miles, I think. Besom will be out front of the hotel to drive us there in jig-time."

"We'll only have about a half-hour after we check in before we'll need to leave," Maggie concurred.

Raine sipped her champagne, reflecting for several moments on the past. "I was just thinking that throughout the years and all of Emerald's escapades– *and there were many*– Grantie's belief that there was goodness in her heart never wavered." She flung a glance to Maggie and Aisling. "Our faith in Em whiffle-waffled," she said, tilting her hand back and forth in a seesawing motion, "especially mine, but Grantie's love and belief in Emerald never faltered."

"Emerald's one-of-a-kind. That's certain," Aisling pronounced. "Just one more shrimp." She popped a fat prawn into her mouth. "Yummy. Grantie told us Emerald doesn't give a hoot that some say it's bad luck for a bride to wear green. 'Green's my signature color, and that's what I'm wearing,' she's declared."

"Cousin Emerald wears green nail polish too," Merry Fay commented. "Even her little car's emerald green."

"Wonder how the old Sunbeam's holding up?" Beau said, paused in his noshing. "Emerald drives too fast and reckless."

"Not anymore she doesn't. Grantie says Jack's been a good influence on her." The Goth gal pondered for a long moment. "When Emerald's research on the Sunbeam revealed its nickname to be the 'Rich Girl's Car,' she was thrilled to bragging about it all over Salem. After acquiring ownership from Grantie of the rare– and I might add *mint-condition*– vehicle, Emerald started having her nails done in the same glossy green as the car. The green, of course, matches her McDonough eyes, as well as most of the clothes in her jam-packed closets." Raine stopped just long enough to swallow a sip of champagne. "She's connived Cousin Darby into keeping the Sunbeam tuned up and purring like a kitten for her, as he did when it belonged to Grantie. Darby's OK with the arrangement. It means he can drive the car on occasion."

"Did you know that green eyes are the rarest of eye color?" Betty asked. "Uh-huh, naturally occurring in only two percent of the world's population. People with green eyes are said to be tough, quick-witted and caring, attracting others like magnets. They're leaders, excellent speakers, and great lovers. Let me think; it's been a while since I read this. I seem to recall it's the only eye color that changes, becoming more green, grey-ish or blue-ish, depending on mood, weather, or surroundings, and that includes what the green-eyed person is wearing."

"Do you agree with all that?" Maggie whispered to Thaddeus, who, in turn, came back with–

"Every word," he winked.

"I wonder," Maggie mused audibly, "if Emerald will be wearing a gown that's *totally* green? I had a vision of her last night, and she was wearing–" she cut off, continuing, "I don't want to spoil it for all of you, so I'll let you be surprised. And wait till you see what her fiancé Jack surprises *her* with tonight at the rehearsal dinner! I saw that in my vision too."

Ian poured himself and Aisling more champagne. "Has anyone heard how Emerald's parents are getting along, now that they've reconciled so many years after their divorce?"

"From what Grantie has said," Aisling reacted with happy air, "Bartley and Maureen get along better now, as friends, than ever they did as man and wife. Naturally, Emerald's elated over the ceasefire."

"Wonder if they'll ever remarry?" Betty asked, as she brushed cracker crumbs from the turquoise velvet dress she was wearing.

"None of us think so," Maggie replied.

"No," Raine agreed simultaneously, "even Emerald realizes and accepts the fact that her parents are much better as friends than mates."

"Have Emerald and Jack purchased a home yet?" Hugh questioned. "I assume they have." He was heartily enjoying the hors d'oeuvres and champagne.

"Oh yes," Aisling answered. "Grantie told us they purchased a charming old home, very Gothic. The house is located in Salem's historic Chestnut District, reputed to be the most beautiful street in all of America, you know."

"'Tis a good thing Jack's family's wealthy," Raine bantered. "He'll one day take over the real estate brokerage his father owns. We wish him well in his endeavors. Emerald's high maintenance– with very *expensive* preferences."

Aisling zipped her brunette sister of the moon a look that stopped further digs.

"Grantie was, of course, tickled pink that Emerald gave in to Jack's desire to live in a historic Salem house. At first, Em wanted something much more modern," Maggie remembered. "Jack plans to ride the ferry every day to and from work in the city, from Salem to Boston's Long Wharf and back again."

Reaching for a cracker, Merry Fay remarked, "Ooooh, that sounds like fun."

"I'm eagerly anticipating lively discussion with your cousin Sean again," Thaddeus stated. He helped himself to a few more prawns, sharing with Maggie. "He's one of the most intelligent people with whom I've ever had the pleasure of debate."

"Sean holds a couple of degrees, one in philosophy, the other, more recent, in archeology," Maggie rejoined. "And I believe he's almost acquired enough credits for a third degree in anthropology. He's a true Celt, not only in looks; but like all the McDonoughs, he's a free-thinker, a free spirit. 'No amount of security is worth the suffering of a mediocre life chained to a routine that's killed dreams,' he's told us.

"He could be making a fine salary at a university, but he's never cared about money or material things. 'I want to fill my life with adventures, not things. I want stories to tell, not stuff to show.' Hence, Sean chooses to teach on an Indian reservation out in Montana. There, he also gives lectures on various subjects near and dear to his heart; and he quietly practices the Craft, along with Native American spiritualism, in the solitude of his remote, rustic log cabin. His large acreage of wilderness land affords him the hermit existence he fancies." Maggie poured herself and Thaddeus a bit more champagne.

"Witchcraft," the redheaded Sister thought to add after a moment, "is a spiritual path. We walk it for nourishment of the soul, to commune with Earth Mother and the Life Force of the universe, to know our animal brothers and sisters better, and to thereby know ourselves better."

"In response to what you said earlier about Sean. There's a lot more to him than the tautly muscled torso and the exotic slant of his eyes. Anyway, he's been after us to come visit him in Montana. It would be too crowded for us to bunk with him in his little cabin, but there's a guest ranch, a working ranch not a golf-course dude ranch, within a reasonable proximity to him that he recommends for our stay." Raine looked to Maggie. "We've been thinking about obliging our favorite cousin during spring break this year."

"I think you should do it," Beau commented. "You deserve a vacation, and I wouldn't worry with you in Sean's care."

"I meant to ask when his name came up," Hugh voiced, "how's your cousin Darby? In good health and spirits, I trust."

"Darby's well," Raine and Maggie spoke in sync, as they ofttimes did.

"Darby's got his funny little ways and his issues with anemia, but he's stronger than he looks," Raine concluded.

"I sometimes worry," said Maggie, "that he's a heroic character wasted in a prosaic life."

"Oh, from what little I know of Darby, I sense he just hasn't discovered his calling yet ... why he was put here on planet Earth. Does he still live with his mother?" Thaddeus queried, though not in a snide or negative tone.

"He does," Aisling replied. "When Grantie passes over, he'll reside in her seaside cottage as caretaker. We'll have to contact him when we wish to occupy the place, and those times, he'll stay at his mom's. It's the way Grantie wants it, so Darby can experience life without his mother, and the historic cottage is never left vacant and vulnerable. When we take possession one day, we'll adhere to her wishes."

"It'll be so nice to see everyone again," Maggie whispered, almost to herself.

"How are the aunts?" Betty quizzed. "Any news on that front?"

"Oh, Aunties Luna and Celeste never seem to change," Aisling stated with a musing smile, "the quintessential good witches, both."

"And Cousin Rowena, Darby's mom, never changes either." Maggie laughed her crystal laugh. "She's just as chatty as ever, still plump as a partridge, with a cheery smile for everyone. Ro's still cookin' up the best potions of anyone in our clan, in addition to the best New England cuisine we ever tasted."

Dr. Weatherby, who had been engrossed in the passing seascapes, bounded back into the conversation. "We're nearing the Common, boys and girls!"

Everyone finished their drinks. They'd all done justice to the hors d'oeuvres; and now it was time to slip back into their wraps, for crystal-like flakes were beginning to descend upon the already snow-blanketed Salem, rendering the old town even more enchanting– the winter wonderland for which Emerald wished.

Winter's eventide was glorious at Salem. Here, the stars always seemed to shine brighter than anywhere else, reflected in the water and twinkling, with the lights of the city, like a faerieland.

"Hawthorne Hotel," their driver announced via the intercom. "Founded by the city of Salem in 1925," the gifted Merry Fay remembered from their last visit to the "Witch City," when the limo driver recounted for them the hotel's history. "Remember, this is a *haunted* hotel. I hope *we* see a ghost!" Before anyone could respond, Merry raced on, "I looked the ghost stuff up, and guess what? *Several* rooms are haunted, especially rooms 612, where a lady ghost is seen by lots-a people; and 325, where the lights and the faucets turn on and off all by themselves. Oh, oh, oh, and apples! People smell apples when there are no apples. D'you know why?" Again, the excited child rushed on, "Because one of the first women to be hanged as a witch during the sickening Witch Trials was Bridget Bishop, and she owned an apple orchard right *here*," she thrust a dimpled hand toward the Hawthorne, "where this hotel now stands. Lots of famous people stayed here, Presidents and movie stars. And *Bewitched* was filmed here too, but I forget the year."

"1970," Aisling supplied. "Some of our relatives were extras in those episodes. Button your coat, Merry Fay."

"*Bewitched* is my favorite show," Merry enthused. "I watch it all the time on Classic TV. Mommy points out the aunts when they show the Salem parts."

Hugh handed Don Karr a generous gratuity, as the chauffeur helped the ladies out of the stretch limo. After all the luggage was removed from the trunk, the driver tipped his hat. "It's a pleasure to serve you. I plan to grab a quick sandwich and a coffee, then I'll return here in a half-hour, at the hotel entrance, to drive you to the Avalon."

Inside the Hawthorne's lobby, the tall, green ferns and bright floral arrangements, together with the comfy sitting nooks and oriental carpets, created a reception area that was inviting and cozy.

"Let's all get checked in and freshened up," Hugh charged. He glanced at his watch. "We'll meet here in the lobby at quarter till seven."

On the way up to their room, Raine remarked to Beau, "Exciting nights and days ahead, big boy!"

As everything was about to unfold – that was an understatement.

Chapter Two

En route to the Avalon, where both the rehearsal dinner and the handfasting ceremony would be taking place, the Sleuth Sisters and their party were again ensconced in the luxury of the black, stretch Besom Limo. Since time was tight, everyone had traveled in what they would be wearing to the dinner; thus, they had only to freshen up in their rooms at the Hawthorne before setting off for the banquet hall.

"It might seem like a modern concept," Raine was saying, "but the idea of a marriage 'for a year and a day,' or 'for as long as love shall last,' is very old. Emerald and Jack, however, chose to legalize their bonds in accordance with Massachusetts' law, so their marriage is sealed until either death or a legal divorce."

"I can understand that," Beau was quick to remark, "about their wanting a permanent bond. After all, they are entering a financial partnership as well as a loving union." He stole a glance at Raine, who pretended not to notice.

"And I have a feeling," Aisling broke in, "they will be wanting children. At least, I believe, Jack will. Then, there's the matter of inheritance. In their case, I deem it was the right thing to do."

"I agree." Maggie attended to her lipstick in her compact mirror, catching sight of the looming Gothic Witch Museum to the left of their moving limo. "Jack's family is in the upper socio-economic echelon; and like Emerald, he's an only child. Yes, for them– and Grantie said they really hashed everything out– it was the best decision."

"Jack's not a practitioner of the Craft, is he?" asked Thaddeus.

Maggie snapped the compact closed with a dramatic flourish. "Not yet," she replied with mysterious tone and smile.

"I think, too," Aisling said with a nod, "Emerald will convert him. And I have a witchy hunch she's already made real progress."

"Does Jack's family accept Emerald's beliefs?" Thaddeus wondered out loud. He stroked his trim, pointed beard. "*Quin* ... Irish Catholic, aren't they?"

"Yes, in answer to both queries." Aisling tarried for a moment, reaching over to adjust the headband in Merry Fay's long, blonde hair. "Surprisingly, Jack's family is accepting of Emerald's convictions. Or perhaps not so surprisingly. Perchance they have a witch or two secreted in their family tree."

"It's a possibility," Raine jumped in. "Salem is, after all, the Witch Capital of the World. A practicing witch since childhood, Emerald has been greatly influenced by Grantie's teachings. She feels it's important to declare the commitments she and Jack share. Irrespective of the civil service this morning, Emerald very much wants to express her own feelings, and she wants Jack to be able to do the same at their handfasting tomorrow."

"Right," Maggie concurred, "they both felt that a secular ceremony would be neutral ground, but not as fulfilling and meaningful as a declaration of love before the God and Goddess– the Lord and Lady– or in Jack's case, the Divine Source, and in the presence of family and friends." She popped a mint into her mouth, passing the small tin round to the others.

"Have Emerald and Jack written their *own* vows?" Hugh queried. And though his words were posed with inflection, the Sisters instantly sensed he knew the answer.

"Indeed," Aisling rejoined, "the vows will be of the couple's own making, and they will express their own needs and emotions. We will not be privy to those vows until the ceremony on the morrow, when the magick circle is cast."

"For a brief moment in time," Maggie inferred with wistful expression, "that circle will become the center of the universe, and what evolves within its sacred space, during the handfasting ceremony, will recreate and reenact the cosmic theme of the great love between the Lord and the Lady, God and Goddess."

"It's very old and quite powerful," Aisling whispered, squeezing Ian's hand. "Usually, if there's to be a civil ceremony, it follows the handfasting; but Jack's parents lobbied for the observance by Jack's father's longtime friend, Judge Sullivan, and since the judge had a European vacation planned, he married the couple this morning in chambers before he embarked on his holiday. According to Emerald's brief text message, the civil ceremony was simple and straightforward, though delivered with all the solemnity that a wedding deserves."

"Anyroad," Raine interjected, "vows, rings, hand-binding, and besom jumping will all take place tomorrow."

"I've never attended a handfasting," Betty commented, "so this is all new and exciting for me." She handed the little tin of mints back to Maggie.

Now it was Hugh's turn to squeeze his beloved's hand. "Perhaps," he halted briefly, his gaze meeting Betty's, "we'll have our own one day … in the not too distant future."

His words prompted an exchange of looks among the others, with Raine exhibiting a satisfied grin.

"So you would want a handfasting?" Betty returned in hushed mien, her turquoise eyes suddenly moist with emotion.

"I would," Hugh delivered to her ear. "We can personalize it to fit *our* desires."

"I'm certain Emerald's handfast will provide wonderful inspiration," she whispered to him alone.

"Aisling," Raine said, "about the civil ceremony taking place before or after the handfasting: The day belongs to the couple, and they can shape it however they wish." She caught a sidelong glance of Beau through her thick, dark veil of lashes. He was watching her with an intensity that forced her to ramble on, avoiding his eyes, "Emerald will have a high priestess as her officiant for the ceremony. High Priestess Wind-Song is well known and highly respected throughout the Salem community, and she's licensed to perform handfastings."

"February is a good month to wed. 'When February birds do mate, you wed nor dread your fate.' And the moon in Leo tomorrow is the purrrrrrrr-fect moon for a handfasting," Maggie affirmed in her soft voice. "The time of day is also significant, and Emerald chose eleven in the morning on Valentine's Day, because that's precisely when she and Jack met. Eleven is near mid-day, which represents the zenith of the day's power."

"I *am* surprised she settled on a Saturday, though I realize Valentine's this year falls on a Saturday. Still …" Raine pondered, flicking a wisp of ebony hair from her eye, "not a good day for a handfasting. Saturday's the day of Saturn, the planet concerned with endings, dissolution, and death."

"*Ah*," Maggie interposed, holding up a finger for silence, "keep in mind that Emerald and Jack were legally wed this morning, Friday, and Friday's a jolly good day to wed, unless you believe it to be the day of crosses. But Emerald's not a Christian, so she accepts that Friday is Venus' day, Venus, the Goddess of Love, hence it's a grand day for marrying. Venus is associated with the sea, and it is for this reason that fish was eaten on Fridays, a custom later adopted by Christians. I'd wager we'll be served fish and other fruits of the sea this evening at the rehearsal dinner. It would be for good luck. And don't forget that Saturday is a good day for preparation, so why not preparation for the couple's life together?"

Raine had been nodding her assent to each of Maggie's points. "Sound reasoning, Mags. I totally agree with you."

"Who will be Emerald's maid of honor?" Betty queried. She opened her purse to retrieve her leather gloves, which she commenced to pull on.

"A kinswoman," Aisling answered. "Cousin Rowena McDonough."

"I love the magickal name *Rowena,*" Raine cut in. "Always reminds me of our favorite musician, Rowena of the Glen, though our kinswoman is nothing like the songstress."

"As I was saying," Aisling persevered, used to Raine's fire that sometimes burst into someone else's dialogue, "the bride is customarily attended by a married woman, albeit our Rowena is a widow. Grantie told us it surprised Ro greatly when Emerald asked her, but it healed an old rift; and Grantie crowed, with unabashed pride, that it showed how much Emerald has grown in the past months."

"Jack's groomsman is a kinsman as well, his favorite cousin, Terry." Raine thought for a moment. "Did you know that in olden times, troubled times, it was part of the groomsman's duty to safeguard the wedding party, and that's one of the reasons the bride stands to the left of the groom, so that his sword arm is free to protect her."

"And did you know that in medieval times, the bride, maid of honor, and bridesmaids, if there were any, *all* dressed in white?" Maggie gave a brisk nod. "So any evil spirits lurking about with intent to spoil the wedding wouldn't know which maiden was the bride." The redheaded Sister was suddenly struck with one of her flash visions that stopped her abruptly. *I wonder if ...* Aloud she said, "Green, as we said, is Emerald's signature color. When she heard that old saying, 'Marry in green, ashamed to be seen,'" the sensual Sis raised a brow, interjecting with lowered voice, "it implied, you see, that the bride had been rolling about on the grass with a lover or lovers, Em became *determined* to defy convention."

Raine laughed, "There's no force equal to that of a determined witch."

"The theme, Grantie told us, of the handfasting décor will be medieval Irish … well, Celtic anyway, and the attire, food, and drink will all reflect that theme." Maggie gave a little sigh. "*Romantic*, isn't it?" She looked to Thaddeus, who, she discovered, appeared to be intently studying her. "You're unusually quiet," she breathed into his ear.

"I usually am when I'm thinking," he answered smoothly. On impulse, he lifted her hand to his lips to bestow a kiss.

"I'm looking forward to the medieval," Betty fluttered her hands in the air, "*ambience* tomorrow. I daresay Hugh and I took great care selecting *our* attire."

"Auntie Raine," Merry Fay smiled, giving the Goth gal's sleeve a tug, "I looked up handfasting on my computer this week, and guess what I learned?"

Raine leaned close to the child. "May I borrow a kiss? I'll give it back. What did you learn, precious?"

The bright little Fay landed a kiss on Raine's cheek, reciting from memory, "The idioms 'getting hitched,' 'tying the knot,' and 'joining hands in marriage' all came from the ritual of binding the bride and groom's hands together with colored ribbons or the groom's tartan, whichever, during the handfast."

Raine's face brightened, and she returned the caress. "That's right. Great galloping gargoyles, most of the wedding customs we use today sprang from pagan rites … the couple's loving cup, the sharing of a cup, symbolic of their sharing everything from that point on; showering the couple with rice, an act of magick so they never go hungry; throwing the bouquet; the tying of old shoes on the couple's mode of transportation. All those rituals hark back to pagan times."

"I meant to mention earlier, that, in Ireland, green is deemed the faeries' color," stated Maggie, who had lived in Ireland when she was married to a man from the Emerald Isle.

"To be sure," Aisling laughed, "and according to Grantie, *that* made our Emerald even *more* determined to wed in green. Her father always tells her she has faerie blood.

"She wore a body-hugging, designer suit this morning for the civil ceremony. Hunter green silk." Aisling extended her phone with a picture Emerald had sent earlier. "No matter what legends are attached to it, if you want my opinion, it strikes me that Emerald would feel **un**lucky married in any other color," the senior Sister concluded.

"And *that* could well draw *bad* luck," Maggie said with slightly lifted brows.

"Well, green is said to bring prosperity, loyalty, and adventure … **so there!**" Raine, who also claimed that witchy color as *her* own, declared with vehemence. She smiled when a sudden image flashed upon her mind. "Emerald has always been so keen on Scarlett O'Hara that even her engagement ring was selected from the literary character's tale. The ring is an exact copy of the one Rhett chose for Scarlett, except that the stones are reversed– Emerald's own little twist, you see, on Margaret Mitchell's creative genius. Rather than a huge, four-carat, pear-shaped diamond surrounded by emeralds, Em's ring holds, for the central stone, a four-carat, pear-shaped emerald surrounded by sparkling, brilliant-cut diamonds. Like Scarlett's, it reaches her knuckle and appears to weigh her hand."

"Emerald loves bold jewelry, so the ring more than pleases her," Maggie interjected. "She loves to flaunt it, though I can't say I blame her. She told us the total weight is nearly seven carats."

"From the images Emerald sent us on our computer, the ring is *breathtaking*. Fiddle-dee-dee," the raven-haired Sister giggled, "the day after she became officially engaged, when showing it to friends– who, of course, nearly gasped over the token *fiançailles*– Grantie reported that Emerald remarked in as level a voice as she could muster, 'Yes, it's sweet, isn't it?'"

"It *is*. Emeralds represent the Goddess Venus, the Goddess of Love, and the gemstone's metaphysical properties are *perfect* for a handfasting– love, loyalty, happiness, joy, and prosperity. Both rings, hers and Jack's, are engraved on the inside band with the Irish words *Mo Chuisle*, meaning My Darling." Maggie peered out the window. "I think we've arrived."

Validating Maggie's declaration, Chauffeur Don Karr announced, by way of the limo's intercom, "Avalon!"

The Sleuth Sisters and their party exited the limousine to a grey-stone, Gothic and imposing, castle-like structure that twinkled with hundreds of tiny, white welcoming lights.

Inside, the Great Hall was equally impressive. Suits of armor, shields, swords, and medieval weaponry dignified the walls, three of which exhibited yawning fireplaces, in which great log-fires blazed, the flames making cozy crackling sounds, as the smell of wood and pine cones pleasantly scented the romantic feudal atmosphere. The ceiling was peaked and beamed, from which hung various, colorful standards, the stone floor warmed with Oriental area carpets in rich reds. The largest, center, carpet was topped with a long, heavy, medieval-style table and carved chairs, the backs of which bore three-dimensional Irish wolfhounds, facing outward to traditionally guard the backs of sitters.

"Wiz–ard!" Raine exclaimed, using her favorite oath. "I feel transported back in time."

"The furniture and fittings look authentic but surely aren't," Maggie whispered. It seemed only proper to hold one's voice to a whisper in such a place as magnificent as this.

"We are to meet in the Secret Garden," Aisling reminded their party, who trooped through the castle in silent awe, their eyes taking in the majesty of their surroundings. "The Lady in Waiting I spoke with at the reception area, when we came in, told me to turn right after we pass through this Great Hall. The Secret Garden should be," she turned her head to point, "down that passageway."

"The handfasting and subsequent reception tomorrow will take place in the Camelot Room, but the rehearsal dinner this evening is in the Secret Garden," Maggie reaffirmed. "Ah, here we are." She indicated the small, flowery sign that told them they were in the right place. The placard above it read *Faerie Gallerie*, with an arrow that pointed in the opposite direction.

"'Who enters there, may faeries meet. With laughter soft, they should be greet,'" Raine giggled, causing Merry Fay to clap her hands. "Couldn't help quoting a passage that popped into my head from an old Nancy Drew Mystery."

At the garden-room entry, the Sleuth Sisters' faction paused just inside the doorway, mainly to get a long view of the conservatory-like area, but also to allow the High Priestess to conclude her discourse with the wedding party, who were just entering, in a group, from the far side.

The domed garden room was surrounded by glass and bursting with greenery, tall and low potted plants and hanging basketry. Torch-style wall sconces protruded at an angle from the narrow wall spaces between the broad segments of glass. Outside, the medieval lighting romantically showcased the falling snow; whilst inside, the baronial, faux-candle chandeliers and wall sconces cast soft, flickering light on the faerie-tale space. As in the Great Hall, a massive Gothic oak table with carved chairs dominated the center of the room.

"I think," High-Priestess Wind-Song was saying in conclusion to the wedding party, "we have the choreography down pat now. If you are happy, I'm happy." She brought her hands together in a pleased manner. "Questions?"

Wind-Song's eyes skimmed the small wedding party before her. When no one put forth a query, she went on, "Then let us adjourn to the Secret Garden," she extended a graceful hand forward, the long, bell sleeve of her ecru-lace gown cascading from her arm, "for what I am certain will be a delicious dinner. Tonight, I advise the bride and groom, especially, to get a good night's sleep." She gave a knowing smile. "Problematic, I realize, since you tied the knot today in the judge's chambers." She extended her hands to Emerald and Jack, "Goddess bless you both. Bathe tonight in lavender scent and sleep with a large amethyst under your pillows, to sweeten your dreams and grant you a more restful night, or," she smiled again, "as restful as you can make it. And on the morrow, remember the rings and your vows. If you don't have your vows memorized, as I told you earlier, it is perfectly all right to read them from a sheet of paper. You can do that if you're nervous, no problem."

High Priestess Wind-Song was a middle-aged woman of medium height and build. She was blonde with a sweet face and a soft, soothing voice that reminded listeners that she served the Goddess.

"The High Priestess looks a lot like Stevie Nicks," Raine whispered to Maggie.

"She does," the redheaded Sister replied.

"I'm getting good vibes from her, aren't you?" Aisling breathed.

"Really good," came the in-sync reply from Raine and Maggie.

Guests were milling into the Secret Garden now for the cocktail hour, which included champagne and an open bar in addition to hors d'oeuvres. Dinner would follow. As the Sleuth Sisters and their party approached the bride and groom, Wind-Song, Grantie Merry, and several others were already gathered round the beaming couple.

"Emerald, Jack, you're positively glowing," Aisling said, stepping forward to embrace first their cousin, then the groom. "We're all so happy for you."

Raine and Maggie followed suit, as everyone greeted one another.

It was an especially poignant moment when Emerald, Aisling, Maggie, and Raine basked in a group hug.

Still in the encirclement, the bride whispered, "Thank you, dear Sisters, for aiding in my … *illumination.*"

A faint smile appeared on Aisling's lips. "You always had the power to shape the winds of change to your will. All you needed was a nudge in the right direction."

"At any given moment in our lives," Raine took up the thought, "we all have the power to say …"

"This is not how the story is going to end," the Goth gal and Maggie concluded in unison.

"Exactly right. You're the author of your own story," Aisling adjoined, "the pen is in your hands. And it looks as though, beginning with this faerie-tale handfast, you're crafting a beautiful storybook, with all the right elements for a 'happily-ever-after' ending. We're proud of you, Em; we really are."

"And I shall be forever grateful to you that you opened the door to a new chapter of my life," Emerald divulged, giving the trio of Sisters another warm hug. "Quite frankly," she leaned forward in conspiratorial undertone, her Irish eyes dancing with naughtiness, "I meant to behave in the past, but all the other options were *ever* so much more fun. To be perfectly honest, I don't suppose I'll ever be a well-behaved woman … not *really.*"

Maggie laughed breezily, and her green eyes sparkled too. "You wouldn't be our Emerald if you were. Always remember that what you *are* is a *McDonough* woman. If you can step out into a storm with a smile and," her gaze lowered to Emerald's glittering green shoes, "your favorite heels, darlin'– the battle is already won!"

Raine nodded in ardent agreement. "Wise women armed with love and ancestral wisdom are an unstoppable force."

"One more piece of advice, Cousin," Aisling said, squeezing Emerald's hand, "and we promise we'll stop pontificating. Be the reason someone, especially that *special* someone, really *believes* in magick."

Singular attention and respect were bestowed, by every member of the McDonough clan in attendance, on Grantie Merry, who appeared to defy Time. Though now a centenarian, the woman never seemed to age past sixty.

"She told us once," Maggie whispered to Raine and Aisling, "that she took Granny McDonough's advice to bathe her face daily in ice water charged with rose quartz to fade wrinkles and keep the skin young and glowing."

"Don't know. What I *do* know is that age is a state of mind," Aisling pointed out. "Grantie lives by the maxim that aging is not lost youth, but rather, a new stage of opportunity and strength."

"And lest we forget," Maggie put in with her mysterious tone and smile, "A witch can be *both* immeasurably ancient *and* forever young."

There came the lovely clink of glasses and serving dishes. By this point, waiters, garbed in the attire of medieval pages, began to circulate with trays of appetizing hors d'oeuvres and flutes of champagne; and waitresses in serving-wench attire began carrying items to the long, set table in preparation for the dinner. At this same time, too, medieval court music began to issue softly from wall speakers.

In the castle-like setting, Grantie looked more regal than ever. Her soft velvet gown was of the deepest purple, and her fingers sparkled with amethyst, garnet, and ruby rings. On a chain of substantial silver, a huge amethyst, nestled in filigree, was suspended from her remarkably youthful neck.

The McDonough *grande dame* was an average-size woman. That is, she was of medium height and build, but her stature was the only *average* thing about this matchless crone. Often, after speaking with Merry over the telephone, people envisioned her as a "*big* woman." She *was*, but not in the way imagined.

A cloud of white hair, which she habitually wore in a loose bun, framed her once cameo-pretty face. Hers was an intelligent, sensitive face, with grey eyes of a peculiar and searching intensity. Grantie's features were what most would term "classical," and for years, Merry used nothing but a soft-pink lip color and powder on her curiously unlined skin.

To look upon this pink-and-white confection, one, if not familiar with Meredith "Merry" McDonough, would think of her as a "sweet little old lady," but Grantie was anything but. Indeed, she would have *cringed* at that description of herself. Not to say that she was unkind and hard-hearted, but she was certainly not made of sugar candy.

Merry McDonough tenaciously believed in "taking the bull by the horns" and "putting the cards on the table" when dealing with life.

Where the Craft was concerned, Grantie was an ultra-talented, multi-gifted, natural-born, solitary, eclectic witch, who, over the long years, honed her skills to near-perfection. Like anyone else, in or outside the Craft, she was sometimes led by the heart rather than by good common sense– *but not often.* Merry had learned, from life's lessons, when to listen to the heart, and when to act from reasoning.

An Aries sun and the Ram in its home sign of Mars kept her youthful, and strong Capricorn and Scorpio influences made Merry a resilient old gal. With typical Scorpio-rising demeanor, this lady was dignified and reserved, secretive and magnetic, with a gaze that was as direct and penetrating as her speech.

Grantie was never known to utter her words with affectation. She never beat around the bush, but cut right to the mark, and no one could ever say there was anything fake or pretentious about Merry McDonough.

The lady's deep sensitivity made her the best and most loyal of friends, but that same trait rendered her the most formidable enemy, and there were a few over the mounting years that found her Scorpio sting to be, succinctly stated, *astounding*– so at odds was it with her affable exterior.

Grantie's moon in Capricorn allowed her to keep a stiff upper lip and to keep going in life, even when patches of rough road made the going tough. This astro-placement also bestowed on the lady a strong sense of duty and reverence for tradition.

Though, for the most part, her magick was white (she'd gone grey a few times in her long life when she deemed it necessary for self-preservation), all in all, Lady McDonough was no one with whom to trifle.

Proper protocol dictated that the Sleuth Sisters and their faction return their homage to the bride and groom.

"Emerald," Hugh spoke with sincerity, picking up her hand to kiss it, "I never thought you could become more beautiful than the last time we were here, but I was wrong."

A faint tint of color rose to the bride's fair cheek. "Thank you, Mr. Goodwin. You're a darling. It was so good of you to come all the way up to Salem to help Jack and me celebrate our vows. We appreciate," her sparkling feline eyes swept the gathering of family and friends, "seeing all of you. Your presence makes our handfasting all the more special."

The Sisters' younger cousin, Emerald Holloway-Quin, looked a lot like Raine, and they both possessed the same fiery disposition. The bride's jet-black hair, however, was not short and wispy like the Goth gal's. Rather it was shoulder-length, casual, with loose waves that framed her oval face. She'd inherited the slanted, vivid green McDonough eyes from her mother; and, similar to the Sleuth Sisters, she accentuated those mesmerizing eyes with bold make-up. Like Raine, Emerald, too, had fair skin and a nice body. In summary, Miss Holloway was a stunning brunette, much smarter than she frequently let on, sassy, sexy, and when she chose, *charming* with a cauldron full of witchy-woman mystique and mystery.

The groom, Jack Quin, was what cinema historically termed "tall, dark, and handsome." Combine that with successful, wealthy, and polished, and you have–

"… the perfect match for Emerald," Maggie whispered to Thaddeus, who answered with an agreeing nod.

Emerald looked drop-dead gorgeous tonight in a lustrous charmeuse dress of her signature color. Her enormous emerald and diamond engagement ring sparkled on her left hand, and around her neck was Jack's wedding gift to her, a six-carat, pear-shaped emerald surrounded by diamonds and set in a glowing, medieval, eighteen-karat gold circlet that could be worn as a necklace or on the crown of the head, so that the emerald rested on the forehead. In her ears, she wore the emerald drops that her father had gifted her mother, Maureen, on their wedding day.

The fair Maureen was an older version of Emerald, though her coiffure was shorter, a little like Raine's feathery do; and for all her forty-odd years, she'd kept her figure. Tonight, her McDonough eyes shone with true happiness. Maureen had been estranged from her daughter and husband for more years than she cared to remember; but since Emerald's troubles the previous spring, troubles the Sleuth Sisters sorted out, the pined-for woman was back in Emerald's life, in Emerald's father's life, too, as a long-lost friend and confidante.

"Long-lost friends are like fine wine," Bart told Maureen; "we're better with age."

Once known in the McDonough clan as "Black Bart," Bartley Holloway was a reticent sort of chap whose intense dark eyes and black hair, sleeked back from a chiseled face, with its pronounced widow's peak and high cheekbones, lent him a devilish appearance.

Nowadays, however, with the wounds of his failed marriage healed and his alliance blossoming with his ex-wife, he was anything but devilish.

At the moment, he and Maureen were happily chatting with their daughter and the groom in a way that bespoke contentment.

Checking her watch, Aisling glanced around the garden room. "My parents rang me earlier to say they might be a tad late, but not to worry about them. They took the ferry over to Boston today to sightsee and do a bit of shopping. In a moment, her face lit up, "Oh, here they come now!"

Given that Aisling's parents resided in Haleigh's Hamlet, she saw them often, though, since her father retired, the couple traveled a lot. Aisling's mother, Kate, a former elementary-school teacher who became a stay-at-home mom when Aisling was born, was blonde like her daughter and granddaughter, of medium stature, and possessed of a happy, carefree nature that seemed to provide her with a visible glow. She wore her chin-length hair in a sleek, shiny pageboy, held in place with a black, velvet headband. Her husband Ronan, Aisling's father and brother to Raine and Maggie's fathers, was a retired police detective. Tall and burly, Ronan's dark hair was streaked with grey, his face somewhat weathered from all the activities he enjoyed outdoors; but, akin to his wife's disposition, his spirit soared.

Once the Ronan McDonoughs paid their respects to the bride and groom and Grantie, they made their way among the others, exchanging pleasant repartee to end with their daughter and her family.

"Did you have a nice time today?" Ian asked his in-laws, grasping his father-in-law's hand to shake it.

"We did," Kate replied, embracing, in turn, daughter, granddaughter, and son-in-law.

"Did you do much shopping?" Aisling inquired, knowing full well what her mother's response would be.

"Does a witch wave her wand?" Kate laughed. "I hit upon a *great* pair of shoes, though I don't know where I'll even put another pair in my closet. Your father says I need a room just for my shoes. And I found an *adorable* Valentine-red jumper for you, Merry Fay. I–" Her words were halted when Aisling interceded.

"Oh, Mother, you buy her so much, you didn't have to–"

"Of course I didn't, but I wanted to. I enjoy it. It was on sale at this charming, little boutique, and …"

The aunts were there at the Avalon, of course, as magnetic as ever. Laughing together over an incident that occurred that morning at the courthouse, Luna and Celeste McDonough were spinster sisters– sisters by blood *and* sisters of the moon.

If one had sent down to the trusty Central Casting for the ideal good witch, either of those sisters would have fit the bill to a fare-thee-well.

Never having married, the "McDonough Sisters," as Salem folk called them, resided in the same house together, the house built in 1886 on Pickman Street in which they were born, the gabled, powder-blue house with the dark-blue awnings and white gingerbread. Now in their late-sixties, the aunts were more mellow than ever, and though set in their ways, they always appeared to be in a good mood. "Laughter becomes you," a would-be suitor once told Celeste, and truer words, in regards to either of the sisters, were never spoken.

Luna had shoulder-length, silver hair that shimmered with the moon's own light. She wore it loose and natural, and her blue-grey eyes were reminiscent of moonstone. Celeste was taller, but both women were of average height. Appropriate to her name, Celeste had sky-blue eyes and cloud-white hair pulled loosely back from her face in a single, long, thick braid that she wore, *à la bohème*, over her shoulder.

Both sisters dressed in an airy fashion, giving the impression that they were painters, sculptors, writers, or of some such calling within the arts. They consistently chose organic fabrics, for comfort and insouciance. The pair took to the lagenlook like proverbial ducks to water. It was the style they were both sporting tonight, layered, long and flowing– Luna in silvery-grey and Celeste in a light, mystical blue– that heightened their witchy looks and gave them an almost ethereal mien.

"Hahahahaha," Luna shook with laughter, as she rested a hand on Cousin Sean's muscular arm. "You have such a quick wit! Oh, darling, you *must* try these smoked salmon deviled eggs."

Giving Luna a peck on the cheek, Sean turned to snatch one of the treats from the tray of a passing server in page attire. When he did, his eye caught Raine's, and he sent her a jovial nod.

The family said the Goth gal's favorite cousin was her male counterpart. Tall, rangy, dark, mustached, and super-sexy, Sean McDonough looked and sounded like Sam Elliott– as the actor appeared in the film *Mask*. Sean's thick, wavy, near-ebony hair he wore slightly long; and his face, now that he'd reached the back side of thirty, exhibited just the right amount of weathering to give him the air of the classic cowboy. His suggestive grin and the Western drawl that carried on his basso voice caused female hearts to flutter whither he roamed.

The previous year at Salem, while immersed in a philosophical discussion with Hugh, Sean said something that pretty much epitomized his character: "I spend most of my life on a horse or a motorcycle, and that has caused some to label me; but *I* know who I am, and that's all that matters." When Grantie asked him why in the world he'd majored in philosophy, adding that he never used it after college, Sean had laughed, rumbling in that distinctive voice of his, "Majored in it 'cause I love it. That's the best reason I know to major in anything. And who says I never use it? I use it every day of my life. Isn't life a pursuit of wisdom, as philosophy itself?"

At the moment, Sean's deep laugh rolled over the chatter, as something Luna said tickled his funny bone. "Our Native American rodeo's not for the faint of heart." He put his arm around the sweet lady, giving her a hearty hug. "Don't worry, Auntie," he responded to Celeste. "Only good reason I know t' ride a bull is to meet a pretty nurse! And Aunt Luna, you got it right about this dang texting that's infected humanity. Folks need to spend less time staring at screens and more time dancing in the kitchen, making love, and laughing under the stars."

Last but not least, Cousin Rowena and her son Darby were the remaining members of the bride's family. A moonchild, Rowena's round face constantly presented a smile, and this occasion was no exception. In her mid-sixties, this was a "wise-woman" of several talents, with cooking topping the list. Rowena was as rotund and talkative as her son was tall, lean, and reticent.

"Darby," she sighed, gazing fondly at her only offspring, "the great Goddess grant that the next wedding we're all gathered for will be yours. You're not getting any younger, but you're a man, so there's still hope."

Pale and angular, Cousin Darby was a timid soul, in his early forties, who suffered from anemia. He was a computer tutor at the high school and around Salem, and he repaired computers in the basement of his mother's house, where he still made his home. No one ever seemed to pay any mind to Darby, so unobtrusive was he. Indeed, this cousin blended into the background of any setting, almost like a chameleon. He'd never married, never even courted a girl, not because he didn't like or notice girls, but because he lacked the confidence to approach them. Now, standing next to his mother, he nibbled on the hors d'oeuvres, content to watch and listen, as the others interacted with one another. Darby learned a lot of things by staying still and quiet, listening and observing.

Actually, everyone was listening– enjoying the Celtic harp, medieval wedding music that began to softly play in the background.

Thaddeus whispered to Maggie, "I recognize everyone in *your* family. Not that many from the groom's clan here though, are there?"

"There won't be," she answered in a muffled voice. "Most of Jack's family is skiing at Haute Savoie in the French Alps. Grantie said they go every year at this time." She moved closer so no one would hear, even those standing nearby. "Emerald knew this, of course, and that was another reason she chose the Valentine date for her handfasting. Apparently, she finds several of the Quins 'stuffy.'"

"So who all from Jack's family then?" Dr. Weatherby asked, his gaze searching.

"Jack's parents; his cousin and groomsman Terry; Terry's sister, Desirée; and an elderly uncle … Maxwell, I believe his name is. *That's it.* Emerald kept changing the date of the handfast, and so Jack's family went ahead and planned their Euro-ski trip as usual. *Then*, she set the date in stone for Valentine's."

"Crafty little minx, isn't she?" Thaddeus remarked with humor in his twinkling blue eyes. "I must say, this hot crab and artichoke dip is excellent. The bacon-wrapped scallops are tasty too."

Distracted, Maggie whispered, indicating with a tilt of her red head, "Jack's parents are over there, chatting with Grantie."

John Quin III and his wife, Rachel, were a distinguished-looking couple. Jack, whose proper name was John Quin IV, resembled his father and was blessed with the same fabulous hair, not quite black (though the father's was greying at the temples), and deep-blue eyes. Both possessed the same fine nose, as Emerald described it, "… the nose of Michelangelo's sculpture *David*." Father *and* son were tall with good physiques. And this night, as often as not, both wore custom dark suits.

Rachel Quin was a striking woman, dark, petite, and elegantly maintained. Like her husband, she gave the impression of being rather reserved. Her dress this evening was the classic "little black dress" that looked as if it came from the *haute couture* house of Chanel. Rachel's long dark locks were parted in the center and sleeked back from her patrician face in a classy low bun. Pearls adorned her ears and neck. Her only other adornment was her diamond wedding band, which held a large, oval center stone.

Maxwell Quin looked very much like a sea captain. There was good reason for that– he'd been a captain in the Merchant Marines before retiring some years ago. His face, despite the regulation cap required on deck, was weathered from sea and surf, his full beard and thick crop of hair as white as the breast of a gull. He had an intense look about him, as though he were sizing up everything and everyone; and his eyes, a brilliant blue, for all his eighty-odd years, mirrored a sharp intelligence and a keen wit. As Thaddeus and Maggie watched, the captain moved to Grantie's side, where he easily slid into the lively conversation flowing between her, the happy couple, Wind-Song, and Rowena.

"And that's Jack's cousin Terry at the bar," Maggie informed. She reached out to snag a crab-stuffed mushroom from a passing "page."

Jack's groomsman's thick, wavy hair was fiery red and his greenish eyes were full of mischief. He looked younger than Jack, though they were the same age, both in their thirties. Terry, too, was a real estate broker, who worked for Quin, senior, at the Boston office.

"Likely the reason Terry appears younger than Jack," Beau commented to Raine, "is that he's more outgoing and fun-loving. Doesn't seem as serious a fellow as we know Jack to be."

"His sister keeps looking over here," Raine replied. "What's her name, and what does she do, have you heard?"

"I caught her name a few moments ago," Beau answered. "Desirée."

Raine tilted her dark head, studying the woman for a long moment. She had the same flame-red hair as her brother, which she wore in a classic French twist, and the same mischievous eyes, though in her case, *naughty* might be the better word. Her chic grey suit fit her like a glove, and her long, shapely legs were encased in sheer, grey stockings, the shoes a soft grey suede that Raine knew must have cost a small fortune. A glittering diamond brooch on her lapel and diamond-stud earrings were her sole adornments.

In that instance, Miss Quin inclined her head and returned the gaze. The Goth gal took a sip of champagne, not lowering her eyes. "I recall now. Maggie told me she's a fashion designer."

Beau responded flatly, concentrating more on the caviar canapés he'd put on his hors d'oeuvres plate, "That's not hard to believe."

"'Tisn't," Raine mumbled under her breath, "she looks like a *designing* woman." Before Beau could utter a return, she shifted her ground. "I think I'll pop into the ladies' before we sit down to dinner. Excuse me."

With a quick bob of his head, her other half helped himself to more caviar.

When Raine re-entered the Secret Garden Room a short while later, she was not surprised to discover Desirée Quin hand-feeding Beau sushi from her plate. She had to admit that the good doctor looked a tad uncomfortable, but she would deal with him later. Right now, she intended to do something about the naked appetite in the shameless woman's luring presence. With startling suddenness, an incident from a mystery she and her sisters of the moon solved several years prior sprang to mind. *Aha! You think you're so hot, we'll see just how hot ...*

Moving to Beau's side, Raine's quick eye noted with accuracy what the cheeky temptress had on her plate. In the time it takes to whisper Bibbidi-Bobbidi-Boo, she fixed herself a duplicate. Luckily– *or perhaps it was magick*– Desirée decided to set her plate on a side table in order to exchange her empty champagne flute for a full one from the tray of one of the wandering "pages." The action afforded Raine the opportunity to make the old switcheroo.

Picking up a sushi roll from "her" plate, Miss Quin said in a purring voice, "Mmmm, I *adore* this avocado sauce." She proceeded to load even more of the green paste onto the small, round morsel. "Soooooooooo good."

In an instant, her face went scarlet– the heat, with vivid color, rocketing from neck to the tips of the ears. Her hand flew to her mouth, as she noisily deposited the remainder of the sushi into a napkin, causing those nearby to gape. "Waaaaaaaaaaaaa-saaaa-bi," she croaked out; and indeed, it almost looked as if smoke poured from those glowing ears whilst she grew steadily redder and redder. Turning on her heel, she hurriedly fled the room, the assembly inside staring after her with dropped jaws and questioning expressions.

Satisfied, Raine turned her witchy McDonough stare on Beau, who looked to be a discomfited combination of stunned and sheepish. Fixing him with that penetrating gaze, she gave a terse inward laugh. *Celtic women*, she told herself, *there's nothing passive about our aggression.* "Revenge is beneath me … *but* accidents happen," she mouthed quietly to her Beau.

Now it was *his* face that flamed red. "I tried to get away," he delivered with lame voice and grin.

Raine replied with an edge to her words, "I saw … but I've seen you move faster."

When Beau opened his mouth to counter, she cut him off, "Consider yourself on probation." With that, she strode off to chat with Maggie and Thaddeus, who were pretending to be unaware of what just transpired.

As Maggie had predicted, fruits of the sea were the focus of what Emerald called their "wicked indulgence." The sumptuous sit-down dinner opened with a lobster risotto, followed by a delightful house salad and, for the entrée, pomegranate glazed salmon with horseradish cream and baby shallot potatoes. A variety of side dishes included a spicy Moroccan shrimp, which set everyone to raving. Afterward, desserts bolstered the Valentine notion that chocolate is an aphrodisiac– dark-chocolate lava cakes for two, colossal chocolate-covered strawberries, and elegant chocolate-raspberry Pavlova.

Conversation at the long Gothic table was breezy and bubbling over with the bride and groom's plans– from their forthcoming handfasting and their extended honeymoon in Ireland, Scotland, Wales, and Cornwall, to interested chatter about their new home.

By chance, *or something more fanciful*, Desirée was seated across from Raine and Beau.

Beware, the Goth gal cast, *I walk my talk.*

At one point, Thaddeus leaned toward the raven-haired Sister, next to him, "You, my little Ram, are so baaaaaaaad."

Locking eyes with Desirée, Raine returned, one ebony brow lifted in emphasis, "You have nooooo idea."

"The secret to having it all … is believing you already do."
~ All the great avatars

Chapter Three

The Witch City of Salem was a winter wonderland the Valentine morning of Emerald's handfasting. A pristine white blanket covered the ground, whilst lacy flakes floated in the crisp, cold air, producing enchantment.

At the Avalon, the Great Highland pipes sounded the old Irish tune "Wearin' of the Green," the kilted pipers lining each side of the Gothic, double-door entrance, as the Sleuth Sisters and their party filed into the hall. The Irish tradition of "pipers a-piping" the first to greet the bride insured that Fortune would favor the couple during a long and happy marriage.

Inside, the medieval Camelot Room, reminiscent of the larger Great Hall with its knights in armor, medieval weaponry, shields and colorful standards, was bedecked with hung tapestries, as well as greenery and flowers that augmented the beauty and romance of the setting– pure white roses representative of the Goddess of Love; the green of ivy for fidelity and wedding bliss; the aphrodisiacs of white lily of the valley and yarrow (that also served as protection); the regal purple of lavender for luck, devotion, and wishes granted. In addition, scattered besoms beset with ribbons and herbs– such as rosemary for remembrance of all the good times, along with cinnamon sticks and ginger to spice things up.

This room, too, boasted a *gigantic*, grey-stone fireplace that housed a dramatic log-fire, flaming and crackling in warm welcome.

"What's wrong?" Thaddeus asked Maggie, when he noticed the tears glistening in her green eyes.

"Nothing's wrong," she answered softly. "Everything's so right." She dabbed at her eyes with a tissue pulled from her glittery black evening bag. "And it's the pipes. They faithfully stir my blood."

"They do *that*," Raine and Aisling chimed in, "if you've but a *drop* of Celtic blood."

The Sleuth Sisters were robed in velvet gowns with long, hooded capes. Raine's gown was forest green, and her cape was black. Maggie's frock was deep purple, her cape dark green; while Aisling wore a gown of gold with silver trim and silver cape. All the men sported kilts, with "Prince Charlies," short tuxedo jackets, under which they wore white tuxedo shirts and black bowties, all, that is, except Dr. Weatherby. His bowtie was his signature cherry-red.

Fur-trimmed sporrans, kilt hose/ knee socks, and ghillie brogues completed the men's attire.

Glancing round, the Sisters saw that, within a few minutes, the carved, medieval-looking chairs were filled. It appeared as though all the guests had arrived and were seated in a timely, orderly fashion.

Presently, the officiant, High Priestess Wind-Song, entered the chamber, and everyone grew quiet. She was wearing a long, ecru-lace gown, with a circlet of ivy, lavender, white roses, lily of the valley, and yarrow topping her blonde hair that she wore loose and flowing in a medieval style. Without delay, she proceeded to clear and cleanse the entire room, including the alcoves, where the bride, her maid of honor, and on opposite ends of the space, the groom and his groomsman waited, so that their entering would not break the circle.

Having smudged with white sage, Wind-Song lit incense of dragon's blood, which drifted over the attendees, permeating the area with its magickal spicy scent. From the altar– a carved chest covered with a runner of pink cloth scattered with rose petals– in the northern quarter of the circle, the High Priestess lifted the athame, the witches' all-purpose ritual knife.

Beginning in the north, she drew the circle to take in the whole chamber, chanting, "I conjure thee, oh Circle of Power, that thou mayest be a meeting place of love, joy, and truth, a boundary between the world of men and the realm of the Otherworld. I raise the power to be a shield of protection between ourselves and the entities of darkness. So mote it be!"

Wind-Song then dipped the athame into the bowl of salt, near the fore of the altar, which held, in addition to the rose petals, fruits, nuts, greenery, a scattering of red hearts, and the silken handfast cords. "Be this salt dedicated to the Lord and Lady to keep us from all negativity and evil, to protect us wholly at this time."

Taking the knife again, the High Priestess dipped it into the bowl of full-moon water, also at the front of the altar. "Be this water dedicated to the Lord and Lady, to keep us from peril and to purify this space."

Pouring the water into the salt, Wind-Song stirred the mixture. Moving deosil/ clockwise around the entire room, she began sprinkling, with her hand, the salt water, as she chanted, "Lord and Lady, cast from us all negativity and evil, so that we become, each of us present here this day, what we must be in your presence. May we be clean, inside and out, so that we are acceptable to you."

With expediency, Wind-Song finished the cleansing segment of the handfast ritual by sprinkling each person in turn. Then, starting at the north, she invoked the Guardians of the Watchtower, to protect and witness the ceremony. She then consecrated the altar candles, pink to symbolize love, red for passion, and green for the heart chakra and unconditional and lasting loyalty.

"I consecrate these candles that they shall represent light and knowledge within this circle and during this ceremony. So mote it be." Wind-Song then lit the first candle, using it to light the others. Finally, she lifted the dish of burning incense and carried it, deosil, round the now-sacred space of the Camelot Room. The cleansing ritual was complete.

When the High Priestess returned to the altar, she announced. "We may now begin." From opposite sides of the room, the bride and groom entered, each accompanied by a piper. The melody was "The Love of a Princess," the love theme from the impassioned film *Braveheart*. The bagpipes inside the Camelot Room were the *Uilleann*, the Irish pipes, which, smaller than the Great Highland pipes, were more suitable for indoors.

As Maggie had envisioned, Emerald's attire was two-toned. Beneath a long, emerald-green tunic, that laced under the bust, her medieval-style gown, with its dripping sleeves that came to a point over the tops of her hands, was fashioned of the finest lace in a shade somewhere between eggshell and ivory. The tunic's generous hood rested on her flowing, ebony hair, beautifully framing her face; and under it, she wore Jack's wedding gift, the glowing yellow-gold circlet with the huge, pear-shaped emerald resting against her forehead. Around her neck, an exquisite emerald and diamond necklace, on loan from Grantie Merry, harmonized perfectly with the bride's other jewelry.

Emerald's bouquet of Irish wedding bells, Scottish heather, and English lavender symbolized love and devotion, protection, and wishes coming true. Into the medley of Celtic flowers, the High Priestess had tucked a single four-leaf clover for good luck. The bride's parents and Grantie Merry had each added three shamrocks for joy.

As the pipes played on and the bride entered, everyone stood. Turning to face her, their whispers and emotions rose in an aura of admiration and love to reflect in a word– *Stunning*.

Emerald was followed by her maid of honor, Rowena, whose gown was similar to that of the High Priestess, though the lace was a darker ecru. The maid of honor's headdress was a floral wreath of baby's breath, white tea roses, and greenery.

The groom, wearing a green-tartan kilt, Prince Charlie wedding jacket, formal shirt and bowtie, full-dress sporran, kilt hose and ghillie brogues, was followed by his groomsman Terry, who was similarly attired.

As soon as Jack appeared across the room from her, Emerald extended a hand to him. He took his place to her left, whilst his groomsman moved slightly to one side, behind him. Rowena stayed to one side, behind Emerald.

The High Priestess nodded to the pipers, who concluded their tune but remained where they stood. "We are gathered here on this joyous day to witness the handfasting of Emerald Holloway and John Quin, the Fourth, in the presence of the Lord and Lady, brothers and sisters of the Old Ways, family and friends. Welcome all those who come in perfect love and perfect trust. Again, I call upon, we *all* call upon, the lovely Lady of the Silver Moon and the gentle Lord of the Wildwood, to bless this act of love celebrated in their honor. So mote it be."

When Wind-Song extended her hand toward them, the entire assembly repeated, "So mote it be!"

The High Priestess then commenced to introduce the bride and groom, by pronouncing their names to each of the Guardians of the Watchtower, beginning again in the north. Afterward, the couple moved to the altar, where the groomsman stepped forward to hand the officiant the rings, which she placed on the altar, atop her book of rituals. Wind-Song next sprinkled the rings with water blessed by the munificent Leo moon's energizing rays the night before.

"The ring is a symbol of eternity and of the sacred circle, whole and unbroken. I bless these rings in the name of the God and Goddess that they symbolize the strong bond of true love between Emerald Holloway and John Quin, the Fourth. So mote it be." The High Priestess beckoned to the congregation, who responded–

"So mote it be!"

Wind-Song now faced the couple. There was a small pause, as she took a breath, centering herself. "John Quin, is it your wish that you shall become handfasted, in accordance with the Old Ways, to this woman, Emerald Holloway, in the presence of the Lord and Lady, the Guardians of the Watchtowers, and in the presence of family and friends?"

"It is my wish to be handfasted to Emerald Holloway in accordance with the Old Ways and before these witnesses. So mote it be."

"And, John, do you pledge on your honor, before the Lord and Lady and these witnesses, that you will strive for Emerald's happiness, and that you will cherish and protect her?"

Jack turned to send his bride a look sated in love, though he was responding to Wind-Song. "I swear on my honor that I will do so."

The High Priestess handed him one of the rings. "Then place your ring on her finger."

Wind-Song regarded Emerald. "Is it your wish that you shall become handfasted to this man, John Quin the Fourth, in accordance with the Old Ways, in the presence of the Lord and Lady, the Guardians of the Watchtowers, and in the presence of family and friends?"

Emerald turned her beautiful face toward Jack. "I so wish to become handfasted to this man in accordance with the Old Ways and before these witnesses."

"And do you pledge on your honor, before the Lord and Lady and these witnesses, that you will strive for his happiness?"

"I do swear on my honor."

"Then," Wind-Song instructed, "place your ring on his finger." She handed Emerald the symbol of their love.

When Emerald slid the ring on Jack's finger, she looked into his eyes and whispered the reply to the question he posed to her the day they met: "I will be your Valentine forever."

The High Priestess picked up the silken green cord and bound together the left hands of the couple, saying, "You are now bound together both by Massachusetts' law *and* by the ancient, sacred rite of handfasting in the eyes of the Lord and Lady, the Old Gods and the Old Ways. So mote it be. Blessed be."

Wind-Song motioned to the assembly, who repeated the ancient ordination, "So mote it be! Blessed be!"

The High Priestess again faced the couple. "John, you may now recite the vows that you have harvested from your heart."

Jack took a long moment to regard his bride. "Three years ago today, Destiny made our paths to cross. Today, on this holiday of love and lovers, I choose to walk through life with you. Our love was born to be, for we are true soul mates." The groom paused for a moment, collecting himself before continuing …

"Our love will bring passion, and we will be warmed by desire. Our friendship will banish loneliness and bring us lifelong companionship. With this handfasting, our fidelity and commitment will bind us ever unto each other. In our life together, I pledge to respect and honor you. I vow to support you as husband, friend, lover, and confidant. I will stand by you in good times and bad. Today, I promise to cherish and protect you–*forever*. All present," his gaze swept the High Priestess, then the congregation, "witness my oath to stay at this woman's side for all eternity, for our love is true; and love, *true love*, like the soul itself, is *eternal*."

Wind-Song bestowed a kindly smile upon the groom, her eyes shifting to the bride. "Emerald, you may now recite the vows you have harvested from *your* heart."

Emerald swallowed, and her vivid green eyes shown with emotion. "I cherish you, Jack, and I cherish this precious love that we share. This handfasting ritual today is my oath, my solemn *promise*, that I will always be at your side, through the joys and the challenges that our life together will bring. Today, I choose with the utmost joy and depth of feeling to bind my life to yours, so that tomorrow and for all the tomorrows ever after, we shall continue our beautiful life together– *as one*.

"*I love you*."

"I love *you*," Jack whispered in response.

That last had not been part of the rehearsal the night before. It spontaneously swelled from the couple's hearts and sprung from their lips on a wave of adoration and mutual respect.

The High Priestess smiled, sending the pair a loving nod. Then she took the colored ribbons from the altar– pink for love, red for passion, green for loyalty, white for purity, and blue for serenity– and lightly bound their hands together, *uniting them as one*.

"May your mornings bring joy and your evenings generate peace. May your troubles grow few as your blessings increase. May the saddest day of your life together, this rite doth cast, be no worse than the happiest day of your past." Wind-Song placed both her hands over the joined couple's clasped hands. "May your hands be *forever* clasped in friendship, and may your life together create the perfect blend-ship."

The High Priestess then untied the ribbons from the bride and groom's hands, dividing them– for there were two streams of each color– then tied each set round the couple's left wrists. "These to stay in place till day's end the morrow."

She lifted the dual-handled loving cup from the altar. It contained red wine. "So may you share all things from this day forward with love and understanding. Drink, and may the cup of your life together be sweet and full to running over. Drink now to the love you share."

Emerald and Jack, each taking hold of a handle, sipped the wine, handing the cup back to the officiant, who gave another satisfied nod.

"May any bitterness that comes your way be sweetened, as honeyed as this wine; and your life together be filled with only good and an abundance of good from the universe, enriched by the God and Goddess' blessings upon you," Wind-Song's eyes rose to take in the assembly before her, "and crowned by the love of family and friends."

"And now for the symbolic act of the Great Rite, the supreme joining of male and female energies that shape the cosmos, the transcendent experience and joyful celebration of being both human and divine. The High Priestess nodded to the maid of honor and the groomsman, who came forward to receive the symbols of the Great Rite to be given, in turn, to the bride and groom, chalice and sword, respectively, whilst the Priestess poured wine into the chalice.

Jack accepted the sword, his gaze set on Emerald, who extended the chalice, whereupon he plunged the tip of the sword into its depths, complemented by a flourish of nine notes from the Irish pipes.

"The Lord and Lady rejoice in your love," Wind-Song beamed. "*It is done.*" She gave a subtle signal to the pipers, who broke into "Mari's Wedding," a lively Irish wedding tune of old. With the visceral beat of the Irish drum, the *bodhrán,* for accompaniment, the gathering of hearts beat high.

"May the God and Goddess bless you forever and a day!" the High Priestess exclaimed. "So mote it be! Blessed be!" She kissed first the bride then the groom, each on the cheek; after which Rowena, Emerald's maid of honor, stepped forth with a besom decorated with the same bright ribbons as the couple wore round their wrists.

"I bid you jump the broom now, *together,*" the Priestess sang out, "so doing, good luck will attend you all the days of your life together."

Jack grasped Emerald's hand, and laughing joyously, the pair jumped the besom as one.

Clasping her hands together, Wind-Song, too, laughed aloud. "As it has been since the beginning of time, and it shall be till the end, two lovers have been joined together and have been made stronger, happier, and greater than they were apart. This wondrous state is the supreme gift of our Lord and Lady, whose love flows through all things."

Raising her athame, the High Priestess opened the circle. "The circle is open but ne'er unbroken! What we have witnessed here today shall remain in our hearts. We thank the Guardians of the Watchtower for their presence; and above all, we thank the gracious Lord and Lady for their blessings." She extended her arms forward. "Blessings be on all. So mote it be."

With a nod from the Priestess, the gathering responded in kind, "So mote it be!"

Reaching skyward, Wind-Song exclaimed, "Let the feasting begin!"

With that, the pipers skirled "When Irish Eyes Are Smiling"; followed by "Kitty's Waltz" (from the film *Michael Collins*); the lovely old Irish tune, "She Moved Through The Fair"; and, accompanied by the heart-stirring drummers, "The Gael" theme from *Last Of The Mohicans*.

Here in the Camelot Room, as the previous evening in the Secret Garden, waiters dressed as medieval pages and waitresses robed as serving wenches began circulating among the guests with trays of drinks– goblets of the traditional mead, an ancient drink made from honey and known as the Nectar of the Gods and the Drink of Love; ale; and mulled wine. Everyone stood about, talking, laughing, and toasting the happy couple.

Glancing to her right, Raine discovered Desirée, standing alone and looking a tad forlorn. Feeling magnanimous as a result of the beautiful ritual she had just witnessed, she glanced shrewdly round. Forthwith, her cat eyes lighted on a handsome young man, who seemed to be on his own and who was looking nearly as cheerless as the Sister's redheaded challenger.

Picking up his thoughts, via focused meditation, Raine inched closer. A few more moments of concentration, and she knew he was unattached and bored with the surroundings. She also learned that he worked at the Quin brokerage with Jack and Desirée's brother, Terry. Quickly, she crafted a love spell and blew it, in a glittering, rose-hued mist, across the goblet of her mead toward the young swain. In a trice his wandering eyes caught sight of Desirée, and it didn't take him long to advance upon her– with purpose.

"Looks like Desirée has met someone *receptive* to her charms," Beau said with what could have passed for humor in his deep-blue eyes. He was unexpectedly there at her side, and the sudden sound of his voice startled the absorbed Sister.

"Looks like," spoke Raine innocently. She took a long sip of her mead, avoiding his gaze.

"I'm not still on probation, am I?" he teased.

"Haven't quite made up my mind," she replied. "I'll let you know at the end of our stay. You'll just have to win me over; and I warn you, I'm not easy to sway, so you have your work cut out for you."

"Nothing I enjoy more than a challenge," he whispered in her ear. "And I warn *you*– I'm really *up* for this one."

Her pulse leaped. However, as she sipped her mead, she kept her thoughts guarded. Something in the sound of his voice had sent an especial thrill racing through her.

At the far end of the room was the raised table for the bride and groom, maid of honor, and groomsman. All of the tables were set with a medieval flair, including pewter goblets and plates, spoons and knives. Forks were conspicuously missing, for they had not been used in that long-past era of knights and their ladies fair.

The white linen napkins bore a single red heart; and wine-red, tasseled runners brightened the long heavy tables. Like magick, the Camelot Room dimmed; and everywhere– *everywhere*–appeared the flickering glow of candlelight, from the faux-candles in the baronial chandeliers, to the torch-style wall sconces and the candle-held lanterns lining the central table. The result was spectacular!

By this time, the pipers were joining the guests for the festivities, replaced by a harpist dressed in a medieval gown of a rich claret color. At the moment, she was playing "Give Me Your Hand," a favorite Irish wedding tune.

"Ooooh," Maggie sighed sentimentally, "this is *so* beautiful. The medieval setting, the flowers, the music, the romantic lighting and costumes … the family all together, and, most of all, the happy couple, who I just know will be even *happier* with each passing year together."

"I'm feeling a happy *satisfaction* that we helped sort out Emerald's troubles last year," Aisling stated *sotto voce* to her two sisters of the moon, "or this day might never have happened."

"Like I always say, 'They don't call us the Sleuth Sisters for nothing,'" Raine returned with a merry laugh.

The servers made certain everyone had a goblet of mead, ale, or mulled wine, before Jack's groomsman stood and clinked his goblet for attention. He looked to the harpist, who was just finishing her first rendition. She bowed her head to signal she understood the formal toast was about to be made.

"Herman Melville once said that 'Friendship at first sight, like love at first sight, is said to be the only truth.' As Jack's cousin, best friend and groomsman, as his co-worker for some years now, I think I know him pretty well, and the truth of the matter is when he first set eyes on Emerald, it was love at first sight. Their time together has proven it was also friendship at first sight. I remember it well because Jack came back to the office that Valentine's Day in a daze. When I asked him if he was OK, he informed me straightaway, "I met the girl I'm going to marry. I've met my soul mate." Terry raised his goblet, smiling at the bride and groom, "May your life together be a million times happier than you are at this moment."

"Hear, hear!" echoed the room.

Everyone began clinking their goblets then, asking for the bridal kiss, which the happy couple readily obliged.

"I'm starved," Raine blurted, throwing discretion aside. "I wish they'd bring the first remove."

Scarcely did those words leave the Sister's pouty red lips when the "pages" and "serving wenches" began carrying in the first course, called in times of yore, a "remove," a savory pottage thick with vegetables. Of course, in keeping with medieval custom, no one began eating until after the bride and groom/ Lord and Lady took their first bite.

"I wish I had the recipe for this soup," Ian commented to Aisling. In the Gwynn home, Ian was the cook.

"Husband," she replied, "all you need do is look and taste, and you'll figure it out, if I know you. You're a born chef."

"I'll drink to that," Ronan remarked, taking a draft of his ale. "And a blessing it is," he tossed a glance toward his wife, "because our daughter never liked to cook; though I must say," he proffered with a glimmer in his McDonough eyes, "she certainly has proven herself a top-shelf detective."

"And wife and mother," Ian added.

"The best," Merry Fay giggled, raising her glass of apple cider.

Aisling sent her family a grin, which they returned with expressions of affection and approval.

Huge, family-style platters appeared next with roasted meats, paté, individual Scottish meat pies, chicken pot pies, wedges of cheddar cheese, salads, and pickled vegetables. All through the meal, and between the enchanting music of the harpist, a variety of medieval entertainment delighted the wedding party and guests– jesters and jongleurs; Irish step dancers; Irish musicians with *bodhráns,* flutes, tin whistles, and the *Uilleann* pipes.

At medieval banquets, eating food with the fingers is acceptable, and good thing, too, for the second remove, along with roasted potatoes and vegetables, included roasted chicken breast. The fare was cooked to perfection and delectably seasoned. Everyone dug in, and a good time was had by all.

The third remove came later, fruits-of-the-forest pie topped with thick whipped cream. Sugared almonds, reminding the couple that life is both bitter and sweet, followed, along with a variety of other confections, such as Tudor flan; medieval oat cakes; red, sweetheart sugar cookies; and a romantic fantasy called "Violet Twilight," a mouthwatering creation made with crystallized violets.

When the musicians took a break in order to enjoy their repasts, as per Emerald's request, the recorded music of Rowena of the Glen fed the assembly's spirits. The bride had chosen, ahead of time, "Ave Maria," "The Cathedral," "Moon Goddess," "Dancing In The Garden," "Purple Galaxie," "My Mother's Song," "Trust Me," "Ice Blue," and "The Witching Hour."

It was some time later in the festivities that the High Priestess gave the silent signal to the bride and groom. Jack rose and crossed to the musicians, seated at the far end of the long guest table near the harpist, who'd just finished a charming trilogy, accompanied by song, of Loreena McKennitt's "The Mystic's Dream," "The Lady Of Shalott," and "The Old Ways."

Presently, the Irish musicians' start of the love theme from *Romeo and Juliet*, "A Time For Us," signaled the groom to lead his bride to the dance floor.

Wind-Song rose to her feet to express to the couple with great joy, "Allow the Universe to wrap you in her magick– and *dance!* Dance to the music of your coupled souls!"

As the newlyweds waltzed round the floor, the flickering candles and flaming, medieval wall sconces reflected the love in their faces, the lights catching the brilliance of Emerald's fabulous jewels.

At the end of the enchanting music, Jack dipped his bride to the applause of the guests, after which, the couple held each other in a close embrace. Everyone began clinking their glasses. The deep kiss that followed was just as timeless, before Rowena of the Glen's magickal "Pagan Lover" set the couple dancing again. Partway through the song, Emerald waved everyone onto the floor to join them, and the dancing officially began.

Rowena of the Glen's earthy whiskey-and-smoke voice delivered her sensual song of love and desire: "I've got a pagan lover/ He's got a wild heart …"

Whilst they danced, Beau whispered in Raine's ear, "Have you been thinking about *our* handfasting, my little witch?"

"He grooves me … oh, baby, he soothes me/ Shake it up/ Hold on tight/ He *moves* me …" The primeval beat throbbed in the Goth gal's essence. Rowena's music always did that to her.

"You know I have," came her unexpected reply. However, before Beau could claim a victory, she added, "But you also know I am not ready … not yet. Not now."

"Thunder in the morning/ Quakin' in the night/ Treats me like a lady/ You know he does me right …"

Thaddeus, too, was doing a bit of nudging. "May I hope that you've been thinking seriously about our handfasting, my Maggie?"

"Of course I have, darlin'," she answered truthfully. "And one day we shall. Not this day, not this month, and not this year, but one day, I promise you– *we shall.*"

"He grooves me … oh, baby, he soothes me/ Shake it up/ Hold on tight/ He moves me …/ He moves me …"

Very nearly simultaneously, both Raine and Maggie spoke the magick words, each to her respective pagan lover, "When we do it, it will be '… for as long as love shall last.'"

Emerald was never one for limitations; thus, when it came to the wedding cake, there were two– a vanilla-almond passion cake, its white icing decorated with green Celtic knots representative of eternity, and a traditional Irish wedding cake chockfull of fruits, soaked in Irish whiskey, and topped with a sweet, white glaze, along with a pair of glittery, green shamrock favors.

When Twilight let fall her curtain to pin it with a star, another of Jack's wedding surprises made its dramatic arrival at Avalon's castle doors– a horse-drawn sleigh that would carry the newlyweds over the snow-covered fields to their new home, where they would spend the night before embarking on their extended honeymoon the next day. After a word from the groomsman, who had charge of horse and sleigh, that their charming transportation awaited, Emerald let fly her bouquet– and Betty caught it.

Jack helped Emerald on with her long, green hooded cape, lined and trimmed with glossy faux fur. A huge, outsized, faux-fur muff completed her riveting attire, as the couple made their way to the castle entrance, the jovial guests following in their wake.

Emerald squealed in delight and clapped her hands with joy when she saw their romantic carriage, complete with bells and cozy lap rug, the big, white steed pawing the snow-covered ground, tossing his head and whinnying his impatience to be on their way, his breath blowing from excited, dilated nostrils and visible in the frosty air.

Jack lifted his bride into the sleigh then took up the reins, as a lone piper, silhouetted against the setting sun, sounded the Great Pipes with the love theme from *Braveheart*——
"The Love Of A Princess."

"When you love a witch– magick happens!"
Aisling McDonough

Chapter Four

Early the next morning, the Sleuth Sisters were en route, with Cousin Sean in his rental car, to Grantie's seaside cottage, Raine in the front passenger seat, Aisling and Maggie in the back.

Covering her mouth, Maggie sighed, her words nearly lost in a yawn, "I'll never be a morning person, for the moon and I are too much in love."

"We really appreciate your driving us out to Grantie's this morning," Aisling said.

"Nooo problem," Sean enunciated slowly, flicking on his turn signal. "Grantie asked me long before you did. She really wants to meet with you in private before you have to leave Salem this afternoon. I'll make myself scarce so you'll be the only ones at the cottage with her. Witch Hazel will leave when we get there. She's going to visit with her family for a couple of hours, while I run some errands, and Grantie has her conference with you." He gave a short chuckle. "The old dear's been keeping me busy. I got up early this morning to clean out her fireplaces, before I got them going nicely. I shoveled snow and swept her walks. While you're there, I'll be grocery shopping for her. She also wants me to stop downtown Salem for a list of items from a couple of the witch shops." His teeth flashed white and his eyes crinkled at the corners. "I think Grantie wants to make certain I'll be gone long enough so she'll have sufficient alone time with you."

"Grantie's well ... *Grantie*," Aisling pronounced with a tilt of her blonde head.

"One-of-a-kind," Maggie rejoined, suppressing another yawn.

Raine was uncharacteristically quiet that morning, en route to the cottage, as she gazed out the rental car window at the passing seascapes. Beau dominated her thoughts. Last night was phenomenal, and she smiled to herself when she remembered how it had felt to hit such a high level of excitement. Even now, her heart pounded when she thought of how masterful her lover had been in his coercion. Of course, she forgave him for his little indiscretion with Desirée. The thought occurred to her that he'd let the woman flirt with him to arouse jealousy. But making up was so much fun!

The way he kissed me ... he left me breathless, drove me absolutely wild. Raine closed her eyes, tingling from the memory of something he'd done when– she started at something Sean uttered, and her face flushed as she came abruptly out of her dream, hoping she had not expressed any of her thoughts audibly.

"I hope you've given serious thought to my invitation to spend spring break with me in Montana," Sean was saying. "My log cabin's too small for guests, but I'd be happy to pay for your stay at a not-too-distant guest ranch. You'll love New Moon Ranch, because, as I told you, it's not a golf-course-type dude ranch, but a real working ranch. The owner, Nigel Hawkes, is a retired British colonel from out in East Africa. He met his wife Marjorie, a native of Montana, when she was on a camera safari in Kenya several years ago. There's always an interesting mix of guests at the ranch which leads to lively conversation at mealtimes and the cocktail hour. You'll especially enjoy the colonel's stories. His family settled in Kenya back in the 1800s; and well, you'll just have to come out and hear all the exhilarating tales for yourselves. I couldn't do them justice, not like Nigel."

"We *have* given it serious thought, Sean," Aisling answered, looking to Maggie, next to her in the backseat. It would just be Raine, Maggie, and I on a well-deserved break. Ian said he doesn't mind looking after the agency and Merry Fay for a week or so without me."

"Thaddeus," Maggie informed, "has some departmental projects prearranged that, since he's in charge, he cannot forsake, and–"

"Beau can't take off for that long," Raine rebounded, "because Hugh and Betty have a trip planned in the spring, and Hugh won't be there to pinch hit for him at the veterinary clinic. So, as Aisling stated, it'll be just the three of us."

"You will *not* be paying for our stay at the ranch, Cousin," the Sisters echoed nearly as one.

"As I said, I'd be happy to do that. After all, *I* invited you," Sean answered.

"That's very generous and thoughtful of you, Sean," Maggie interjected, "but the excursion will be a welcome break for the overextended Sleuth Sisters. And anyway, we haven't had a holiday with just us in years, so we're eagerly counting down the days to it, and to visiting with you on your turf."

"It's enough that you'll be escorting us about," Aisling rejoined in firm response.

"That's right," Raine acknowledged. "We know you'll make the perfect guide, and we're quite looking forward to a great getaway."

"Well, ma'am, I say life's too damn short for cheap coffee, stale conversations, and passionless sex, so spring for the gourmet, hash out the esoteric and mystifying, and make love like your life depends on it– because it does." Sean rumbled his low laugh, "A cowboy can be a force of unbridled temperament, and I ain't just talkin' rodeo here."

"Cowboys, Indians, time in the saddle ... hot dog! *Lots o' time* in the saddle, and the place will be awash with history and majestic scenery. Oh, lest we forget, bears, mountain lions, elk, mule deer, bighorn sheep, even Canadian lynx." Raine turned partway round in the front seat to regard Aisling and Maggie. Reading their thoughts, as she often did, she confirmed to Sean, "So unless something changes, we'll tell you our answer to your invitation is an emphatic– *Yes!*" *Sometimes we need a getaway to cleanse the bitter taste of life from our souls, and my witch's intuition is that, come spring, such an escape will be just what the doctor ordered.*"

"Good!" Sean shouted. "It's settled then. Let me know the exact dates, and I'll assist you with your ranch reservations. If you let me know soon, I'll try my best to take my vacation concurrently, so we'll have more time together. And make sure you contact me with the date, time, and number of your flight, so I can pick you up at the Billings Airport."

When they reached Grantie's seaside cottage, one of Salem's most historic dwellings, the Sisters piled out of Sean's rental to take deep gulps of tangy sea air.

"The salt air is soooo invigorating, isn't it?" Maggie asked, not really seeking an answer. "I love it here. Just the smell of the ocean brings back so many happy childhood memories. Each visit with our Grantie was a wonderland."

"A witch's wonderland!" Raine said, raising her arms and spinning round.

"C'mon, our time is limited, since we have to catch a plane later, so let's not tarry, Sisters," Aisling reproved, shepherding Raine and Maggie inside.

As soon as they opened the cottage door, Witch Hazel, Grantie's longtime friend and live-in caregiver, slapped the sheet, with which she was struggling, down atop a pile of folded laundry. "It must take a *powerful* witch to fold a fitted sheet properly. A *super*-witch," she laughed. "I'll deal with the maddening thing later." She hurriedly pulled on her hooded, black wool cape, greeting the visitors with her ready warm smile. After embracing the Sisters, one by one, she said, "Now that you're here, I'll be on my way. Put your minds at ease, I'll be back in a couple of hours, and Sean will be back by then too."

"I will," he concurred. "I just want to stir the fire before taking off on the shopping errands Grantie wants me to run."

"I just tended to that, so you can go on and get started," the caretaker said with a shooing gesture. "Merry is chomping at the bit to have her private meeting with the girls, and she's getting antsier by the minute," Witch Hazel informed. She looked to the Sisters, wagging a finger but holding her smile, "Now, don't tire her out. She's waiting for you in her room. And keep a weathered eye on those two fireplaces. She wanted a fire lit in *both* to chase the dampness, so mind you tend to both while Sean and me are gone."

Hazel Cooke, a plump, jovial witch whom the Salem community had nicknamed "Witch Hazel," was known, far and wide, for her chowder. No one, not even the culinary talented Rowena, could whip up a pot of good, creamy, New England clam chowder like Witch Hazel.

"See you later then," Sean waved, as his long legs took him out the door to his rental car.

The Sisters strode into the dining-living room area, the space Grantie referred to as the "Hearth Room," with Raine calling out, "Grantie, we're here!"

Aisling took a few moments to properly fold the troublesome fitted sheet and set it neatly atop the pile of clean laundry.

In Grantie's seventeenth-century, cedar shake cottage, the hearth room was a happy-feeling, all-purpose room. Merry long ago christened her home "The Mews," apropos for reasons of her cats and the fact that it *was* a sort of hideaway from the rest of the world, as Merriam-Webster defined the word. Moreover, and even more fitting, it looked out onto Cat Cove.

One end of the cottage's main area served as the kitchen, with its antique, black hooded stove. The refrigerator was disguised as a wooden cabinet, the stain on the wood matching the polished rosewood throughout the small home's interior.

Every inch of space was cleverly utilized. There was a small, diamond-shaped, leaded-glass window, fitted with shutters, over the tiny kitchen sink. Copper pots and pans hung from one of the rustic walls, along with kitchen utensils and a collection of interesting baskets, in different shapes, sizes and colors– souvenirs from Merry's various jaunts to some of the world's most interesting locales.

Bins held potatoes and onions, other foodstuffs and miscellaneous items. Wooden shelves displayed sea-blue crystal goblets, as well as a set of grey stoneware dishes, decorated with small, blue flowers. A variety of dried flowers and herbs hung from the thick ceiling beams.

Two hand-carved, wooden cupboards stood tall and ornate, facing one another, against opposite kitchen walls. Merry's magickal tools filled one. The other contained sundry kitchen items and canned goods. Witch Hazel had recently burned dragon's blood incense, and the pleasant odor of cinnamon hung in the air. For the Sisters, it was a homey, familiar scent.

An antique Colonial table, with matching twin benches, dignified the center of the kitchen-dining space that flowed into the living area where the large, grey-stone fireplace was the focal point. The hearth retained its original iron swing arm, known in Colonial times more fancifully as a "witch's arm." A trio of unique besoms stood in the corner by the hearth, and select antiques graced the mantel. Two giant, cast iron black cats served as andirons, their amber glass eyes enlivened by the fire's leaping flames.

A pair of comfortable easy chairs faced the hearth, both covered in dark-green fabric; a sky-blue afghan, that Merry knitted herself, lay at an angle over the back of the one. The couch was an eye-catching shade of scarlet; and glancing about, one could readily see that the mistress of this home rejoiced in color. Splashes of color brightened the entire cottage.

"Like scent, color is a power that directly influences the soul," Grantie often said.

Interspersed with magickal odds and ends– poppets, gargoyles, gemstones and stones from a range of sacred places in the world, candles, and other such witchy items– the shelves overflowed with books, including Grantie's grimoires and rare antique volumes on a variety of arcane, esoteric subjects.

Included in Merry's sacred stone collection were a male-and-female pair of moqui balls, also called "shaman stones," from the Navajo sandstone formations of the American West, for strong protection, deeper meditation and astral journeying; shiva lingam stones from India's Narmada River for keener intuition, boosted energy, and healing; sacred golden quartz from the Nagqu River of Tibet, dream stones to connect with loved ones passed over to the Summerland; Cornish hag stones, faerie stones with natural holes fashioned by the sea, from Merlin's Cave at Tintagel, for windows into the faerie realm and protection from evil and evil spirits. Among several others were Apache tears from the American Southwest, lava stones from a variety of volcanic sites across the Globe, a large, high-grade Besednice Moldavite from the Czech Republic, and a nice-size chunk of noble silver Shungite from Russia, believed to be over two billion years old.

On the remaining wall of the living area, suspended from an ancient lance, a riveting hand-made quilt depicted the rich history of Salem, including the Witch Trials. Grantie purchased the treasured item at a Salem witches' meet decades earlier from an elderly sister of the moon, who knew that her time for passing into the Summerland was near and who told her, in a voice that warbled from age and weariness, "Real art must always involve some witchcraft."

The cottage's rosewood floor, containing its original wooden nails, gleamed like a fine wine, reflecting, in the glow from the fireplace flames and lighted lamps, the multi-colored books, knickknacks, and antiques that filled the cozy hearth room. Two bright rag rugs added to the array of colors and broke the monotony of the hardwood floors.

The pair of small, stained-glass lamps were Tiffany, a birthday gift from Merry's long-passed husband, who had loved her as the sun loves the moon.

On each side of the hearth room was a door. One led to the bedrooms, the other to the den, which opened to the backyard and herb garden that overlooked the sea. There, on the small patio, a variety of wind chimes, each with a link to magick, tinkled and rang a Merry music.

A faerie mound and tiny fountain in the center of the backyard space added a touch of the Celtic to the picture-perfect New England home.

Years before, Merry commissioned a second bedroom and the den added to the rear of the cottage. At the time, when the addition was constructed, this tradition-minded mistress of the house made certain that the contractor did not destroy the integrity of the original structure. Dipped in buttermilk, dried, and then installed, the new shaker shingles possessed the same, weathered greyish tinge as the rest of the cottage's façade.

The small den was artfully decorated with New England Colonial charm. It was evident here, as in the living-room area, that Grantie McDonough had always been an avid reader, for books crammed the shelves lining the den walls. Nowadays, even with her reading spectacles resting on her nose, Grantie needed the magnifying sheet she placed over each page; or Witch Hazel read aloud to her.

The den's leather-bound tomes were accompanied by several family portraits, framed vintage photographs, and a small tapestry depicting a witchy *Samhain* scene. Gifts from the sea– a spectrum of sea glass (what Grantie called "mermaids' tears") that sparkled in the sun's radiance but resonated with the pull and allure of the sea, seashells, seahorses, sand dollars, and starfish– all shared space with the expanse of books and topped the old pigeon-hole desk that had belonged to Merry's father.

"A seashell is never empty," Grantie repetitively enthused. "It's filled with wondrous energies, such as the sounds of the crashing waves and the songs that mermaids sing."

The child Raine, upon arriving at Grantie's for a visit, unfailingly made a beeline for the largest spiral conch, holding it to an ear to listen for the rolling sound of the waves as they met the shore, as well as the sweet enchantment of the siren's song.

Only in the past few years did Merry finally consent to a computer, and never did she use it without setting her Shungite on the terminal to block free radial output. The "confounded device with a mind of its own" occupied a scarred, old table in front of a shuttered, leaded-diamond window that looked out on the sea. A short file cabinet covered with a fringed, vintage shawl; a couple of Morris chairs, so comfortable for reading; and Grantie's seldom-used television, secreted inside a rosewood cabinet, completed the den's furnishings.

A small rustic bathroom separated the two sleeping chambers, Merry's from Witch Hazel's, the walls covered with soul-stirring New England and Irish seascapes, from whence the Sisters swore they could actually *hear* the storms depicted. There was no shower, but rather a fabulous, old claw-foot tub for "soaking and soothing," as Merry was wont to say.

"'Bout time!" Grantie called out in answer to Raine's announcement that the Sisters had arrived. "Stop your prattlin', and come in here."

"Were you calling us, Grantie?" Raine asked, as the Sisters entered Merry's room.

"Of course, I was calling you! Who else would I be calling? The cats are here with me. Come over here and give your auntie a kiss."

Merry's bedroom was the larger of the two sleeping chambers, though both were small rooms.

The heart of Grantie's bedroom was the stone fireplace, where the flames leaped and crackled in cheery salute. The bedroom hearth's thick mantel supported a large, glass-domed, lunar-phase clock encrusted with seashells, together with Grantie's sepia-tone wedding portrait in a silver oval frame. In the image, the bride is standing behind her dark-haired, mustached husband, Shamus McDonough, with one hand resting on his shoulder. He is seated in a fancy, curly-back chair, and though the couple is not smiling with their lips, their bliss is evident in their eyes.

Next to the fireplace hung a brass, eighteenth-century bed warmer that Merry actually used. Witch Hazel had cozied her bed with it before she left, in fact. At the moment, Grantie, a green knit shawl covering her shoulders and looking somewhat impatient, was sitting up in bed with her cats around her– a large brown tabby, a black, and a blue-point applehead Siamese.

At the foot of the four-poster bed was a large trunk– oak and lacquered a dark green with hand-painted gold leaves and flowers, faded, but still eye-catching in its appeal. An old-fashioned quilt, in a multi-hued, autumn-leaf pattern, created by Merry's own hand, covered the double bed and comforted her old bones on a day as chill as this one.

As in the hearth room, the ceiling, here too, was beamed; and from its center hung a Colonial chandelier that had been electrified, the circle of "candles" topped with amber flame-bulbs that, when lit, bathed the room in a soft glow much like the radiance that had issued from the original fixture.

A massive, free-standing wardrobe, ornately carved in a goddess theme, held Merry's clothing. There were two large dressers, opposite one another, one with doors that opened to shelves, with deep drawers beneath. A small nightstand and a harvest-style

Hitchcock rocker, positioned before the fireplace, completed the furnishings in Merry's bedroom.

Other than the trunk, the furniture was cherry. As in the other rooms, a bright and colorful, hand-fashioned rag rug, treated so not to slip under Grantie's cane, enhanced the hardwood floor.

Moments after their arrival, the Sisters entered the bedchamber, exclaiming in sync, "Why are you abed, Grantie?"

"Are you feeling poorly?" Aisling asked, as they each bent to bestow a kiss on their beloved great-auntie.

"Only a bit weary, my dear girls," the centenarian replied. "The handfasting was *unaccountably* fatiguing for me."

The Sisters suppressed the urge to smile.

Very much *la grande dame,* Merry patted a hand on the bed. "Come and sit with me. I told you I have some very special items to give you, and we must *get to it*, before you have to leave for the airport."

Raine and Maggie sat on the bed, one on either side of the imposing woman, whilst Aisling parked herself at the foot of the bed. Raine, especially, could hardly contain herself, so excited was she about the forthcoming gifts.

Sensing this, the dowager pointed a gnarled, bejeweled finger that shook slightly, "Raine, go to my dresser and open the top drawer. Inside you'll find a red box. Bring it to me."

Never one to dally, Raine sprang up and, finding the velvet chest, danced it across the room to place it in Merry's waiting hands, whilst anticipation tingled within each Sister's breast.

Without further ado, Grantie lifted the hinged lid to extract a gold locket, beset with rubies, fashioned in the shape of a heart, and bearing the raised image of Cupid. When she held the locket up, the Sisters saw that it was suspended from a sturdy, gold chain.

"The gold," Merry began, "represents the sun and power. Gold assists in clearing negativity from the chakras. It is also a great activator and will help you mobilize into action, giving you the self-confidence to make this shamanic journey. You might be questioning why the image of Cupid on this locket cast with a shapeshifting spell, and why rubies?

"Let me begin with the rubies. They are a most helpful gemstone for attraction, love, passion and desire; and that's the state of mind and heart you must be in to successfully shapeshift. It requires a lot of 'juice,' as I like to say. Rubies are also a marvelous gemstone of protection, so you see why the rubies. In my opinion, rubies are one of the best gemstones for holding energies.

"You know Cupid as a chubby cherub, winged because lovers are flighty and often change their minds. He totes a bow and arrow because love enflames the heart, and it can wound. But lest we forget, Cupid has several guises ... semblances ... *manifestations*, if you will. For instance, when he is blindfolded, it reminds us of the old adage that 'Love is blind.' When he is depicted riding a dolphin, it symbolizes how quickly love can move."

Grantie cocked her snowy-white head, "And the water ... the sea represents the power of love, the *emotion*, just like Cups in the Tarot symbolize emotion. Cupid riding a sea monster represents the *wild* ride love can create. A sleeping Cupid signifies absent or languishing love. The crying Cupid as the honey-thief being stung by bees conjures the powerful sting of Cupid's arrow, for when the rascal ran crying to his mother, Venus, asking how anything so small could hurt so badly, she shook with laughter to answer, 'You're small, yet your arrow is most powerful!'"

Grantie waited, studying her grand-nieces to determine how well they were listening. "Oh yes, then there's the *mischievous* Cupid. Remember the song popular years ago, 'Stupid Cupid, Stop Picking On Me'? Like Peter Pan, Cupid is the child who never grows up, and that's to remind us that true love never grows old. Venus, Cupid's mama, represents, to me, feminine power; and she, like the rubies, are a mighty deterrent against negative energies. You should feel wholly protected when you use this charm to shapeshift, my dear girls, *but never allow yourselves to be careless*."

"The spell I'll be telling you about has been in our family for hundreds of years." Merry seemed to slip away for a moment into private reverie. "Ah, to be a witch is to know the ways of the Olde." She patted the locket. "The original piece of jewelry cast with the spell is long gone. Worn out it was. Well," she sighed, "as your cousin Sean, or his Cheyenne friends, say, 'Nothing lasts forever, only earth and sky.'

"Let me begin my directive by saying that meditation and visualization are the key elements to making shapeshifting work, not to mention, of course– and this is a given– that you *believe*. You know from experience that you must believe, and *strongly*, in your own abilities to make *any* magick work."

Merry's brows rushed together as she pontificated, "You know what the issue is with this world?" Before the Sisters could answer, she ran on, "Everyone wants a magickal solution to their problems, but everyone refuses to believe in magick! By *everyone*, I mean, of course, muggles, as I've heard you refer to the non-magick folk.

"Obviously," Grantie advanced after a deep gulp of air, "one cannot be disturbed or interrupted in any way when conducting magick. Make sure you're *unplugged*, to quote again your generation.

"I should mention, too, that I've always liked to preface my magick by taking a long soak in the tub with a pinch of sea salt in the water, along with a few drops of whatever essential oils you feel drawn to at the moment. Go with your gut as to what feels right to you, but oils that purify, protect, and enhance meditation are the best, such as frank and myrrh. And, whilst soaking, I like to bathe myself with a frankincense and white sage smudge soap. I purchase it right here in Salem– mar-r-r–ve-lous for ridding any residue of negativity from oneself before conducting magick.

"Candlelight is the best lighting for magick. It's softer and more soothing than modern lighting, yet it raises energies. I know you're aware of that, but doesn't hurt to reiterate it. I like instrumental Celtic music softly playing in the background to set the mood. Harp instrumentals are good for me. Medieval music like we enjoyed at Emerald's rehearsal dinner. And do make certain, if not skyclad, you're garbed in loose, comfy clothing. Much easier to unwind that way.

"But to return to what I'd started to tell you: The shapeshifter must *visualize* the person, creature, or animal that he or she wants to become. When doing this or any magick, you must, I hardly need say, be within a circle of protection, *centered* and *focused.* Breathe deeply," Merry said, bringing her hands up from her lower abdomen and out and away from her lips. "You must strongly *visualize* how you want to appear to allow these energies to enter the auric field.

"The aura, as well you know, is the electromagnetic field that surrounds the human body and every animal or object in the universe. When a shapeshifting spell is properly cast, the auric field will then inform and influence the body, which, in turn, will create a physical manifestation and change– resulting in what we sometimes call in the Craft a 'Glamour.'

"I'm certain you understand that shapeshifting is not in any way an attempt to take over the spirit or body of the entity the shifter wishes to look like. Never do we interfere with Free Will, which, as you also know, goes hand-in-hand with the Great Secret, the most precious gifts of the God and Goddess. Shapeshifting is a spell created so that others see the shapeshifter as the entity the shifter wishes to look like— that's why visualization is so important, as well as the pictures you will place in the locket. I'll get to that in a moment.

"The shapeshifting spellcaster," Grantie went on, "must take pretty much the same precautions as a witch who is astral projecting— which, by the bye, is what prompted me to think of the other gift I have for you today, but we'll get to that later too.

"Right now, I want to finish my instructions on shapeshifting. Basically— and you've had plenty of experience with this, so you'll know what I'm talking about— when you attempt this particular shamanic journey, you must embark on it with a definite date and time for *ending* the connection. I hardly need tell you to be *specific* in your intent. *Intent with specifics, visualization and focus, and belief in your own powers.* That's always the formula.

"Oh, lest I forget, if you choose, at times, to shapeshift to an animal, rather than a human, then it helps to place your body in a position to properly align with that animal. What I'm saying is this: If you wish to shapeshift to a cat, then position yourself like a cat." Merry guffawed. "Not a difficulty for you, my dear girls, and especially not for *you*, Raine."

Grantie reflected for a moment. "I'll never forget how your convincing interpretation of Maggie the Cat in your community theatre's production of *Cat On A Hot Tin Roof* caused a seeing-eye dog in the audience to react!"

"My stars," the raven-haired Sister replied, "I had *no* idea my acting would cause a problem. The dog barked and made all sorts of weird sounds, causing everyone in the audience to react. When I made my apologies to the owner after the show, he told me *nothing* ever distracted his well-trained guide dog— *except for a cat.*"

Grantie fixed Raine with her stare. "What better review could you have wanted for that performance? To get back to our discussion: Shapeshifting, as I told you before, will be one of *your* special powers, Raine," the wise crone charged, "though this locket is meant for all of you. Just as I gifted Athena, the crystal ball, to the three of you, though it's Maggie's forté. As in the past, there will be times, in future, you will want to cast with the Power of Three, when using each of my bestowed magickal tools."

The Goth gal appeared especially excited.

"Like anything else, inside or outside the Craft, practice makes," Grantie gave a little beam, "purrrrrrr-fect. Just remember to set a definite time for the spell to end, so you can transform back to your own physical self, no matter where you are.

"To help you to believe with all your essence, think of shapeshifting in this manner: Those of us who follow the Old Ways know that no one, nothing, ever really dies. They merely change form. 'Tis the cycle of life. All people, things, whatever, constantly change shape; it's a natural occurrence, so shapeshifting is *not* really *un*natural, you see. Not at all, at all.

"An infant becomes a child who grows to adulthood, to old age, to death, and again he's reborn. The Native Americans understood ... *understand* this so well– everything moves in cycles within the Great Circle of Life. Anyroad, everyone and everything is continually shapeshifting. Cycles ... shapeshifting– semantics. Not so strange. Certainly *not* impossible. You can do this– *and you will.*"

Grantie twinkled at the Sisters. "You're dependably good at believing in the so-called *impossible.*"

History professor Raine, whose heart was soaring, slapped her knee in a startling clap. "Napoleon once said that *impossible* is a word found only in the dictionary of fools!"

Grantie gave a resolute nod. "Indeed. And you'll use this shapeshifting tool, as you use your other magickal tools– *for good. For only good.*

"Now," Merry sighed, bringing her hands together as if in prayer, "after following my preparatory advice, you simply place, on the left side of the locket, an image of the witch– w-h-i-c-h-slash-w-i-t-c-h of you– who will be shapeshifting; and, on the opposite side of the locket, on the right-hand side, an image of what or whom the shifter wishes to transmute to.

"Contrary to what you might be thinking, and unlike your Time-Key chant," Grantie extracted a card from the red velvet box, "this shapeshifting chant is quite simple. It is written in a sort of Old English ... well, Old Scottish, actually. For instance, if you wish to shapeshift into a cat: 'I sall gae intil a catt–'" Merry broke off deliberately, as her eyes widened, "I shan't recite it here and now, out loud, for this is a very, very powerful spell, and we don't want manifestation to occur at the moment."

Grantie handed Raine the card with the handwritten spell. "For the Sleuth Sisters' very special *Book of Shadows*. One more thing about shapeshifting, it can be done on three levels, as, doubtless, you suspected. On mental, physical, and astral planes. Start with mental, then physical, and do not attempt astral until you've mastered the first two. You'll discover more about all this in your *Book of Shadows,* put there by your granny. And goes without saying, you can always call upon me, your granny, or both of us whenever you need extra assistance."

Her old eyes locked with Raine's. "Just be sure to use good common sense, good judgment, and a goodly measure of *self-discipline.*"

"Grantie," Raine ventured, "if I ... *we,* I mean me; oh, fiddle-dee!" She tried again. "If I wanted to shapeshift a cat to human form, will the locket aid us just as strongly?"

Grantie tilted her head to scrutinize her sometimes over-zealous, too daring great-niece. She stared at her across the bed covers for a weighty moment, her eyes sharp and curious like a bird's. "It will," she replied at long last. Merry's gaze dropped to one of her cats, the large brown tabby, causing the Sisters to believe that she had done this herself and often. "However, I'll give you fair warning that to shapeshift from animal to human, to give a cat, for instance, the glamour, the appearance, of a human, requires, as I'm prone to say, a whole lot more 'juice.' Let me cap that with this: Good judgement comes from experience, and experience often comes from bad judgement. But," said she after a slight pause, "we learn more from mistakes than we do from triumphs."

The wise crone cleared her throat and reached for the glass of water on the nightstand, Maggie assisting her, as she took a long drink. "Thank you, dear. Your shapeshifting skills will have to be fine-tuned to properly shapeshift a cat to human form and behavior." That last was directed to Raine, who appeared to be occupied with her own thoughts.

Merry raised a knotty, bejeweled finger, the gesture asking for her great-nieces' full attention. "But, to reiterate, always remember that the word *impossible* does not exist in our vocabulary. No McDonough worth his or her salt," her old eyes kindled, "no *witch* worth his or her salt would ever think to mutter the word. Even the spelling … get what I'm saying to you, the **SPELL**ing," she raised her brows, "of the word itself is *I'm possible!* Enough now about the locket. I'll repeat what I said earlier, for some things are worth repeating– practice makes perfect."

After having the girls tend to the two fireplaces, again Merry opened the red box that was still on the bed, next to her. "For my other gift to you today, I have here a very powerful ring to aid in astral projection, one of Aisling's special gifts. If she hadn't astral projected to Ireland when first you used your Time-Key, you would not have been successful in your initial time-travel attempt. Then and there, more than ever, you needed the Power of Three."

The Sisters exchanged quick looks, with the boldest of the trio voicing, wide-eyed, the question that was resonating on their minds: "You have astral shapeshifted to watch us more than once over the years, haven't you, Grantie?" Dribs and drabs of remembrances were skittering across Raine's mind.

The wise crone could not help but laugh. In fact, she rocked with Merry laughter. "You already know the answer to that!"

When the Sisters yet again looked to one another, Grantie added, "Your granny is not the only one watching over you, my dears."

The threesome gave a unified nod of conformity, as Aisling reached out to grasp their great-aunt's wrinkled hand. When Maggie started to say something, Merry raised her free hand.

"Our time is limited today, so let me speak. It will be most helpful for you to use Granny McDonough's Easy Breezy Flying balm when you astral project, just as you now do with your Time-Key when time-traveling." Grantie fixed her penetrating gaze on Raine to say in a chiding tone, "Only *one* drop is necessary for *astral* work."

The color rose in Raine's cheeks, but she stayed silent.

"And," Merry continued, extracting a few crystals and a pair of moqui balls from the red box, "these shaman stones will also aid in astral work. They will help in overcoming any deep-seated fears while journeying outside of the body. By the bye, the word *moqui* is a Hopi Indian word meaning 'dear departed ones.' Legend says that the Native Americans of the Southwest used these stones to play games with the spirits of their ancestors in the evening hours when spirits are permitted to visit Earth. The left-behind 'marbles' remind the Natives that their loved ones are happy and well.

"The moqui also thwart any negative energies or entities from attaching themselves." Grantie lifted from the red box two other stones, holding them up for the Sisters to see. "Angelite and celestite are both high-vibration stones infused with Divine energies. These will facilitate conscious contact with the angelic world." Grantie picked up the remaining crystals, naming each, "Ametrine, sapphire, and clear quartz. Ametrine rids the aura of negative energy and stimulates the intellect. If one walks in fear, ametrine will reveal the hidden warrior within. Sapphire, as you are aware, is the 'Wisdom Stone,' so appropriate for seekers of Truth. Quartz, an amplifier, enhances the other stones."

Merry held up the ring. It was a beautiful piece of jewelry with a generous, high-domed mounting in fancy silver filigree in which was nestled a brilliant-cut ametrine, which "… since it is comprised of both amethyst and citrine, has the metaphysical properties of both gemstones, in addition to what I've already told you about ametrine. Amethyst, especially, possesses age-old, *timeless* knowledge and protection. Citrine rids negativity and releases fears and phobias … emotionally balances."

The ring's shank bore ancient engravings of magickal symbols, including those of strong protection.

Grantie coughed and lowered her voice to a conspiratorial timbre. "This astral ring, like the locket, is very old and very, very powerful. I know I need not tell you to use them only for good, the good of all, and to use them wisely, but I am saying exactly that– *because I must.* You can see," she turned the ring, "that there is a portal on the back of this magickal tool that will allow your spirit to pass through, so to speak, when you chant.

"As I am certain you know, with astral projection, the spirit leaves the body attached to a silver umbilical-type cord, that some witches, including our Aisling here," she indicated with a wave of hand, "can actually see. I've found, since total relaxation is a *must* with astral spells, that reclining is good. Always worked best for me, but you'll have to experiment with this to see what works best for each of you.

"After your bath or shower and anointing with your oils, cast your circle of protection and lie with your body at a north-south axis, with your head pointed toward the magnetic north. If you decide to go skyclad rather than don your ritual robes, then cover yourselves with a light blanket or sheet to maintain your body temperature. I found that to be a help as well. As to what other magickal jewelry to wear, with the astral ring, I leave that to your instincts. I know you've been trusting your gut feelings as to which pieces of your enchanted jewelry to wear during any and all of your magickal doings. Each is a journey in itself, in more ways than one, and each is unique, so continue to go with your gut on each. In fact, I'll remind you to always trust your instincts– they are messages from your soul.

"With an out-of-the-body experience," Merry pressed on, "again atmosphere and state of mind are important." The *grande dame* inclined her head to the side. "When Buddha was asked what he gained from meditation, he answered, '*Nothing*. However, let me tell you what I've lost,' he said, 'anger, anxiety, depression, insecurity, and fear of old age and death.' Soooo," Merry let out her breath, "in a quiet place within a circle: meditation and focus, intent with specifics, and strong belief in your own powers. Take deep, deep breaths to focus and relax even more into your altered state of consciousness. This promotes the shifting of your brain frequencies, boosting your travel to the fifth dimension. Visualize yourselves rising, floating, to the ceiling. Have a clear and specific intent and know *completely* that you will succeed in whatever you wish to accomplish on your journey.

"When you are ready to return, simply *will* yourself back into your physical body, with the knowledge that you'll remember everything you saw, heard, and experienced. Afterward, do what you always do after spellcasting– thank, release the conjured deities, and open the circle; then be sure to ground yourselves fully, as you do after a session with your crystal ball. Water and a light snack, a glass of wine, or a bracing cup of tea.

"Again, the chant is a simple one: 'Through the charged air, out of my body I go without a care–'" Grantie interrupted herself, saying, as she handed Aisling a card with the handwritten chant, "I have written it down for you for your special *BOS*. I shan't chant it here and now, for, like the shapeshifting spell, it's a powerful incantation, as you will discover."

Merry closed her eyes and issued a little sigh.

"Are you feeling all right, Grantie?" the Sisters asked.

Merry smiled. "I've been better. Tired today. Let me conclude with this, my girls: Sacred items come to each of us when we're ready for them. I hope you realize that I am gifting you with these tools because I know *you* are *ready* for them. I can give you no better compliment than that. I know your granny and all the ancestors are pleased with the work you've been doing. As I'm sure you've noted over the years, I am not one for gushy compliments, but you have all three *earned* these tools. You've worked hard, shown fortitude, courage, and true concern for the innocents who have called upon you for help. You've gone above and beyond, and I want to say here and now how proud *I* am of you."

The Sisters moved to embrace their great-aunt, each voicing gratitude for the wise crone's faith and trust.

At that supreme moment, each Sister felt the presence of the ancestors– with their granny's warm smile. "Go that extra mile," she frequently told them, "it's never crowded."

Merry gave a knowing nod, her eyes glistening. "Always be grateful for your struggles, girls. Without them, you would never stumble upon your strengths."

The dear lady then took up the individual items, rubbing her hands over the charmed objects, seeming to memorize each, or at best to recall to memory how she'd used each during her long and vibrant life, before she replaced the treasures to the red velvet chest. Then she closed and patted the lid, heaved another sigh, and handed the box to the senior Sleuth Sister. "Here you go, my darlings, use these, and all your magick, wisely, for only good and in good health. So mote it be."

"*So mote it be*," echoed the Sisters with the passion that was surging through them.

En route, with Cousin Sean, back to the Hawthorne, where the Sisters needed to prepare for their departure to the airport, Raine decided to check in with their housekeeper Hannah Gilbert, who, with her husband, Jim, was staying at Tara in their absence. She fished her cell from her bag and placed the call.

"Hal-low, chickadees!" Hannah sang out. "You're gonna be mighty pleased with what hubby and I got done this weekend. I got a real good jump-start on the spring cleanin', and Jim has made all the repairs to the stable and the paddock fence. The stalls are clean, the horses brushed, and the cats bright-eyed, bushy-tailed and anxiously awaitin' your return, especially those crafty black ones."

Raine could hear the kitchen radio playing in the background, crooning with the country music for which Hannah had a persistent hankering. "Any news on the home front?" the Sister asked, catching, as soon as the words left her mouth, an ominous feeling that there was indeed news.

"I hope you got a good rest up there in Salem," came the feisty housekeeper's immediate reply. "Looks like there just might be a maniac loose on Haleigh Campus!"

"Life isn't about waiting for the storm to pass, it's about learning to dance in the rain."
~ Dr. Raine McDonough, PhD

Chapter Five

Early Monday morning, Raine and Maggie were motoring up the long, snowy avenue of stately oaks that led to Haleigh College.

The campus grounds were shaded by the wealth of trees from the various countries the institution's founder, coal czar Addison McKenzie and his wife, Haleigh, had traveled. The Sisters especially loved the majestic weeping willows that stood sentinel, in all their glory, along the campus' picturesque lakefront.

"Only women know why the willow weeps," Granny used to say. "They are the same women who confide in the moon and listen to voices in the wind."

As Maggie's vintage, green Land Rover passed the line of willows, the early morning sun glinted through the frozen cascading branches– ghostly in their shimmering cloaks of silvery-white, like trees from the faraway land of faerie.

The coal baron's former mansion, a virtual castle with turrets and wrap-around verandahs, housed many of the small college's classrooms. With the passage of time and Haleigh College's growth, a large addition was made to the McKenzie mansion, at the rear of the brick structure, that blended nicely, and did not mar the Victorian integrity of the architecture.

This was the building affectionately called by one and all "Old Main," the incentive for the college's Student-Union-sponsored Valentine Fest. The majestic structure's "facelift" would include a new roof, new wiring, plumbing, and general restoration; though, once again, the college was determined to keep the Victorian essence of the beloved, old manse.

Addison McKenzie's impressive brick-and-stone stable had been converted to the faculty offices; the carriage house, to the administrative building. The long garage that Addison built to house his fleet of carriages and motor cars, including three Rolls-Royces, became the college's first dorm. Over the years, however, two nearby mansions, both within walking distance from the main house/classrooms, were also converted to student dorms.

All in all, the campus was "rustically beautiful" and "idyllically enchanting," phrases applied to the whole of the faerie-tale place known as Haleigh's Hamlet by anyone lucky enough to live or visit there.

Feathery flakes of snow swirled and drifted toward the Land Rover's windshield as the Sisters entered the college grounds. Hither and thither, passing students, with backpacks or cradling books in their arms, and hurrying professors with briefcases were attired in costumes befitting Valentine's. The Sisters noted, though the masqueraders were sporting winter coats or jackets, several Cupids, what looked to be a shivering, caped Venus, and a number of participants swaddled in red.

Splashes of red were everywhere! There were red tights and leggings, red skirts, red pants, red sweaters, red jackets and coats, red hats, and red scarves. Pink was another prevalent color. A popular look was tights or leggings with tunics or long sweaters and scarves sprinkled with red, pink, or white hearts. All in all, the Sisters could see that dear, old Haleigh College was steeped in a festive Valentine mood.

"I was planning to wear my Queen of Hearts costume today and everyday till the end of the fest; but since we've that meeting this morning in the dean's office, I decided to hold off till tomorrow. We want to appear as stern and serious-minded as we can before those wayward students," Raine remarked to Maggie, who was sitting next to her in the passenger seat. Maggie did not like to drive in the winter, leaving that to the more venturesome Raine.

The redheaded Sister gave a quick nod to the stern, serious-minded reference. "I agree." She smiled to herself. "I just thought of something Granny imparted to us when we were teenagers. 'A well-bred girl is always particular to wear the right clothes for the right occasion.'"

Raine smiled too. "I remember. The occasion when we were each inducted into the National Honor Society our senior year at Haleigh High. It was one of the few times I recall Granny opting for convention." The Goth gal thought for a moment, adding, "Of course, the 'right clothes' for us, for the most part, are anything but conventional."

"True. I'd started to say," Maggie picked up her train of thought, "originally, I thought I'd dress as Venus but decided Friday last to go as Freya. As you know, she's the *Norse* goddess of love and beauty, so I can dress *warm*. The costume I rented from Enchantments has a nice, cozy fake-fur robe over the velvet gown, with a generous hood that's most becoming. I don't usually wear grey or silver, but it *is* a redhead's shade."

"Hannah's news didn't surprise us, did it?" Raine put in, of a sudden, to her sister of the moon.

Maggie shook her head, answering, "Not really. Both incidents involved someone being grazed with an arrow on campus at night. First a female student, strolling, hand-in-hand, with her boyfriend; then, Saturday evening, just after dark, one of our professors, Professor Hass, was struck in her ample derrière with an arrow, as she was bent over, putting her briefcase and books into her car."

"She wasn't wearing a coat, only a short jacket; so she's damn lucky she was carrying a small, hardcover copy of *The Art of Sarcasm* in the back pocket of her skirt, or that arrow might have done her an injury." Raine tarried whilst a grin manifested on her kittenish face. "For once Hass the Ass' sarcasm has served her well!"

"I hate to say this, because I rather like Old Bull's-Eye, but our campus archery instructor and Hass were overheard in a blaringly heated row late Friday afternoon by numerous faculty and students in the Student Union annex of Old Main. Tut-tut, Professors Hass and Longbough," Maggie pronounced, shaking her head. "Those two have a colorful– or perhaps *garish* is a better choice of word– history of arguments and insults; and they both have quick, hot tempers," Maggie reminded.

Raine turned pensive, saying almost to herself, "But surely Professor Longbough didn't–" She broke off, asking, as she pulled the Land Rover into their reserved space in front of Old Main, "What was the quarrel about; did you find out?"

Raine and Maggie shared an office in one of the building's high turrets that overlooked the campus with a panoramic bird's-eye view. A few years before, their history classes met there, but the college's increased population changed that. The Sisters wanted to pop into their office first, before reporting for their meeting, also in Old Main, with the Dean.

"Yes," Maggie voiced in answer to Raine's query, "I got the lowdown on the latest Hass-Longbough clash when I rang Dr. Yore early this morning. I know she likes to rise with the birds, you see, so I knew she'd be up. Lizzy told me the dispute erupted because one of Hass' English students wanted to be excused from Longbow's archery class on Friday, so he could attend Hass' lecture on romantic figures from literature that she was giving in keeping with our campus Valentine theme. I don't like Hass, b–"

"Who does?" Raine interjected.

"But," Maggie carried on, "she told the student she could not free him from Longbough's class, that would be entirely up to Professor Longbough, whether or not he excused the student from his class to attend her lecture. Apparently, she penned a short note to Old Bull's-Eye to explain why the young man wanted to attend her lecture, leaving the decision, and rightly so, up to him. He either didn't take the time to read the whole note, perhaps exploding when he saw *her* name on it, or … who knows what the *student* conveyed to him? We both know how students like to twist and mold information to suit themselves. There's no telling *what* the involved student told Longbow."

"Could be he was still vexed over losing his gym to the Valentine vendors. That's where they all are, you know, in the gymnasium. When he learned that the college was commandeering *his* gym for the sellers' tables, you remember what he said, before he stormed out of our last faculty meeting: 'Haven't you people ever wondered why Cupid rhymes with stupid?'" Maggie thought for a moment, as a memory jolted her. "You know Longbough abhors anything that smacks of Valentine's."

"Ooooooh yeah," Raine replied. "But the particulars have temporarily escaped me. Wait a minute," she snapped her fingers. "It's coming back, but go ahead– refresh me."

"Professor Longbough was married years ago. One Yuletide, he and his wife attended a sports banquet, where she met a dishy pro football player and fell instantly and madly in love, like she was hit dead-on with Cupid's arrow. She ran off with the guy at Valentine's, and later, they were married. The clincher, for Old Bull's-Eye, was what *she* said to a reporter who spotted them out together shortly after she left Prof Longbough, and the snoopin' scribe asked what the couple planned to do, since she was already married. She retorted that she'd rather have one day of true bliss than a lifetime of boredom."

"Ouch, that left a mark!" Raine waited as all the salacious gossip flooded back to her. "A *bad* blow, that."

"A *low* blow, that!" Maggie quipped.

"Certainly explains why our poor ole archery coach abhors Valentine's," Raine concluded. "It's no wonder, but *I* can't help wondering if …" she let her thought drift away like smoke, when Maggie spoke again.

"Strange to say, for some reason, *whatever* reason, Longbow *did* excuse the student from his class to attend Hass' talk.

"Later, however, when he encountered Hass in Old Main, he let loose some pretty pointed arrows, so to speak, of his own, wheeling on her accusingly and *demanding* to know why she thought *her* class was more important than his. The scenario rose to high drama, when she in turn rushed forward, with clenched hands and two bright splotches of color in her jowly cheeks, to bellow at the top of her voice: 'I merely explained in my note *why* the student wanted to attend my lecture, but I left the decision up to *you,* you baboon!' He hurled her words aside, ranting on and on about how she constantly belittles phys ed, to which Hass snorted with indignation to roar back, 'Hold on. **Hold on!** Let me get this straight. *You* made a decision, and now you're angry with *me* for a decision *you* made. I'm trying my absolute hardest to see things from your perspective, but I just can't get my head that far up my ass!'"

Raine giggled, "Did she really? In front of other faculty *and students*?"

"You bet your besom she did. It was a *fierce* exchange, to put it mildly, that *raged* on for another ten minutes before both profs stormed out, in opposite directions, but not before hurling final insults at one another." Maggie's face broke into a grin. "And more scandalized expressions Lizzy said she doesn't ever recall witnessing."

"Well, neither Hass nor Longbow has ever been known for what anyone might describe as *tact*," Raine chortled.

"True. Not an ounce of *savoir faire* between them. As a matter of fact, both can be extraordinarily obtuse and …"

Distilling their sensations into a single word, the Sisters concluded as one, "*Cantankerous!*"

"Can you picture all this?" Maggie shrieked. "Great Goddess! Needless to say, Dean Savant got wind of it straightaway and ordered them both, first thing this morning, to his office." The redheaded Sister checked her face in her compact mirror, replacing the enchanted item to her purse with meditative expression. "Would've loved to have been a fly on the wall in there, huh?"

"I can image it all right … Hass blaming it on 'That horrible man,' as she likes to call our Haleigh's Old Bull's-Eye. You know what?" Raine thought abruptly and aloud. "I believe Longbow excused the student from his class just so he could jump Hass in front of others and humiliate her. He seemed to have forgotten, though, that she's old Haleigh's *star* of sarcasm. I can imagine his tizzy when his ruse backfired. Everyone laughing behind his back, and his backside still smarting from the cruel Valentine joke Cupid and his ex played on him.

"I don't think Longbow will be the *only* prof on this campus in a tizzy after this morning," Raine mused. "If the dean suspends the cheaters– and I expect he will; Dean Savant won't let the fact that the girls come from prestigious families stop him from doing what's right– then our theatre director, Dr. Lear, will also be in a dither."

Raine was referring to the three students whom both she and Maggie had caught cheating on exams the previous week. Since then, it looked as though at least one other professor would be coming forward with the same charge.

Maggie considered this information, replying, "Oooooh, I get it; the cheaters have significant roles in our Valentine Fest's production of *Romeo and Juliet.*" After a moment, she shrugged, "Things happen, as well we know from our involvement in community theatre. That's why they invented understudies … and prompters."

Raine opened the car door to step out. "We may have some hard moments in the dean's office, Mags. You ready to deal with what's sure to be a sticky situation?"

Maggie gave a curt nod, "Ready as I'll ever be."

Dean Savant's office was at the end of the long hallway on Old Main's second floor. It was a small room, as unobtrusive as the man who occupied it. The pragmatic Savant had chosen the quiet, out-of-the-way space himself, for it was not nearly large enough to accommodate a classroom. There were only three faculty offices in Old Main– the Dean's; Raine and Maggie's shared office in one of the turrets; and, in the other turret, the office of Dr. Barron Whitman, the head of Haleigh College's English department. The turrets made charming offices but were too small nowadays for classrooms, Old Main's chief function. The rest of the faculty offices were located on the opposite end of the campus, in the brilliantly converted brick-and-stone McKenzie stable.

When Raine and Maggie reached the Dean's office, the Bitchy Bees, as the Goth gal privately defined them, were sitting in folding chairs in the hall, sulkily waiting to be called inside. Feeling their shrewd eyes looking them up and down, the Sisters greeted them in passing with a simple, "Good morning," after which the girls' leader, Liza Berk, replied in typical insolent attitude, "What's good about it?"

"Well now, that remains to be seen," Raine cracked wise, as she and Maggie entered Dr. Savant's office.

***

"So you see, Dean Savant, we caught these girls cheating in *both* our classes," Raine delivered in summation, "caught them red-handed in the act, and we feel that the only recourse–"

"I think you're being totally unfair to us!" Liza blurted. "This is our first infraction of any rule here at Haleigh. We've been *model* students; but lately, due to the Valentine Fest, we've been swamped with extra-curricular activities."

Déjà poo, Raine thought, *I've heard this crap before.*

Waggle my wand, Maggie was thinking, *that sort of bombast is so tiresome.*

"We've been working like dogs to help raise money for Old Main through our sorority," Liza flung at the dean, "*and* the Student Union, and it's been grueling!"

Liza Berk was an overbearing, overweight bleached blonde with short frizzy hair and an even shorter temper. Her teeth resembled horse teeth, too big and prominent for even her broad face. The only *small* thing about the girl were her mean eyes. With the exception of her two constant cohorts, Liza wasn't popular with either the students or the faculty; but her father gave large sums of money to the college, hence she felt and acted privileged.

Insufferable snobbery oozing from every pore, the obnoxious girl voiced in a demanding tenor, "You need to let us retake the tests, in each of your classes. We deserve a break, in view of how hard we've been working for Old Main; and, after all, this is our first offense."

"Working hard, are you, for the restoration of Old Main?" Maggie and Raine responded closely in sync.

"We looked into that, since you mentioned it Friday last when we collared you, and not surprising to us, we couldn't find one single thing that you three have contributed to the project thus far," Raine stated evenly. "Regardless, you *cheated* and were caught dead to rights in each of our classes, so *first offense* hardly applies, now does it? Furthermore, we believe there's a pattern of behavior here that we intend to uncover. As for being model students– model students are never insolent to their professors. You, on the other hand, take that tone recurrently."

"A thousand pardons," Liza muttered, bowing from her chair in a mocking gesture.

Keep it up, smartass, Raine thought. *It's called Karma, and it's pronounced Ha, ha, ha!* Turning toward the dean– who was fixing Miss Berk with a look that was sternly disapproving–the Sister gestured toward the impudent student, voicing aloud, "I rest my case."

"I strongly advise you," Dean Savant cautioned the girls, "to keep civil tongues in your head and to show respect for your professors, this office, and this institution!"

"Dean, this *is* our first offense," Liza spewed out, totally oblivious to his dour stare. "Check your records, why don't you?"

"As the Dr. McDonoughs have pointed out, having been caught in *both* their classes rules out first offense, which, by the way, is *no* defense, since we have at Haleigh a no-tolerance cheating policy," the dean replied.

"There are extenuating circumstances here, Dean," Liza said in a challenging voice. "The Valentine Fest has put a lot of pressure on us, and–"

"Valentine Fest or not, our cheating policy here means just what it says– *no tolerance*," Dr. Savant responded with dignity.

A quick, signal-type rap on the door resulted in the appearance of one of the professors from the English department. "Clearly not a first offense, and not even their first-time caught. *I* can attest to that," Professor Annabel Lee announced, as, motioned in by the dean, she stepped further into the office. She was a young, attractive brunette with a slender figure– *ethereal* is the word Granny McDonough would've used– with a natural grace and elegance, a woman who gave the impression that she might be a ballerina by profession. "I want to express my sincere regret to you, Dean Savant, for not coming forth sooner.

"I caught these students cheating last fall, but they *begged* me to give them a chance to retake the exam and not report them, telling me, then, that it was their first offense. A sob-story accompanied their pleas. I subsequently came to seriously doubt that the cheating in my class *was* a first offense for this trio due to other infractions, including the insolence you," she looked to the Sisters, "brought to light. I am deeply sorry I did not report them when I caught them last October. It was not only foolish of me, but wrong," Professor Lee apologized.

Annabel settled her gaze on the girls, testifying, "Over the weekend, I overheard them bragging to other students, in a downtown café, about how they've easily duped teachers at the schools they attended, from grade school to college. They laughed like hyenas over how they'd duped *me* and how they intended to do the same with *you* today," she looked again to the Sisters. "As soon as I heard about their cheating in your classes," the instructor nodded toward Raine and Maggie, "I knew I needed to come forward with *my* information."

Dean Savant indicated that Professor Lee should sit in the remaining empty chair across from his desk. He was a tall, robust man, with a slight paunch, in his early sixties. His sandy-colored hair was heavily threaded with grey, and his face was plain and rather non-descript. He took a long look at the girls, before saying, "This is your senior year. I am wondering how many times you've cheated since you started here as freshmen."

"Dean Savant," Tiffany Browne, the pretty, slender brunette of the Terrible Three– another of Raine's private appellations for the girls– pleaded, "Professor Lee *misunderstood* what we were talking about in the café. We weren't bragging about cheating. In fact, we weren't even talking about ourselves. We were laughing about a movie we'd seen."

The most boisterous of the clique, Liza caught Tiffany's eye and burst in with, "That's right! *You*," she rudely pointed a finger at Professor Lee, "obviously missed the beginning of our conversation."

"All nonsense! A string of lies," the professor countered, regarding the students with contempt, her voice crisp and businesslike. "I overheard every word you uttered, since I was seated on the opposite side of the partition, just inches away, though completely invisible to you."

In the interim, Raine couldn't help but think: *What liars these girls are! But I'm not worried. Won't be the first time the dean has confronted students fluent in bullshit.* To the wayward three, she cast with her witchy stare: *Never underestimate my ability to know a lie when I hear one. Just because I don't call you out on it, doesn't mean you have me fooled.*

"Dean Savant, you have to believe us. I tell you we were talking about a movie we'd seen. Professor Lee got it all wrong!" Tiffany shouted. Her lips trembled then hardened again, as she stared for a defiant moment at her instructors to see Annabel lock eyes with the dean and then shake her head in negative reply to the second attempt at explanation.

"What was the name of this alleged movie?" the Dean fired at Miss Browne.

The girl's face blanched. "I-I don't remember now. I'm so upset, I can't recall. Professor Lee and *both* Doctors McDonough have never liked us," the panicky girl tried yet again, switching gears. "They're constantly finding fault ..." the girl stammered, her wild eyes darting to Liza then back to the dean. *"You have to believe us!"* she repeated, her voice going shrill.

Savant threw her a reproachful glance. "I don't *have* to do any such thing. Let me repeat: We have a no-tolerance cheating policy here at Haleigh. It's stated quite clearly in our handbook; and I believe it's already been established that you have cheated more than once, lied to your professors, then bragged and jested about your reprehensible conduct to others. I am afraid I have no choice but to suspend you until further notice. This means–"

Liza jolted bolt upright. "You *should* be afraid," the surly girl cut in characteristically with razor-sharp sarcasm, "if you want my father to continue as benefactor to this dinky college." Her gaze swept her accusers, resulting in a superior snort. "Who do you think you are anyway? You make me sick. All of you!" The small, mean eyes glinted bizarrely. "I guarantee, if you go through with this, my father will see to it that each of you is fired!"

A sharp tongue's the only edged tool that grows keener with constant use, Maggie whizzed to Raine, who came back with–

Hers certainly has.

Dean Savant's normally poker face took on a look of austerity the likes of which the Sisters had never before seen. "This means, of course," he pushed on, louder and with a sharp edge to *his* voice, "you will *not* be permitted to participate in any of the Valentine Fest activities, nor will you be permitted to participate in any of your sorority happenings until further notice."

"Oh, please, *please* don't do this, Dean, because we have roles in the college production of *Romeo and Juliet*. *Leading* roles! *I* am playing Juliet!" screeched Sylvia Blair, the curvaceous redhead. "Dr. Lear is depending on me," she shot a desperate glance at her cohorts, "on all of us, and I am sure you're aware that the proceeds from the play will go toward the restoration of Old Main."

Liza looked up to lock regards with Raine– and was startled to find those McDonough eyes cool and amused. Tearing her gaze away, the girl rose partway out of her seat to shriek a totally different argument at the dean. "That's right! We're all *three* in the play, and we *all* have *leading* parts," she trumpeted loudly. Her air was gallingly smug, and it was obvious she did not expect the dean's answering comment.

"I suggest you stop playing the fool. Or is it that you think *I'm* the fool?" the dean prodded, his voice hard. "Either way, it isn't working."

Liza's wide face flamed with her rant of defiance, "You can*not* do this!!"

"Oooh, I assure you, I *can*, and I shall," Dean Savant replied calmly, his air and tone disarming for two of the wrongdoers before him. "Let me be clear. No school play, no Valentine's dance, no sorority activities, no college activities of *any* kind. Your present conduct has not helped you, I must say." He pulled himself up a notch in his padded chair. "You will remove yourselves from this campus when we finish here, and you will await my decision, via letter, as to how long your suspension will last, though I can tell you now, it *will* last through our Valentine Fest. What's more, I intend to investigate this matter thoroughly, and depending on what I uncover, disciplinary action could well be *expulsion* rather than just suspension. It goes without saying that your cheating offenses, as well as your conduct here today, will be *permanently* attached to your academic record."

Liza shouted with brazen impertinence, "You are going to rue the day you ever–"

"**That will do!**" the dean cut in strongly.

Tiffany began to cry. "Dean, it's going to be *impossible* for us to catch up if you suspend us now. We might not get to graduate with our class!"

"And if you expel us with this stuff on our permanent records, we might not be able to get into any decent college in the whole country! How can you do this to us?" Sylvia completed Tiffany's thought, her voice rising to a wail, *"Ple—ase* reconsider!"

By this point, the near-hysterical Tiffany and Sylvia were both openly sobbing. "Please, Dean, be fair!"

"I am being fair," the dean answered in the blunt and direct manner that suited his position. "And to respond to your question, Miss Blair: *You've brought this on yourselves.* Cheating is a serious violation of our rules here at Haleigh. A serious transgression at any school. The repercussions of cheating vary by institution; and again, I reiterate, here at Haleigh, we have a *no-tolerance* policy. *It is our right.* If this derails your plans for your futures, you should have thought of this before you decided to break the rules– and then brag about it publicly."

When the vociferous girls began protesting discordantly, the dean barked, with suddenly penetrating gaze on an exceedingly outraged Liza, whose open mouth shut quickly enough. "Hold your tongues! I've heard quite enough from *you!"*

When Maggie stole a glimpse at Raine, she saw that the latter, with knit brow, was frowning.

"A bit of advice," the Goth gal couldn't refrain from saying. "There's no such thing as getting away with something. Doesn't happen, girls. Everything we do in life, good or bad, comes back to each of us– three-times-three. *That's a law.*"

Only Liza of the *triade terrible* remained dry-eyed. Her big, red face was screwed in an ugly snarl, and her mean, and unquestionably shrewd, eyes fastened intently on Raine, Maggie, and Professor Lee, narrowing with blatant hatred– *and revenge.*

The day after the showdown in the dean's office, Professor Lee had a painfully embarrassing occurrence befall her. She'd been chosen to speak about the college's Valentine Fest at the televised meeting of Haleigh Hamlet's town hall. The talk was planned to better acquaint the public with the fest and hopefully encourage more merchants to participate in the fundraising for Old Main's restoration, in addition to garnering more customers for the sellers from the community. Professor Lee hoped also to encourage donations from the public for the renovation.

Annabel habitually kicked off her morning with a Danish and a good cup of coffee from Sal-San-Tries, the popular café-deli downtown, that several of the college profs frequented. The morning of the televised meeting, she set the continental breakfast on her desk, but was called away for several minutes when a note was slipped under her office door. After hurrying to the library to meet with the Sleuth Sisters, as the note fervently entreated her to do, she discovered that neither Raine nor Maggie sent her the missive. She rushed back, gulped down her breakfast of coffee and a roll and took off for the town hall.

No sooner did she step to the microphone to open her presentation, when she was nearly doubled over with violent diarrhea, causing her to literally run from the room to the nearest ladies'. No way could she return to complete her talk. She spent the rest of the day near, in fact, *quite* near, a toilet.

The subsequent morning, when Annabel started her car, the engine began to sputter, knock and hesitate, eventually losing power. At the close of her classes that day, she sputtered to the nearby Auto Doctor, left the vehicle in their care, and drove home in a loaner. That afternoon, the words out of the mechanic's mouth over the phone startled her: "You must've made an enemy among your students, professor. Someone dumped a bag of sugar in your gas tank. Easy for anyone to do with an old car like yours."

Raine and Maggie, on the other hand, cast a strong protection spell to aid them against the trio of *enfants terribles*. Thus far, the only thing that befell the Sisters was a pizza delivery man ringing their doorbell in the wee hours with an unsolicited, unwelcome order.

*** *** ***

Wednesday afternoon, whilst Raine and Maggie promenaded across campus toward the college gymnasium, where they planned to browse the vendor tables, they were deep in discussion about the disturbing events developing at Haleigh. To help fend off negativity and to get into the Valentine spirit of campus activities, the Sisters were sporting their fun costumes.

Raine's Queen of Hearts outfit suited her perfectly. The shimmery white gown had long, dripping sleeves and a huge, black, Gothic-style stand up collar that framed the face. The black tunic exposed the front of the gown that was sprinkled liberally with red hearts. An ultra-wide, black corset-belt and a sparkling, crystal crown in her raven hair completed the bewitching attire. To ward off winter's chill, the Goth gal chose, from the back of her own closet, a long, red wool cape with a faux-fur-lined hood.

Maggie's Freya costume conveyed to perfection the *Norse* goddess of love and beauty. As the redheaded Sister had related, the silvery-grey, fake-fur robe over the snow-white velvet gown was warm and cozy; and the long cape's generous hood was flattering to Maggie's vivid coloring.

"I was thinking the other day," Maggie considered, "that the only person who could get away with a *real* bow and arrow on campus is our archery instructor, Professor Longbough. Campus security would apprehend anyone else, and after the first errant arrow, security was intensified. Two wayward arrows, the first targeting the female in a pair of college lovers strolling the campus grounds at twilight, and the second hitting Hass, Longbow's longtime nemesis, as she was about to get into her car in the college library parking lot. It's so obvious. *Too* obvious, if you know what I'm saying?"

Raine set her lips firmly together in a grim line. "I do. Someone might well be staging this to pin the blame on Old Bull's-Eye. And that's another thing: Both arrows did no real harm. If the archer wanted to do harm, he isn't a very good shot, and our Longbow's a former Olympian."

"Yes," Maggie said sharply, "but might be that the perverse archer's *express* goal is to blight our Valentine Fest. If *that's* the case, he's right on target."

"So it would seem. A most unaccountable business, this whole campus mess, but we'll get to the bottom of it. It's occurred to me more than once," Raine mused aloud, "that the wild archer has no intention of killing or wounding his targets. Then again," she rambled, "everything one does is intentional. Every time you forget a name or a face, for example, it could be that, unconsciously, you *wish* to forget it. And every time you have a slip of tongue, it has *meaning*," she maintained.

"And the dreadful things that have been happening to Professor Lee!" Maggie exclaimed, more or less unmindful of the other's ramblings.

Raine came back with, "Oooh, I don't think we need to reflect too long and hard about who *that* might be. The Bitchy Bees either have an accomplice on campus, or they snuck over here to work their devilment … easy to do in the guise of a costume. Annabel admitted to us she neglected to lock her office when she rushed to the library to keep what she thought was an emergency summons from us. *Anyone* could've darted in there, though everything points to the Terrible Three."

"Hard to *prove* at this juncture. As for the vandalism to Annabel's car, the vengeful students could've dumped the sugar in her gas tank when the car was in the driveway of her home, rather than here on campus," Maggie reasoned. "As for our delivery from that all-night pizza shop, Liza's probably savvy enough to use a burn phone for her nasty tricks, so we wouldn't be able to trace the call."

Raine chewed on her full lower lip. "Yeah, it's going to be hard to prove the Bees are the guilty parties."

Maggie could feel Raine's mind ranging vividly over all the possibilities.

Outside the gymnasium building, salespersons from the Hamlet's Sugar Shack hawked steamy, fragrant mugs of their popular hot chocolate. Inside, tables with a variety of wares covered the floor, from one end of the gym to the other. The goods and services were all connected to the Valentine love theme and were for sale to students, faculty, college personnel, and the public at large, since the college was promoting the fest in the Hamlet and round about. Browsers and buyers wandered from table to table. Groups of students stood or sat about chatting and laughing, and at the entrances, Student-Union reps oversaw matters in an orderly fashion.

Vendors had to agree to the rules, including the one regarding the proceeds. Sixty percent of each seller's proceeds would go to the renovation of Old Main. There were a few, however, who volunteered to donate their total profits to the Cause, including Raine and Maggie.

There were perfumers selling his and her fragrances with dreamy names that conjured *allure*, music stores and home-grown musicians offering a spectrum of wistful love songs, restaurants with romantic dinner-for-two gift certificates, representatives from the Mountain Chateau in the nearby Laurel Highlands armed with holiday and spa vouchers, book stores and authors touting romance novels, video shops with love-themed movies to buy or rent, florists whose array of flowers ranged from traditional red roses to old-fashioned bunches of deep-purple violets, candy peddlers with heart-shaped boxes of chocolates, travel agencies hawking romantic getaways, clothing stores and local seamstresses displaying tasteful items for starry-eyed ladies, dance studios with tickets for couples with dance fever, gift shops with sundry items for the "incurable romantic," and farmer's markets with pretty baskets brimming with assorted goodies.

"Those handcrafted chocolates we purchased from The Hamlet Candy Bar," Maggie remarked, indicating that particular stand, "are first-class. I'd like to get more, but we'll gift them to someone before we're tempted to open a second box."

"Good idea."

"Oh look, Mags, there's the author whose history works we've used in our classrooms, Ceane O'Hanlon-Lincoln. I heard she's one of us donating total proceeds to the Cause."

"Correct," Maggie replied. "She authored a respected collection of romantic short stories entitled *Autumn Song* that she's selling here. We should get a signed copy."

"Lets. Oh, and remember, her name's pronounced SHAWN-ee, or Shawn for short. I wonder how our perfume and love potions are faring?" Raine queried, as they approached the spot where their housekeeper, Hannah Gilbert, was manning their table. Hannah had offered to fill in for the Sisters, during periods when they were in their classrooms, or otherwise occupied with their college duties.

"I was just wondering that myself," Maggie replied in regard to the sale of their witchy wares.

Raine and Maggie were selling their newly concocted Be My Valentine Love Potion, as well as Lover Come Back, a powerful potion their granny had perfected years before. Made with herbs; oils; and items that represented and carried the energies of the intentions therein, such as selected gemstones, all bonded together with strong magick, the McDonough potions were legendary throughout the Hamlet and beyond. Also on the Sisters' table was their love-spell perfume, Witchy Woman.

"How's it going?" Maggie questioned, giving Hannah a hug, after which the older woman responded with an animated thumbs-up. To Raine the redheaded Sister said, "Going to grab those items we said we wanted. Shan't be long."

Hannah's well-scrubbed face wore a broad smile. "I'm practically sold out of your love potions. Don't worry, I'm tellin' customers *exactly* what you instructed me to say: "Dab the stuff behind ears, on wrists, or over the heart, throat, or even on the back of the neck. I'm rememberin' t' tell them they kin also dress candles with these potions, just like you tole me to do." She pointed to the ribboned scrolls in a white box decorated with red hearts, positioned on the table next to the potion and perfume bottles. "I give each buyer a little scroll of instructions with each purchase. Makin' a tidy sum for the Great Cause, as I heard some of the kids callin' this here fest." She neatened the remaining bottles in an attractive arrangement.

It seemed odd to see Hannah without her colorful muumuu, her signature cleaning outfit that she habitually wore with purple sneakers. Today, her stout body was clad in a corduroy skirt and bulky wool sweater, both purple; and when she stepped out from behind the table to greet the Sisters, they immediately noted her trademark purple sneakers. "As you kin see by the number of bottles left, business really picked up today. Been selling your bewitchery, left and right, ever since I got here this mornin'."

Though Hannah's voice and manner were brass, her heart, as the Sisters asserted, was "pure gold." And despite the housekeeper's tendency toward the bossy, along with her penchant for gossip, she was a *nurturing* soul. She took good care of the Sleuth Sisters and Tara, scrubbing and polishing the old house with almost religious fervor, and she regularly looked after Aisling's preteen daughter, Merry Fay.

"Your Witchy Woman perfume is just about sold out too," Hannah said proudly with a flourish of hand over the bottles. "I tell everyone it kin charm the birds outta the trees!"

"We've more at home. We made huge batches of both the potions and the perfume, so we'll need you to keep selling, Hannah," Raine enthused.

"I'm enjoyin' it." Hannah inclined her grey head with its tight bun, lowering her voice in a secretive manner, "Gets me outta real work."

"Remember, when you need a break, get one of the badge-wearing Student-Union members to hold down the fort for you," Raine reminded.

"I remember." She tapped her grey head, "Got everything stored up here." Gazing down at the potions, she said, "I should be sold out of this batch sometime today, and I'll just turn all the money over to the Student Union, like you tole me t' do, then go on home and fix ole Jim his supper." Hannah snickered. "It would serve the ole man right if I bought a bottle of your Valentine love potion to use on him. All he does at home anymore is sleep."

"Sweets for the sweet," Maggie said, sweeping in from her shopping errand to gift Hannah with the box of chocolates she purchased. "Thank you for what you're doing for us and the college."

Raine saw that the O'Hanlon-Lincoln short-story collection protruded from the top of Maggie's bag. Noting her gaze, Maggie extracted the paperback. "The author signed it for us." Her green eyes scanned the blurb. "Says *Autumn Song: Romantic Interludes* is the perfect bedside-fireside reader … sixteen stories … thought-provoking twists and turns … surprise endings. Can't wait to curl up with it tonight!" She tucked the book back into the side pocket of her purse.

"Hannah, before I forget, go ahead and take a bottle of our Be My Valentine Love Potion," said Raine in her low husky voice, "and be sure to let us know how it worked for you," she winked. "Fair warning: Be prepared for *sizzling* results."

The housekeeper howled. "In our house, when we talk about 'Gettin' any,' we're talkin' *sleep.*"

As the Sisters continued to chat with Hannah, two of the English professors paused at their table, Professor Annabel Lee and Dr. Barron Whitman. Dr. Whitman was relatively new to Haleigh College, having come from his native Boston the previous year to head the English department when his predecessor passed away. The son of one of Boston's elite families, Barron had graduated from Harvard *cum laude* after having gone straight through for his doctorate. Yielding to his mother's pleas, he'd taught at Harvard for a few years before accepting the department head at Haleigh. To his mother's argument that Haleigh was backwater and small, he answered in truth that the distinguished Pennsylvania institution was considered one of the best private colleges in America.

Looking every bit the aristocrat, the forty-ish Dr. Whitman was tall, suave, and meticulously groomed, his appearance and manner as posh and polished as his speech. His dark hair was only slightly touched with grey, at the temples; and his features, like his demeanor, were decidedly patrician.

"Good-afternoon, ladies," Dr. Whitman greeted with a half-smile, his gaze sweeping the gym. "It is gratifying to see so many people from the village participating in our fest."

When greetings and introductions were completed, Maggie regarded Professor Lee with tilted red head and searching eyes.

"You're looking especially happy today, Annabel. In fact, I'd go so far as to say you're positively glowing."

Annabel looked to Dr. Whitman, who gave a subtle nod, after which she held up her left hand, the ring finger adorned with a fabulous, antique-style, diamond engagement ring, the glittering, mine-cut diamonds set in platinum. "Barron and I are engaged. It's *official*," she beamed.

For an instant, anyway, the Sisters were bowled over, prompting Dr. Whitman to enlighten. "It surprises you very much, does it?" Without waiting for their responses, he went on, his eyes on Annabel, "We succeeded, then, my dear, in keeping our courtship quiet; but now it's time, I think, that we share our bliss with our families, friends and fellows."

Raine and Maggie quickly congratulated Dr. Whitman, telling Annabel what a beautiful bride she was going to make, as she gazed up at her fiancé adoringly.

Behind the couple, Maggie noticed that Dr. Rex Lear, head of Haleigh College's theatre department, who'd been tying his shoe lace in a nearby corner, straightened, picked up his signature umbrella and briefcase and started toward them. Suddenly changing his mind, he did an about-face and bustled off toward the nearest exit. *Poor man's got a passel of things to deal with nowadays.*

Pleasantries were exchanged for several minutes at the Sisters' selling table, after which Annabel's smiling eyes dropped to the love brews, remarking, "Potions! What fun! I've heard about these. There's no end to your talents."

From somewhere, out of nowhere or so it seemed, Trixie Fox, the graduate student whom Dr. Lear was mentoring in preparation for a career in theatre, appeared at the Sisters' table. She was an extremely pretty young woman, sexy, with a mane of auburn hair and hazel, come-hither eyes. Her body was perfect, and the foxy lady never failed to show off her assets with the figure-hugging clothes she wore.

"Potions, did I hear you say? Well, well," she cocked her head, picking up a vial, only to set it back down with a pooh-poohing gesture. "I suppose *some* girls," her feral gaze flicked over Annabel, "might have *need* for that sort of thing, but not me. I rely on my own, *natural*," she eyed Raine and Maggie with a haughty air, puckering her lips in a mock kissing attitude, "*witchcraft*."

The Sisters swapped quick thoughts, "Of that, we have no doubt," they replied in saccharin voice.

"Ta ta!" With a frosty smile and a saucy toss of her long hair, Trixie sauntered off in the direction her mentor had exited.

What a half-baked sly puss she is! Raine communicated to Maggie.

Hannah gave a sharp click of her tongue. "Witchcraft? More like *bitchcraft.* What does that gal have against *you*?" she prodded Raine and Maggie. The words had slipped out, but Hannah found that she wasn't a bit sorry as she steamrollered on. "I was just about to tell her that she could use a potion in good manners. A slap upside her head would also do the trick, an' a lot quicker t' boot!"

"Hmmm," Maggie mused, staring with troubled aspect after the hip-swaying tease, "I wonder ... . Trixie Fox doesn't even know us. *Of* us, perhaps. Maybe she caught us watching her yesterday, when she and Rex were lunching in the cafeteria. I hope we didn't stare." The Sister paused to reflect, and Hannah seized the opportunity to cut in.

"Oh poo, no class, that one. A classy woman is one who's got everything to flaunt– and chooses not to," the housekeeper recited in what she fathomed was a posh tone. "Pinched that from the newspaper this mornin'. It was one-a them 'fillers' they use between articles."

"I wouldn't worry about it, Maggie. I'd say it's a case of envy, pure and simple," Dr. Whitman said with staid, unsmiling expression. "On the other hand, her manner was, to put it mildly– *barbed.* 'Beware of jealousy,'" he began, borrowing from the Bard. "'It's a green-eyed monster that makes fun of the victims it devours.'" He regarded Hannah, and his brown eyes crinkled at the corners. "Dear lady, I love your rhetoric. Cuts right to the mark. Bravo!" Seeing the puzzled look on her face, he clarified. "You seem to possess a natural gift for choosing the precise word or phrase that fills the requirement of the occasion."

Hannah gave a short, guttural laugh. "I jus' call 'em as I see 'em, professor." She turned her head to face the Sisters. "You be careful of that yella-eyed vixen, hear? I didn't like how she looked at you." The protective housekeeper tossed a glance in the direction Trixie Fox had departed, wisecracking, or as Raine put it, "cracking wise" with– "Witch with a capital B!"

In the intervening time, Annabel was looking closely at the fancy little bottles on the Sisters' table, asking the magickal pair, "Have you a potion that will make a future mother-in-law love me? It would have to be *super* strong."

The Sisters regarded one another, not sure of how they should respond, when, in an attempt to smooth the awkwardness of the moment, Dr. Whitman quickly spoke. Clearly, he was embarrassed by Annabel's airing of such a private matter.

"All in due course. My mother just doesn't know you yet, darling. She's always been somewhat reserved. It's a family trait, I'm afraid. When she's here for her visit, you'll see, she'll return home with as much tenderness for you as I hold." His smile was rather thin, however; and, as empaths, the Sisters acutely felt the chill of his displeasure at Annabel's remark.

She sensed it too, murmuring, "I'm certain your mother and I will come to love one another very much, Barron. I've high hopes. As a matter of fact, I'm quite looking forward to her visit."

He sent his fiancée another smile, this one more genuine. "Mother's a tad reticent, but we all have our little quirks. I'm elated she'll be here to enjoy the Valentine tea with us as my guest. She's expressed a desire, on more than one occasion, to accompany me to a faculty tea. My letters glow with praise for our Haleigh."

Dr. Whitman glanced at the gold Rolex on his wrist. "Excuse us. We must be off. We each have another class this afternoon. I will wish you a good morning, Hannah. It was a *pleasure* meeting you, and," looking to the Sisters, he enunciated with a lilt to his words, "it is, on every occasion, *enchanting* chatting with you. Make it a great day, ladies."

"Thank you," the Sisters returned.

"We'd better be off too," Maggie alerted. "I have another class in twenty minutes, and Raine has a conference with a graduate student in a few."

Hannah waved the Sisters in the direction of the exits, "Go on, go on and do what y' have to do, chickadees. I'll hold down the fort."

"You're doing an excellent selling job, Hannah. They'll be a nice bonus of gratitude for you in your next paycheck," Raine declared.

"G'on now," the beloved housekeeper countered, "no need f'r that. If I can't do for my own– and you know all three-a you girls are like daughters to me– who can I do for?"

As they walked across campus, Maggie remarked to Raine, "The news of Annabel's engagement is going to be a shock to our theatre director. It looked to me like he fell head-over-heels in love with her from the moment she began teaching here."

Raine thought before answering, "Perhaps, but my guess is our shy Dr. Lear worshiped her from afar." She shrugged. "If he did make his feelings known to her, I can't believe she led him on when she obviously didn't return those feelings. Annabel's not a flirt. It never looked like she encouraged him."

"No, no, she isn't a flirt," Maggie put in. "I imagine she ignored Rex's ardor for her, if she was even aware of it. *We* were aware of it, but then again, we're both empaths; however, she might not have been aware, because I doubt very much he made any overt advances toward her. Rather a shame, isn't it, about Dr. Lear? He's handsome, creative, charming, and hard-working, but he always seems unlucky in love. Now it looks like the graduate student he's mentoring, that Trixie Fox, *is* leading him on, I think, to gain what she wants from him. I saw them together yesterday in the cafeteria. That tricky little fox is a *real* player."

"Yeah, I didn't want to say anything in front of the others, but after we saw them yesterday, I did some checking up on her. *Interesting* reading, I must say. Hannah was right, a good slap upside her stupid head would benefit the little minx tremendously." In a moment, the raven-haired Sister burst firmly into speech, "Oh, Rex'll move past Annabel's engagement and all the Trixie Foxes who come along. He pours himself into his work. You know what I think? I think *theatre* is his one *true* love; and right now, he's got his hands full with his *Romeo and Juliet* production. Getting three understudies ready to step into leading roles with Shakespearean dialogue for a fast-approaching opening night is, without exaggeration, nothing short of nerve-wrecking. You know what a consummate perfectionist he is," Raine reminded. "Bless my besom, I nearly forgot to tell you what I happened to remember about Trixie Fox! She had a real thing for Dr. Whitman."

"She did?" Maggie reacted with genuine surprise. "She didn't even acknowledge him when she blustered over to our table."

"Yes, I was aware of that; but the fact is," the Goth gal informed, "she did everything but hold a gun to his head to get him to fall for her. He wasn't interested, let her know it in no uncertain terms, and

… you know what?" she exclaimed of a sudden. "I believe Trixie overheard Annabel announce the engagement."

"Ooooh, you're probably right," Maggie replied. "I'm *sure,* now that you mention it, I caught her sending Annabel the Evil Eye. I mean, if looks could kill!"

Raine smirked. "I wouldn't put anything past that bag of tricks. Did you note how her eyes raked Annabel when she snidely mentioned that *some girls* might have need of love potions, and that's when she targeted us with her spite … as if–"

"*We* brewed Annabel a love potion that resulted in Barron's marriage proposal!" Maggie, in sudden insight, completed the thought. Well, at least we know, or I *think* we do, why Trixie Fox acted as she did– both toward Annabel *and* us."

They arrived at Old Main, and as Raine pulled open the door, she spoke again. "I'm caught up, as of today, with my college duties, so now I can experiment with Grantie's shapeshifting locket. *I can hardly wait!* By the bye, Mags, isn't Annabel's engagement ring to die for?"

Little did the Goth gal realize how literal her non-literal language would soon become.

"I love the woman I am because I fought to become her!"
~ Dr. Raine McDonough

Chapter Six

The Trio of Sleuth Sisters were seated across the desk of Haleigh Hamlet's Chief of Police. Since Thursday was a light day at the college for Raine and Maggie, and Aisling had no pressing business at the detective agency, they decided the evening before to pay the chief a visit in the afternoon; and now, they were glad they'd listened to their instincts.

Chief Fitzpatrick was a burly, middle-aged fellow with a thick crop of white hair and a high color to his fair Irish complexion, a big, comfortable-looking man with a deceptively mild manner, who, at times, seemed to actually radiate power and vitality.

"Fitz, we just want to make certain you're OK with us doing some sleuthing around campus," Raine said. "This whole business with the errant arrows is puzzling, to say the least. There's more to it than what we're seeing on the surface. *Much more.* We don't wish to alarm you, but we feel it's deeply rooted in something dark and sinister, which is why we stopped in here today."

Maggie bobbed her red head. "We've a definite foreboding."

"A most disturbing feeling that we can't throw off," Aisling gravely interjected.

The chief gave a brisk nod of empathy. "I welcome your help, as I always do. And as I tell you at the onset of each new case, keep what we say in this office between us. I know you realize this, especially you, Aisling," he added, "but I have to voice it; it's my job."

"We understand," the Sisters replied in unison.

As a former police detective, Aisling understood *fully* what the chief was saying. "What can you share with us at this point?"

"Campus security called us right away. They were taking no chances ... in this day and age. We checked those two arrows, and they are the same kind used in Professor Longbough's archery classes. We checked for fingerprints, though I realize that archers use gloves."

"Not always," Raine cut in. "Sorry, do go on."

"Found the victims' prints on the arrows, and the boyfriend's on the one that grazed the female student. There was a full print on one arrow and a partial on the other, both belonging to Professor Longbough.

"When we questioned him, he told us the arrows *looked* like his." Fitzpatrick's blue eyes widened, and his voice rose an octave, "What *could* he say? He got ruffled when I pressed him; and he roared like a banshee: 'For God's sake, I'd have to be either crazy or stupid to be the person who shot those arrows! And I assure you, I'm not either. They're marked 'Property of Haleigh College,' and *I'm* the archery instructor and coach. The idea's almost laughable!'"

The chief looked keenly at the Sisters. "I *assured* him I wasn't laughing. In any case, he kept answering my questions with questions of his own, ranting on and on—" He cut off. "What do *you* think of Ken Longbough? I value your opinions."

The Sisters looked to one another, with Aisling saying, "I'll let Raine and Maggie answer that, Chief, because I really don't know the man."

"We like Longbow," Raine stated evenly.

"Longbow?" the chief broke in. "Am I mispronouncing his name?"

"No, Professor Longbough is known— affectionately I might add— around the campus as Old Bull's-Eye and Longbow. He can be somewhat eccentric, and—"

"Word is," the chief interposed, "he has a pretty bad temper." He slipped the info in offhandedly, but his eyes were sharp and interested.

"He does, but we've never seen evidence he's a maniac, and he's a *fair* man. It's hard to believe he's the one shooting people with arrows," Maggie responded. "Someone could be shooting those arrows, not to hurt the victims, but to hurt Professor Longbough."

"I have to admit, it does look that way," Fitz concurred with an agreeing nod. "A mare's nest," he rubbed his jaw with the back of his hand. "We *could* have a mare's nest here, *or* Longbough could be the one shooting the arrows, thinking that the obvious is often overlooked, ignored, or ruled out."

"Tell the chief what you know about the professor's abhorrence of anything that smacks of Valentine's," Aisling suggested.

Raine and Maggie obliged, relating the story of Longbough's wife running off with the pro football player at Valentine's, whilst Fitzpatrick digested the information with a tilt of his white head.

"If the guy has a bad temper," Aisling interjected, "like as not he's made a few enemies along life's road, and it could be that one of them has thought of a way to seek revenge on him for something."

The chief acknowledged the truth of that, fixing Raine and Maggie with his somber regard. "Anyone come to mind?"

"Longbow's nemesis on campus, for several years now, has been Professor Hass of the English department, but *she* is one of the victims. Again, the obvious, Chief." Maggie turned to Raine. "Can you think of anyone else?"

"Not off the top of my head," the Goth gal replied.

"Could be a student that he reprimanded is trying to frame him for these shootings," the chief mused aloud. "How well known *is* that story about Longbough's wife running off at Valentine's?" Fitz inquired.

"Oh, I'd say just about everyone on campus has heard it at one time or another," Maggie spoke without hesitation. "It's been bantered about for years, by students, faculty, and college personnel, as well as by just about everyone else in this small town."

The chief nodded, retreating in his own thoughts.

"You know, don't you, Chief, that Professor Longbough's archery classes and the archery team's practice is being held at the Hamlet Sports Club's indoor archery range for the duration of our Valentine Fest. It's only a short hike across campus– the sports club's property is adjacent to the college– but Longbow wasn't too happy about that. The archery classes and his archery team normally use the gym. They have a long canvas backdrop behind the targets, and–"

"Yeah, yeah, Longbough told us that." Fitz leaned back in his padded desk chair to ponder over something that was taking form in his mind. "Would I be correct in saying that the old boy has student helpers to lug equipment around?"

"Right," Raine and Maggie established, foreseeing what the chief was going to say next.

"Sooo ... what if a helper neglected ... forgot, whatever, to take a couple of the arrows back to the gym's equipment room, and someone at the sports club who had it in for Longbough ... well you see what I'm getting at," the chief let the thought coast.

"We questioned the professor, of course," Fitz went on, "as to his whereabouts when the two victims were hit with arrows on campus. When the female student was grazed, he said he was at home, in his apartment, alone. He lives in one of those condos on the edge of town, so perhaps someone saw him come home, saw his car there ...

we just haven't found anyone yet who can back up his story that he was at home when the first victim was struck.

"When Professor Hass was hit, Longbough claims he was at The Man In The Moon pub, having a couple beers and a bite to eat. Said he left the campus between five and five-thirty. He couldn't give us an *exact* time when he drove off the college grounds, since, he said, he didn't check his watch. He told us he drove straight to the pub, ordered a beer and a sandwich, and was eating when the six o'clock news came on the bar television.

"We looked into that when we conversed with the publican, Ron Moon, and the professor's story checks out; except that Moon told us Longbough arrived at the pub at twenty till six, and that means he could have shot Hass with that arrow. She knows for sure that she was struck at five-thirty, because she checked her watch when she exited the campus library to get in her car and drive home.

"The archer would have been concealed in that dark copse of trees adjacent to the lit library parking lot," the chief finished.

Aisling and Maggie were taking notes the whole time the chief was talking, but it was Raine who spoke.

"Uh-huh, those trees are close to the parking lot, and Hass' big, wide derrière made a fine target, especially since she was wearing a short jacket and bent over, putting books into her vehicle. What I'm saying is– the archer didn't have to be a toxophilite."

"A what?" Fitz asked.

The Sisters could feel the chief parsing Raine's words.

"*Toxophilite*, an expert archer," Maggie explained, "like our former Olympian, Professor Longbough. Whoever the wayward archer is, he … or *she* could have been an archer with *average* skills." The redheaded Sister reached up to adjust the black beret she was wearing.

"We appreciate your telling us what you garnered thus far, Chief," Aisling remarked, closing her notebook. "We'll keep our eyes and ears open, and we'll do some sleuthing of our own."

"Needless to say, we'll report to you with any clues or info we dig up," Raine added.

"Ian and I will see if we can find anyone who can corroborate Longbough's alibis," Aisling volunteered. She stood and began pulling on her black leather jacket. Raine and Maggie followed suit, slipping into their warm, black trench coats. Since they knew they'd be visiting the chief, they'd foregone their Valentine Fest costumes today.

"I'd be grateful," the chief responded, standing to escort the ladies to the door.

***

When they left the police station, Aisling drove home in her own vehicle. Raine dropped Maggie off at Thaddeus' home, where she planned on spending the night. Then the Goth gal drove on to Tara, where she was anxious to try Grantie's shapeshifting locket. She knew she would not be interrupted in her spellcasting, for Beau had surgeries scheduled at his veterinary clinic. Once Raine's mind was made up, as was her habit, she did not lose a second.

The first thing she did, after arriving home, was to strip off and take a nice, long shower in which she used her favorite frankincense-and-myrrh soap. She'd purchased the soap as a Yule gift to herself because, in addition to frank and myrrh, the soap also contained white sage. In fact, it was labeled a "smudge soap."

Emerging from the bath cleansed, optimistic, and bent on intent, she proceeded to her bedroom with her Merlin-cat familiar, Black Jack O'Lantern. Setting him purring on the bed, she hurriedly dressed in a fresh, loose-fitting, black tunic and cozy, black leggings. Then she took a steadying breath, letting it out slowly.

Make sure to unplug, Grantie had cautioned. She'd done that, en route upstairs. Another deep breath and she picked up her small grimoire, quickly leafing to the pages on which she'd written Grantie's shapeshifting directives. With quickening pulse, she turned her attention to her altar.

The locket was there, waiting for her. Indeed, it seemed to call to her with a familiar voice from afar.

Raine closed her eyes and visualized her cousin Sean for a long, vivid moment. Her plan was already formulating. Without further delay, she cast her circle, calling on God and Goddess for protection, assistance, and guidance, as well as on her spirit guides, angel guides, guardian angels, and last but not least, the Guardians of the Watchtowers. Then she lit a fresh bundle of white sage and slowly paced deosil/ clockwise round the circle, allowing the good-smelling smoke to smudge the entire room free of all negativity, as she chanted a cleansing mantra: "Smoke and Air, Fire and Earth, cleanse and bless this home and hearth! Drive away all harm and fear! Only *good* may enter here!"

Next, she moved to the altar for Grantie's gift. Inside the locket's opened case, in the left oval recess, she placed a readied photo of her familiar, Black Jack O'Lantern; and on the right side, a prepared photo of Cousin Sean. She made certain to use actual photographs, because photos capture energy, zeroing in on frequency.

Pressing the open locket to her breast, she whispered with a veteran witch's intensity, "*I believe.* I believe in my own power, and I believe in the power of this locket."

To take it up a notch, she lit a purple candle that she dressed with her own special mojo oil, along with frank-and-myrrh oil. The purple color she chose for protection, mastery and power. With belief in her own abilities as a witch, she stated her intent, incorporating specifics and end time, that she set for midnight, when Black Jack would transform back to his physical feline self.

One final read over the handwritten pages in the shapeshifter segment of her *Book of Shadows*, then she scooped up the locket, along with Jack, and sat, crossed-legged on the floor, facing the cat.

Deciding that the lotus position would work best for her, she adjusted herself to comfort, closed her eyes, and holding her familiar, she breathed from her diaphragm, relaxing to what she referred to as his Number-Three Purr.

The universe supports me in everything I do. The universe loves and supports me in all my endeavors.

After several moments, she was centered and focused, hence she began to visualize Black Jack in human form, with the Glamour– that is, the *appearance*– of Cousin Sean. Lifting the muscular cat, she held him before her, visualizing him looking like Sean, sending those energies– with all the power in her and all the power in the universe– to the familiar's auric field. Jack continued to purr with half-closed eyes that suddenly began to widen. *The spell was working.*

Black Jack's telling me himself that the magick is stirring!

All that was left to do was to commence the chant, which she did, in the Old Scottish language that she'd practiced, for proper pronunciation and lilt, several nights in the solitude of her bedchamber.

Believing with all her heart, *with every fiber in her*, she kept her focus, as she recited the chant, with deeply felt fervency– nine times.

It was her own idea to chant the spell, exactly the same way, *nine* times, since she knew that 3x3 equaled *mega-power*– so mote it be!

Her pouty lips curved in a little-cat smile. *I **am** the spell. I have the power!*

As she chanted, she stared into Black Jack's mesmerizing pumpkin-colored eyes, and with each recitation, she could sense and *see* that the cat's electromagnetic field was receiving and processing the energies she was launching.

Upon chanting the spell the ninth time, Raine closed her eyes again to visualize and whisper– ***"I believe."***

She uttered the words with such a profound passion, conjured from the depths of the most secret chamber of her heart, that she could actually *feel* the energy streaming from her body, down her arm, and out her finger tip that was pointed at what looked to be a mesmerized Black Jack O'Lantern.

She sucked in one last mouthful of air, releasing it with anticipation. *It was done.*

When she opened her eyes, Jack was resting on his haunches on the floor, continuing to stare at her with a curious intensity.

Suddenly, she felt a **ping** in the charged air between them.

Rising on his hind legs, the black, panther-like cat stood straight up, his clearly visible aura elongating and brightening to explode into a virtual column of dazzling light, out of which emerged– a purrrrrrrrrr-fect likeness of Cousin Sean, complete with tautly muscled body and exotic McDonough eyes! In his feline form, Black Jack's eyes were slanted to begin with, so in reality, all that changed was the color, from pumpkin to emerald.

As per Sean's photograph in the locket, the shapeshifted Jack was dressed totally in black from head to foot– black turtleneck sweater; snug black jeans that fit so well Levi's would've hired him on the spot as one of their top models; black motorcycle jacket; and hefty, black motorcycle boots. His midnight hair was casual, tussled, and a tad on the longish side. The morphed Black Jack sported Sean's thick, ebony mustache; and when he spoke, even his sexy voice was Sean's.

"Well now, are you just going to sit there like a big-eyed owl?" he asked in mellifluous drawl. Sean's easy humor leaped into the McDonough eyes that, for a moment, startled the gaping Sister. "I thought we had errands to run."

***

Twenty minutes later, Raine and her fine-looking "cousin" were rolling downtown Main Street in the Sisters' winter vehicle, Maggie's green Land Rover. Raine pulled into a space on the square, switched off the ignition, and turning to Black Jack, said, "Now, this is an important test run today. It's the first time I've shapeshifted ... er, you have, in the manner I crafted, so cut me a break and behave yourself. I know how ornery you can be."

"Ah, cool your jets." Jack tilted his dark head, and laughter danced in his emerald eyes. I won't let you down. Have I ever?"

"I don't have time to think on that. I just wanted to caution you. And remember, you're supposed to be my cousin; that way, if we run into anyone I know, and they've seen me with Sean in the past– well, you know what I'm saying. If it's someone who's never met Sean, then I'll introduce you as Sean."

"Where're we going first?" Copy-catting her, he reached for his seat belt, the ensuing struggle producing a definite growl from deep in his throat.

"Here, let me get that." Raine leaned over and released the belt. "Animal House is our first stop. I want to–"

"Good, the pet store; now you're talkin'! We're out of catnip. I've been trying to tell you that all week, but your mind has been elsewhere. You really need to keep a list of the important things we're out of." He cocked his head to one side and scratched his ear. "And while I can, I want to recommend a book to you, *The Care And Feeding Of Your Familiar* by one of the best– I.M. Pyewacket."

"*Catnip*," she pronounced, weighing the word on her tongue. "I'll get you some, but you can't have it till we get back home, clear? I don't want you bouncing all over the place. People will think you're ... that *my cousin's* on dope."

"You know, of course, you're a tyrant. Oooooh, and how good it feels to be able to verbalize that to you!"

When they entered the pet store, Black Jack slinking forward with the aplomb of a *Cait Sidhe*– the fearsome hunt-cat from Ireland's rich store of legends– the shop went hurly-burly. He crept onward another inch, and–

It was utter chaos!

Double, double toil and trouble, quailed Raine with widened eyes and shrinking bravado.

- 128 -

Near the entrance stood all the bird cages with the parakeets, canaries, parrots, and cockatoos. Within moments– and everything began unfolding in rapid succession– **the whole area was filled with feathers, squawking, screeching, and screaming!**

"Awwwwk! **It's a cat! It's a cat!!**" a blue parrot shrieked in frenzied fluster, as it rocked to and fro, then started pacing back and forth on its perch. "**Awwwwwk! It's a CAT!! AWWWWWWWWK!!**"

Meanwhile, the rapid-fire movement of Jack's jaw was producing bird-watching chattering sounds, as he began to salivate.

To add to the mayhem, **all the dogs started barking, setting up an ear-shattering chorus of yips, bays, howls, snarls and growls!** From somewhere in the rear of the store, **a Siamese in heat yowled a loud cat call** that caused Raine to jump and Black Jack to sniff the air with open mouth in what looked like a grimace.

It was a nightmare!

Frozen in her tracks, Raine wailed, "Oh, no! What was I thinking?" as she copped a glimpse of her cat-man eyeing a huge tropical fish tank. *Hecate's crown! He's like a kid turned loose in a candy store!* Frantic, she grabbed Jack's reaching arm, in the nick of time, rushing him outside. "You'll have to wait for me out here," she said firmly. "Do *not* move from this spot! I am *counting* on that. Do I have your word?"

"Spoilsport," he spat. "I feel like sushi today."

"We'll see. You stay right here till I come out … and it'll mean *double* catnip plus your favorite treats. Deal?"

His response was to touch his nose to hers.

With flushed face, Raine dashed back inside, determined to make her purchases as quickly as possible.

"What happened out here? I just stepped in the back for a few moments, and it sounded like all hell broke loose!" the shop owner challenged, gawking at all the feathers floating in the air and littering the floor. "All right now, settle down. *Settle down*," he coaxed, in an attempt to soothe his fur and feathered wards.

"Gosh, I'm sorry, Mr. Behr," Raine replied, releasing her held-in breath. "All I did was open the door, and the birds went crazy. Then the dogs started up. They must've been frightened by a sudden gust of chill wind … or something," she finished weakly.

The proprietor eyed his customer oddly. "May I help you, Dr. McDonough?"

"No, no, thanks," she answered with a weak smile. "I know what I want, and I'm kind of in a hurry, so I'll just use a shopping basket," she said, slipping one over her arm, "and breeze through on my own."

When Raine exited the pet store, she was relieved to find Jack waiting for her out front. She saw immediately, however, that, sly as any cat with whiskers, he was poised to pounce upon a squirrel that darted across the street toward them. "Don't even think about it!" she warned, as she snatched his arm and held tight.

"I'll carry that for you," he contended, grabbing the bag of feline goodies before she could stop him.

When they started off in the direction of the Land Rover, they chanced upon an acquaintance of Raine's from the community theatre. The stylish blonde was carrying, in a sling-bag over her chest, a tiny Yorkie sporting a cute red bow at the top of its little head, the only part of the dog that was visible.

"Raine, how good to see you!" the young woman uttered in pleasant surprise.

"Hello, April. Fancy running into you today. It's very nice to see you too. This is my cousin Sean McDonough from out West. Sean teaches on an Indian reservation in Montana. He's visiting us for a few days. Sean, this is April Curtin, one of my thespian friends from Whispering Shades. I know I've mentioned our 'little theatre in the woods' several times."

April's eyes roamed over Sean's muscular body with its panther-like grace. "Only here for a few days? What a shame," she husked. "You look like the actor, Sam Elliot … when he was younger, of course. I'll bet you hear that a lot."

Before Raine could intercede, Jack took a step closer to the love-struck lady, rubbing up against her. When he began to knead April's arm, however, the Goth gal ordered him, via mental telepathy, to *Knock it off!*

April, in turn, cocked her blonde head, posing the disquieting question, "What's that sound? Do you hear a motor running?"

Raine need not have fretted over Black Jack's blatant display of affection, for as small breeds of dogs will ofttimes do, the Yorkie began to assert himself, barking wildly at Jack and prompting him to react with an unmistakable hiss accompanied by a swift but harmless swipe at the minuscule canine's nose, missing the pooch by a whisker.

"Oh Ja ... Sean, don't tease!" Raine speedily amended, pinching her familiar's tush, which brought forth another loud hiss. She glanced at her watch to say, "Oh my, we better be off. We've got several more stops to make."

After she and Jack were in the Land Rover, she yanked the bag of goodies away from him; then, leaning over, brushed catnip from his mustache, muttering, "Grantie tried to tell me, but did I listen? *No, no*, I had to prove I could do Advanced Shapeshifting, rather than begin with Shifting 101."

"Where we going to eat?" Jack asked, licking his lips. "You owe me sushi." He swiped his tongue over his fingers; then, with brisk motions, wiped the remaining specks from his mustache before flicking his right ear.

"Stop that! We're eating at The Gypsy Tearoom, and again, I warn you. Behave yourself and act like the gentleman I know you can be ... when you want to." She pulled her phone from her purse to check for messages. "*I'm sorry*. I don't mean to be cross. This is more my fault than yours. Ooooooooh, Jack," she sang with abrupt humor, "April thinks you're *adorable*. Yes, that's the word she used. She wants me to arrange a date." Rolling her eyes, she poked her familiar in the ribs. "She doesn't realize what a tom cat you are, Jackie."

"The sweet lady's not my type," he jested. "Too fair. Looks like a ghost."

Raine chortled, dipping her hand into her purse for the car keys and opening the windows to freshen the air after a truck burning diesel rumbled by. At that express moment, a Great Dane on a leash, sauntering down the street with its owner, started barking loudly at Black Jack, who calmly placed a "paw" over the power button to close the window, turning his head to ignore the huge dog with silent but unmistakable– *disdain*. Raine couldn't help herself. She burst out laughing and was still laughing as they drove off.

"Hey, I thought we were going to get something to eat!" Jack protested, when Raine pulled the Land Rover into a space in the Auto Doctor's parking lot.

"We will … after we get this car inspected. It won't take long. C'mon, let's go in and find out how long. And goes without saying– behave yourself."

"I hope you don't intend driving all over town today with me. You *know* I cannot abide long periods in the car. You don't want me to spew a furball on Maggie's nice clean upholstery, do you?"

"Hush now. Hi, Kathy!" Raine called, as she and Black Jack approached the counter. "You said on the phone you had a cancellation, and I could get Maggie's Rover inspected. I'm a little early, but I thought perhaps they might be able to start sooner." *As I programmed it.*

"You're in luck. Hold on; I think they can do it now. Won't take long. About an hour, I'd say." She pulled a file, scanning it adeptly.

Known throughout the Hamlet as "Savvy Kathy," Wise was exactly as her surname proclaimed. A middle-aged woman with a much larger personality than her petite frame belied, she possessed a head full of know-how and knowledge. The classic go-to gal, Kathy knew the answer to most questions, and she knew just about everyone in Haleigh's Hamlet and round about. Her super-short hair was spiky and heavily blonde-tipped, her clothing stylish. In summary, Kathy was streetwise, cute as a button, and someone the Sleuth Sisters always had an urge to hug.

"Where'd you park?" She was gazing beyond Raine to the entrance. Before the Sister could answer, Kathy aimed a perfectly manicured finger at the vintage, green Land Rover she spied through the glass, "Ah, right out front!"

"That's it. Here're the keys." Raine handed them to Kathy, who gave a courtesy nod.

"OK, you're good to go." The receptionist picked up the phone and barked the order into the receiver, while replacing the file. "Say, you're the Sisters' cousin from out West, aren't you?" she directed to Jack, whose tip-tilted eyes were half-closed in the sunbeam into which he'd stepped.

"Indeed, I am. Your wish," he roused with a graceful bow, "is my command," a blink of the droll leaping into his eyes, his theatrics bringing Raine's elbow to his ribs.

"Sorry I didn't introduce you, but I thought you'd met our cousin when he brought my MG in that time to be inspected." To Black Jack, Raine said, "Sean, you remember Kathy Wise."

"It would be impossible to forget such a … *bewitching* lady," he replied in Sean's sexy cowboy drawl. A pleasure, ma'am," he grinned seductively.

"A p-pleasure," Kathy stammered in the uncharacteristic role of silly parrot, her eyes skimming over him, "it *is*. *R-raine*," she rasped, dragging her gaze away from Jack, "I'm glad you came in today." She leaned across the counter, closer to the Sister and lowered her voice to a whisper. "Someone was in here earlier to get a bulb replaced in a taillight on a Corvette, someone from the college. I couldn't help but hear the person talking on their phone. You know me; I'm not one to spread gossip, but this is different. I think I'd better share this with you …"

***

"Now look here, Raine, you said we were going to eat. I know this place, it's the vet's office! What are you trying to pull?"

"Oh, for goodness sake, I'm not trying to pull anything. I just want to stop in for a moment to ask Beau what time he'll be through tonight and if he's coming over." She unbuckled her seat belt, then reached for Jack's.

"Oh. No. You. Don't. I'm not going in there!" he recoiled, as if Raine were about to steal one of his lives. "I heard you telling Maggie yesterday that it would soon be time for Black Jade and me to get our anal glands expressed. *No way* am I going in there. I know a trick when I encounter one," his eyes held hers, "and a con man … *woman* when I meet one."

"You *are* going in with me. I promise no tricks. I told you I just want to check something with Beau. Now, come on!" She unbuckled his seat belt and began pulling him toward her, but he clung tenaciously to the door, refusing to budge. No matter how hard she tugged, she could not pull her cat-man out of the car.

"You're not going to drag me in there, Raine, so give it up. Hisssssssssssssssss!"

"If you come in with me, I'll ask Beau for those tasty little treats you like, and I promise no tricks. *Word of honor.* We're in and out, and we go to eat. I'm starved too."

When Raine and "Cousin Sean" slunk into the office, Beau, who happened to be in the reception area, looked up with a broad beam.

"Well now, isn't this a happy surprise? Hul–lo, Raine. How you doin', Jack, m' boy?"

It was a wide green-eyed gaze that confronted Dr. Goodwin. Quickly then, Raine looked round for Beau's receptionist, Jean, who was away from the counter and in the back.

"How did you know?" the Sister asked in a stunned whisper.

"One, I just happened to think that your cousin Sean is not visiting you. If he were, you'd have told me, but you did tell me about the shapeshifting locket, so there's your answer."

A twinkling later, when she and Jack were back in the Rover, she told her happily-munching familiar, "I guess what Beau said *does* make sense."

With bulging cheeks, Jack held out the opened bag of cat indulgences in a proffering gesture, croaking indistinctly, "Have some?"

Oblivious of his jest, Raine exclaimed, "But he knew *immediately*– as soon as we walked through the door– before he even had time to think!" She glanced over at a superior-looking Black Jack. "**What?** You're looking at me the way you did when I read aloud to you from my dissertation."

"Tsk, tsk, tsk, Raine. I was born at midnight, but not last night. At risk of the captious judgment of which you accuse me, then and now, I think," Jack replied, with a particularly cunning air, "that you were seeking the answer to a question other than what time tonight Beau might be coming to Tara." He nonchalantly popped another treat into his mouth, twitching his nose as if he could smell the twisted truth. "And now you're wondering if the answer you got is correct. Or, more significantly, if the answer you got is *the one you wanted.*"

***

Raine took her time on the road, not only to think, but to enjoy the snowy scenery. Like a true daughter of Pennsylvania, she took pride in the beauty of her state, in the rolling hills and valleys, the deep, ever-mysterious woods, and the cities and towns rich with history.

Winter's twilight was settling over a sleepy Haleigh's Hamlet when she and Black Jack entered the restaurant.

The Gypsy Tearoom was an intimate café with romantic, flickering wall sconces and intimate seating. Located in the lowest level of what had once been the Hamlet's original armory– a 1907, red-brick, fortress-like structure built in the late Gothic Revival style– the comfy seating began life as horse stalls.

The historic building was purchased by the Tearoom's proprietress, Eva Novak, when the new armory was built several years earlier. During renovation, the roomy box stalls were transformed into booths, ideal for the readings that Eva's clientele often requested along with her special teas and the delectable Tearoom fare. Like her ancestors, Eva read palms and tea leaves. The Viking runes were another of the ancient oracles she consulted on occasion, following them with the more specific tarot cards.

The Gypsy Tearoom's ground floor was the banquet hall, reserved for groups and events. Eva used the third floor for her private quarters. Her living room occupied one of the building's twin turrets, her bedroom the other, making her feel, as she often said, like a queen in a castle tower.

Renovation of the edifice had been as the definition of the word affirms– cleaning, repairing, and reviving with as little actual remodeling as possible, for Eva, like others who purchased the village's noble old buildings, was set on keeping the historic structure's integrity.

In the basement-level Tearoom, wood table-and-bench seating filled each horse-stall-turned-booth. The walls of the cubicles were covered with dark-red, tufted leather, against which the occupants could comfortably rest their backs. Too, the booths' thick, padded walls provided additional privacy.

Gothic-style tables and chairs occupied the center of the room. Miniature stained-glass lamps topped the tables, and on the opposite wall from the stalls was a magnificent stone fireplace. The ceiling flaunted the original walnut beams; the walls, exposed brick, the same aged brick that covered the building's exterior. Massive, sliding barn doors, with medieval-looking, black hardware, separated the dining area from the kitchen.

Hardly did Raine and Jack enter the cozy establishment, when Eva, in colorful Gypsy attire– black, off-the-shoulder, low-cut blouse and flowing red skirt belted with a lacy black shawl– emerged from the kitchen to greet them. Snatching up a couple of menus, she sang out, "Welcome! Welcome!"

Each time Raine looked into Eva's face, she saw her honest heart, and it enduringly filled her with light and made her smile. "It's good to see you," the Sister replied, returning the pleasant woman's warm embrace. "Eva, this is my cousin Sean you've often heard us mention. He lives out in Montana, but he's visiting with us for a few days. Sean, this is our dear friend, Eva Novak."

"Charmed," Black Jack purred, bringing Eva's hand to his lips, his jewel-like eyes looking into hers.

"Ooh," the café owner breathed. "Oooooh."

The proprietress showed the McDonoughs to the Sisters' favorite booth, Raine and Jack sliding in to sit across from one another.

Handing them the menus, Eva asked, "Shall I bring you my special brew?"

"Bring it on," Raine answered. "A bracing cup of your tea will do me good." She tossed her cat-man a look. "I'm a bit stressed today."

"I'll have a glass of milk," Jack ordered, settling back against the tufted-leather seat. "And none of that nasty skim stuff. Whole milk, please."

Making swift use of one of her special gifts, Raine sped her familiar a telepathic message: *Nooooo milk! You'll have the litter-box runs.*

"On second thought, have you cream? A nice *full-bodied* cream?" Black Jack was quick to query, at the same time reaching under the table to swipe Raine's knee, a tiny squeal escaping her, as she sent him a warning look. "I have no wish to order an insipid blend of milk and cream, my dear, a *mélange* that can't seem to make up its mind which it is."

"I do have heavy cream." Eva was somewhat taken aback by the unusual request, and she looked hard at the cowboy imposter before her. "But let me get this straight. You want to order a glass of cream for your beverage?"

"I do indeed," Jack responded firmly. "Yes indeed. I fancy myself a cream," he brought his fingers to his mouth to kiss and release them in a global gourmet's gesture, "*aficionado*."

Raine was pretending to search for her reading glasses in her purse, at a loss for something to say, a condition from which she rarely suffered.

"Ooooooo–kay," Eva conceded. "One glass of cream and one–"

"Make that a small glass of cream, Eva. Sean has to watch his cholesterol." She sent Jack another cautionary glance before slipping on her reading glasses to peruse the outsized menu.

"Right." The Gypsy-souled sister watched "Sean" speculatively for a secretive moment, sweeping her keen regard over him, as though measuring and appraising this newcomer, who appeared to be sniffing the air like a hungry panther. Finally, she found her voice. "*Soup du jour* is caramelized onion soup with Gruyère and croutons. And the entrées today are my special Tuna Surprise and Chicken Kiev."

"Hmmmmm," Black Jack mused, running his tongue over his lips, "difficult choice. *Tuuuu–na* … suppose you surprise me with the tuna, *chère madame*."

"And I'll have the Chicken Kiev," Raine stated. "That way, Ja … *Sean* and I can share."

Eva pried her eyes away from "Sean" to catch the nervous smile Raine was sending her.

"Is the Kiev your herb-butter stuffed and breaded chicken?" the Goth gal speedily asked, hoping to divert the proprietress' attention.

"Yes, *darlink*, and it comes with mashed cauliflower and a light mushroom sauce."

"Excellent. I'll have a salad too," Raine added. "Your salmon and shrimp salad."

"Perfect. I'll get your orders underway, but first, let me get your drinks."

When Eva moved off to the kitchen, Jack leaned across the table to murmur to Raine, "Well, did you like how I greeted your friend?"

"You referring to the hand kiss?"

His smile and demeanor were unquestionably catlike. "I saw it in a late-night movie we watched together once. I thought I executed the move rather elegantly, if I do say so myself."

Raine giggled. "You did, you crafty copycat. And that's why I ordered the salad, so you can have all the salmon and shrimp. I'll share my chicken with you too," she said, scratching his chin.

The distinct sound of purring filled the space, as his lips turned up in a feline grin, and he blinked thrice. "May I suggest scones or fruit with clotted cream for dessert? Lots and lots of clotted cream …"

***

When Raine and Black Jack exited The Gypsy Tearoom, the latter remarked, "That woman is very astute; I hope you know. She may have been on to me."

"Eva is an excellent psychic, so thank the great Goddess she was too busy to really visit with us, though I have to admit, you behaved astonishingly well in there. Other than washing your face after your cream cocktail, that is."

"Old habits are hard to break, baby. When I finished my tuna surprise, it took a lot of restraint for me not to lick the plate; I'll tell you that!"

Raine giggled. "You did pounce on that tuna."

Eva's parking lot was nearly empty as the pair approached the Land Rover. Raine had parked under a lamppost, and what she glimpsed startled her. "Oooooh, no!" Forgetting caution, she dashed forward, coming up on three figures, dressed all in black and wearing ski masks, who were crouching down on the opposite side of the Rover. "You there, stop! I'm calling the police!"

Instead of running off, the ruffians moved menacingly toward the Sister, the one out front carrying a crowbar.

JACK! The cry *reverberated* inside her head, yet she knew she did *not* utter the name or anything else aloud when she swallowed the little flutter of panic that threatened to seize her.

The leader raised the iron in a threatening stance, and spry as a cat, "Sean" leaped into the glow of one of the parking lot's lampposts.

Raine had handed him a pair of sunglasses to wear out of the restaurant, as soon as she became disturbingly aware that the pupils in his eyes were beginning to elongate in a most feline manner, and the irises were transforming from green back to their staggering orange shade. She deduced her spell hadn't been strong enough to last till midnight. It was nigh on to ten now. Jack, however, remained calm, chortling out the mysterious words, "Everything happens for a reason."

After having sprung to Raine's side, her stealthy champion puffed himself up to his full, muscular height, whilst he yanked off the glasses to send the would-be assailants a blistering glower accompanied by a loud, protracted **"Hisssssssssssssssssssssss!"**

Catching a clear view of his slanted, slit-pupiled, pumpkin-hued eyes in the lamppost's radiance, the figures froze in horror, as Time halted, and–

Jack swiped the air between them, sending forth another drawn-out hiss that released the trio from their shock and sent them stumbling over themselves and one another to race off. "Go smudge yourselves!" he called after them, laugher rolling from his throat. "Cats' pajamas! Did you see their faces? *Priceless!*" Turning to Raine, he asked, "You OK?"

Staring after them, she mentally cast: *What you hurl at me, be returned times three. Head to toe, skin and nerve, may you get what you deserve!*

"Yo," Jack prodded her upper arm. "You OK?"

"Thanks, Jack. I think I know who they were," she growled, her dark brows shooting together in anger, "the Bitchy B–"

"Keep it clean," he teased, sidling closer, the energized heat of his aura radiating with hers, "and don't disturb the molecules. Those three are a special kind of stupid, aren't they?" For a second time, he tottered with laughter. "*Priceless*," he repeated. "What Granny McD would've called a 'Kodak Moment.'"

Raine regarded Black Jack for several heartbeats, a whole circuitous route of emotions swirling within her breast, as he touched his nose to hers.

Cocking his dark head, he spoke with alacrity, "No need to thank me. I'm your Watcher, and no matter what form I take, or what plane I'm on– I'll *always* be watching over you. It's a forever thing, baby." He blinked and began kneading her back, as he pushed her toward the vehicle. "Let's go home. Step sprightly. I miss Black Jade, and our nice, warm radiator is calling to me."

Raine smiled, suddenly remembering something an old and beloved shaman once told her and Maggie, years before, whilst they were accompanying their parents on an archeological dig out West. "A Native American legend says there's a bridge humans cross over when we die, the Hanging Road to the Other Side. At the end of this bridge waits all the animals every human encountered during his or her lifetime. Based on what they know of each person, the animals decide which humans may cross the Hanging Road and which are turned away."

"I *CAT*egorically agree!" Jack yowled with enthusiasm.

Relieved to see that no harm had been done to Maggie's Rover, Raine repeated her gratitude to her familiar, lowering the sunglasses to his nose and shaking her head at the vertical pupils in what were now his stunning, pumpkin-colored irises. "My Jackie," she whispered, adjusting the glasses to cover his feline eyes. *"I love you so much."*

"Empowering, isn't it?" he rumbled in his deep, Sam Elliot voice, as he clamped a caring arm around her shoulders. "You, Mags, and Ash are forever babbling about the McDonough eyes; but a cat's eyes, like a magick wand, have the power to make anything happen– anything we choose. That harks all the way back to Bastet, ancient Egypt's cat goddess of protection. Bast, as you know, was especially shielding of women and children," he chattered on. "Oh, and you'll like this– *secrets*, women's secrets …"

Chapter Seven

When Raine, Aisling, Maggie and Thaddeus entered the Student Union annex to the rear of Old Main for the Valentine faculty tea, they lingered in the doorway to absorb the festive scene.

Aisling was taking a bit of time away from her Black Cat Detective Agency to attend as Raine's invitee. Each faculty member was permitted one guest.

Due to limited seating, Student Union reservations had to be made in advance, so they would know how many table settings they would need. Orchestrated entirely *by* the Student Union, the tea was $100 a plate with the total proceeds going to the restoration of Old Main. Since the students arranged for everything to be donated for the event, and they were doing all the food preparation and serving, they'd net 100 percent profit. The Hamlet's Sal-San-Tries café-deli, The Gypsy Tearoom, The Man In The Moon pub, The Sugar Shack, and the Espresso Patronum coffee house (so named because the owner was a Harry Potter enthusiast) had all donated food and beverages.

"Wiz–zard, it looks as though most of our 'eighty' are here," Raine observed in reference to Haleigh's faculty, as she glanced eagerly about. The Goth gal's kimono-style tea gown was midnight-black, as might be expected, with exquisite embroidery and lace.

"Could be a scene from one of *Titanic*'s elegant teas," Maggie cited of the gathering's quaint attire. The striking redhead's near-ankle-length Edwardian tea dress was peacock blue, a ꜱhade that quite complimented her vivid coloring.

"Great Goddess, let's not program anything disastrous," Aisling chided in a quiet voice. The blonde with the wand's tea gown was the color of fallen leaves, cocoa-brown and sleek with the rains of winter. The elbow-length sleeves were sheer, over which she wore a long, black shawl that harmonized well with the dress' black-lace trim.

Costumed as they were, their black capes draped over their arms, the Sisters were promptly caught up in the festive mood of the tea. Thaddeus sported a black cutaway; snug, grey trousers; and a shiny black top hat. Though he was wearing his contacts, he'd thought to augment his outfit with a monocle. Of course, his white, high-collared shirt bore his signature cherry-red bowtie.

The Student Union ordained that the faculty Valentine tea be a romantic, old-fashioned Victorian affair. Though it was not mandatory, everyone was encouraged to dress the part, and it looked as though most of Haleigh's professors happily embraced the idea of traveling back in time via proper afternoon attire.

"Reminds *me* of a scene straight out of *Downton Abbey*. Oooooh look," Raine pointed out, "they've blown up antique Valentine cards to poster size for the walls. What a lovely idea!"

"The Student Union's done a bang-up job with the decorations and the tables," Thaddeus remarked, making use of his monocle.

Snowy-white tablecloths with scarlet-red runners graced the tables that filled the long room. Red carnations, donated by several of the florists round about, brightened the place settings, whilst ubiquitous red hearts and chubby-cherub Cupids reminded Haleigh faculty and students alike of the love they shared for Old Main.

"Oh, don't Professor Lee and Dr. Whitman look nice?" Maggie remarked, waving to the engaged couple, who were conversing with others across the room.

"I'll find our seats," Raine volunteered, heading for the tables to look for their name cards. Quickly finding their places, she beckoned her companions over, after which she greeted Professor Karel Hass, already seated at the table, with a flat "Good-afternoon."

"Good-afternoon," Hass returned in her usual sharp manner.

In a brown pullover, tweed skirt, and blazer, the mannish Hass hadn't bothered to dress for the occasion. As her gaze swept the Sisters and Dr. Weatherby, her face took on an expression that made it appear as if she'd caught wind of an offensive odor.

"Oh, what darling favors!" Maggie commented, picking up a small, white gauze bag tied with red ribbon. Nestled inside was a chocolate heart. The red heart on the bag bore the silver words in fancy script: "Sugar-free. All-natural, organic ingredients make this dark-chocolate-almond truffle a heart-healthy treat. Enjoy!"

"Our good friend, Eva Novak, made the truffles," Raine stated. Eva told us that Professor Longbough suggested to her, while dining at the Tearoom, that she donate some healthy-choice treats. He informed her that several of our faculty were fitness-conscious, including him, not to mention that a couple of our professors are dealing with medical issues. She took his advice."

Dr. Weatherby assisted the Sisters as they slipped into their places, then they all sat back to enjoy the soft, romantic music playing in the background, which the professors recognized as the nostalgic love theme from the classic Franco Zeffirelli film, *Romeo and Juliet.*

Most of the faculty were seated by now, and Student Union members were beginning to serve the tea. Taking their places across from the Sisters and Thaddeus were Dr. Barron Whitman; his fiancée, Professor Annabel Lee; and Dr. Whitman's mother, Mildred Whitman.

Great Goddess' nightgown! Raine exclaimed to herself, *poor Annabel looks stressed.* "Good-afternoon," the raven-haired Sister said aloud. "I meant to ask when we chanced upon one another at the vendor tables the other day, have you two set a date yet?"

The Sisters could not help noticing that Mildred Whitman made a definite eye-roll.

"Before I answer your query," Barron replied, "I'd like to introduce our table to my mother, Mildred Whitman."

"So nice to meet you," the Sisters answered, with Thaddeus' greeting of "Welcome to Haleigh College. We hope you enjoy your stay with us."

"Mother, these are the widely celebrated Sleuth Sisters, Doctors Raine and Maggie McDonough, who have professorships here at Haleigh in both history and archeology, and Aisling McDonough-Gwynn. Aisling and her husband, Ian, own and operate a successful detective agency. And lest I neglect to present the esteemed head of our history department, Dr. Thaddeus Weatherby, a man of great wisdom and experience."

Thaddeus acknowledged Barron's description with a gallant bow of his head.

Across the table, Mildred's pale-blue eyes scanned the foursome. "Good-afternoon," she condescended with a curt nod. "My son has mentioned each of you on different occasions."

Whilst Dr. Whitman completed the introduction, the Sisters decided that Mildred Whitman was likely in her seventies, though she looked years younger due to the privileged life she enjoyed in Boston. Her short, white hair was coifed in a sophisticated style that suited her patrician face and manner, while her clothes and glittering jewelry screamed *Expensive.* The woman's makeup and attire– a garnet-hued tea gown trimmed in black– were *flawless.* In fact, if the Sisters would have been asked to choose a one-word description of Mrs. Whitman, it would irrefutably have been– *soignée*. Both she and her son fairly *breathed* elegance.

"To answer your question, Raine, Annabel and I have decided on an autumn wedding. Autumn is our favorite time of year, so it will be worth the wait."

"And since October is eight months away, they'll have time to decide if they really are right for one another," Mildred put in with terse voice. Her manner more than suggested that she hoped the couple would make the decision *not* to marry.

When the Sisters' unified gaze veered to Annabel, they caught the hurt in her eyes.

An uncomfortable pause hung in the air. In fact, the only one who looked contented was Professor Hass, who seemed to be enjoying the situation, for a rare look of humor established itself on her jowly face.

Visibly discomfited, Barron shifted the conversation. "I have heard that the menu today will be first-rate."

"I'm certain it will," Maggie rejoined, glad that the awkward silence was broken. "The eateries in town that have donated to our Great Cause are famous round about for their culinary delights." Maggie couldn't be sure, but it looked like Mildred gave another eye-roll.

The Sisters were relieved to see Dr. Yore, wearing one of her characteristic long capes, this one Valentine red, and carrying her tall, forked staff, come sailing over to sit down next to them on their side of the table.

"A very merry good-afternoon to all!"

After acknowledging everyone– the heartiness of her greeting a welcome respite– Elizabeth Yore rested her staff against the wall in the corner behind them, then shucked out of her cape to place it over the back of her chair. Lowering herself into the seat next to Maggie, she said, "I was thinking about wearing some sort of Victorian getup, but this," she gestured toward her staff, "is who I am, and I'm most comfortable dressed as myself." Glancing quickly round the spacious room, she uttered with satisfied expression, "*Quite a turnout!* I'm glad. The Student Union's been working very hard." She looked down the table, catching the eye of Dr. Weatherby. "I have a sneaking suspicion that was your Model-T I saw out in the parking lot. Am I right?" Liz asked.

"Your hunch is correct," Thaddeus smiled widely, obviously proud of his new acquisition. "America's first affordable automobile," he beamed, ever the educator. "Isn't she a beauty? She's completely and, I daresay, *beautifully* restored, a 1926. All-steel body, wire wheels, with the sweetest red leather interior. There's even an art deco, sterling silver rosebud vase on the interior passenger side. I won't bore you with a recitation of stats, but suffice it to say that T-For-Two's been restored as a one-of-a-kind auto, and done just right. A great riding classic that, I'm certain, won't disappoint. Traded the bullet-nose Studebaker for her."

"You traded your 'missile'!" Yore blurted.

"I did indeed." Thaddeus' face developed a grin, and turning toward Maggie, he favored her with a secret wink. To Dr. Yore, he declared in a mildly teasing fashion, "If you and I were still keeping company, I would've been tempted to call her after her most popular soubriquet, the 'Tin Lizzie.'"

Liz' laugh was open and friendly. "I like the name you gave her. 'T-For-Two' is perfect, and I love the artwork on the driver's door."

The art to which Dr. Yore was referring were two steaming teacups, each personalized with a name, *Thaddeus* and *Maggie*, toasting the white Edwardian script, above, that spelled out the glossy black auto's cozy name.

"Maggie and I intend on taking her out for a spin on special occasions– for leisurely Sunday drives in the country, in clement weather of course, as well as in our Hamlet parades," Dr. Weatherby informed.

With her crystal laugh, Maggie stole into the conversation. "Thaddeus wasn't overstating his new toy. The 'T' does provide a charming ride. I know next to nothing about cars, but I do love that rosebud vase." Her emerald eyes fastened on her man. "Almost as much as I do the name. I say, though, it has the most piercing Klaxon I ever heard ... more irritating, I think, than our antique doorbell at Tara."

Hass groaned, "For God's sake, Weatherby, you're so 'Once upon a time.'"

The remark went unanswered, when everyone at the Sisters' table turned to regard Dr. Lear, who was just arriving and appeared to be winded.

Of average height and weight, the middle-aged Lear's rather boyish face exposed his sensitive, gentle nature, with a touch of the scholar.

He removed his black silk top hat and ran his fingers through his tousled, dark hair. "Thought I'd be late '… for a very important date,'" he quipped, catching his breath and reminding the Sisters, momentarily, of *Alice in Wonderland*'s White Rabbit.

"I'd foolishly forgotten about the faculty tea last week when I scheduled a student meeting in my office, so I had to *rush* down there to reschedule." Dr. Lear pulled off his leather gloves and slipped out of his long, black cape, adding, o'er la Rabbit, "I'm forever rushing about these days." The theatre director allowed his white, silk scarf to remain round his neck. Lear was never without a scarf, no matter the season, or his umbrella that he carried merely as an accessory.

"Rex," bade Dr. Yore, "your son will be graduating from Haleigh this year, won't he?"

Lear gave a brisk nod, adjusting his cape over the back of his chair, after which he sat at table to let out another breath. "He will, yes."

Dr. Lear is the only man I know who can carry off sporting a cape, Maggie zipped telepathically to Raine and Aisling.

The head of the theatre and drama department looked very much like a gentleman of *la Belle Époque*– even without the costume this afternoon, which included a maroon frock coat and Victorian-collared, white dress shirt.

"I loved having William in my archeology classes," Yore was saying, "he's a fine young man. Will he go on for his graduate work?"

"Yes, he's decided to go straight through for his doctorate," Rex broke in. His voice had an expected dramatic quality about it that did not exclude credibility. "I encouraged him to do that, and I'm glad he's taken my advice … *on that anyway*." Dr. Lear's air implied that his son didn't take his advice on much of anything; but again, the talk swung to something else, when Professor Longbough entered the conversation.

"So what's the menu today? I thought it would be printed out, but there's nothing here on the table." His tone struck the chord for everyone that he was disgruntled over the entire Valentine's proceedings. In his late-forties, Longbow still looked like a jock, though his face could appear puffy at times, and his brown hair was thinning.

Raine threw a glance to Maggie and Aisling with the thought: *I'm surprised he's shown up here today given the way he feels.* Aloud, she answered the archery coach's query, "I think when they bring out the sandwiches, followed by the pastries, there will be little heart tags denoting what everything is," Raine replied, picking up her newly filled teacup to sip the refreshing Darjeeling she'd selected.

Barely had the Goth gal spoken when Student Union servers began carrying tiered trays of fancy sandwiches to the tables, whilst others of their number continued pouring tea.

While they waited for the food to reach their group, conversation bounced round to why Dr. Whitman wanted to leave Harvard to come to such a small college as Haleigh.

"Why indeed?" grumbled Mildred with yet another of her annoying eye-rolls.

Keep rollin' those eyes; maybe you'll find a brain back there, Raine simmered in silent provocation.

"I wanted to escape from the hurly-burly of a big city and an Ivy-League school and settle into small town, liberal arts campus living, where I'd be more inclined to write," Barron responded levelly to his mother's remark, shooting her a frosty glance. "I could *not* write at home in Boston; I needed a change. For a long while, I was indecisive about where I would go after Harvard. I considered several locales beyond our Hamlet, favorite places I frequent when I travel, including Portland, Maine; the Santa Fe region of New Mexico; and Sag Harbor, New York. I even considered New York City's Hunter College, but something indefinable about the Hamlet drew me. Here, I *know* I'll be able to finish my novel." He closed his eyes for a reflective moment, concluding, "It's a combination of things– the aesthetic beauty, the quiet atmosphere, the overall ambience. It feels as though this whole area is instilled with inspiration."

"Haleigh's Hamlet has produced some fine authors over the years," Raine stated with pride.

"Haleigh College may be small," Dr. Yore put in firmly, fixing her astute gaze on Mildred Whitman, "but we are a well-respected *and* well-endowed institution. Among numerous awards and accolades, Haleigh is listed among the top fifty liberal arts schools in the nation."

"It's a far cry from Harvard," Mildred muttered under her breath, though her thoughtless comment was not missed by the others at table.

Maggie tilted her red head to put the leading question to the woman she'd immediately sensed was a parvenu, "Did *you* graduate from Harvard?"

Mildred seemed taken aback by the directness of the query. "I did not, but my husband and son did, as did all the Whitmans since Harvard's beginning year in 1636."

"Had you a career?" Raine, on the same wavelength with Maggie, presumed to put forth. *In addition to being an overbearing control freak, that is.*

"For a few years before my marriage, I was a nurse with a master's degree … a nurse practitioner in today's terminology," the controlling woman answered after a tremor of hesitation, a *telling* pause that strikingly signified she had not wished to divulge the fact that she'd ever *had* to work for a living.

Tea was replenished and sandwiches served, whilst the conversation died to some extent as everyone enjoyed the appetizing cuisine. The tiered trays were loaded with traditional English afternoon tea favorites: cucumber with mint-herbed butter sandwiches, smoked salmon with dill and crème fraiche on pumpernickel, watercress egg salad on whole wheat, cress and goat cheese on multi-grain bread, tuna salad with capers on toasted bread, and cheese and pickle rounds.

"I'm glad to see that they're familiar with good tea here in this backwater …" Mildred caught her son's displeased countenance and completed her sentence, "*village.*" When asked what tea she preferred, she was visibly surprised when they poured her request of Earl Grey.

"Oh, yes, we even have running water and indoor plumbing," Raine joked in a questionable good-natured timbre. The Goth gal touched her diamond magick-wand brooch pinned to the bodice of her tea dress. *Abracadabra … nope, she's still Nurse Ratched!*

"Glancing around this room, I'm reminded that so many of us went to school together, from grade school through college," Professor Longbough noted.

Aisling gave a nod of concurrence as–

Professor Hass, unusually quiet that day, gave another low groan. The way she was stuffing her face, it was all she could manage.

A similar sound escaped Dr. Lear, a strange sound that could have translated to just about anything.

The Sisters glanced toward the head of the English department, then to one another, with Maggie remarking, "When you're born and reared in Haleigh's Hamlet, you never want to leave; and if ever you do, the Hamlet inevitably pulls you back."

"You mean you can take folks out of the Hamlet, but you can't take the Hamlet out of their hearts?" Dr. Whitman said, paraphrasing a popular metaphor.

"Something like that," Raine dimpled.

Professor Longbough's face grew morose. "The Hamlet's a hard place to leave. I *know*. I tried it once and found I couldn't do it; though, as I'm certain you all know, I've some unhappy memories attached."

"You know what they say," Professor Hass jibed, "'If at first, you don't succeed, try and try again.'"

There was a loaded silence, after which Longbow, upon flashing Hass a hostile face, resumed talking. "Most of you probably thought I wouldn't attend the faculty tea, but I've nothing to hide, nothing to be ashamed of. You all know my story." He lowered his voice a tad to bob his head in what looked like sad reflection. "Everyone has a chapter of their lives they don't read out loud … don't want discussed aloud, though I guess everyone has heard mine, huh? You know I've no ardor for anything Valentine's; but," his eyes scanned his fellows as he nodded to the table, "like you, I want to support the restoration of Old Main."

"We're glad you made it," Maggie affirmed in her soft way of speaking, prompting several of the others to voice like-minded comments. Hass, on the other hand, seemed to have contracted Mildred Whitman's eye-rolling bug.

Again, Dr. Lear uttered the peculiar sound from deep in his throat, and again, the Sisters found it impossible to interpret. They became aware that Lear looked as though he were studying Professor Lee and Dr. Whitman; but then again, *they* couldn't resist watching Annabel themselves, so edgy did she appear.

Haleigh's theatre director cleared his throat to speak in his strong, resonant voice. "Annabel, Dr. Whitman, I wish to extend my very best wishes on your engagement. I would have done so sooner, but as I said," he smiled, resorting once more to *Alice in Wonderland*, "'No time to say Hello, Goodbye'; I've been rushing about like a madman for the past several days." He paused for a beat, raising his teacup and enhancing his felicitations with, "May your hearts be forever entwined."

Annabel gave the impression of lighting up, for a few moments at least, to reply, "Thank you, Rex. Our friendship has always meant a great deal to me."

"Such an odd thing, friendship," Dr. Yore interjected.

"Why do you say that?" Raine queried, setting her sandwich on her plate.

"Because friends are capable of bringing out the best … or the worst in us," she answered.

"Yes," Thaddeus replied with a touch of the wistful, "I think that's true, Liz."

"Ahem!" Dr. Lear looked as if he wished to speak again. "I might interpolate that *true* friendship, like true love, is rare," he remarked in a philosophic tone.

"I quite agree," Dr. Whitman put in.

"To true friendship … and true love," Raine smiled, raising her teacup, now too, in a toasting gesture.

Repeating the Goth gal's salute, *most* at table followed suit.

Presently, Maggie spoke. "Dr. Lear," she began, "how's it going with your understudies? Raine and I were talking about this last evening, and we'd be happy to pitch in backstage. We," she looked to her sisters of the moon, "have been members of our community theatre for several seasons; so if you like, you can put us to work at whatever task or tasks you might see fit."

"And I just *might* take you up on that. I could use you as prompters." Rex Lear replaced his teacup to its saucer, as again his bearing took on a theatrical flavor that was his alone. "To answer your question, I am uneasy– and that's putting it mildly– about understudies taking over three significant roles with challenging dialogue at nearly curtain; but I totally support your reporting those students for cheating. It was time they got their *just deserts*, Liza Berk especially. My student actors tell me I'm a tough director. I know I was tough on Berk. I was hoping a leading role in this play would help her to achieve some level of responsibility, but obviously that has not happened. That girl has an incredibly *mean* streak, as I've told Dean Savant on more than one occasion. You caught them cheating too, didn't you, Annabel?"

Professor Lee, who, at the moment, appeared to be a million miles away, came back to earth with a start, "Y-yes," she faltered, "I did."

"It wouldn't surprise me if the police find those girls guilty of more than just cheating, though that in itself should get them expelled," Professor Longbough took the opportunity of verbalizing. "I had to throw Liza Berk off my archery team last semester for a list of infractions, mostly alcohol-related. The culture we here at Haleigh have established and persist to reinforce to our student athletes is integrity and accountability in all we do. When that culture is threatened by the Student Athletic Code of Conduct or Team Rules, disciplinary actions must be imposed. She left me *no* choice but to eject her from the team. As I told the defiant girl *and* her parents, participation in intercollegiate athletics is a *privilege* not a right."

Longbow's comment, in turn, incited Professor Hass to paraphrase, in audible mumble, a Shakespearean line, which she delivered with a heavy crust of her usual sarcasm, "And seem a saint, when most he plays the Devil."

Dr. Lear gave another of his grunts that, this time, could have been a throat-clearing cough, prodding the Sisters to wave it aside with the thought that he might be struggling with a cold or sinus infection, both of which were running rampant on campus that winter.

It wouldn't take me aback, Raine mused, regarding Professor Hass for a studying moment, *if somehow, some way, she staged this arrow business to cook up trouble for Longbow. If one of those errant arrows hadn't hit her in the ass ... but she could have ... yes! She could have ...* She let the notion waft away when her eyes caught Longbough's dark expression. Hass' sarcasm was not lost on Old Bull's Eye, who, turning to his arch-enemy, was about to retort when–

Wishing to prevent World War III, the astute Dr. Yore intervened. "I am certain your Valentine production of *Romeo and Juliet* will be as stellar as your litany of plays from the past, understudies or no, Dr. Lear."

Rex's face mirrored his gratitude. "Thank you, Dr. Yore. I have long appreciated your amiability, as I've admired your genius."

At once, the atmosphere became less strained, and the flow of conversation recommenced with small talk until Longbow directed a query to Annabel.

"Professor Lee," the archery coach asked, "have the police made any headway on the vandalism to your car?"

"No, I'm afraid not," the distracted professor replied, her eyes darting to her future mother-in-law.

It's as though Annabel's afraid to utter a word today, Raine shot automatically to Maggie.

Right, Maggie rocketed back. *If I'm reading the signs correctly, she's fearful of being belittled or mocked.*

And **we** *don't need to deliberate on who the offender might be,* Aisling sent her sisters of the moon.

Raine directed another thought-wave to Maggie and Aisling: *I shan't mention the three ski-masked thugs. I reported the incident to Chief Fitzpatrick, and for now, let's keep it hush.*

Good thinking, Aisling zipped back.

"There's a rumor making the rounds that you've been the victim lately of a number of nasty pranks," Professor Longbough pressed, his eyes on Annabel, "all begun after those girls were put on suspension."

"I'm afraid that's true," Annabel answered quietly, praying Old Bull's-Eye wouldn't mention her humiliating intestinal episode, likely schemed by the girls, that hit her at the televised town meeting. *That's all my future mother-in-law would need to hear!* the frazzled Annabel fretted. *Why does Professor Longbough keep harping on this?*

"The police will get to the bottom of all the campus shenanigans," Dr. Whitman said, sending his fiancée a concerned look. "Are you all right, my dear? You've hardly eaten a thing."

"I'm feeling slightly tired." Annabel took a sip of water. "It's all the excitement, I suppose."

"When you spoke the phrase 'just deserts,' Dr. Lear, I was reminded that I'd been under the mistaken belief that our Valentine tea would be *just desserts*; but what a happy discovery these gourmet sandwiches!" Dr. Yore held a satisfied mien, nodding to a server to refill her cup with the green tea she enjoyed.

The Sisters picked up straightaway on Lizzy's motivating sentiment. Perceiving that Annabel was uncomfortable talking about her situation as the victim of malicious acts, Dr. Yore, ever the peacemaker, was again attempting to smooth matters over with her *just deserts* comment.

"So many people today misspell the second word of that old expression," Professor Hass jumped in with her usual harsh tone; and true to her practice, this professor's gravelly voice bespoke cold superiority. "Deserts in the idiom 'just deserts,' is spelled with one *s* and means," she fixed the now poker-faced Longbow with a piercing glare, "'that which one deserves.' The 'just deserts' phrase is the last refuge of an obsolete meaning of *desert*."

"Well," Dr. Yore voiced, picking up her teacup and sitting back to study her fellows, "that old adage that you learn something every day is true, isn't it?"

The Sisters darted quick looks to one another.

The head of the archeology and anthropology departments was a very knowing, perceptive lady; and the Sisters sensed immediately that her thoughts were harmonious with theirs– thoughts that had relatively nothing to do with grammar and spelling.

"Speaking of desserts," Yore repeated, "here they come."

The servers spread out, each carrying a tiered tray, to place the sweet treats on the tables, prompting everyone to comment nearly at once.

"Wiz–zard," Raine exclaimed by way of her signature expletive, "would you look at that!"

There were hot, buttered crumpets; a variety of fruit scones with clotted cream; a spectrum of jam tarts; an array of faerie cakes; British sponge cake; madeleines; trifles; fig and almond squares; and an assortment of fancy cookies, counting red hearts and pink-sprinkled Cupids.

"My, it's difficult to choose," Dr. Yore considered, as she helped herself to a crumpet, scone, and madeleine.

"Haven't the students done an extraordinary job?" Dr. Whitman asked no one in particular.

"They have, a most *admirable* job. However," Raine added, leaning forward to whisper in a conspiratorial tone, "our good friend– and a great friend to Haleigh College, I might add– Eva Novak, is in the kitchen, supervising."

"I didn't think our Eva would trust her tarts, scones, and madeleines to chance," Maggie commented with a girlish giggle. "Hmmmm, I haven't tasted crumpets this buttery good since I moved back home from Ireland."

"Darling, aren't you going to have any dessert?" Dr. Whitman put quietly to Annabel.

In response, Professor Lee set her teacup down to sit back in her chair. "I think not. You know I never eat sweets."

"The dark-chocolate-almond truffle has no sugar," Mildred was quick to remark. "It's the favor in the white gauze bag with the heart on it. *Here*," she indicated, picking up Annabel's to hand it to her. When she turned to her future daughter-in-law, the thin lips twisted in a sardonic smile.

"Thank you, Mrs. Whitman." Gladdened by the woman's unusual attempt at kindness, Annabel accepted the token, opened the little bag, and bit into the heart.

"Ooooooh," Aisling crooned, "this lemon madeleine is almost too pretty to eat." She took an expectant bite of the rich French confection, shaped like a seashell and dusted with powdered sugar, as her face shone with unspoken gratification.

"Madeleines actually have an exquisite literary reputation, having served as Proust's muse in his *Remembrance Of Things Past*," Dr. Whitman remarked. "I feel certain the nostalgic Marcel Proust would have written wistfully about these *petits gâteaux*."

No one noticed that Annabel's face was flushing bright red, until she began gasping for air. Dropping the remaining bit of truffle, her hand flew to her heart, which was pounding through her chest.

"Annabel, what's wrong?" Barron asked, abruptly abandoning his madeleine to reach for his fiancée's hand.

"I-I-I don't k-know," she wheezed, swaying in her seat. "I-I f-feel dizzy, and I-I c-can't … get … m' breath!"

Mildred lifted the panicked woman's wrist to check her pulse. "Her heart is *racing*. Call 911. This woman has a congenital heart disease." She picked up a glass of ice water, holding it against Annabel's scarlet cheek. "Try and relax," she said in a professional manner. "Breathe deeply, and let your breath out slowly." With a nurse's competence, she then unbuttoned and loosened the high Victorian collar on Annabel's tea gown. "Come on, breathe … breathe deeply."

"Ambulance is on its way!" Aisling announced. The Sister had started calling 911 before Mildred proposed it.

Since several people had risen and began crowding round the wheezing woman, Barron interceded loudly, "Please back off and give her space to breathe."

Unable to speak, Annabel choked, grasping her beloved's hand, her eyes large with fear.

A moment later, she clutched at her heart and collapsed, lapsing into unconsciousness, her body nearly sliding from the chair.

"Annabel!" Dr. Whitman shouted. "Annabel!" He shook her, trying to get a reaction.

Feeling again for a pulse, Mildred said in an icy-calm voice, "Get her on the floor so I can perform CPR. Looks like a sudden cardiac arrest."

The thought struck Aisling: *Ten to one that's what we're meant to think!*

Swiping the remnants of the truffle from Annabel's mouth with a napkin, Mildred expertly opened the young woman's airway, tilted the chin, and immediately began the CPR, doing the chest compressions, then covering the mouth and blowing into the nostrils. She continued the resuscitation steps until the emergency medical team arrived on the scene and pronounced the victim–

"*Dead.*"

"No!" Dr. Whitman shouted, rushing forward to take his fiancée's face between his hands. "Annabel ... speak to me!"

"It's no use, Barron. No use at all." As Mildred turned from her son, a curious presence passed fleetingly over her features to express rather too eloquently what was in her mind and heart. Though it was there but an instant, the Sleuth Sisters recognized–

Smug satisfaction.

Three pairs of McDonough eyes quickly scanned the table to make yet another observation.

Two other faces exposed to the Sisters' view– the same startling reaction.

Mildred grasped for the small remains of the heart truffle that had fallen from Annabel's lap, inciting the Sisters to exclaim virtually in sync, Aisling's hand shooting out to stop the former nurse, "**No,** don't touch it! Don't anyone touch anything!" She spoke with the voice of authority. "We rang the police right after we called 911 for the ambulance. They'll be here any second."

Longbough stiffened, bellowing with alarm, "Why the police? I don't see why you've called the police! No crime's been committed here!"

"We don't *know* that," Aisling stated firmly, angered by the man's impudence. "But, I'll tell you this– we're sure as hell going to find out."

Chapter Eight

Raine rolled over and stared, for a fuzzy moment, at the alarm clock on her dresser. *Seven-fifteen. Can't sleep. Might as well get up.*

The Goth gal enjoyed sleeping in on the weekends, but this Saturday morning was different. She hauled herself out of bed, pulled on her cuddly, green robe, and stumbled into the bathroom. Then she headed downstairs. When she entered the kitchen, she was not surprised to see Maggie sitting at the table, sipping her Irish breakfast tea and looking absorbed in thought.

"Couldn't sleep either, huh?" Maggie came out of her reverie to address a yawning Raine, who hadn't bothered to brush her tousled hair. "I scarcely slept a wink."

"Tossed and turned all night," the raven-haired Sister groaned. "The errant arrows, the three thugs in the parking lot the other night, the vandalism and mean-spirited pranks that tormented Annabel, and now her untimely death– everything just keeps spinning round inside my head, and I can't seem to connect the dots. Not with any satisfaction."

"I know. I feel the same way. I keep sifting through the evidence, but to no avail. I cannot, for the life of me, arrive at a satisfactory conclusion." The redheaded Maggie sipped her tea, mulling over the disturbing occurrences. "Tell you what," she said, "let's have a comforting breakfast, then dress for the weather and go for a nice, long walk. That always helps us sort out problems and puzzles. What say you?"

"I say it's a *wizard* idea, Mags. A tranquil toddle through the woods is just what we need. And then tonight, we'll light a candle to make good use of Granny's Sleep Spell. The one that goes, 'Goddess above, Queen of Night, help me sleep in your healing light. Restful sleep come to me. Relax my body; let my mind be free."

A little over an hour later, the pair entered Haleigh's Wood that bordered their property. Since only a dusting of snow lay on the ground, they were able to hike the paths at a brisk clip. Both Sisters were clad in hooded jackets, with eternity scarves round their necks;

thick, black pants and sweaters; gloves; and flat-soled, fur-lined boots.

"After speaking with Chief Fitzpatrick late yesterday afternoon, I'm even more convinced that Annabel was murdered," Raine stated with conviction.

"So am I, and Aisling feels the same way," Maggie replied.

"Fitz was sure glad we had the presence of mind not to let anyone disturb what we believed was a crime scene." Raine drew in a long gulp of frosty air. "Ah! I love long tramps in the woods any season." Her eyes scanned their snow-dusted surroundings. "Biologists say that trees are social beings. Did you know that? They can count, learn, and remember. They nurse sick members, warn each other of danger by sending electrical signals across a fungal network, and they keep ancient stumps of long-felled companions alive for centuries by feeding them a sugar solution through their roots.

"You know too," Raine chattered on, "that the further we remove ourselves from Nature, the more negative thinking and feeling we experience, and it follows that we have far more stress. Clinical studies have proven that a couple hours of Nature reduce stress hormones and activate DNA known to be responsible for repairing and healing."

A pensive Maggie responded with a soft sound of agreement, and the Sisters traipsed smartly along, side by side, without speaking, in order to better soak up Earth Mother's rejuvenating gifts. Sensing that Maggie preferred to listen to the soothing sounds of the forest, Raine refrained from speaking– for a while anyway.

Like all witches, the Sisters were reliably recharged by Mother Nature. Animal brothers and sisters; the quiet and majesty of a wood; the sound, smell, and sight of the sea; birdsong; sunrise and sunset; thunder, lightning, and rain; the delicate beauty of a snowfall; the stars and constellations; a full moon; in fact, each of the moon phases the turning wheel of the seasons– *all* are enchanting and magickal to a witch. "Not all classrooms have four walls," the Sisters were prone to say.

After several minutes, Raine took a deep breath. "As we walk, let's fill our lungs with fresh air to clear our minds; place the palms of our hands on tree trunks to feel emotionally healed; and raise our faces to the sun to connect with its power and our own."

"I almost suggested we saddle up the horses, but I don't like to ride when it might be icy," Maggie admitted.

"They get outside in the paddock nearly every day," Raine answered, "but we should be able to ride before too long. We always seem to get an unseasonably warm day or two come this time o' year."

"Hmmm, then the wind changes overnight, and the next day it's winter again. I've been thinking, darlin'," Maggie began with her trademark Sweet Nothing, "that no one actually saw that arrow strike Hass in the derrière. *She* could've stuck the damn thing in her skirt's back pocket that held the small book of sarcasms."

Raine giggled. "Talk about a smart ass! I thought of that too. Yes, she could've easily done that herself. Did you notice how she was goading Longbow yesterday at the tea?"

"How could I, or any of us for that matter, have missed it?" Maggie sucked in her breath, letting it out with gradual release. "You know something? I wouldn't put *anything* past Hass when it comes to brewing trouble for Longbow."

"*Nor would I*," Raine punctuated with terse pitch. "I never particularly liked or trusted Hass," she fairly hissed the name, thinking aloud, "not one iota have I ever trusted that ... *woman*, and I use the word loosely."

The raven-haired Sister paused for an instant, after which her voice rose. "Guess what I found out last night when I was on the phone with Beau? Great balls of fire, I nearly forgot to tell you! Hass had an intense dislike for *Annabel* too. Beau's receptionist, Jean, told him she overheard Hass venting to someone at one of the Valentine vendor tables that Haleigh College had *no* business asking Annabel to represent the school at the televised town meeting. Hass ranted that her tenure at Haleigh was many years longer, and *she* should have been the one speaking to the public about the fest, not a virtual newcomer like Annabel. Get this: Hass concluded that *it served Annabel right what happened to her!* This was before our Professor Lee's death, so what Hass was referring to was the violent attack of the 'runs' Annabel got when she stepped up to the microphone that morning to speak."

Maggie jerked her head in her sister of the moon's direction. "Hass is always bellyaching about being unfairly treated at Haleigh. Her complaints are relentless. *Makes me wonder.* You know what? There are just too, too many obvious clues in this mysterious maze with none of the loose ends tying up satisfactorily. I remember skipping over the obvious early on when solving a mystery in the past; but then, we ended up coming round to it at the last. Oh, I made a rhyme! Could signify that's exactly what'll happen again. Oh, none of what I said came out right, but you know what I mean."

"I do," Raine responded with an understanding pat to her sister of the moon's shoulder. "I almost always know what you mean, Mags."

"Yes," Raine was saying, "it's come to my notice that the palpable indications in this spider's web are ever mounting." *Spider's web* … "I wonder if our suspicions about Annabel's demise will turn out to be true? Fitz told us he should have a report from the crime lab on that truffle she ate as early as today. He's pushing for it, even though it's the weekend."

Maggie's foot snapped what she thought was a twig on the forest floor. Looking down, she spotted the arrow. "Raine, look," she pointed, bending down, with gloved hand, to pick up the feathered missile and examine it. "It's the same kind that Longbow uses in his archery classes." Turning it over, she looked for the words *Property of Haleigh College*. They were *not* there.

"There's another one!" Raine exclaimed. She moved to it, picked it up, and studied it for several seconds. Finding nothing of interest, her gaze lifted to the horizon. "Maggie, we must have walked about four miles. Do you know who lives over there?" she pointed through the trees at the clearing ahead.

"I do," the redheaded Sister answered.

"C'mon," Raine breathed, "let's have a closer look."

The Sisters crossed as quickly and as quietly as they could to the tree line, where they stopped dead in their tracks.

"Hay bales," Maggie muttered.

"As used in archery practice," Raine proclaimed with sudden realization.

Maggie stared at the bales of hay. "Rather an intriguing business, this."

"Hmmmm," Raine mused, "our secret archer doesn't want the hay bales close to the residence, so no one can see. We've got to clue the chief in on this."

As if on cue, the Goth gal's phone sounded with the magickal music of Rowena of the Glen.

"Dr. McDonough here," her deep voice rumbled.

"Raine, Fitzpatrick here. I want you to meet me at the coroner's office this morning. Can you all three be there? Aisling didn't pick up, so I left her a message."

"Coroner's office? On a Saturday? Will Ben *be* there?"

"He will. My years in uniform are telling me we dare not drag our feet with this thing."

"Our witches' instincts are telling us the same thing, Fitz. What time do you want us there?"

"Would an hour be too soon?"

"Not for us!"

When Raine, Maggie, and Aisling stepped through the door of the white-tiled autopsy room, where Chief Fitzpatrick had bid them come, they saw immediately that he was already there.

In lab coat and mask, the chief was standing on one side of the sheet-covered body of Professor Annabel Lee. Coroner Dr. Benjamin Wight was on the opposite side of the stainless-steel table positioned in the center of the sterile room. Both men looked up as the Sisters, pulling on the masks Fitz left for them in the anteroom, entered the cold chamber.

"Good, they're here," the chief commented to Wight.

Perfunctory greetings were quickly exchanged.

"Thank you, Dr. Wight, for consenting to our presence here today; and Chief, we appreciate your personal invitation," Aisling courteously remarked, sending a nod of deference to each of the two men.

"I unequivocally respect and trust you three," the burly, uniformed officer replied in his no-nonsense voice. He cocked his snowy head to the side, and the usually bright blue eyes above his face-covering seemed to darken. "Looks like we've another tricky mess to sort through." He looked from the Sisters to the coroner, who was staring down at the body.

"Glad you could make it," Wight proclaimed in an absent sort of way. He continued to stare at the corpse, and when he spoke again, his voice seemed to be coming from afar. "I remember telling you in the past that we can learn a lot from the dead. I'll restate that today."

The comment caused Maggie to shiver. *It feels colder in here than it did in the woods*, she told herself. *But my frisson is not just from the chill. Ben thinks Annabel was murdered too.*

Dr. Benjamin Wight was a tall, fastidious man in his mid-fifties with slightly wavy, black hair frosted to near grey. His eyes, too, were the color of steel, and though he looked like he strode straight out of the silky pages of *Gentlemen's Quarterly*, it was steel he was made of. In brief, the distinguished Dr. Wight did everything as meticulously and as accurately as humanly possible– *perfection* was his life's credo– *and it showed.*

The Sisters took recurrent notice that Ben's office and surroundings at the morgue were as pristine as he was. It always made them wonder if working with dead bodies had increased his natural tendency toward impeccability.

"So tell us, was our suspicion on target?" Raine asked, not able to wait a moment longer for the verdict.

"Wholly," answered Dr. Wight without preamble. "She was poisoned all right. Cause of death– *cyanide*. No doubt about it. Note the color of the skin," he said, pulling the sheet back a little.

The Sisters could clearly see that Annabel's skin was a bright cherry-pink. Maggie began dabbing at her eyes, whilst Raine and Aisling shook their heads in sad response.

Poor Annabel, Maggie slipped to Raine, whose own eyes were now brimming with tears.

God and Goddess rest her, the Sisters petitioned.

"We'll find out who did this and give her spirit rest! Raine sped to her sisters of the moon.

"Cyanide is a deadly poison. *Deadly,*" the coroner repeated. "It works by preventing the body from using life-sustaining oxygen. In other words, cyanide keeps oxygen from getting to the red blood cells. When the cells are deprived of oxygen, they die. The heart and the brain use a lot of oxygen; thus, cyanide is especially deadly to those two vital organs.

"This was potassium cyanide, a fine, white powder."

"I've heard of it … hateful stuff," Raine blurted.

The coroner resumed speaking. "Dissolved in water, potassium cyanide's even stronger, though that sounds like it would be quite the reverse. Alcohol and sugar can lessen this poison's effect, but there was no alcohol served at the faculty tea, and none in her blood. Chief Fitzpatrick informed me that you told him the victim did not eat sweets. The stomach contents revealed the truth of that. The truffle that was dosed with the cyanide was sugar-free."

Wight took a breath, continuing, "Signs and symptoms can be difficult to detect– to connect what's happening to the victim with a poisoning, that is. There would have been general weakness, confusion, dizziness … shortness of breath. The body is simply starved for oxygen, you see."

"Yes," Aisling responded with a nod, "we noted all those signs."

"Needless to state, you did the right thing calling an ambulance immediately; but this poison, especially with this victim's congenital heart disease … this poison is fast-acting. It's a rapid kill. Death can occur within a minute. Doesn't take much either, not for a woman of her size and condition. As little as 100 mg can be lethal, and there was far more than that in her system. That large truffle was loaded with cyanide, about 300 mg. The killer likely injected the liquid cyanide into the heart truffle with a hypodermic needle."

Maggie pursed her glossy red lips. "It's a wonder Annabel didn't–"

"Virtually no taste," Dr. Wight interposed, "but there would've been a slight, bitter almond odor that, since this was a dark-chocolate-almond truffle, wouldn't have been detected. The dark-chocolate is a tad bitter, as well as the taste of almond; so there you have it– the poison effectively undetectable in that truffle. Cyanide's odor is very faint. Even without the dark-chocolate and the almonds, some people … dare I say *many* would have difficulty smelling it.

"And lest I fail to mention," Wight concluded, "the victim's blood had a purple tinge. Another indication that she was poisoned with cyanide."

"Where would the murderer get his hands on cyanide?" Raine asked no one in particular.

"His?" The chief jumped on the word in anticipation.

"His or her. One tends to say *his* for convenience is all," the raven-haired Sister answered.

"Cyanide is used in certain industries," the coroner went on, "such as gold and silver mining, but we don't have such mining around here," he stated. "Cyanide is also used by many jewelers in electroplating, and it's–"

"By jewelers?" Raine cut in with sudden concept.

"Yes," Dr. Wight answered, mistakenly thinking that the Goth gal had *actually* posed a question. "And cyanide is used in the pesticide industry as well as in chemical laboratories."

"I'm on the same wavelength as Raine," Aisling revealed. "I'm getting the feeling, quite a strong *gut* feeling, in fact, that the killer got the poison from a jeweler."

"So am I," Maggie put in. "I actually got a quick vision– just a flash, mind, but nonetheless, a *vision*– of a bottle, with skull and crossbones and the word *danger*, on what looked like a jeweler's work bench."

"Tell you what, Chief, we'll," she darted a glance at her sisters of the moon, "visit all the jewelers round about to find out if anyone connected to Haleigh College, including the mother of Dr. Whitman, visited a jeweler lately," Aisling directed. "With a bit o' luck, we'll find a jeweler who was visited of late by someone linked in some way to Haleigh."

"And if the same jeweler discovered that a bottle of cyanide went missing from his worktable," Maggie added.

Not long after, as the Sisters were exiting the morgue, Raine was reminded of that haunting poem by Edgar Allan Poe: *The wind came out of the cloud by night, chilling and killing Annabel Lee.*

"I have a suggestion," Maggie said, after the threesome piled into Aisling's black Escalade. "I've been thinking about something Longbow brought up at the faculty tea yesterday. He said many of the people in that room went to school together, from grade school to college. Sometimes there are deep hurts that occur during the formative school days … especially during the teen years, leaving scars that remain with people all their lives."

"Go ahead," Aisling prompted. "What are you getting at?"

"What I have in mind is this: Suppose something happened to one of our professors during his or her teen years that started the ball rolling toward," she shrugged, pausing when Raine pronounced–

"Murder?"

"Dead right," Maggie quipped.

"You said you had a suggestion," Aisling pressed again.

"Sorry." Maggie cleared her throat. "I got off piece. I suggest we stop at The Man In The Moon and speak with the publican, Ron Moon. His family's owned that pub for years, and I'll bet my wand he's garnered hordes of information from and about our local citizenry. Publicans, bar tenders, are like confessors or 'shrinks' in that people tend to tell them their woes, their sad stories. You know what I'm saying, drinkers tend to unload and vent their troubles in bars, cry into their beer, as the saying goes; and The Man In The Moon is a favorite watering hole of our professors."

The suggestion instantly appealed to Aisling. "Your idea's a good one," she said, starting the SUV's ignition.

"And," Raine adjoined from the backseat, "we can order Ron's delicious English sandwiches. I'm starved."

Adjacent to the small but picturesque Moon Lake with its tall stately pines, The Man In The Moon was located just outside the Hamlet proper. Patterned after an English pub from the Forties' era, the antique, wooden tavern sign, from England, depicted a man-in-the-moon, the orb golden, the face merry.

The present publican's father, J.R., had been stationed in England with the 8th Army Air Force, the "Mighty Eighth," during World War II, returning home with a love for England and its people forever etched on his heart. He opened his English pub on the outskirts of the Hamlet in 1950, which rapidly became popular with the locals, as well as wayfaring strangers. The entire pub was pure English, complete with a "red Brit phone box" and dartboards. The fare was typical English-pub food, including fish and chips and bangers and mash; and, of course, the establishment offered English beers and other British drinks. Music from the Forties' era was a charming part of the rustic atmosphere.

The lunch rush was over when the Sisters entered The Man In The Moon. Ron Moon was polishing a pint glass at the bar, and in the background, Glenn Miller's "Moonlight Serenade" was playing softly on the old-fashioned jukebox.

"Ey up, the Sleuth Sisters!" Moon exclaimed in typical English style. "Welcome! It's a long time since you've been in here. *Too long*. Where've you been?" He set the sparkling glass in its proper place and leaned on the bar toward the Sisters with a smile that closely resembled the man-in-the-moon on his tavern sign.

"Been keeping busy," Aisling returned the smile. "Three bitters, please, Ron, and menus."

"Comin' right up."

In next to no time, he set the drinks before them, along with menu cards on which was printed, in a sort of Gothic script, the bar fare.

"We really enjoyed your English sandwiches yesterday at the tea," Raine opened. "Made us hungry for more."

"Glad you liked them." Ron glanced quickly round and, seeing no one about, posed the question, *sotto voce*, that was on his tongue since the Sisters arrived, "Do they know yet what happened to that professor who died so sudden-like? Heart attack was it?"

Not wishing to divulge information just yet, Aisling replied, "Seems like it. Professor Lee had a congenital heart disease." It wasn't a lie.

Ron shook his head. "Shame. She was so young. The *Hamlet Herald* said only thirty-two. Damn shame," he repeated with another shake of his head.

Ron Moon was a congenial chap, with a round face that totally fit his surname and the fact that he was a Cancer. Of medium height and weight, he was exceptionally youthful for a man in his seventies. Ron knew everyone in the Hamlet, and the Sisters never heard him utter a negative remark about anyone. In return, the Hamlet liked Ron. Over the years, his pub became *the* popular haven for that quiet drink, a good and satisfying meal, and the place to rendezvous with friends, old and new.

Raine put down her menu. "I'm for your cheese and pickle sandwich."

Maggie looked to Aisling, who gave a quick nod. "Make that three," the blonde with the wand stated.

"Chips or crisps?" he asked, using the British vernacular for French fries and potato chips respectively. "We make both here."

The Sisters traded looks– and a thought.

"We love your homemade potato chips," Raine answered.

"Three ploughmen with crisps!" Moon called through the opening behind him and into the kitchen.

"Ron," Raine began in a voice that bespoke secrecy, "there's another reason we stopped in here today, in addition to your tasty fare, that is. We were thinking that publicans hear a lot of gossip, acquire a stockpile of information too. Folks tend to open up when they drink. We've known you a long time, and we know we can trust you to keep this in the strictest confidence."

Moon leaned toward the Sisters again, saying in a muted voice, "I already know what you're going to say. You're working with the police, and you think there just might be more to that professor's death than her congenital heart problem. Am I right?"

The Sisters' regard bounced from one to the other.

"You are," Aisling whispered. Her emerald eyes swept the empty room behind them. "Can you help us?"

Ron's dark eyes opened wide. "To probe a mystery? You Sleuth Sisters are full of surprises! I'm flattered. *Of course* I'll help you, if I can. I'm well aware of the good works you do."

"Like we said," Maggie replied, holding her voice to a whisper, "when folks drink, they talk. Has anyone, especially anyone from the college, ever unloaded or vented anything to you that stands out in your mind and might help us, anything at all ... even if you think it not connected in any way to this case."

Ron ran his fingers through his straight brown hair. "Hmmmm, let me think on this. More than a few of the professors from Haleigh frequent my place. Several of them have been comin' in here for years. This is going to take some careful thought, ladies."

The waitress passed the platters of sandwiches and crisps through the opening to Ron at the bar.

"Here you go." He set a plate before each Sister, as in the background, Glenn Miller's 1943 hit, "That Old Black Magic," began to play, the notes drifting from the jukebox to dance round the Sisters and Moon in a way that verily bespoke– *magick*.

Listening to the music and relaxing, the Sisters drank and ate in silence, as Ron, puttering round the bar, pondered over what they'd said. Now and again, he started to say something but broke off.

All of a sudden, he flinched, and his brown eyes opened wide. Moving closer to the Sisters, he said, "That old song has triggered a memory, more than one, in fact."

The perceptive sleuths, sensing that Moon was uneasy, exchanged looks but stayed silent, so he could tell them what he remembered before he lost his nerve.

"It wasn't quite a year ago ... maybe ten months, somethin' like that. At any rate, one of the professors from the college ... wait a minute." He swung round to slide the little door shut between the bar and the kitchen, closing the opening. "As I was saying, one of my regulars–" he cut off again, fixing the Sisters with an imploring look. "Please, I'm trusting you as you're trusting me. Don't ever tell anyone I told you this. I've made it a practice never to repeat to anyone anything I hear in my place, *please–*"

"Take it easy. You know you can trust us," Aisling assured, reaching out to pat his hand.

Ron gave a nod, continuing then, "Well, one of my regular patrons came in late that night, late for this particular professor on a school night. Usually this prof was not a heavy drinker, but that one night, the drinks flowed. In fact, I had to cut– Well, as I'd started to say, that ole song triggered my memory. And 'Old Black Magic' it sure sounded like to me!"

Moon cocked his head, as though attempting to envision the customer and how it had all gone down. "You're right about liquor loosening the tongue. Honestly, a lot of times, I don't even hear what's being said in here, especially near closing time. Words, phrases, the chatter all go in one ear and out the other. But this particular night, I was all ears because the talk pertained to World War II England; and as you know, my father was stationed in England during the war, so this story captured my interest, from beginning to end. I remember it perfectly … I would say *verbatim*, 'cause I have to tell you, it *stunned* me. As a barkeep, I've been pullin' beers for more years than I care to remember, and I thought I'd heard and seen everything, but this takes the biscuit. No one was in here at the time, only me and the professor; in fact, it was late, and I was about to close. Never have I told this tale to anyone, not even to my wife."

Aisling nodded rather impatiently.

Raine, especially, was getting antsy. "Oh, I can't stand the suspense another moment! Tell us, Ron. *Tell us* before someone comes in."

Moon glanced quickly round and then launched into the tale that, truth be known, stunned the Sisters too; and at this point in their lives, it took a lot to stagger the magickal trio.

"Then," said Ron, "just the other day it was, the same professor mentioned something else; but," he faltered, noting the Sisters' peculiar expressions and forestalling their question, "I don't know if there would be a connection. That's a poser and would be difficult to say." The publican paused a second time, remembering something significant. "However, and again, my recall is verbatim 'cause it, too, was odd, *bizarre* in fact. *It was as though someone else was lookin' out that professor's eyes and speaking through the mouth!*"

At eventide, the Sisters were at Hugh and Beau's home, next door and through the woods from Tara, where they were enjoying a pickup supper with their Sleuthing Set. Hugh and Betty, Raine and her Beau, Maggie and Thaddeus, and Aisling with hubby Ian were all present, spread out over the Goodwin's living room, each with a tray holding a big bowl of Betty's Witches' Stew– that looked and tasted delightfully like thick, dark and savory, old-fashioned beef stew– crusty bread, and a green salad. The long coffee table held condiments, as well as wine, fruit, and cheese.

"Great stew, Betty," the Sisters acknowledged.

"Exactly like our granny used to make," Raine effused.

"I'm so glad you like it. I found the recipe on one of the witchy Facebook sites you told me about. Hugh and I whipped it up hastily, so I wasn't sure it would turn out good, but it *is* good, isn't it?" she looked to her beloved, who answered with a butterfly peck to her cheek.

"Now that's 'cause it was made with love– the most important ingredient to any meal," the elder Goodwin proclaimed.

Pleasantries and small talk were exchanged for several minutes, after which Aisling proposed, "Let's get down to it, shall we?"

"Let's," Betty responded, rubbing her hands together with growing eagerness. "My excitement is killing me!" The former librarian and mystery buff was always more than ready to tackle a sizable scoop of secret sleuthing.

"Raine, you start," Aisling directed.

The Goth gal set her tray on the hassock next to her. She was sitting on the floor, as was her habit, with her back against the wall. Beau was parked beside her, with Hugh and Betty sharing the love seat, Maggie and Thaddeus occupying the couch, and, to complete what actually was a circle, Aisling and Ian in separate easy chairs. Hugh's sibling German shepherds, Nero and Wolfe, were lying, heads on paws, in their winter haunt– on the hearth rug before a lively fire. The dry apple wood snapped, crackled and popped pleasantly, giving off a nice fruity aroma that permeated the cozy room.

Since their Sleuthing Set was sworn to absolute secrecy via a solemn, binding covenant, Raine filled everyone in on the errant arrows, the harassments done to Professor Lee as well as to Maggie and herself, including her near attack in the parking lot of The Gypsy Tearoom, everything they'd seen and heard at the faculty tea, what they'd discovered in the woods and the clearing, and what they'd learned from the coroner. She ended with the information Ron Moon provided them at the pub.

After pausing to take a sip of wine, Raine said, "I think Maggie and I ought to do as much research as we can to ferret out everything possible on the professor Ron spoke about."

"I agree," Aisling stated. "Also in the works, we need to find out if anyone linked to Haleigh College visited a Hamlet-area jeweler lately, including Dr. Whitman's mother. If so, if any cyanide went missing from that same jeweler." She glanced over at her husband. "Ian's willing to handle things at the agency while I make the jeweler rounds."

"Good." Maggie considered for a beat. "That's in no way a stiff assignment for you, and it frees Raine and me for research and whatever else we'll need to do to fully investigate the professor Ron Moon clued us in on. This is a matter that demands reflection … a great deal of reflection. After muddling through all this info today, Raine and I both feel strongly that we'll uncover a whole chain of occurrences, *hidden hurts* that took their toll and just may have unhinged a formerly balanced person, driving that individual to murder. We'll be making good use of our crystal ball, Athena, soon too."

The raven-haired Sister swallowed another sip of wine, whilst a cunning expression manifested on her face. In the time it would take to wave a wand, she made up her mind to the idea that thrust its way into her brain.

With sudden suspicion, Beau eyed her archly, delivering a tap to her temple as he blew in her ear. "What's brewing in your crafty cauldron, Raine Storm?"

He knew her so well. In effect, she'd already begun to craft a daring plan as to how she would use the shapeshifting locket again, with the help of her familiar. "Nothing that involves you," she retorted slyly, giving him a quick kiss on the lips. She smiled, shooting the message to Maggie: *I'll share my plan with **you** later.*

Betty poured herself and Hugh more wine, passing the bottle to Beau. "So, Longbow is the one who put the bee in Eva Novak's bonnet to make a few healthy, sugar-free desserts, including the heart truffle favors, right?"

"I wonder if he knew that Annabel Lee never ate sweets? Was he a former beau?" Hugh asked.

"Not that we know of. But remember, they both taught at Haleigh; and thus, they would have broken bread, so to speak, together in the canteen, at the various teas and other social affairs at the college," Maggie divulged. "Like as not, Annabel mentioned on other occasions that she never ate sweets."

"Makes sense," Hugh nodded. He glanced over at Betty, who looked to be brooding over something. "A penny for your thoughts, dear."

"I was just thinking that Professor Lee was not the kind of girl to get herself murdered."

"If you mean that everyone loved Annabel, you're right about that," Raine returned. "People were full of admiration for her, both on campus and in the village. She was good company, warm-hearted– she had a lot of friends."

"People have been known to get poisoned by their friends," Hugh commented. "The question begging might be: When is a friend not a friend … or no longer a friend?"

"There was no darkness surrounding Annabel," mused Maggie, glancing over at Betty. "Like you, I should never have thought of murder in connection with our delightful Professor Lee."

Raine disclosed then, with Beau's input, Professor Hass' nasty remarks concerning Annabel and the thwarted Valentine-Fest talk at the televised town meeting.

"OK, the question *here*," Maggie posed: "Was that simply Hass being Hass? I mean for as long as Raine and I have known her at Haleigh, she's never uttered a kind word to or about anyone; and she spouts a long litany of complaints and grievances about the college, involving fathomed 'injustices.' *Or* were her remarks about Annabel significantly more sinister?"

"Jealousy?" Betty questioned, picking up a bunch of grapes to share with Hugh. "It can provide a *strong* motivation for killing. Along with it, you might even discover that layered wounds," Betty made imaginary quote marks with her fingers, "'*injustices,*' drove this pugnacious professor to murder. Just saying. It's good to put this all *out there*."

"To sort it out– you bet! But to be clear, Hass is not our top suspect, *thus far*, but we could amend that at any time. I can't help remembering Hass' face, her enjoyment of Annabel's discomfort at the tea," Raine stated. When Barron's mother made that unfeeling comment about October being eight months distant, you know, time for the couple to see if they were really right for one anoth–"

"***The faces***," Hugh cut in, "that you noted at the tea, whose expressions displayed smug satisfaction when Professor Lee expired, let's talk about them …"

"Does anyone gain particularly by Professor Lee's death?" Betty queried some time later.

"We don't think so," Maggie answered. "Annabel wasn't well-off, if that's what you mean."

"More reasons to kill than just for money," Hugh remarked in swift voice, "though some people would do anything for money … even murder. However, murder for monetary gain is not at the top of the motive list. People also murder to keep a dark secret; for concealment, that is to cover up another crime; for revenge; for lust, love or hate. Jealousy, yes. But let me go on. People murder to protect someone or something. Then, there are those murderers who kill simply for the thrill of it; and there's personal vendetta, or did I already say that?" he asked himself.

Betty was ruminating over what Hugh listed. "The question that just popped into my head: Was Annabel murdered to cover up another crime? Perhaps she knew too much about something or someone. However, whoever did it did not silence her, because as Dr. Wight says, you cannot silence the dead."

"I'm guessing that Annabel's murder was due either to jealousy, revenge or personal vendetta," Ian, the seasoned detective, stated.

"I'm thinking along the same lines," Aisling concurred. "But hot passion at the root of the crime or not, Professor Lee was murdered in cold blood."

"Oh, it was coldly calculated; that's for certain," Raine replied.

"Yes," Ian agreed, with Aisling adding–

"And it was an especially *wicked* thing to do, which points, as Ian deduced, to motive connected to jealousy, revenge or personal vendetta."

"I follow your thinking," Betty replied. "I set forth, for discussion, the cover-up query, but I definitely follow your reasoning."

Raine and Maggie exchanged a long pensive look, with Raine blurting, "Trixie Fox! She might *well* have harbored a strong jealousy against Annabel. She had the hots for Dr. Whitman, who soundly rejected her. Aisling, you know that Mags and I are quick to notice reactions, so we didn't miss the black glare she shot at Annabel when she heard about the engagement. And Goddess only knows what that vixen is capable of."

"Your reasoning certainly is logical. Poison's usually a woman's murder weapon," Hugh reminded, sipping his wine in thought. "Not to say there are no male poisoners in the dark history of crime, but there are far more women poisoners lurking about the world than men, or so it's believed. Women murderers seek to avoid physical confrontation, you see, so poison's an equal opportunity weapon, a great equalizer."

"Yes," Betty agreed, "and poisoners tend to be especially cunning, sneaky, even creative murderers. They can design the murder plan in as much detail as if they were writing the script of a play. Isn't Trixie Fox working toward a master's in theatre?"

Raine and Maggie responded with a resounding, "Yes!"

"Your reference to the words *sneaky* and *cunning* took me back to something else. So before I forget to mention it, we found out that Longbow kicked Liza Berk off his archery team last semester for a string of infractions, the most serious of which were alcohol related," Maggie informed.

"Ahhhhh, I see what you're getting at. She had reason to seek revenge on Professor Longbough, Professor Lee, and both of you," Betty digested, looking to Raine and Maggie. "Maybe even on Haleigh College itself."

"She did, and trust us," Raine replied grimly, sending Maggie a darting glance, "that girl is mean as a rattlesnake, and she's definitely vindictive. From what Mags and I have collected, she's a real party girl too, well on her way to becoming a confirmed alcoholic."

Beau put in the question he'd been wanting to ask for some time. "D'you think the jerks in the ski-masks who nearly attacked you were Liza and her two cohorts?" He slid his arm around Raine.

"That's my ardent suspicion," she responded without hesitation. "Whoever they were, it was obvious they were targeting Maggie's car; and then they came at me, perhaps only to frighten me, but nonetheless, it was a *threatening* gesture. I got the distinct sensation that the would-be attackers got real pleasure out of putting me in a spot … though fleetingly. I reported the episode to Chief Fitzpatrick straightaway to have it on record."

Beau gave a brisk nod. "*Good.*"

Picking up Beau's thought, the Goth gal added, "Don't worry about me. I choose my fights wisely, and I never get into one to lose."

"Yeah, we all know you're a girl with a lot of spirit, and you enjoy a good battle," Beau retorted, "but I'll never stop telling you to be careful. You're *not* invincible, my Free Raine."

The Sister frowned, but before she could say anything else, Hugh posed a query of his own.

"Have the police connected those three girls to what happened to Professor Lee's car? Or are they keeping that under wraps?"

"Curious circumstance, what happened to that car," Betty murmured, nibbling a buttered chunk of crusty bread with the piece of cheese she'd selected.

"The incident certainly points to the girls who were suspended," Hugh huffed into his cavalry mustache.

"To answer your question, if the police have connected the Terrible Three to the vandalism of Professor Lee's car, the answer is *no*. But my witch's intuition is telling me that someone in this Hamlet saw them, and it's only a matter of time before that someone talks to the police," Maggie said. "I realize that witchy intuition is not evidence, but when one of us gets a premonition, we're usually right."

"I'm glad you mentioned Professor Lee's car, Hugh," Ian remarked. "Aisling or I can question the professor's neighbors. From what we've gleaned thus far, we believe the vandalism was done in the wee hours, in her own driveway."

"Do that!" Hugh blustered. "Talk to the folks who live near Professor Lee's house. Every neighborhood has at least one nosy neighbor, or one who suffers from insomnia."

"Right," the Sisters answered together.

"Understood that Professor Lee was the one who proved to your dean that cheating and lying were ongoing things with those wayward students," Betty pondered. "But would Liza, a young girl like that, go to the extreme of *murder* to seek revenge?"

"Ooooh, there have been proven *child* murderers on record in the annals of crime," Aisling put in, "*way* younger than this Liza character. Many murderers begin as children, quite young children, whereupon the perp is ofttimes referred to as a Bad Seed."

Brrrrr, Raine thought, *someone's walking over my grave!*

"Dreadful," Betty winced.

"*Chilling*," said Maggie aloud with a shudder. "Wouldn't be the first student to have it in for a teacher enough to do real harm– even murder."

"We can't wave away the Liza clique's actions as mere follies of youth; that's for sure," Raine interjected. "If Dean Savant *expels* them from Haleigh– and keep in mind that the cheating and whatever else they've done that can be proven will go on their permanent records– we may just have *motive*."

"A shadow of a motive anyway," Betty shrugged.

Raine and Maggie linked gazes. "No, *motive*, but with the emphasis on *shadow*."

"There are a number of suspicious characters with what could be motives here," Betty retorted. "And that number seems to be growing."

"By the way," Beau happened to think, "did you find anyone who could corroborate Prof Longbough's alibi that he was at home when the first errant arrow struck that student on Haleigh's nighttime campus and at The Man In The Moon when Hass was hit with the second arrow?"

"Ron Moon still swears Longbow didn't arrive at the pub until twenty to six," Raine answered. "That would've given him sufficient time to shoot Hass with that arrow. And, to date, no one can corroborate his story that he was at home when that female student was grazed by the first arrow."

"That explodes Longbow's alibis," Ian stated. He set his wine glass down to pick up a wedge of sharp cheddar.

"Jealousy's a *strong* motive, so keep tabs on Trixie Fox," Hugh reminded. "You know what I'm suggesting here– *a woman scorned*. And from what you've said, that vixen has sharp claws. But let's not lose sight of the fact that the hostile future mother-in-law was a former nurse. She's certainly a candidate for Annabel's murder. Keep in mind that the coroner's educated guess was that Annabel's killer injected the heart truffle through the gauze bag with a *hypodermic* needle."

Raine came back with, "Oh, Dr. Whitman's mother's in the running all right. Nurse, dragon lady, watchdog and controlling mum, to cite a few of her qualifications for this murder."

Betty raised her wine goblet in a gesture of accord. "Certainly no lack of motive there!"

"True, but let's be careful to reserve judgement till we have all the facts," Aisling cautioned, "lest we miss other clues and suspicions."

"We're of the same mind, of course," Maggie answered. "Nonetheless, remember this: We noted that Mildred Whitman swiped Annabel's mouth clean with a napkin before she began the CPR. When she did, she administered the chest compressions but *no* mouth-to-mouth ventilation. Rather, she held her hand over the victim's mouth and blew into the nose," the redheaded Sister pointed out.

"In today's world," Betty began, "with so many deadly diseases, that may be the preferred ventilation step during CPR, or–"

"Mildred Whitman *knew* there was cyanide in that heart truffle and didn't want to risk ingesting any of the deadly poison," Raine finished with grim utterance.

"You mentioned that Professor Annabel Lee and her fiancé, Dr. Whitman, along with his controlling mother were already in the Student Union hall when you arrived," Hugh recalled. "They may have gotten there before anyone else, and somehow Dr. Whitman's mother found a private moment to dart the heart. And you said Professor Hass was already in the hall too."

"*Dart the heart*," Raine repeated, musing. "Cupid's arrow to a vulnerable heart.   Now that makes me think …" She broke off in reverie, saying aloud, "You know what? I'm starting to think of this tangled web in terms of theatre. Sets, lighting, entrances, exits, dramatis personae, noises off. Then, of course, there's the audience … and their reactions. All very interesting. Very interesting, indeed."

"You informed us earlier that 'Nurse Ratched,' aka Mildred Whitman, exhibited a smug look of satisfaction on her face when Annabel was pronounced dead," Betty was saying, with a quizzing regard toward the Sisters.

"She did," Aisling replied flatly. "Without a doubt, she did, but so did two other suspects we told you about."

"I'd go so far as to say that all three smug expressions appeared to be *deep-felt*," Thaddeus chimed in. He had been quiet till now, but opined this last with conviction.

"Those arrows you found in Haleigh's Wood … and the hay bales," Ian deliberated. "The evidence against your *top* suspect seems to be building, and my years as a detective are telling me this will be a short-lived mystery."

"To use your phrase, Betty, *curious circumstances* that suggest … no, **translate** murder," Thaddeus said aloud as he absently stroked his beard.

Ian concluded what he'd started to say. "Yes, I believe we'll be connecting the dots sooner than we think."

"Oh, I hope this can all be cleaned up quickly," Aisling responded, sending her husband a glance, "and with the least amount of trouble. But we all know that murder can be anything but trouble-free."

"We're used to trouble," Raine chortled. *And I can't wait to tackle the next phase of it!* she spun to Maggie, as a temptation curved her mouth in a smile, and her emerald eyes sparkled with her secret.

"Some days I feel extra witchy!"
~ Dr. Raine McDonough, PhD

"C'mon, out with it! Tell me what you're up to," Beau cajoled, as he began undressing Raine, peeling off one article of clothing at a time, unhurriedly, teasingly. With rapid drafts of pleasure, their kisses became more and more heated as they fed off each other's strong energies.

When she was completely nude, he whispered into her ear, "Tell me, baby."

"You'll see," she sang. *Once it's done.*

With a quick, deft movement, he gathered her into his arms and kissed her soft mouth.

In the dancing light from the green marble fireplace in her bedchamber, Raine's eyes flashed desire. They had Tara to themselves, since Maggie was spending what remained of the weekend at Thaddeus' mountain cabin.

"C'mon, what crafty little plan have you cooked up?" he murmured against her lips. "C'mon ..."

She broke the kiss. "*You* come on ... wrap your body around mine, and let's make magick with love."

"Tell me!" he said again, his actions causing her to draw in her breath, the kiss deep and passionate before his lips and mustache began feathering a trail of caresses to her ear, her neck, and lower, ever lower, as he knelt before her.

"Beau," she sighed, "a long time ago, I learned never to explain things to people, it misleads them into thinking they're entitled to know everything I do." Catching the fleeting look of hurt in his eyes, she bantered in a sweetened voice, "I might be tempted to tell you what I'm going to do, if you continue what you're doing."

Beau paused in what he was about, his touches tantalizing that left her literally aching for more.

"Play with me, Beau," she purred. "I need it." She ran her kitten-pink tongue over her top lip, as her ebony nails lightly raked his back and shoulders.

"I'm not playing, you naughty girl," he growled, picking up where he left off. "Playtime's over. Now it's time to get serious."

"Ooooooh!" she virtually screamed a few minutes later. "Ooooooooooooooh, yes, yes ... YES!"

"Hmmmmm," she released her breath, "it's amazing what a person can do with practice. Mmmmm, yes. That was *good*, Beau. *Deliciously* good."

"You liked that, did you?" he rasped, standing and sending her a sexy glimmer.

"Let me show you how much," she answered, reaching fervently for his zipper.

"Topping last night is going to be difficult," he countered, his hands seeking to deliver more pleasure.

"Oh, but don't you just love a challenge?" she mewed. She grasped his buttocks and pulled him closer, as she gently sucked then nipped his lower lip. "I've been thinking about this all day and, I confess, *of very little else.*" As if she were enjoying the most scrumptious ice-cream cone, her tongue swirled round his in a circular motion, and they both hit sensual overload– which spurred him to reciprocate with a move of his own.

"Oh, great Goddess," she moaned, gripping him for support, "you're going to make my legs buckle."

"We can solve that." He smoothly swept her up and crossed to the bed.

With a knee on each side of her, he capably renewed his lovemaking, kissing, tasting, and touching until she begged him for more still, and they indulged, for several long, blissful moments, in the soul-grasping kisses about which Raine was so crazy.

"Oh, Beau, please. I'm on fire ... so good ... and ready." The words came out in a breathy, uneven whisper, as her hand slid down her stomach, and her eyelids fluttered shut.

"I know you're good, but I'm not entirely sure you're ready," he returned with wicked façade, a lock of ebony hair falling over his forehead.

"Yes, yes, yessssssssss!" she gasped, biting his shoulder. "Ooooooooh, yes! That was soooo *hot!* I love it, *love* what you do to me. Have *always* loved it."

"You're going to love it even more after tonight. *That*'s a promise. And you know I never break my word. Do I, my little witch? *Do I?*" he said louder, with a thrust that took her breath.

"Oh, Beau! I never want to be without you. *Soul mates forever ... for ... ever and ever ... and ever.* She arched to meet him as pleasure surged, and her cry echoed in the hearth-lit room, renewed desire flaming within her.

"I love you, Raine. Much more than you know." His words were so soft, she barely caught them, and what she did catch was a misty fragment.

She couldn't be certain, but she thought he whispered, "... strong magick between us."

"*Soul mates forever,*" she repeated softly, as she inspired him to create even more magick between them, ever-stronger *magick* of a much more ancient sort– and they erupted with starry explosion together.

"Mmmmm, *I sooo needed that*," she sighed several minutes later. "I've been on edge since we got back from Salem. And you've got the best medicine I know for stress release, doc." She ran a finger over his lip, light as a feather, then traced its outline with her tongue. "Did I ever tell you how much I love your lower lip? Yeah, stress relief, that's your main job."

"My job as a man," he informed, pulling her closer, "is to make sure you never need or want any other man."

She snuggled against his chest, closing her eyes. There was such peace in Beau's arms.

"Tell me again … how you never want to be without me," he breathed into her ear.

"I *don't* ever want to be without you," she obliged in a keen whisper. Her emerald eyes shone with the intense love she harbored for this man, and her short, ebony hair fell over one eye and wisped about her rosy face, as she stretched, catlike, on the bed. "I put a spell on you," she goaded.

"Really? How do you know *I* haven't put a spell on you?" Beau stared at her for a studying moment, as a look of humor and some of the familiar defiance leaped into the feline gaze that met his. He could read those eyes, as he almost always had in the past. They seemed to be speaking to him from another time and place, from that distant star whence they both felt an inherent allure: *Oh yes, you conquered me, but only because I permitted it. I'll savor my destruction for a moment longer, then I'll become independent once again.*

"You still haven't told me what you're up to," he said, grabbing handfuls of her raven hair, to kiss her open mouth.

Her eyes closed. "I'll tell you when I'm ready."

"And you're not ready now?" He trailed a hand down her nude body.

"Not for that," she whispered, jumping up to straddle him as a suggestive grin played about her pouty lips. "Those were for me, and now– this one's for you."

"Oh, wow … you always deliver." Maggie clung, quivering, to Thaddeus, as they both took a moment to catch their breaths in the whirlpool bath. "I've looked forward to this for days. Making love with you is every time extraordinary, but in water … hmmmmm, it's always over the top. There are so many *perks* to being a witch."

"Yes, aren't there?" he replied, his voice carrying a hint of the mysterious.

She was soft, smooth and slippery, and his hands slid over her with rekindled desire, as she leaned in and kissed him full on the mouth, as if she could never get enough. "I'm continually spellbound by your creative lovemaking, darlin'," she murmured against his lips. "I daresay it is– *impressive*. *Wildly* impressive."

The romantic bath smelled of the patchouli oil Maggie had tossed, along with her own creative intent, into the water. For a few moments, the couple did not speak, savoring the silence, save for the sigh of the mountain's winter wind; the sight of the falling snow on the gently swaying trees through the leaded-glass diamonds of the window; and the flickering scented candles circling the hot tub.

"The snow's sooo peaceful," Maggie whispered. "There's something to be said for deep winter. I could stay here forever."

Surrounded by a Colonial-style rail fence, the charming log cabin, that Thaddeus christened Wood Haven, was situated high above Haleigh's Hamlet, in a forest clearing of the beautiful Pennsylvania wilds known as the Laurel Highlands. The professor purchased it for a retreat, away from everything and everyone, and over the past few months, the place was proving to be a most *satisfying* investment.

"Do you like your Valentine present?" he asked with busy fingers.

Her laugh rolled from low in her throat. "You're going to have to lace me into it."

The Victorian, red and black lace corset was the perfect choice, and Maggie had squealed with delight when she opened the package.

"Tomorrow, with black silk stockings and four-inch spike heels," she whispered. "It's a promise … *and will accompany my Valentine gift to you.* For now, I want us both to envision it with," she grasped his shoulders, pulling herself against him and blowing into his ear, "*anticipation.*"

"I am imaging it now," he said, making her squeal again, "the way the twin globes of your breasts will overflow the top, and the way the twin globes of your fine bottom will entice me when I turn you around."

"Do you know what I think?" she trilled her crystal laugh, reaching over to playfully tweak his van dyke. "I believe that corset is more a present for you, Dr. Weatherby, than it is for me."

He suspended his lovemaking to tilt his head in thought. "A point well taken, but you will most definitely benefit from it; I assure you." Now it was his turn to chortle, as he remembered the catalog description when he purchased the erotic item. "The corset I chose ends at the hips; hence, the wispy, black thong 'for easy access' it said under the picture."

"Ver-ry easy," Maggie smiled seductively. "Now, I think you'd better convince me again, why you want to …" she breathed the remainder of the sentence into his ear, biting the lobe then flinging her head back in ecstasy when he brought her again to the summit of her super-sensuality, the magick between them blazing.

"That was a very wicked suggestion, my little red bird." Yanking her closer, he kissed her, and she moaned anew as the kiss deepened. He turned her around and began running his hands over her front, squeezing her full breasts, then soaping them with gentle massage. Dousing the soap in the water, he began caressing her with erotic, circular motions. His hand moved to the small of her back, and he commenced to leisurely soap her buttocks.

She pushed against him and parted her legs, enjoying the massage and exploration. "Each time, my wish is that … it will never end," she panted. "It's … that good. Mmmmmmmm. Ooooooooooh, that feels soooo go—ood … oooooooooooh …"

He entered her easily. "It's never going to end, my darling. It will only persist in getting better, each time surpassing the last. That's *my* promise," he whispered with an especially breathtaking move. "And you know I never make rash promises. Think of a fantasy," he breathed into her ear, "and I will make it come true, for I intend to keep you smiling and satisfied. *Very … very satisfied.*"

Her heart beat rapidly. She could hear it throbbing in her ears, like the pounding Irish surf in a westerly storm, as again the excitement built– and intensified.

Maggie reached down to touch herself, dancing her watery fingers over her love button. She was always so aroused by this man that the pleasure was nearly unbearable. He'd taught her so much, releasing her of any lingering inhibitions. Here was a woman who had believed herself to be sexually liberated, who had experienced many lovers– but never one as erotic, as sexually polished as Dr. Thaddeus Weatherby, PhD.

"It *can't* stop, professor. I … am … totally and irreversibly … *addicted* to you," she panted, screaming his name as she closed her eyes to better enjoy the magick.

Her time with Thaddeus *was* magickal. Dreamlike, *freeing*, and empowering with the enchantment of a true and abiding love.

"As much as you want, my Maggie. Every time … as much as you want."

The next morning dawned bright and almost spring-like, prompting Maggie and Thaddeus to take an early-morning tramp before breakfast through the picturesque snowy woods that surrounded their cabin.

"If you could use the Time-Key to solve any mystery in history, which would you choose?" he asked, looping her arm through his.

"But," she started, stopping in her tracks on the path, "we can't use our Time-Key for anything but helping innocents! We don't dare use it to promote ourselves or satisfy our own selfish curiosities. Why, cracking unsolved historical mysteries would be– No, quite out of the question. We couldn't do that … well, not unless," she paused there, not venturing to verbalize the remainder of her thought. "Never forget that our job is to help innocents … *and* to protect our Time-Key." Maggie blew out her breath.

"I know that." Dr. Weatherby's intense blue eyes twinkled in amusement. "*Perhaps better than you, luv.* If you recall, you and Raine were, at the onset, planning to incorporate the Time-Key into your dissertation, before I–" now it was he who stopped abruptly, pausing to seemingly choose his next words with great care before continuing. "Let's just say before I planted the idea in your heads to think hard about what you were doing. If you recollect, I was immensely *relieved,*" he bellowed, "that you came to your senses in time to protect yourselves and your Key!"

Before she could respond, he rushed on, the humor he initially felt swiftly swelling to agitation. "If you would've made your Time-Key the focus of your doctoral dissertation, as you originally set out to do, you would've had every historian, every history buff, every news reporter and commentator, as well as every treasure hunter in the world … along with every *wacko* you could shake your wands at coming out of the woodwork to accost you. Your very lives would have been in jeopardy. Turned upside down to boot! I love you both, and I did not want that to happen."

He heard the sharp intake of her breath.

Maggie stood with open mouth for several seconds before she spoke. "I've never seen you so ruffled, darlin'. I was merely reminding you that we can never use the Key for going back in time to solve mysteries that would only serve *us* and not–"

"Forgive me," the professor interpolated, a somewhat uneasy expression manifesting on his noble face. "I was *not* suggesting we use the Time-Key for anything other than that which it was bestowed upon you three. I was simply asking a rhetorical ... *thought-producing* question. An intellectual exercise," again his bright blue eyes sparked, "purely for amusement."

"No need to apologize," she said in her normally soft tone. "I understand."

"You don't need to understand. I've got my reasons," he said gently, kissing her cheek. They began once more to walk, side by side, her arm through his. "Hence," he added quickly, "are you ready to be amused?"

"Well, there are so many captivating mysteries in history from which to choose," she answered, delighting now in his little game. "Though there are several theories as to what happened to her, the mystery of Amelia Earhart is ever compelling; oh, and the Lost Colony riddle of Roanoke Island; then, of course, there's the enigma of Loch Ness; and the Ghost Ship Mary Celeste." Maggie ruminated over matters, as more baffling historical puzzles drifted across her mind. "The Bermuda Triangle, Jack the Ripper, Sasquatch, the Holy Grail, the Shroud of Turin, the Ark of the Covenant ... *so many!* But your subject of debate was which of history's mysteries would *I* choose. Hmmmm," she ruminated with serious face. "That's a tough one ... though I've forever been partial to the Lost Colony mystery. Yet," she blurted, with pointed finger raised in asking for a moment, "I've repeatedly gravitated to mysteries with paranormal attachments– oh, I can't choose! It's *impossible* to choose just one. I'm grateful I don't have to."

Thaddeus patted the hand that rested on his arm. "Very well, let's play another game."

She began to feel excited. "Hmmm, I love your little games," she replied in a manner that was in every way seductive.

"Yes," he laughed, "I've noticed. Do you know what game I like best to play with you?"

In a teasing mood now, she twitted, "No, but I'd bet you a Jameson and soda you're about to tell me."

"The game I like best with you is a *wishing* ... or should I say *witching* game?" He brushed her red hair back from her ear to breathe an especially erotic fantasy that made her purr with pleasure. "But that's for later. For now, tell me to which mysterious locales you would like to travel ... with me. *Mystical* places, or places with hauntings or mysteries attached."

"Another tough question, Dr. Weatherby," she hummed, locking eyes with him to adjust the scarf round his neck. His fantasy so enflamed her, it was some moments before she spoke, as she willed herself to return to the moment. "Are you aware that witches believe," she cleared her throat of the huskiness his sexy words had brought on, "there are places in the world that are holy, sacred wells where the power of the ancients can still be summoned?" She rambled on, ignoring the look of amusement that had returned to his face.

"There's Peru's Machu Picchu with its ancient Inca city. Oh, and that country's Nazca Lines, the weird and wonderful geoglyphs depicting spiders and monkeys. There's Easter Island with its strange carved effigies. The Great Pyramids of Giza, and lest we forget the incomparable Stonehenge. I love Tintagel with Merlin's Cave in Cornwall too, and all the places with faerie circles. There's Arizona's unique and spectacular Sedona and the spellbinding Superstition Mountain's cougar shadow ... oh, and the sacred Nagqu River area of Tibet that left me with deep impression; and though I've visited all those sites, I'd most certainly love visiting them all over again– with *you*.

"Then, of course, there are so many tempting haunted sites. Gettysburg is conceivably one of the most haunted locales in America; I've visited it several times. New Orleans is another of the most haunted cities here in the States, with some *chilling* vibes. I might choose to re-visit it, since I've never had sufficient time to check out *all* its ghostly sites. Oooooh, I mustn't overlook Ireland's Leap Castle, said to be one of the most haunted ancient strongholds in the world." Maggie struck an attitude of contemplation. "And I mustn't neglect to mention the sacred Hill of Tara, ancient seat of the High Kings and one of the Emerald Isle's most *revered* spiritual sites. There, druids held festivals, priestesses were trained, and shaman rites were performed. You know, of course, that those who hear voices in the wind at Tara are said to possess faerie blood." When Thaddeus didn't respond, though his keen, blue eyes danced anew with their spark of humor, she said, "Let me think harder.

"There's the Hoia-Baciu, that eerie dark forest in Romania, reported to be not only haunted but where several people, over the years, have disappeared. Yes, *vanished without a trace.* All sorts of paranormal activity there. Even the trees and vegetation in that place are bizarre. I've never been, but let's rule that one out," she said almost immediately. "I really do *not* want to go there. But you asked me to choose *one* place. Impossible! Again, I can**not** do it." She gazed at him speculatively. "What about you, darlin'? Which spot would you choose?"

Thaddeus' laugh was a soft, mysterious chuckle, as he sensually pulled off a mitten, bringing the hand to his lips. "A no-brainer. I would follow wherever *you* go, my love."

And though their discussion was oratorical, it went deeper– much deeper than mere words.

"Our cats protect us from evil."
~ The Sleuth Sisters

Chapter Nine

Aisling pulled up to Joel Goldman's home, turned off the ignition of her Escalade, and sighed, saying aloud to herself. "Last jewelry store on my list. Granny used to say, normally it's the last key on the ring that opens the door. Goldman will be *the one*."

She exited the vehicle and marched briskly up the stone walk to the lower door, where a sign read: ENTER. When she opened the door, a bell sounded inside the workshop and studio, where the jeweler was working at his bench.

The rotund, good-natured Joel Goldman was a popular Hamlet jeweler, whose shop was in the basement level of his modern contemporary residence, a house that could have been designed by Frank Lloyd Wright, so harmonious was it with Earth Mother. In a wooded setting, with the circular movement of the Guggenheim Museum in New York City, the home gave the impression of a treehouse.

"May I help you?" Joel asked, raising his magnifying glasses from his nose to his bald head.

"I hope so," Aisling expressed pleasantly. The Sister introduced herself, quickly relating that she was working with the police on a case and had a few questions to put to him that, *answered*, might help them solve it.

With sudden realization, the middle-aged artisan burst out with, "You're one of the Sleuth Sisters! I thought I recognized you when you came in." His eyes appraised Aisling. "My, my, where crime is concerned, you three are the goods. I'd be happy to assist you in any way I can. What do you need from me?"

"Thank you, sir. I appreciate your cooperation, and I'll try not to take up much of your time. Was anyone connected to Haleigh College in here lately?" Aisling pulled a notebook and a pen from her purse.

"Let me think." Joel passed a hand over his jaw in a pensive gesture. "In the past couple-a weeks, I had two customers connected to the college. The first was …"

Aisling gave a brisk nod, writing the name the jeweler uttered on the pad. It did not shock her. In truth, it was the name she expected to hear. "Can you provide me with a date for that visit?"

Goldman rose and went to a ledger he pulled from under the counter. "Give me a second. Ah, here it is. I was wrong. It was only ten days ago." He reversed the book to allow Aisling to see the entry. "Came in to have a battery replaced in a watch."

Aisling raised her eyebrows. "Really? Don't most people just buy a new battery and replace it themselves?"

"Some watches are tricky to open. I actually do that for my clientele."

"I see. You mentioned that you had *two* patrons linked to the college within an approximate two-week period. Who was the other one?"

"I don't know if she's actually associated with the college itself, but the customer was Dr. Barron Whitman's mother, who's visiting him from Boston. She came in to have an item engraved for her son. It was to be a Valentine gift for him."

"Just out of curiosity," Aisling probed, "what was the item, and what did she have engraved on it?"

Goldman tilted his head, and it looked as though he was diffident about whether or not he should answer. "I don't like to discuss my clients' affairs, but I do trust the Sleuth Sisters, so I see no harm in it. Mrs. Whitman brought the item in with her to be engraved. She said she happened to think that personalizing it would make it more special. It was a gold– nearly solid gold, in fact– signet ring. A superb, museum-quality medieval piece, with amazing detail. The letter on the ring, depending on which way it was worn on the finger, was either a W or an M. Mrs. Whitman remarked that it could stand for Whitman or Mother. She commissioned me to engrave the inner shaft with the words– *Forever my son.*"

Aisling wrote that down, and again asked the date of the visit, entering the info in her notebook. "Mr. Goldman, do you use potassium cyanide when electroplating?"

"Yes, I do. I live alone; I'm a widower, and I don't have any pets, so I don't worry about anyone touching the stuff. I've worked with it for years, so I know what I'm doing."

"Has any of it gone missing of late?"

"Missing?" The jeweler's face reflected his surprise. "No, I keep it over there," he gestured behind him, "on my workbench."

"Could you please check and make sure that none has gone missing."

With a shrug, Joel moved across the room to the worktable, where he looked for the cyanide. "What the– **it's gone**! I kept it right here." He began moving items to see if perhaps the cyanide was hidden behind something else on the table. "Haven't needed to use it for a while, but this is where I *always* kept it." He turned to face Aisling, his chubby face flushed scarlet. "It's gone!" he repeated in what looked to be an attempt to convince himself.

"When do you last remember seeing it, *for sure?* Think hard."

"Well, I electroplated a bracelet for a regular customer about two weeks ago. That was my last electroplating job. Let me check my book." After moving back to the counter and perusing the ledger, he raised his eyes to meet Aisling's. "Just before the two people from the college paid me their visits. Oh, dear." He shook his head, brooding over what the missing cyanide could mean. "Dear me."

"Do you remember leaving the room either time those two individuals were here?" Noting the chary expression on the jeweler's cherubic face, Aisling, a seasoned detective, was adept at dealing with that one. "Look, the information you're sharing with me is more than helpful, Mr. Goldman. It will not only aid us in solving a current case, *it could save lives.* I want you to know that, for I know you're a man of good conscience." Having thus charmed away the man's tentativeness, Aisling hadn't long to wait for his next words.

Goldman gave an understanding nod. "I'm uncomfortable discussing my consumers, especially regulars, but I want to do the right thing. I do recall leaving the room when the professor was here. He wanted to see my photo albums, in which I catalog pictures of my custom designs. I'm a silversmith and a goldsmith, in addition to a watch maker and a gemologist. So many jewelers today are simply salesclerks. You know what I'm saying; they send out all their jobs." Joel flashed an on-and-off smile. "But I digress.

"I left the room to go upstairs and get my newest album," he said, reverting to the matter at hand. "I'd added a couple of photographs to it and then neglected to bring it back down to my shop here. It was upstairs on the kitchen table. When I exited my workshop, the professor was looking through the older books that were down here. As you see, I keep the photo albums of my designs on the counter," Goldman indicated, "for interested parties to leaf through. The professor started looking through the albums, then inquired if I had any more."

"How long were you gone, do you think … when you went upstairs to get the new album?"

"Ooooooh, ten minutes maybe. I asked my customer if he wanted a coffee, and he said no, but I grabbed a cup when I went upstairs to fetch the album. I also popped into the bathroom for a second, then returned back down here, with my coffee and the photo catalog. I didn't worry about anything being stolen. I never keep jewelry on display, only the pictures. And I've known the professor for a long time. He's a regular customer, and a good one."

Noticing the change that suddenly came over Joel's face, Aisling asked, "What is it? You look as though you just remembered something."

"Well, I happened to think that the professor's visit that last time wasn't his usual flying visit. He seemed to be lingering–" the jeweler stopped with an abrupt lift of his shoulders. "I can't be sure … maybe my imagination's running wild. Forget I even said that."

Aisling was recording everything in her notebook, and for some moments, neither she nor Goldman spoke. After she jotted down the final annotations, she queried, "Do you recall leaving the room when Mrs. Whitman was here?"

Joel tightened his mouth, pondering over the question for a long moment. "Y–yeah, I did leave the room for a short while, now that I think back on it. The Fed Ex man came with a package. When he rang the bell, I stepped outside for a few seconds to sign for it." His brown eyes widened, and he exclaimed, "When I turned around and re-entered my studio, she was standing over by my workbench. I asked if she was looking for something. She gave me that impression, and she answered that she walked over there to peer into the adjacent room, looking for a restroom. I showed her where it was, and she used the facility I have down here, while I finished the engraving. We then completed our transaction, and she left."

Aisling dashed off a few more bits of information, before slipping the notebook and pen back into her bag. The tête-à-tête ended, and the Sister rose to her feet. "Thank you, Mr. Goldman, you've been a *huge* help."

Once inside her vehicle, Aisling programmed Annabel Lee's address into her GPS. Since she'd completed her jeweler rounds, she had time to question the victim's neighbors to find out if anyone had seen or heard anything the night the professor's car was vandalized. Even though the police already spoke to the neighbors, the blonde with the wand strongly suspected that someone knew something they were not telling.

When she arrived at Annabel's house, the Sister immediately saw, at the residence next door, a woman's face peering from behind the curtain of an upstairs window. *Just what I'm looking for, a nosy neighbor. I'll start there,* she decided, switching off the engine.

With a plan of action, she walked briskly up the drive to the pillared porch, rang the doorbell and waited. Finally, she could hear the sound of approaching shoes on a hardwood floor, and the door opened just wide enough to reveal a petite elderly lady with white, pixie-short hair. The hair, though cropped ultra-short, was flattering to the well-shaped head and small face. Gold wedding-band earrings hugged the ears, and the eyes– a light shade of blue that bore a resemblance to glass– were frightened.

"Yes?" the voice sounded a bit frail, but nonetheless, the fear came through– loud and clear.

Aisling carefully explained who she was and why she wished to speak, in private, with the woman, whose features, for an instant, stiffened.

"Please," Aisling entreated with the ease of long practice, "may I come in? I promise not to keep you back from whatever you might have planned for today. This is very, very important."

To the Sister's amazement, the old lady quickly ushered her inside. "Yes, do come in. I'm *relieved* you're here."

In the living room, after introducing herself, Mrs. Peepers gestured for Aisling to have a seat on the couch, as she sat on the opposite end, facing her.

"I'm ashamed of myself," the elfin crone began without preface. "Ashamed for being so tongue-tied." She fidgeted some, twisting an old-fashioned hankie between nervous fingers before she spoke again. "I didn't tell the police what I saw. *I was afraid.* But, you see, we here on this cul-de-sac have an agreement that we watch out for one another, and I am *ashamed* that I let poor Annabel down, and now she's dead! I feel so bad about it all. The paper said she had a heart attack. It was probably from stress. Stress can kill, you know. My doctor told me that. Oooooh, I feel like I let Annabel down."

Ada Peepers daubed her tears with the handkerchief, shaking her head in sorrow. "I meant it when I said I'm relieved you're here. Normally, this is a safe neighborhood. We ... the residents, have this pact, and I broke it when I didn't tell the police what I saw," she repeated, as if desperate to receive absolution.

Aisling leaned forward to take the older woman's hand, answering in as gentle a tone as she could, "Don't beat yourself up over this. You can help Annabel *now* by giving her spirit closure–so she can rest in peace."

A rush of fresh tears kept Mrs. Peepers from responding immediately. "If *I* had a problem, I would want my neighbors to come forth to help me, so I have to do the same thing for any one of them. I was going to call the police, today in fact, to ask to speak again with that nice Chief Fitzpatrick; but affable as he is, I'd rather speak with you." She looked Aisling up and down. "The blonde one," she murmured to herself. "My, my, you're just like I thought you'd be! I know *all* about the Sleuth Sisters. How you get mixed up in one murder after another."

Aisling explained modestly that she and her cousins didn't actually get mixed up in murders, but that they aided the police in solving them.

Ada tittered. "Of course, my dear. I didn't mean that you *committed* any murders," she forged a quick smile, "but you're very good at them! Oh dear," she lamented, "that didn't come out right either, but you know what I mean. I've followed your careers, you see, for years; and well, it's easier for me to talk to one of you than to the police, since it's like I know you."

The diminutive woman's blue eyes got as big as saucers. "It's *disconcerting* talking to the police. And I didn't know if I'd be in some sort of trouble for not revealing to them what I saw in the first place. I was also afraid that the criminal would, perchance, see the police car out front of my house and come back and do me harm. After all, I am an old lady, living alone."

"I quite see your point of view," Aisling admitted with genuine sympathy. She pulled her constant notebook and pen from her bag.

"I've felt *so* alone since Arthur died," Ada grieved with sad eyes.

"Your husband?"

"No, my cat. My husband passed over years ago."

"Please, Mrs. Peepers, just relax. Take your time and tell me everything you saw and heard the night Annabel's car was vandalized. I promise nothing bad will happen to you," the blonde with the wand stated with conviction.

Wiping away another tear, Ada whispered in a confidential attitude, "Well, it's not that I am a *nosy* old woman, though there are those who might slap that label on me," she frowned. "I must admit, I do enjoy sitting at a window or on what I call my 'jeepers-creepers' side porch– some people around here call it 'Peepers' jeepers-creepers'– watching what goes on in the neighborhood. After all, at my age, what else is there to do? I usually take my husband's World-War II field glasses with me, and–" she stopped short, noting how the Sister's brows had shot upward. "That's not illegal, is it?"

Aisling merely smiled, patiently hoping Mrs. Peepers would get to the point. She knew the elderly were given to a great deal of rambling conversation, hence she decided to give the old lady a few moments.

"At my age," Ada said, after a bit more prattling, "you have to get up several times a night to visit the bathroom. So, long about 2:45 in the morning– I remember glancing over at the lighted alarm clock on my nightstand– the night Annabel's car was spoilt, I thought I heard something outside. My toilet sits right in front of the bathroom window, which, of course, I keep shuttered and curtained. What I'm saying is, I was on the toilet, and that's another reason I hated conversing with the police," she said primly. The old woman made an almost humorous face. "No delicate way to word that; now is there?"

When Aisling didn't respond, Ada went on, the last shred of reticence leaving her, as she plunged into full recital. "I opened the curtain a tiny bit and lifted one of the shutter's louvres to peer out. I saw a solitary figure wearing all black. Even a black ski mask covered the head. I couldn't tell, to be honest, if it was a man or a woman. Well, not a hundred percent anyway; but I'll tell you this– whoever it was, was young and spry.

"I have a nightlight that burns all the time in the center of the bathroom, so I don't trip over anything when I get up during the night. The fact that I didn't turn on a light– you know what I'm saying, a *bright* light– meant that I could see what was going on outside, and whoever was out there couldn't see me.

"Anyway, I could see *clearly*," Mrs. Peepers emphasized, "that the person was holding a package. It looked like a package of flour or sugar from the grocery store. The culprit opened Annabel's gas tank and dumped the entire contents into it. Annabel drove an older car, so a criminal could do that … get into the gas tank, you understand."

Aisling lifted a hand to signal her eyewitness to halt in the account. "Was there only one person involved, or did you see more than one?"

"All I saw was that *one* lone figure, like I told you, dressed all in black."

"Short or tall, slender or stout? Tell me whatever you can remember?"

Ada Peepers tilted her head with its cap of short, feathered white hair. "I would say medium height, chubby … hmmm, more than a little on the chunky side. *Youthful* though, with movements that led me to believe that the *perpetrator*– that's the word, isn't?" Before Aisling could respond, Ada declared, "I read mystery novels, so I think that's the correct word. As I was saying, the movements led me to believe that the perp– that's the police word for it– was youthful, which didn't remotely surprise me." Ada made a grimace. "You know what these kids are nowadays! I'm constantly reading in the newspaper what one or the other of them has done to get themselves in Dutch with the police. But to get back to what I was saying: The movements also led me to believe the culprit was a female rather than a male. The way it moved about …" Ada pursed her lips, "oh yes, my deduction– *and I'm pretty observant*– is that it was a female."

Aisling made an encouraging sound, and Mrs. Peepers talked on.

"Once the person emptied the contents of the package into Annabel's gas tank, she–" Ada paused with another tilt of head. "I guess, since we're not absolutely sure of the perp's sex, I should say she **or** he *ran* off; and a moment later, I heard a car door out front, in front of *my* house, not Annabel's. So I went, fast as my old legs could take me, the short distance across the hall to the front bedroom; and when I looked out, I saw the person driving away in a white sportscar. One of the taillights was burned out, and I saw the license plate, clear as day, under the Victorian lamppost I have out front. Usually, I would not remember a license plate, but I remember *this one* because it was one of those kind that people order special. It was a name. I mean, I *think* it was a name."

Aisling came alive, yanking the pen from behind her ear and looking up from her notes to lock eyes with the witness. "Do tell!"

Ada Peepers obliged without hesitation, sending the name Aisling anticipated to echo through the Sister's core with goading purpose.

***

During the time Aisling was conducting her interviews, Raine and Maggie were doing some sleuthing of *their* own at the Hamlet's Addison McKenzie Library. They each had to reschedule their two afternoon classes, due to the fact that so many of the student population were suffering from a stomach virus.

"Don't take this the wrong way," Raine said, slipping on her reading glasses, "but rescheduling our afternoon classes to the end of next week is a *boon* for us. Gives us time to gather the info we need before we meet tonight with Aisling."

"I just hope *we* don't catch that damn bug," Maggie huffed, drawing from her bag her own reading glasses. "It's short-lived but virulent."

"We won't catch it," Raine stated with conviction. "No way will that virus get past Granny's energizing elderberry elixir!"

Maggie laughed. "Of course you're right, darlin'. Powerful stuff, Granny's elderberry brew."

On a library table before them, they spread various yearbooks, both grade school and high school annuals, from which they were pulling names.

"This is a good idea, Mags, but it could take us several days to navigate through all these names in order to hit on just the right one. What we need is a miracle." Raine scrawled another entry in her notebook, pausing when someone placed a hand on her shoulder to peer over her at an open Haleigh High yearbook.

"Oh my God! That's me," the woman indicated with pointer finger. "Would you look at that hair! Big Hair they used to call it."

Raine and Maggie looked up from what they were about and into the face of the lady who ran the Biblio Bistro, the library café. "Hi, Jo."

Raine looked to Maggie, then asked Jo Nosh straight up, "So you were in Haleigh High's Class of 1989?"

The Goth gal attempted to keep her tone as flat as possible, as her excitement grew. The Sisters knew Jo, knew they could count on her for facts and not gossip, and the witchy feeling that was mounting was that they just might have bumped into their miracle.

"We've been doing some reminiscing, time-travel via old yearbooks. You know how it is. You start leafing through one, and before you know it, you're hooked. Yearbooks are like peanuts or potato chips, you can't consume just one," Maggie joked.

"Do you have a few minutes?" Raine requested with a gesture toward an empty chair. "Won't you join us in our sentimental journey?"

"Sure. I just closed the café for today, so I'm free to chat for a bit."

The Sisters exchanged thoughts, with Maggie asking Jo, as casually as she could, whilst she indicated two of the yearbook's black-and-white senior photographs, "What were these two fellows like in high school?"

Jo settled into a seat across the table from the Sisters. "Pretty much the same as they are today, I'd say."

A salt-and-pepper, fresh-faced brunette, Nosh was not really a pretty woman. Rather, she was the type that, if properly made-up and coiffed *could* be pretty. Robust and sturdy, Jo Nosh, who used no cosmetics or artificial aids to youth, was what Granny McDonough might have called "hale and hearty."

Raine pointed to one of the yearbook photos, asking if Nosh knew that particular former classmate well.

Having followed the Sister's ebony fingernail along the glossy page, Jo responded with zeal, "I'll say I did! We grew up right next door to one another, and we were nearly inseparable during our school years, from grade school through high school." Nosh paused, considered a moment, then clarified, "We were never more than friends, but we were *good* friends– *confidants*. We told each other everything. I remember he worried about how he was going to afford college. He had to secure a *full* scholarship to make it happen." She stopped talking for a few seconds, privately reminiscing. "Dredging up the past like this, brings to mind my telling him that we should both stop worrying, especially about what people thought of us. We knew the truth about who we were, and that was all that mattered."

Again, the woman broke off, letting her thoughts carry her back in time, as a far-away expression passed over her face. "See, I was a tomboy, and we both took a lot of taunting for being such close friends. The same a-holes teased other kids in our class too. That sort of thing will either make you or break you. It made me stronger

... molded me into the person I am today." She lifted her shoulders and pursed her mouth. "I'm sure it did the same for him. He's realized his dreams.

"Anyway, back then, all I cared about was sports. Even though my kindred spirit and I shared several common denominators," she deliberated for a few seconds, groping for the right words, "he, um ... he– You know what? I'm not comfortable talking behind his back." Nosh knitted her brow, "Times have changed ... to some degree, but," the café owner stopped, adding after a beat, "ah, the more things change, the more they remain the same." Her brow cleared, and she gave a somewhat sad little smile, a crabbed smile that was difficult even for the Sisters to read. "I don't want to say anymore. He had his ways ... but hey, don't we all?

"Bottom line," Jo went on, "we gravitated toward one another, hung out together, were real pals, all through school. After graduation, my best friend went on to college, and I started working at the glass factory over in Pleasantville. We drifted apart, but I still consider him a friend." Jo's face suddenly morphed into something the Sisters had never before seen on this usually amiable woman. "I've waited a long time to see the people who tormented us in high school get what's coming to them, and something tells me that time is fast approaching."

Whoa! Might we end up with a collusion here? Of perhaps two or more people in a complicity? Maggie zipped to her Sister of the moon, causing Raine to burst out with–

"Why do you say that? That you think your teen tormentors will soon be getting what they deserve?"

"Because," Jo replied with an unreadable shrug, "everyone eventually gets what they deserve, don't you think? The bullies have kids of their own–" she let the rest of the sentence go unfinished, outwardly befuddled before she completed her thought, "college age b' now. See how they like it when someone hurts their kids! It's *going* to happen."

"You seem *sure* of that," Raine blurted, though she kept her voice low and level.

"Of course I am," Jo answered. "That's the way life is. What goes around comes around."

Seems like she's kept track of the bullies through the years, Maggie whipped to Raine, *but surely Jo's not the type to seek revenge!*

*We both know that revenge is a **powerful** motivator. Let's keep her talking*, Raine whooshed to Maggie.

The Sisters continued their conversation with Nosh for several minutes, surer now than ever that they'd chanced upon their miracle.

"Jo," Maggie said finally, leaning forward toward the older woman and lowering her voice to a confidential level, "we," she jerked her head toward Raine, "the Sleuth Sisters, could use your help. Your old friend might be in trouble. At this point, we're not really sure, but we are asking you to help us to help him."

Jo's dark eyes were round with dismay. "He did look as though he had something pressing on his mind when I saw him last week. It was … an *angry* look. Ah, maybe it's just that time of year at the college when he feels more pressure. You guys teach at Haleigh. You know what I mean."

Raine stole a quick glance at Maggie, who, regarding Jo with a raised brow, asked–

"I thought you said you hadn't seen your old pal in years?"

The befuddled expression returned to Jo's face. "I-I didn't say that. I said after high school, we went in different directions, to make our way in life. You said my friend was in trouble. What sort of trouble?"

"We're not at liberty to discuss an ongoing investigation, but let me ask you this," Raine queried flatly. "Do you trust us?"

Nosh didn't have to ponder the question put to her. "I do," she yielded with a brisk nod.

"Then *please* help us to help …" Maggie whispered the name, glancing furtively around to see if anyone else had come into the library's Pennsylvania Room. No one had. They were alone.

"What do you want to know?" the café owner acquiesced, her face reflecting her willingness to cooperate.

"Tell us everything you can," Raine tapped one of the yearbook photos with a bejeweled finger, "about your old friend's childhood and high-school years; and then, we beseech you in all earnestness, please keep this interview between us. As you might suspect, we don't want any of this to get out."

Over an hour later, when Raine and Maggie settled into Maggie's Land Rover, that the former had parked behind the library, the Goth gal heaved a huge sigh of satisfaction. "We were right, Mags, right about everything."

"It would certainly appear so. At risk of seeming dogmatic: shorn of verbiage, the facts are simple. Well, all truth is simple." The redheaded Sister took out her lipstick to glide the glossy crimson color over her full lips. "Now where?"

"The ex-wife's?"

Maggie checked her watch. "I wonder if we'd be lucky enough to catch her at home? She and her husband reside in Ligonier. If we leave the Hamlet now, we might be intruding on their dinner hour, but it would be good to pop in on her, without giving her a chance to really think about what to tell us."

"Right," Raine said, turning on the vintage's car's ignition. "We want unrehearsed responses; that's for sure. As for being lucky– why, this is our lucky day!"

"To be a witch is to know the ways of the Olde."
~ Granny McDonough

Chapter Ten

"Aisling," Raine exclaimed into her smart phone, "you won't believe the clues Mags and I gleaned today! I can't wait till we meet tonight, so we can fill you in."

"I reaped some pretty hot leads today too. In fact, I just got off the phone with the chief. I wanted to report what I uncovered straightaway. I advise you to do the same."

"Will do. We're in the Rover, en route home from Ligonier," Raine informed. "We were just about to phone Fitz with our latest findings."

"Make that priority. What time do we meet tonight to attend Professor Lee's candlelight service?" Before the Goth gal could respond, Aisling answered her own question. "Shall we say right after supper? Ian, Merry, and I are just finishing up. An hour or there about?"

"We're famished. No time to eat since this morning. Give us a chance to stop for a quick sandwich, and we'll meet you at Tara in roughly an hour. We'll drive over to the campus for the service in one car, after which we'll return to Tara to compare notes on today's discoveries, then craft a needed session with Athena."

"Sounds good," the blonde with the wand replied. "See you then."

Raine glanced over at Maggie, "Sal-San-Tries?"

When Raine and Maggie entered the café-deli, the first thing they noticed was the Terrible Three, who were seated at a table toward the front. Seeing the two professors, the wayward girls immediately put their heads together to whisper and snicker in a most offensive manner. Liza, especially, stared at the McDonoughs with a barefaced defiant regard that was downright despicable.

Raine and Maggie totally ignored them. At the fore of the café, they looked over the specials on the chalkboard near the entrance, their gaze lifting to the mirror above the counter when the phrase "Snoop Sisters" skated to their sharp ears, subsequent to which the Sisters quickly swapped a thought.

A loud burst of boorish laughter followed another whispered exchange betwixt the errant students, whereupon Maggie and Raine completed their order and made their way to the back, warily passing the girls' table en route.

When the buxom, redheaded Sylvia leaned over to pour another wisecrack into Liza's ear, her arm bumped a tall glass of ice water, spilling it into her lap.

"Oh!" she jumped, mostly from the shock of the frosty deluge. "Ooooh, look at me! I'm soaked!"

Maggie's eyes shifted to Raine, who, with innocent expression, was ostensibly studying her ebony fingernails.

Concurrently and in high-speed chain reaction, Sylvia's sudden shriek gave Tiffany– who was about to salt her fries– a start, resulting in another "mishap." Unbeknownst to the petite brunette, the shaker's lid was loose; thus, nearly the entire contents "Rained" onto the startled girl's plate of food.

At nearly the same time, Sophie's waitress, holding high a tray with the day's special– a footlong loaded with the works and a double-chocolate milkshake– was passing by the troublemakers' table to attend the only other patron in the place, a middle-aged salesman reading a newspaper. The server's foot slipped on the salad dressing Liza purposely spilled on the floor after the Sleuth Sisters had come in. Losing her balance, though *phenomenally* managing not to fall, she dumped the entire order over Liza Berk's frizzy blonde head.

With an angry scream, the obnoxious girl loudly vented her anger on the poor waitress. "Look what you've done, you idiot! Do you know how much this sweater cost? You're going to pay for a replacement, because *no way* will this mustard– this *mess*– come out of my white cashmere!"

Raine and Maggie stood, uttering sharp exclamations of irritation. "Oh no, she's not! You're lucky she didn't fall and injure herself."

"We saw you deliberately spill that oil onto the floor," the Goth gal stated firmly.

By this time, Sophie, the pony-tailed, calico-aproned café owner, was out of the kitchen and approaching the girls' table, with a look stamped on her normally pleasant face that let the others know she meant business. Fixing her bright blue eyes on the ringleader, she said, hands on hips, "Never mind about paying your bill. Get out, and I never want to see any of you in here again. This isn't the first time you've caused me trouble, but it *will* be the last. **Now get!**" she yelled, flinging her arm out in the direction of the door. "*Quickly and quietly*, or I call the police, and me and the Sleuth Sisters inform the chief what we know. **Out!**"

Sophie's quick-witted warning appeared to have struck a nerve, for the guilty faces went ghost-white. Without another word, the girls rose and exited the café, just as a group of college boys were coming in.

"Yuck!" the guys remarked, their eyes on a suddenly red-faced Liza, as they burst into whoops of derisive laughter:

"You're supposed to eat it not wear it."

"Maybe she missed that big mouth of hers."

"No chance of that."

"Hey, maybe that's Berk's idea of take-out!"

"Hahahahahahahahahaha!"

***

At Tara, whilst Maggie prepared their crystal ball, Raine and Aisling traded information and opinions on their day's findings.

The Sisters had just returned from the campus candlelight service for Professor Lee, where they learned that Dean Savant decided not to cancel the remainder of the Valentine Fest as per the request of Annabel's family.

"It was a beautiful service," Maggie said, swiping a tear from her eye.

"Yes, I could *feel* Annabel's sweet spirit there with us," Raine replied.

"Take heart, Sisters, we'll give her spirit peace," Aisling avowed. "Did you pay special attention to the faces I asked you to watch?"

"We did," Raine and Maggie answered.

"I believe we're all of the same opinion. After what I uncovered today, together with what you and Maggie collected from Jo Nosh and from our top suspect's ex, there's not one shred of doubt now that we're on the right track," Aisling concluded, sitting back in her chair. "At this point, we can't be a hundred percent certain, but, as I said, we're definitely on the right track."

"I feel sure Athena will help us. What do we ask our oracle this night?" Raine put to the senior sister of the moon.

Aisling waded through what they already knew, answering, "We simply ask her to show us what she wishes to reveal at this stage in our investigation."

"I think we should be more specific," Maggie voiced softly, setting the huge, amethyst crystal ball in its stand on the table they used for their scrying sessions. "I have crafted a chant."

Attired in their long, black ritual robes, the Sisters three were in Tara's attic. As always when magick was afoot, the Merlin cats– Black Jade and Black Jack O'Lantern and Panthèra– accompanied them. The two other cats– Tiger, the distinctly marked brown tabby, and Madame Woo, the seal-point applehead Siamese– were exactly the opposite. Winters, they preferred Tara's warm radiators or one of the comfy, sun-splashed window seats to spellcasting.

Raine scooped up Black Jack to walk the circumference of the attic room with her deosil, clockwise; whilst Maggie went, with lighted lantern, to the wooden bookstand that bore their ultra-thick *Book of Shadows.*

The huge tome's black leather cover was embossed in gold gilt with full-blown Triquetra, the ancient Celtic knot symbolizing all trinities– *and infinite power.* Above it, from a thick oak beam jutted a hook; and that's where Maggie hung the lantern, splashing the colorful, hodgepodge room with the soft glow of light and the mystery of shadow.

Supporting their granny's grimoire and occupying a place of honor before three grand stained-glass windows, the vintage bookstand had been prized by Granny McDonough because it was the lectern used by the celebrated orator William Jennings Bryan when, at the turn of the last century, he delivered an eloquent speech at the Hamlet's Addison McKenzie Library. By accident of fate, the reading stand was crafted of the same dark wood as all of Tara's woodwork and finished with the same soft gleam.

A former maid's quarters, Tara's attic was eclipsed by its trilogy of stained-glass windows, the tall center one the largest, displaying the symbol and soul of Ireland– a golden harp. The two smaller, flanking, stained-glass windows each depicted a bright-green shamrock, another symbol of Ireland, and one of the supreme Trinity.

There were two stairways, the "front" and the "back" (the back being the "servants' stairs"), leading to the attic, the Sisters' sacred ritual room that they referred to as the "Heavens." It seemed a fitting name since it was the place where they did most of their spellcasting, weaving powerful magick; and it was here they conjured their dear granny. Tonight, however, they would be conducting another ritual– the ancient ritual of scrying.

"Which," Raine was explicating to her sisters of the moon, "the dictionary describes as divination of distant or future events based on visions in a ball of rock crystal. Scrying comes from the Old English word *descry* meaning 'to reveal,'" she finished. "Looked it up for the fun of it, you know, to see how muggles regarded crystal gazing."

The spacious attic's furniture was a collection of odds and ends, touched by Time and not fitting enough for the rest of the manse, but too steeped in memories to cast away. Granny and Grandpa McDonough had purchased a few of what became the attic's keepsakes during the "Grand Tour" of their European honeymoon, such as a green velvet couch and two– now somewhat lumpy but still handsome– easy chairs in a claret shade of a fabric from *Belle Époque* Paris.

An antique spinning wheel stood in one corner of the attic, the wheel of which had a female ghost attached to it. The apparition was a crone named Nancy Hart, who was born when Thomas Jefferson was President of the United States. A much later owner gifted The McDonough with the wheel when Granny healed the woman of a most virulent winter fever. Every once in a while, Maggie or Raine got a flash of the original owner, old Nancy, at the spinning wheel before her hearth; and sitting next to her, her black cat, staring drowsily into the flames.

In another corner of the attic was a stack of curious old hat boxes, a couple from Edwardian London that held cunning little hats with black nylon netting that dropped down over the upper half of the face. Maggie, especially, enjoyed sporting these witchy chapeaux for the added mystery their veils afforded.

Atop two cabriole end tables rested a pair of porcelain lamps. Chipped from years of use, the glowing lamps' bases depicted romantic scenes of eighteenth-century lovers engaged in a waltz. Once, after a particularly strong conjuring session, Raine reported to Maggie that she'd actually seen *and heard* the dancing couples swirling in a spin-two-three Viennese waltz.

On each end of the attic room, two domed trunks occupied places under the eaves; whilst the center of the scarred-wood floor was enhanced by a worn, though still valuable, French carpet, its floral design faded by Time, sun, and the treading of countless feet. There was a soft sheen about that once-luxurious rug that glinted in the mellow attic light and whispered *silk*– along with a myriad of remembrances.

Whenever they meditatively regarded the attic carpet, Raine and Maggie could hear Granny's musical brogue: "So manny waltzin' feet have tripped th' light fantastic over this rug! Sure 'n it holds so many magickal memories an' energies, I cannot bear to part with it, even if it's as old as the hills."

One piece of furniture in Tara's Heavens was not chipped, faded, worn or shabby, though it was most certainly old.

This was the tall cheval glass that accompanied Aisling Tully McDonough, "Granny" as the Sisters called her, on her fateful journey from Ireland to America. The antique mirror was likely worth a fortune, so ornate was it in carved giltwood with Irish symbols and heroes from the Emerald Isle's turbulent past. Bestowed on her by a doting uncle when she was just a slip of a girl, it had been Granny's most cherished keepsake from the Old Country.

The Sisters wanted to preserve as much of Granny's essence in that memento as possible; and so, they kept it draped, when not in use, in their sacred attic space with a protective ghostly sheet. Hence, no one else ever handled and confused the energies of this treasured family heirloom.

On one side of the mirror hung Granny's Irish knit shawl; from the opposite side dangled a favorite necklace, a long, thick rope of pure silver from which hung two round, silver Gypsy bells. Granny had purchased the charmed necklace as a lass in Ireland, "… from an especially talented tinker." She joyfully declared that the bells' delightful tinkling soothed away her troubles and brought to mind the shell chimes she remembered hanging in the windows of the Old Sod's seaside cottages. In a spider-web design, the black-as-jet shawl sparkled with dozens of tiny aurora borealis crystals. Granny's widow's weeds had enfolded style, as well as a great deal of magick.

Raine abidingly made it a point to choose something of Granny's to hold in her hand from a small treasure box of things that rested on one of the cabriole tables. This evening, 'twas a brooch fashioned in a circle of colorful gemstones. As was her custom, she stood for a few quiet moments at the tranquil trilogy of stained-glass windows, peering out, through the clear portions, at the glittering, nighttime, faerie-tale Hamlet below. In a mysterious way did a mist oft hover over the beautiful but contrary Youghiogheny River.

To center herself, the Sister drew a deep breath, letting it out with measured release. The sight of the curving ribbon of river never failed to relax her, freeing her mind of unwanted thoughts and anxieties. Now, she could see a few small boats on the light-splashed water. Once in a while she would hear the lonely, nostalgic sound of a horn from one of the boats, as it navigated the fog pockets. In the fog, sounds carried a long distance, seeming ofttimes to echo. It was a beguiling thing, that. Sometimes, Raine even imagined she heard voices in that misty fog.

Perhaps she did.

The Goth gal remained, staring through the clear segments of stained-glass at the night. The virtually dark attic room allowed her to see that thick clouds scudded past, obscuring the moon. The snow was falling more heavily now, crafting everything in shadow. For a long moment, she seemed to be gazing *through* the shadows into somewhere far off and strange– or not so strange. Her bosom rose and fell, and her lips parted. Caught in a sudden rift of wind, the snow made a soft, spitting sound on the windowpane; and on the river, a boat signaled its lonely cry. The swish brought her out of reverie, stirring her to the tasks at hand.

After having set their poppet, Cara, down on the chair where she would be sitting, Maggie used her wand to draw a second circle of protection around the attic room, calling upon the God-Goddess; the spirits of the four elements, the guardians of the watchtowers; as well as their angel and spirit guides, to secure their sacred space.

Aisling was busying herself with the lighting of four white, beeswax candles, whilst Raine touched her lighter to a frankincense-and-myrrh incense cone that she set in a brass burner. With the aid of a large, purple feather, she fanned the smoke, allowing the aromatic fragrances to permeate the entire area before placing the activated cone on a stand.

Successively, Maggie lit three small bundles of white sage, each in a big, fan-shaped seashell; after which, she handed them to her sisters of the moon, keeping one for herself. Carrying the smoking sage in a clockwise motion, the Sisters cleansed the room of negativity, all the while chanting a smudging mantra.

"Negativity that invades our sacred place, we banish you with the light of our grace. You have no hold or power here. We stand and face you with no fear. Be you gone forever, for now we say– this is *our* sacred space, and you will obey!"

"Together we cleanse," Aisling advised, activating another chant. "We cleanse this area completely free of any and all negativity!"

The Sisters began walking deosil, chanting and cleansing in perfect accord, as Tara's attic room took on the pleasing mingled aromas of burning white sage, candle wax, and frank and myrrh.

At that, Maggie swished across the attic room, her black robe fluttering behind her, to switch off the lantern hanging above their lectern-held *Book of Shadows*. Before she did, however, she opened the grimoire and thumbed through it to check the ribboned page a final time.

Having properly smudged their sacred space, the witches seated themselves about a small round table from which they temporarily relocated a Himalayan salt lamp in the black metal design of sun, moon and stars, the salt chunks bathed with a relaxing amber glow. The lit lamp, now the attic's only illumination, rested on a trunk positioned behind the colossal, amethyst crystal ball that, decades before, their Great-Aunt Merry of Salem had christened "Athena."

"We must always address our crystal oracle by her name," Maggie reminded. "Raine and I gave Athena a nice cleansing just before you got here," she told Aisling. "As per Grantie Merry's instructions, we bathed her with a soft cloth in tepid water and a mild, good-smelling dishwashing soap."

"Perfect," Aisling replied. "We must keep her physically clean. It will cleanse her energies as well." The senior Sister placed her hands lovingly on each side of the ball, whilst she spoke quietly. "Before we program Athena today, we'll also have to smudge *her* with white sage. Remember, we'll need to smudge her, *before* and *after, each* session, so no negative energies will ever do her *or us* any harm."

Once they'd smudged Athena, Aisling, the firstborn Sister, again took the initiative. "As in the past, you lead us, Maggie. *You* had the vision that time of Grantie and Granny handing *you* Athena, and you're the most gifted with a crystal ball. Have you and Raine read over Grantie Merry's instructions, that you transferred to our *Book of Shadows*, so we can be certain of hitting all the steps?"

Raine and Maggie answered concurrently, "We have, Sister."

"All right then. As before, let's begin by making physical contact with Athena," Aisling directed. "Stroking the ball, before using it, energizes the crystal and strengthens our psychic bond with our oracle. We need to do this now– *together*."

For several moments, simultaneously, the Sisters caressed the amethyst crystal ball, gently passing their hands over the cool, smooth– and quite lovely– purple surface. Athena was so large, this action was effortlessly accomplished, as Maggie hummed: "Our crystal Athena, eye of the Fates, part the veil and the Otherworld gates. Bless our vision to awaken threefold, past, present, or future for us to behold."

Balancing their poppet Cara on her lap, Maggie reached into the pocket of her ritual robe for the Lemuria oil she'd put there earlier. At a signal from Aisling, she dabbed a touch of the oil on the third-eye area of her forehead, passing the ampoule round to Aisling and Raine.

The redheaded Sister, thenceforth, began a breathing pattern, allowing all the stress and negative energies to flow completely out of her body as she exhaled. During the meditation, her two sisters of the moon followed suit, breathing deeply, each at her own rhythm: *Healing energies in ... negative energies out. Healing energies in ... negative energies out ...*

"Healing energies in ... negative energies out," Cara echoed in her wee voice.

There was a silence as the magickal three, with their poppet, applied themselves to the task. It was at this juncture of the ritual when Raine, especially, began to feel eager. Quickly, she did her utmost to tame her ardor. It would *not* do to be expectant, not for crystal-ball scrying.

After several minutes, Maggie opened her eyes to fix them on a section of the ball that expressly drew her. "Focus," she pronounced in her silky voice, "focus on an area of Athena's crystal depths that tugs at each of you."

Several quiet, peaceful moments lapsed, after which Maggie began to chant softly, "Athena, as we go into a trance/ Bestow on us the magick glance/ Take us back in time today/ Reveal what happened come what may/ Back in time less 'n a fortnight chime/ To Jeweler Goldman's in-home shop/ To witness the cyanide a killer did cop/ Then take us back to the Valentine tea; the image at Haleigh for us to see/ Who darted with cyanide the chocolate heart; for this we need afore we part/ For deep, dark secrets to be unlocked/ Within the hours of the clock/ That you have chosen for us to learn/ *The facts!/* For *that*, we now return!"

As the colossal crystal ball's powerful energy commenced to flow, the seated, black-robed Sisters imaged their vibratory levels rising to harmonize with the antique sphere, henceforth to craft their needed psychic link.

*The magick was working! All three witches could **feel** Athena's super power coursing around them and through them like an electric shock.*

Within mere seconds, each of the Sisters began to experience a tingling sensation. As in previous sessions with their crystal oracle, a swift surge of heat flared through Maggie and Aisling, whilst a cool wave broke over Raine. The Sisters were adjusting to the ball's vibration– each in her own way.

"Expectation is *not* helpful," Maggie reminded softly, keeping within the trance. "We know from experience, we must clear away any and all expectancies. We will see what Athena wants us to see, nothing more, nothing less."

Thrice Maggie chanted their petition. When she'd repeated for the third time the line " … deep, dark secrets to be unlocked," Aisling could not help but think– *sinister secrets.*

"Let us allow our minds to become as clear as the crystal. *Relax* … and look into the ball's mysterious crystal cavern. Hold your regards, Sisters– *entranced.*"

Cara melodiously caught at the word: "*En—tranced.*"

"Grantie counseled that sometimes making connection with Athena takes what seems like eons, other times not. We *know* we can do this. We've *done* it. Yes, we …"

"Shall see what we shall see," the poppet, swaying rhythmically from side to side, crooned from her position on Maggie's lap, blending her reedy little voice with the Sister's low melodious intonation.

Keeping their gazes on the ball, not blinking an eye or moving an inch, the Sisters smiled inwardly as, within a few heartbeats and the big crystal ball's mystical amethyst depths, a ghostly mist was appearing.

"Our connection with Athena has been made," Maggie drawled softly. "The door is opening. Keep your focus. Let Athena's mists draw us in. That's it," she droned. "*Good.*"

"*Ver-ry, ver-ry good*," Cara warbled quietly.

Inside the amethyst ball, the ethereal mist swirled, slowly at first, then faster, then slowly again, before the crystal began to clear.

"Hmmmm," Maggie hummed serenely, "now we drift. Light as feathers, let us float inside Athena's crystal cave ... for like Merlin's, it will show only Truth."

"Carry us away," Cara piped in. "Away... *a–way.*"

"Soon now, the light and sound images, indestructible and eternal to the universe, will reveal to us what we seek–"

"At what Athena lets us peek," chimed the poppet.

"*Whatever* will be..." Maggie whispered.

"Whativer we see ..." Cara interjected, intercepting the redheaded Sister's next words.

"Remain calm," Maggie finished her thought, "*calm,* so not to break the trance with emotions."

As the mists cleared, Maggie, careful not to raise her voice, cautioned softly, "We might see and hear what we do not anticipate. Often, this is so, but Athena knows best what we need to know," she rhymed smoothly.

"A spell in rhyme wor–rks every time," Cara trilled.

"Yes ... ye–s." Maggie's full lips were open slightly, as she sighed softly. "Do not try and make sense of anything till everything has faded away, for attempting to sort out will only break our spell and our bond with Athena today.

"Simply *allow* the scenes, one into the next, to flow. *Calm and centered as we go.* That's it, Sisters, keep feelings at bay. When the magickal movie ends, everything will fade and slip away." Maggie drew a fresh breath, freeing it as she kept her focus and her gaze.

Her fellow sisters of the moon and their poppet did likewise. They were discovering that each session with Athena was easier than the last. Within the Sisters' sacred circle of protection, even the Merlin cats appeared wholly sedate, sitting in purring contentment with half-closed eyes, sending out, each of them, what Raine referred to as their comforting Number-Three Purrrrr.

Meanwhile, out of the evaporating mists inside the crystal ball, emerged a nighttime image of Haleigh College. Two people, a young man and a girl, were strolling, hand-in-hand, across the snowy, starry campus. Of a sudden, the image showed, secreted in a nearby grove of trees, a man poised with a bow, making ready to loose the arrow. Though the face was in partial shadow, *there was no doubt who the archer was.*

All three Sisters struggled to control a rising excitement, for they had not even asked Athena to show them this scene, since the unveiled clues and their inquiries ultimately pointed *to* this person. But it was good to have their suspicions verified by their crystal oracle, and they were grateful. Hoping the magickal movie had not ended, they reined in their emotions, as the huge amethyst ball filled anew with its smoky mists.

In a flurry, another image began taking shape inside the crystal; and again, what they were viewing was a campus scene. This time, they were looking at Professor Hass, bending forward to slide an armful of books onto the passenger seat of her car. Behind her, in the shadowy lair of trees adjacent to the college library's parking lot, they saw, once more, the poised-in-readiness outline of an archer. The drawn-out thunnnnnnnnnnnk of the arrow being released reached their ears; then they glimpsed a flash of the bowman's pleased expression, his mouth curled in a sardonic smile.

As Athena's swirling grey mists effaced the scene in her crystal depths, Maggie's soft voice helped keep the Sisters centered and focused. "*Relax*. Athena will show us what she wants us to know, nothing more, nothing less."

"Re–lax," parroted the poppet. "There be more … *more* ..."

Sure as death and taxes, another image was taking form within the ball. Slower to manifest this time, but emerging clearer and clearer, arose the image of Jeweler Goldman's workshop, though Joel Goldman was absent from the scene. At the counter, upon which rested an open photo album, stood their top suspect.

Moving quickly, before the Sisters' watching eyes, the man made a dash for the workbench, there to snatch up the bottle of potassium cyanide, its label marked with skull over crossbones and the single word– *Danger*. Slipping the container into the inner pocket of the jacket he was wearing, the "person of interest" nipped back to the customer side of the counter, where he again busied himself with the album.

Raine could not believe how calm she was, though the soothing sound of Maggie's voice helped. She stole a quick, sidelong glance at Aisling's profile to see that she, too, appeared tranquil.

The familiar grey mists returned to wipe out the image, as almost immediately yet another scene began taking shape.

"Be still and focused," Maggie was saying, "there may be more to see… we shall see …"

"What we shall see," Cara chorused in time with the redheaded Sister.

Straightaway then, they recognized the Valentine-festive interior of the Student Union hall– the tables with their white cloths and red runners; the poster-sized, vintage Valentines, interspersed with hearts and cupids, adorning the walls. The spacious room was empty, but the Sisters could hear voices, snippets of chatter and laugher, coming from what they knew was the kitchen, for they could also hear the sounds of pots and pans, the clink of glassware and dishes.

"Steady on now," Maggie whispered, "and keep your eyes on Athena."

"Steady on," Cara harmonized.

Within the crystal, the Sisters were given a view of the Student Union's doorway, where, once more, they spotted their top suspect– *waiting*. In a blink of an eye, the killer ducked into the hall, located Professor Annabel Lee's name card and, pulling a loaded hypodermic needle from a jacket pocket, promptly injected, through the gauze bag, the chocolate heart truffle with the deadly poison.

Before the Sisters could let out their held-in breaths, the vision was gone, expunged by Athena's effacing grey mists, to leave the ball crystal clear. The Sisters knew now, for certain, that Athena's magickal movie had ended.

After they properly completed their scrying ritual, cleansed their crystal oracle, and thanked and released the conjured entities, the Sisters opened their circle, then slipped out of their ritual robes.

It was at this instant when Aisling said, "We are grateful, because we know we were right, *that we're on the right track*; **but** we also know we can't use any of this in a court of law. We need *hard* evidence. We've got to produce rock-hard, concrete evidence."

"And we shall!" Raine answered with her usual vim and vigor.

When Aisling took her leave, the Goth gal collapsed against Tara's closed front door to announce to Maggie, "OK, here's what I'm going to do, and you're going to help me– you and Black Jack."

"Cats possess numerous charms,
and anyone who has ever loved a cat has fallen for its magick."
~ Granny McDonough

Chapter Eleven

Maggie, Raine, and Black Jack, in his human persona of "Sean," were seated in Maggie's Land Rover, with Maggie behind the wheel. It was after nine the same evening the Sisters had scryed with Athena.

"I hate car rides," Jack, aka Sean, hissed. "Always have, always will. I can't help but associate a car ride with the panic attack of a veterinary visit."

Raine gave a huff. "I assure you we're not going to the vet's. And for the life of me, I can't imagine why you let visits to Beau stress you out."

"White-coat syndrome," Jack muttered. "Beau isn't Beau in that place, he's Dr. Goodwin. Big difference when he's–"

"Pull over there," Raine ordered, cutting in and leaning forward to point from the backseat. "I don't want our top suspect to come home and find this car in his driveway. Jack and I will tramp through those trees to come out in his backyard. You stay here, and if you see our person of interest coming home, you ring me *straightaway* on my burn phone. You've got the number."

"I do, but I wish you'd told Aisling what you're up to," the redheaded Sister said with trepidation.

"No way would I have done that!" Raine replied, unbuckling her seat belt. "She would've tried her damndest to talk me out of it; and besides, just *knowing* what I'm about to do could jeopardize her detective's license."

The raven-haired Sister bounded out of the car, which Maggie parked along the curb, about a block from the target house, on the edge of a wood. She opened the passenger side of the vehicle and undid Black Jack's seat belt, after which he, too, leaped from the Rover. "Stand right here, Jack, and don't move. I don't care what sort of night critter makes a sudden appearance, you keep in that wily mind of yours that you're here with me as my guardian and helper."

"I think the correct word is *accomplice*," Jack retorted smugly. "*Partner in crime* is also applicable."

"Ooooooh, Goddess, protect them," Maggie whispered tensely. "I don't like this, don't like it at all, at all," she moaned.

"*Wily* indeed," Jack grumbled, pouncing on the word Raine used to describe him. "I am your best critic, dear Raine, but at risk of rubbing you the wrong way with what you frequently deem my *captious* judgment–"

"Knock it off!" the Goth gal sizzled. "Do you two want to program something negative? You know I'm a regular Nancy Drew when it comes to this sort of thing. Think positive!"

"I'm trying," Maggie groaned. "I really, really am."

Lifting a brow and stroking his black mustache, Black Jack jested in Sean's basso, cowboy dialect, "Maggie, I'd say you're as nervous as a long-tail cat in a room full-a rockin' chairs."

Lunging into the car, Raine pulled a canvas bag from the backseat. "Mags, I'd do just about anything for you, but I don't intend to get myself killed just so you can say 'I told you so' when we meet one day in the Summerland." She rolled her eyes to look skyward, chanting, "Serenity now! Serenity now! I am attracting everything for my highest good. Serenity now!"

Raine had cloaked her figure with the old work clothes, all black, that she'd taken from what she referred to as her "cat-burglar kit." Worn over her regular clothing, they made it unnecessary to wear a jacket or coat, which afforded her more freedom of motion. The kit held a black ski mask that she quickly pulled over her head; flashlight with extra batteries; small digital camera; surgical gloves, into which she took the time to work her fingers for a comfortable fit; lock picks; a ring of skeleton keys; burn phone, the number of which Maggie and Aisling both carried with them; plastic Ziploc bags; tweezers; pepper spray; and various other small, lightweight items.

Plucking a second black ski mask from the pocket of her baggy pants, she handed it to Jack. "Pull this over your head."

"Why?! No one's going to recognize *me*. I hate it when you dress me up. Remember those bloody antlers that memorable Yule?" He stared at the head covering, sending Raine a cautioning hiss. "No, this is where I draw the line!"

"Someone might recognize **my cousin!**" the Goth gal hissed back. "Even though Sean lives out West, people around here have seen me with him over the years. Now don't give me a problem. Put this on!"

Hurriedly then, Raine double-checked her cat-burglar kit to be certain it contained everything she would need to search the killer's home, taking an extra moment to test the flashlight. "If my lock picks fail me, I can force a lock, if necessary," she said more to herself than to her two companions. "*Or*," a sudden grin split the seriousness of her face as she produced an item from the kit to hold before them, "I could break a window with this baseball. It would look like kids playing ball in the field next to the target house hit a ball through the window, and the suspect won't realize that someone broke into the place, since I don't plan on taking or disturbing anything inside."

"In the winter? What kids would be playing baseball in the winter?" Maggie snapped.

Raine stuck out her tongue. "I didn't say I was actually going to *use* my baseball ploy. Anyway, spring's just round the corner. A gang of kids *could* get baseball fever and– dragon's dung!" she uttered in exasperation. "I could play the same ruse with a hockey puck, which," she whisked from her goodie bag, "you'll note I also carry. The iced-over pond is only yards from here."

"Oooooh, Goddess," Maggie carped again as uneasiness took possession of her.

Staring at the ski mask dangling from his hand, Black Jack O'Lantern's sourpuss said it all, though his throat emitted a low, audible snarling sound.

Raine gave another huff of annoyance. "Pull yourself together, Jack." With the frosty winter air swirling between them, she yanked the thing from his hand and jerked it over his head, snagging a nail in the process.

"Damn it!"

"Don't ya hate it when that happens?" Under his mask, Jack grinned slyly.

As before, he was dressed *all* in black, snug jeans and turtleneck sweater, leather motorcycle jacket and boots. "I'm cold standin' here," he griped, stamping his feet and blowing into his hands. "If you're set on doing this, then stop pussyfootin' round. I want," he covered a sudden yawn, "to get back home to my nice, warm radiator. Let's move!"

"You'd *better* get moving," Maggie concurred. "It's getting late. The killer should be returning home in an hour or less!"

"Keep your ears and eyes open, Mags, and ring me straightaway if you catch sight of him heading up this winding lane. Oh, and keep *that*," she indicated the brimmed, green corduroy hat Maggie was wearing, "pulled down over your face. And for mercy's sake, stop fretting! With his acute sense of hearing and his nighttime vision, Jack will make the purr-fect lookout for me."

"I suppose driving the getaway car is better than acting as lookout, as you used to have me do for you," Maggie conceded.

Raine gave "Sean's" shoulder a brisk knock, "C'mon, Jack."

The pair pushed through the woods as fast as they could. At one point, a rabbit darted out in front of them, and it was all Raine could do to prevent her feline familiar from taking off after it.

"Cool your jets, mister!" she admonished. "Don't even think of running off. I need you big time this night."

When they reached the suspect's backdoor, Raine flexed her fingers sheathed in the surgical gloves. Dipping them into the cat-burglar kit, she felt for her favorite lock picks, expertly opening the door within seconds. "Thank the great Goddess there was no deadbolt," she whispered. Stepping into the kitchen, she dared not turn on a light, but rather, used her flashlight to make a quick scan of the room.

"*Crafty*. I'm impressed," Black Jack purrrred, closing the door behind them. His face took suddenly a tom-cat mien. "What a *sly* baggage you are, missy!"

Glancing about, Raine shrugged. "Duck soup when there's no deadbolt. The homeowner's not going to have to worry about break-ins, however. I'm pretty sure he'll be moving to a secure, gated community before too long."

When Jack responded with a baffled tilt of his head, Raine sputtered, "*Prison!* No place more secure or gated than the state pen." She took a few steps forward. "Stay close to this window, but out of sight. I want you to warn me *immediately* if you see anyone coming up that lane. Don't touch … disturb anything. We don't want our killer to know that anyone was in here, and don't turn on any lights. I'll case the place as fast as I can."

"Go ahead. Window watchin's right up my alley."

"Let's hope it's not a blind alley."

Jack smirked. "You know how sly *I* can be. Piece-a cake!"

"Good kitty." With the beam from her flashlight guiding her, Raine moved from the kitchen into the dining-living space, each shadow taking on the appearance of something alive. On the wall, above the fireplace, hung a huge painting of a beautiful woman, her back turned, as she gazed over her shoulder with a look that brought the Goth gal to a standstill. It was little short of *eerie*.

Great balls of fire! No wonder ...

Moving through the dark, two-story dwelling as quickly as she could, Raine was becoming discouraged that she'd found no evidence anywhere. Bathroom cabinets, closets, a desk, *nothing* held rock-hard substantiation that their top suspect was the killer.

What a dark, dreary night, the Sister thought, glancing quickly out a window. *Not even a moon.* Her thoughts on the weather ended abruptly when–

Creeping toward what she decided would be the last closet, she recoiled when a sharp breeze rattled the window, and timbers groaned. *Mystic minions! I thought, for a moment, someone was trying to get in. I'm ashamed of myself.*

The clock on the living-room mantel chimed ten, as Raine stole, with careful but hurried steps, back into the kitchen to find Black Jack standing in front of the open refrigerator, sniffing an unsealed container he'd lifted from a shelf.

"Jack!" she rasped. "Whatthehell are you doing?"

"Tu–na," he replied, his mouth full, his ravenous McDonough eyes, in the dazzle from the refrigerator light, rendering him more catlike than ever.

"Put that back. Now! We don't want our number-one suspect to know anyone was in here!"

Poised to lick the inside of the lid, Jack reacted to Raine's rebuke with a shrill yowl.

In a flash, she'd snatched the plastic container of tuna salad away from him to reclose it and set it back in the fridge. "Behave yourself, and I'll open a fresh can of Gourmet Kitty when we get home, the tuna stew you like." However, attributable to the gleam of light from the refrigerator, she caught sight of what she figured was the cellar door. "One more place to investigate, then we have to get outta here."

"Yeah, we do. You've made me hungry with your crafty talk of duck soup and tuna stew." He began to lick his fingers clean of the residue of tuna that remained after he'd scooped out a pilfered portion.

Jack's comment and antics were lost on Raine, who was more interested in the newly discovered door. Turning the knob, she realized it was locked. *Now why would anyone who lives alone lock a cellar door ... especially when there's no outside entrance?*

Reaching into her cat-burglar kit, she promptly found the ring of skeleton keys and began trying them, one by one. After the second key, the lock turned. "Jack," she whispered, "I'm going to leave the keys in this door, so I can relock it fast when I come up. Keep watch. I'll b' back b'fore you can say 'Gourmet Kitty.' And stay out of the 'groceries'!" she tossed over her shoulder.

Using her beam of light to guide her, Raine gingerly descended the cellar steps, narrow and steep, into the musty-smelling basement. Even in the cellar, she dared not risk turning on a light, not wanting the illumination to shine through the glass-block windows to the exterior. At the bottom of the steps, she used the flashlight to scan the area.

It was the typical old house, unfinished basement with the usual muddle of exposed pipes, water heater, paint cans, boxes of holiday decorations and old books, a washer and dryer, and a tool bench with two deep drawers. Over the workbench, tools hung from a pegged wall, whilst shelves with sundry items, including canned goods, lined two other walls. Adjacent was a small furnace room with a window that looked as if it hadn't been opened in years.

Like Tara, this house had a coal furnace at one time, and that window was the coal chute.

An instant later, Raine's searching eyes took special notice of several archery things tucked away under the steps. *No surprise there.* She channeled her light. *Now where?*

The workbench, she thought, heading for it. Yanking open the bottom drawer first, she found a jumble of odds and ends, including a roll of duct tape, a dusty ball of twine, a roll of wire, and a box of thumb tacks. Closing the lower receptacle, she attempted to tug open the hefty top drawer, her hand jolting to a brusque stop– it was securely locked. *Now why would anyone who lives alone feel the need to lock a drawer in a locked basement with no outside entrance?* Not to be thwarted, she said aloud, "I'll soon find out."

Swiftly, she dug into her canvas bag for the lock picks, releasing the catch and opening the drawer only to draw in her breath. *Eureka!*

There, before her, was the potassium cyanide bottle with the skull over crossbones and the warning *Danger*, just as, first Maggie, then Athena had revealed. The drawer also contained a hypodermic needle, as well as a few other curious items– a razor blade, packets of sweetener, a clear-drying glue, a small funnel, surgical gloves, and a small vial of amber-colored glass.

Now what do you suppose the killer is doing with– "Oh great Goddess!" she exclaimed again, this time aloud. "I think I know what he's planning to do next!"

Without further delay, she made a hasty assessment of the drawer's contents, snapping a couple of pictures with her burn phone whilst being careful not to move anything. She expertly relocked the drawer; then using her light to guide her, she scurried up the steep cellar steps, resisting the urge to take them two at a time.

At the top, she gave a start, suppressing a scream when she nearly stepped on the dead mouse lying there, at the entrance to the kitchen. "Jack!" she shrieked. "Is this your work?"

He was at the window seat, crouched down on the overstuffed pillows, his chin resting on the tops of his hands. Instantly he stirred, his expression reflecting his hurt feelings. "It's for you. You must admit, I'm an *extraordinary* mouser. Wasn't easy in human form," he sulked. "If you don't believe me, you should try it sometime."

Raine reached out to grasp his arm. "You're a *champion* mouser, a great hunter, but we haven't time for this. Cut me a break; pick *that* up," she pointed to the vermin carcass, "and toss it outside when we leave, which we're going to do right now." She relocked the cellar door, dropping the ring of skeleton keys into her bag.

"**Uh-oh!** I just saw a flash at the end of the lane," Jack voiced in an alerting tone, his keen eyes riveted to the pinpoint of light through the window and the tangle of trees beyond.

At that express moment, Raine's burn phone sounded. "Mission accomplished. We're outta here!" she fired into the receiver at Maggie, as she jerked open the backdoor. She and Jack scurried out of the house, with cat-burglar Raine relocking the door in the very nick of time.

A moment later– and the killer's oncoming vehicle, crunching forward on the gravel lane, would have caught them in the headlights.

When she and Black Jack were safely away, Raine paused for want of breath. "We can walk the rest of the way, but let's catch a breather," she said, pulling off her gloves and chucking them back into her kit. "You did a fine job of watching. Saved me again." She gave him an intense hug. "I love you, Jack. Thank you."

"Sean" lifted his wide shoulders, smoothing his ebony mustache. "It's what I do. I'm a Watcher. More to the point– *your* Watcher," he concluded, blinking at her and bringing a smile to her lips.

Her grin widened. "Oh, I can tell you're quite serious."

He took a step back, drawing himself up to his full height. "Be assured I never joke about magick … and especially not about my personal *raison d'être*."

She could sense that he was a tad insulted, though she most certainly had not intended an affront to his fragile feline dignity. "And don't think I don't appreciate your adept mousing skills. I do. *At Tara*." She planted a kiss on his cheek, combined with another hug.

He blinked again, gliding to her side to put his arm over her shoulders in a protective gesture, as they started off at a brisk gait, with "Sean" chattering happily–

"I realize I'm no better than a serial killer when it comes to rodents, but as I told you before, old habits …"

The following morning, Raine telephoned the chief soon after she woke to ask him to meet her on the campus for a quick bite of lunch. She had such a full day of classes, she couldn't take time to go to his office, and she didn't want to relate what she'd uncovered over the phone.

Promptly at the noon hour, Chief Fitzpatrick caught up with the raven-haired Sister outside Old Main. She was just exiting the building when she saw the burly officer sit down on one of the park benches under a copse of the lofty trees that were part of Haleigh's charm. As per her request, a top coat hid his uniform, so it looked as though he were in mufti. It was a warmer day than it had been for several weeks, but it was still cold, with a slight breeze.

"Let's walk, and I'll give you the rough gist of things," she suggested, handing him one of the two hot dogs she'd purchased inside from a Valentine-Fest vendor. "I don't have much time till my next class, but what I have to tell you could *not* wait till later this afternoon when I'll be free."

Raine quickly passed on all that she and Maggie had uncovered through their encounter with Jo Nosh at the library, as well as what they'd detected from the top suspect's ex-wife.

"We didn't expect to like the woman," Raine revealed. "We told her who we were and why we were paying her a visit. After our questions were asked and answered, we decided we did like her after all. As she told us, 'with the mind-set and the negative baggage' her ex-husband was toting, it's no wonder the marriage failed."

Then, taking a deep breath, she confided in him what she'd discovered in the killer's basement, handing him the photos she pulled from her purse. "Very good evidence, indeed, that any court in the land would accept.

"We realize we can't make use of any of this stuff without a warrant, and you need probable cause *for* a warrant; but at least we know who the killer is and where the stash of evidence is *when* you issue that warrant ... which let's hope will be soon." She bit into her hotdog, hoping, too, that Fitzpatrick's response wouldn't be too reprimanding.

"I don't need to tell you that you were taking a helluva risk, entering and searching the person of interest's house," Fitz replied in a reproving tone. Used to gulping his food, he swallowed the final bite of his dog, as he scrutinized the photos.

The Goth gal answered with a dismissing shrug, "I hoped for the best. Chief, one can hardly go through life without risks, and for us, certain risks are necessary. Aren't you the one who said, 'The Lord hates a coward'?"

Fixing her with his Irish blue eyes, he retorted, holding his voice to a low tone and stuffing the pictures into her shoulder bag, under the open flap, "Girl, you–" he skidded to a stop, at a loss for words. "You're like a cat with nine lives, the way you so often just miss bein'–" He cut off again, blurting, "You *never* told me *any* of this. I know *nothing* about it. Nothin' about the pics. ***Nothing!*** Understand?"

In spite of his reproof, she sensed that he was favorably impressed. "Right."

The pair strode in silence for several seconds, whilst each mulled over the situation, after which Raine said, laying a hand on the chief's arm, "Fitz, we're on track now; and as a result of my break-in, I think I know what the killer is planning to do next. A couple of things, in fact. Give Maggie, Aisling, and me a chance to do some of our *magickal* sleuthing, and then we'll tell you what, how, where, and you can catch him dead to rights."

The chief's bushy brows shot up, and he opened his mouth to speak, when–

Looking at her watch, Raine cut him off, "Must fly. All we need is a day or so, and we'll get him, Fitz. We'll get him sure as witches have familiars!"

Later that afternoon, all three Sleuth Sisters were back in Tara's sacred attic space for another needed scrying session with their crystal ball, Athena.

After having followed all the proper preparatory steps, Maggie expertly steered them through their magick-carpet ride to the huge amethyst ball's crystal depths.

Then, the redheaded Sister began to chant softly, "Athena, as we go into a trance/ Bestow on us the magick glance/ Take us forward in time today/ Reveal the future come what may/ Who will Annabel's killer target next?/ Show us, Athena– who be hexed!/ Take us forward for us to learn/ The who, where, and when/ For that, dear oracle, we now return!"

As the colossal crystal ball's powerful energy commenced to flow, the seated, black-robed Sisters imaged their vibratory intensities rising to synchronize with it, henceforth to craft their sought-after connection.

Within moments, the Sisters could feel the powerful magick swirling around them, just as they could see Athena's familiar smoky mists eddying from the crystal's cavernous nadir.

"The magick is working," Maggie breathed. "Stay calm and keep your focus. Athena is answering our plea."

"Easy does it," their poppet crooned, her usually tinny little voice sounding almost like Granny's musical brogue.

Granny used to say that, Raine and Aisling thought in sync.

The ball's mists cleared as an image swam to life. It was a location the McDonoughs clearly recognized. They had no difficulty identifying the people in the tableau as well. Then, on the wall within the scene, their eyes found the calendar and clock. With a sigh of relief, the magickal trio realized they could save the killer's next victim.

Once the Sisters ended their ritual with the proper steps, Aisling turned to Raine. "I can't remain angry with you, Sister, when your daring deed will likely result in a saved life." She put her arms around her cousin and hugged her close. "I'm sorry I was cross with you, but I worry about you, Raine. You're far too impetuous and impulsive. Far too–"

"Come now, you just said you weren't going to do that," the Goth gal chided. "And besides, I wasn't alone. My Jackie boy was with me."

"Listen, you two," Maggie cut in. "The next few days, these final days of the Valentine Fest, are going to be trying, tricky, and mighty tiresome, so let's reserve all our energies for what we've got to do."

"It could get rough, but we can do this," Raine answered.

"Let's be sure to keep the chief abreast of what we're doing," Aisling stated, starting down the attic steps. "*That* I do insist upon."

***

The following day, it began again to snow– big fat flakes that drifted lazily to settle on the Hamlet like down from an angel's pillow.

"Isn't it beautiful?" Maggie asked from the Land Rover's passenger seat, as she and Raine pulled into their parking spot at Haleigh's Old Main. "Feathery Kisses from Heaven."

The beauty of the snow silenced their words for a long moment, as the two witches appreciated the wonder of the enchanting scene. Witches relish Mother Nature, in addition to the wild nature within their own essences, to align themselves with the cycles of the earth and the phases of the moon.

"Let's dash into the canteen for that quick cup of coffee we talked about," Raine said, dropping the Rover's keys into her bag. "Besides, we'll need a shot of ambition. Busy day today!"

"Right," Maggie answered, stepping out of the car. "We've *got* to be quick. Classes start in twenty-five minutes."

Inside the canteen, Maggie made straight for the counter to get their coffee, when Raine spied Dr. Lear sitting by himself, a teacup before him. A second cup rested on the table at a vacant chair across from him. Professor Longbough, his back to the Sisters, stood next to Dr. Lear. It looked as though the two were conversing.

"Good-morning," Raine called, "Dr. Lear, Professor Longbough." She took a step closer to the table. "I don't mean to intrude," her green eyes darted to the empty chair where the other cup of tea awaited. "But when I saw you," she looked to Lear, "I thought I'd pop over to reassure you that Maggie and I will be at the auditorium early tomorrow, ready to go to work. We won't let you down. By the bye, Rex, how are your understudies doing?"

"Surprisingly well. Perhaps not so surprising since I've been working them hard." Haleigh's theatre director looked tired, almost drained. Lines of fatigue showed clearly on his face, making him look older; the dark hair at his temples seemed more flecked with grey; and there were bags under his eyes as though he were suffering from some sort of sleep deprivation; but the Sister could sense that he was attempting to put on a heroic face. "However," he hastily stipulated, "I'll be depending on your expert prompting."

"Not to worry; you *can* depend on us." She picked up the two sweetener packets lying on the table near the absent person's cup. "I like to keep a few of these in my purse, in case I need them when I'm out."

"Here," Lear said, reaching for a glass container holding an array of sweetener packets. "Take a few of these instead. Those," he pointed to the ones she held in her hand, "were here when I sat down. You don't know who had their hands on them, and with that stomach virus going around–" He left the sentence unfinished as a plea. "I don't want *you* coming down with it, not with curtain tomorrow night."

Raine leaned forward, "No problem. They're sealed, and my granny's elderberry brew never lets us down. A shield of protection, Granny's elixir." She dropped the packets into her purse.

Professor Longbough appeared suddenly anxious, bursting out with "Gotta go!" as he stole a glance at his watch. With that, he hurried toward the exit.

"Bless my boline! Was it something I said?" Raine queried in a semi-joking tone.

"I wouldn't worry about him," Dr. Lear shrugged. "He appeared in a bit of a flurry when he called us," the theatre director gestured toward the other teacup with its vacant chair– "Miss Fox is in the restroom– over to this table to speak to me about my son. William missed Longbough's mid-term, so he asked me to convey the message for him to reschedule."

"The sinister stomach virus, eh?"

"Not really sure."

At that moment, Trixie Fox emerged from the ladies' to take her place in the chair at which the tea awaited.

"Morning, Dr. McDonough," she greeted pleasantly, though Raine picked up her instant displeasure.

"Morning, Miss Fox." *Take the mask off when you speak to me. I see right through it anyway.*

"I told Rex," she sent him a look that Raine found insidious, as a crafty light came into the young woman's eyes, "you can relax and enjoy the play with the audience. I'll be happy to prompt for him." She slid a hand possessively over Dr. Lear's, causing the professor to immediately break the caress.

Ever the coquette. "No, a promise is a promise," replied the Goth gal aloud and in distinct voice.

Trixie frowned, and the cunning expression filtered down over her face. "I suppose some people have these urges to go about doing good deeds, figuring to make the world a better place," she sniffed. Her eyes fastened on the Sisters, and the frown became a scowl. "Good luck with that!"

A most contemptible young woman. Raine delivered her sweetest smile, the dimple in her left cheek deepening. "Rex, Maggie and I will be there tomorrow– with bells on."

"Speaking of bells, our little Trixie's secret lover has put a *ring* on her finger," Dr. Lear announced with one of his clever play on words.

Miss Fox wiggled her left hand for Raine to admire her diamond which, sparkling brilliantly, rested in a high king's-crown setting.

"Oh, Rex," she laughed, sending him a coy look, "Scott was never a secret. I just never mentioned him to *you*."

Striding forward to hand Raine her coffee, Maggie said to Trixie, "Best of wishes and good fortune." She meant it, zooming the notion to her raven-haired sister of the moon, *This tricky little Fox is going to need luck– to make it work with any man.*

*Good luck to her **fiancé***! Raine chortled, bouncing the brainwave back to Maggie, ***He's** gonna need a **bonanza.** Poor bastard!*

Trixie was smiling now, though it was not a pleasant smile. In fact, it was so falsely hearty that even Dr. Lear was looking at her oddly. "Conversations with you," she smirked, her gaze fixed on Raine, for she could see the storm in those emerald eyes, "could prove dangerous."

There was no longer even a shred of doubt in her mind as to the character of the woman when the Goth gal retorted, "Conversations are always dangerous– if you have something to hide."

For a few moments longer, the Sisters stood chatting, whilst Dr. Lear and his protégée, with sidelong sneer leveled at Raine, polished off their tea. Then, they all exited the canteen and headed for their classrooms.

Chapter Twelve

Later that same afternoon, upon completing their teaching duties, Raine and Maggie drove, without delay, to Chief Fitzpatrick's office at the Hamlet Police Station.

Handing him a small, plastic Ziploc bag containing the two packets of sweetener she'd taken from the canteen table that morning, Raine said, "Please have these analyzed in your crime lab, Fitz, as quickly as you can make it happen. I'm pretty sure they'll find potassium cyanide."

The Goth gal then filled the chief in on what transpired that morning in the canteen, prompting him to question grimly, "Did you," his perceptive blue eyes shifted from Raine to Maggie and back again, "*either of you*, witness our top suspect taking *these* packets off his person to set them on that table?"

Raine gave a sigh. "No. To be honest, we didn't. We knew, from our conjured magick, to go to the canteen and *when*. We even got there *earlier* than the time we knew to be there; but–" she broke off, shaking her head with regret, "when we arrived, the way everyone was positioned … no, we didn't witness our top suspect actually putting the packets on the table. Then again, after what I discovered in his house …" her face fell, along with her voice, as she rambled further, "which we can't use … but I just *know* you'll find that sweetener loaded with cyanide."

"Purely *circumstantial*," Fitz challenged. "We need *direct* evidence. Hearsay and circumstantial evidence won't bring a conviction." In the tick of a clock, the frustrated chief shook his head. "Sorry. You very likely saved a life this morning. Good work! We're all doing the best we can, but this murderer's clever, *far too* clever. If only we could catch the devil– *in the act. We've got to catch the killer in the act!*"

"You'll get your direct evidence, Chief, because *we*," Raine looked to a brooding Maggie, "believe we know what the killer's going to do next. Or, I should say, *attempt* to do next."

Fitzpatrick recognized the look that manifested on the brunette Sister's face. He leaned forward, waiting.

Raine's eyes narrowed. "Now, here's what *we're* going to do to match wits with this clever-as-a-fox murderer …"

***

Come evening, the Sisters were at Hugh's home for dinner and an overdue session with their Sleuthing Set. Everyone was present. Hugh and Betty had prepared a huge tray of lasagna. Maggie and Raine stopped off, after classes, at Sal-San-Tries for a big bowl of her garden salad sans dressing. (They planned on dressing the salad at Hugh's). Aisling and Ian dropped by The Gypsy Tearoom for a variety of Eva's fruit tarts, and Thaddeus supplied the Chianti.

"I feel guilty that I haven't brought anything to our supper table tonight," Beau stated, kissing Raine on the cheek as he stepped into the kitchen from the attached clinic. He was finishing late at the veterinary surgery, but the others waited dinner for him.

"You've brought *yourself*, son, and that's good enough for me," Hugh replied, giving him a pat on the back. "You look all-in. Tough day?"

Beau gave a nod. "Mrs. Washington parted with her cat today. You recall she lost her other cat last July; and now, her last one. I always told her she had the oldest cats in Braddock County. Over the years, all her cats lived to twenty or near-twenty." He smiled a little sadly. "She said the secret was lots of love. Today was the most difficult thing, I think, she ever had to do, for this last one was her all-time favorite; but Angel Baby's in a better place. She made the right decision; it was time."

Beau looked as though he were tearing up, but he artfully hid it, turning away from the doorway to wash his hands. "I've treated her cats for years. I'll miss her office visits. We often swapped cat care. Gladys was a fountain of holistic wisdom."

"How old is Gladys Washington now?" Hugh asked.

"I'm not sure, but certainly eighty," Beau answered, drying his hands and again facing the others through the open archway, who were seated in the adjacent living room, sipping wine. He accepted a glass from Raine, swirled the ruby liquid in the goblet then took a long sip. "She told me she won't get any more pets now. Afraid she'll go before them, and she has no one to whom she can leave them." He tightened his mouth. "Gladys and her fur baby slept together every night, his paw in her hand. She used to get so angry when she'd hear someone say that animals don't have emotions or a

- 232 -

spirit. 'Tarnation,' she'd howl, 'if it has a heartbeat, it has emotions and a spirit, and that spirit goes on forever, just like a human's!'

"Gladys took Angel Baby's little sweater off so she could cuddle it nights. She said the sweater would always hold his energy. I asked if she wanted to take him home, and of course, she did. Her neighbor will bury him alongside her other cats, in her backyard, where she told me an angel statue watches over them." Beau took another swallow of wine, staring into the fireplace flames, before which the shepherd siblings, Nero and Wolfe, were napping, side by side.

Raine picked up his thought that parting with them one day would be heartrending. She leaned over to kiss his cheek, bristly with evening shadow. "Beau," she whispered, "if Mrs. Washington wants another cat, Maggie and I will take it in, if she crosses over before it."

"Thank you, baby," he smiled, suddenly lighting up. "I'll talk to her about that. It's too soon now, but before long, I'll broach your suggestion to her.

"Now," Beau spoke abruptly, slapping his hands down on his thighs, "fill us in on your sleuthing."

"Everything's ready, so how about we chat while we eat?" Betty suggested, rising to head into the kitchen. "Everyone be seated, and Hugh can help me serve."

"So there you have it— a review of our harvested clues," Raine said, taking a couple of swigs of water to wet her whistle after her long-winded account.

"Since my interview with Ada Peepers, Chief Fitzpatrick talked with her again," Aisling reported. "She was the only one of Annabel Lee's neighbors to witness anything the night the professor's car was vandalized. Of course, I also told Fitz what Savvy Kathy related to Raine at the Auto Doctor's. Kathy overhead Liza on the phone telling one of her cohorts that the 'Snoop Sisters' better be careful, that she intended, in her words, to 'fix' us. I informed the chief, thanks to Kathy, that Liza's white Corvette had a burned-out taillight when she did the dirty deed to Professor Lee's car. Mrs. Peepers remembered that the white sportscar she saw the culprit drive away in had a burned-out taillight, likewise the bold— and knowing her as we do, *brazen*— LIZA license plate. Looks like Miss Berk will be charged with Criminal Mischief," the Sister concluded.

"Don't let the word Mischief fool you," Ian presaged, "this could result in jail time for the girl."

"Of course, her parents will do everything they can to get her cleared. I blame them for the brat's conduct in the first place. Spoiled her rotten," Raine put in.

"What about Liza's two cohorts?" Thaddeus inquired. "I'd wager they each owned up to what they did during interrogation."

"Yep, sang like canaries. When Fitz questioned them, *separately*, they each broke– ratting out their leader in the process and confessing to all the pranks they'd played on the late Professor Lee. But, again, let's be clear," Ian stated, "there's a significant difference between pranks and Criminal Mischief. For one thing, the admitted threat on Raine was nothing to scoff at."

"I look for the three of them to be permanently expelled from Haleigh," Maggie commented.

"So do I," Raine concurred, "and rightly so. They've a history of cheating, bullying, alcohol abuse, and downright meanness. They deserve to be expelled."

"Oh my!" Maggie voiced with sudden intensity as a vision played upon the computer screen of her mind. "You won't believe what just flashed across my brain! I fancied I saw ..."

Several minutes rolled by with the Sleuthing Set discussing what Maggie revealed, after which Betty queried, as she passed the sprinkle cheese and pepperoncino around the table, "I've been meaning to ask: Have there been any more arrow episodes on campus?"

"No. I don't think our top murder suspect wants to take a chance with that. Campus security has really been beefed up of late," the redheaded Sister informed, "and he would most certainly be aware of it."

"Right. And now, it looks as though the killer has bigger fish to fry," Raine added.

Betty toyed with the chunky turquoise bracelet on her arm. "You're convinced the archer and the poisoner are one and the same?"

"We are," the Sisters answered in sync.

"The info we gleaned from both Ron Moon and Jo Nosh were the keys we needed to unlock this cryptic case," Maggie stated. "The lasagna is delicious, by the way. *Excellent.*"

"Thank you," Hugh and Betty acknowledged, with Hugh sending Betty a wink.

"*And* you think you know what the killer will try next?" Beau said, looking to Raine. It was a question, though it hardly needed to be.

"Yes, we believe we do. And that's why ..."

"Anybody for seconds?" Hugh rose from his chair at the head of the table.

Everyone raised a hand, and Betty stood too. "There's plenty. I'm so happy you're enjoying it."

When everyone's plate was replenished, Hugh remarked, "I'm of the mind that after Ron Moon's recollection, everything started pointing to the obvious. Then came Jo's stories and–"

"Let's not forget what the ex-wife told us," Raine reminded.

"Pretty clear *now*," Maggie concluded. "Funny thing, that. We were batting the obvious around at the very beginning of this case," she broke off, lost in her own ponderings.

"This time, we're *not* overlooking the obvious. One of them anyway," Raine commented.

"Great Goddess!" Aisling exclaimed, "We must try and do everything we can to prevent this, this ... *thing*, for lack of another word, from repeating itself."

"Oh, we will!" Raine said with spirit. "Maggie and I have already talked about what we must do to stop this bane from continuing; but first, *first*, we must be certain to stop the murderer from killing again tomorrow."

***

The next afternoon began with a phone call from the chief. "You were right. The sweetener packets contained poison. They were filled with three-quarters sweetener and a third potassium cyanide. More than enough of the deadly stuff in either packet to kill again."

"*That* was fast," Maggie voiced into her smart phone from the passenger side of the Land Rover.

"I asked the lab to get it done ASAP, emphasizing that the killer was *determined* to strike again, and we *have* to stop him," Fitzpatrick thundered.

"Oh, we'll stop him," Raine said from behind the wheel. "Tonight's the play, and Maggie, Aisling and I are *just* as resolute. *More* so," she pronounced with the grit of her lionhearted McDonough ancestors.

The seasoned officer countered with, "I think I'd better attend that play."

"With all due respect, Fitz," the Sister interposed, "you're too recognizable. You stand out in a crowd. If the killer spots you in the audience, we might not have the result we want. We'll stay connected. Trust this to us, *please*."

"Be careful. Don't take any chances. And know this– I'll be close at hand." Fitzpatrick rang off, with Maggie turning to Raine.

"Hey, you're not going to park this car at the auditorium, are you?"

Flinging her redheaded sister of the moon an annoyed look, Raine spluttered, "Have you gone, as Granny used to say, *scatty*? Give me more credit than that, Mags. I figured we'd park in the library lot. Library's not far from the auditorium. We'll duck into the trees and come out at the auditorium's stage-door entrance, the service door, where I'll make use of my trusty lock picks. Got my cat-burglar kit in the backseat."

"Right," Maggie replied, using her favorite declaration of accord.

Within the next few minutes, Raine pulled into the library parking lot and shut off the ignition to prod her companion, "Let's move. We want to get in there *well* before the killer does. I'd rather we wait for him to show, than we miss our chance again to be eyewitnesses to his dirty work."

The Sisters darted into the trees next to the library and headed for the Addison McKenzie Auditorium that housed the college theatre, Raine with her cat-burglar kit over her arm.

When they reached the side of the building, the Goth gal glanced slyly around to see if anyone was about. Seeing no one, she extracted her preferred lock picks and set about opening the stage entrance.

"Just as I thought," Raine whispered, "easiest door ever! **Anyone** could get in here with just about any kind of pick."

The old door groaned as she gingerly pulled it open. Slipping inside, the pair stood still, allowing their eyes to adjust to the semi-darkness.

The superstitious Dr. Lear insisted on the old theatrical convention of a "Ghost Lamp." (The practice was *so* old no one knew who started it, or where or when it began.) As in all theatres that held to the convention, the light here burned downstage center, dimly illuminating the set and the backstage clutter of set pieces, props, and costumes.

Since, in theatre tradition, most theatres are haunted, the light is said to keep the ghosts at bay, an appeasement to deceased thespians who want never to relinquish their place in the spotlight. Thus, when the company and crew leave for the night, the stage is restored to the theatre ghost so that he or she may return to his or her eternal performance.

Hence, an empty theatre's perpetually burning light is known as a "Ghost Lamp," sometimes referred to as an "Equity Light" required in some contracts as a safety measure on a dark stage. The Sisters were reminded of this bit of colorful theatre history as, mission suspended, their eyes adapted to their shadowy surroundings.

"Door's locked again, so no worries if someone decides to use that entry for any reason. Stay behind me, and have a care where you're stepping." Raine tiptoed nimbly to the stage wings, where she peered with some attention around the open curtain to the cavernous auditorium. The place was empty, and she let out bated breath, staring for a protracted moment at the blood-red seats and the long, murky aisles, echoing with silence. *There's nothing more eerie than an empty theatre*, she thought.

Having snagged Raine's musing, Maggie filled the pause quickly, "Never mind that. Let's find a good hiding place with all haste. The killer could arrive at any moment." Her eyes skimmed over the ghostly, medieval *Romeo and Juliet* set, with its arches, pillars, and steps. "We must choose carefully. We have to be able to *witness* what our top suspect will be doing. We *cannot* miss *seeing* him grab the prop we know he'll be after, *but* we *have* to be well hidden."

Raine's eyes, too, were searching. "Behind the curtain. He won't be tampering with it, and–"

"But how will we see what he's doing behind the heavy–"

"C'mon!" Pulling Maggie with her, Raine scooted behind the red velvet curtain, exploring the folds. In a moment, she whispered, "Wiz-zard, we're in luck. When I was thinking about finding the perfect hidey-hole, I suddenly remembered something you said once about this old rag. Here's a gap big enough for us to watch anyone coming into this wing area where the props are laid out on that table yonder. See … *here*."

Maggie moved nearer to Raine's side, where the latter showed her the peep hole. "Thank you, Goddess," she breathed. "Let's move back a tad. We don't want the killer to see a bulge behind the drape."

"Shush," Raine hissed. "Someone's coming."

The distinct sound of a door groaning open followed by footfalls *with sinister measured tread* stiffened the magickal pair silent and barely able to breathe.

Fearful she might sneeze so close to the dusty curtain, Maggie put her hands over her nose and mouth, as two pair of emerald eyes watched the man they'd been expecting walk to the readied props and, with gloved hand, swipe a small, amber-colored vial from the table.

His attitude was cautious, as he cast sharp, uneasy glances to his right, left, and behind him. Swiftly then, he switched the pilfered vial for one he produced from his coat pocket, taking the substitution from a sealed plastic bag and placing it on the table in the exact spot where the snatched vial had been. Both ampoules were amber, and both contained liquid.

After glancing furtively about once more, the killer stole away, his quiet steps fading then ceasing, after which the Sisters heard again the sound of the groaning door, opening and closing.

"Let's wait a bit, to make sure he's not coming back," Raine admonished in Maggie's ear.

The redheaded Sister gave a slight nod, unable at that moment to speak.

After a minute or so, the Goth gal whispered, "OK, now we make our *own* switcheroo, thenceforth a wary exit."

Moving noiselessly, but at the double-quick, to the table, Raine plunged her hand into her cat-burglar kit for the vial, containing tea, they brought with them. Since she had seen the small, glass vessel in the drawer of the killer's basement workbench, she knew exactly what type to get to replace it. "A perfect match," she grinned, setting her vial down and picking up, with a tissue from her bag, the one the killer put there. In smiling silence, then, she deposited the killer's vial into one of the plastic Ziploc bags she carried in her kit.

Scanning the stage, readied for the play, Maggie whispered a line from *Romeo and Juliet*, "I dare no longer stay."

"Dead right, Mags, let's get th'hell outta here!" Raine rasped with a brisk tug on her sister of the moon's cloaked arm.

At the stage-entrance door, the raven-haired Sister paused, with Maggie so close on her heels, they nearly collided. "Whoa, Sis, let me peek out first." Opening the heavy door but a crack, Raine whispered jubilantly, "Coast's clear. Let's fly!"

The pair escaped through the trees to the library car park, where they got into the Rover and let out a huge sigh of relief.

Raine pushed the kit out of sight under a mackintosh on the backseat. "Now we drive to the auditorium, park in the front, stroll inside and announce ourselves reporting for prompting duty."

"Before we do, let's ring Fitz," Maggie bade.

"Yes," Raine agreed, reaching for her phone, "we want to tell him we'll have exactly what he needs right after curtain tonight."

When Raine and Maggie strode into the lobby of the auditorium a few minutes later, they saw Professor Longbough talking to William Lear. To their left, the janitor, perched on a ladder, was replacing a light bulb.

Attractively decorated for the Valentine Fest and displaying *Romeo and Juliet* posters and photographs of stills from the show, including images with bios of the leads, the lobby awaited the magickal hour of curtain. Printed programs in neat piles topped a counter.

"Planning on lending a helping hand backstage, professor?" Raine cast to Longbow, as the Sisters advanced on him.

The archery coach appeared almost to recoil. "*No.* I saw William here lurking about and I wanted to catch up with him to reschedule his mid-term." It wasn't a question, but a query leaped into his eyes, which he hurled at the young man. "You gave me the impression you were trying to dodge me ... or someone."

William looked a tad embarrassed. "I-I ... wasn't trying to dodge you."

Lurking ... what an interesting word choice! Raine exchanged quick thoughts with Maggie. "What about you, William, will you be pitching in backstage?" the raven-haired Sister asked aloud.

Again, the idea seemed to startle, and the young fellow furrowed his brow, answering, "That's all my father would need– *me under foot.*" He flashed a strange smile. "I'm afraid he'd think I had a dark motive behind *that* idea. We don't have the most agreeable relationship, you know; and," he faltered, shifting gears, "I just popped in here to wish him well, break a leg, or whatever the proper theatre jargon is. He's been totally stressed lately. Oh," he looked beyond the Sisters to the door, "here he comes now."

"See you tomorrow morning, young man. Eight sharp, in my office," Professor Longbough ordained. He shot a glance at the Sisters then, "Beg pardon, but I have to run."

En route out, Longbough sent Dr. Lear a lackluster nod, as he made haste to the door. Through the glass front of the building, the Sisters could see him getting into his vehicle.

It seemed as though Lear didn't even notice Professor Longbough, as he entered the lobby in an equally brisk manner. Passing near the janitor, still on the ladder, the theatre director remarked, "Ah, I came in through the lobby to check on that. Spotted it yesterday. There's another one over there," he gestured.

"I already changed that one," the janitor answered.

"Good man!" Dr. Lear enthused. "We want everything to be perfect." He came forward to kiss each Sister lightly on both cheeks in the Continental way of greeting friends. "Thank you for coming early." Noticing his son, he regarded him with frank interest, exclaiming, "Hello, William, what brings *you* here?"

"I know how frazzled you've been lately, and I wanted to stop by to tell you to break a leg. I hope your cast gets a curtain call or two tonight."

Lear looked taken aback. "*That* is very thoughtful of you, son. Not *typical* but thoughtful."

William's friendly boyish face grew suddenly austere and hard. He raked his rich brown hair with his fingers to reply, "Wow, even when I try to be nice … er, before you correct my word choice, I guess *sympathetic* or *considerate* would be a better word, it's no use." His handsome face darkened even more. "There's no pleasing you, is there?"

The Lear elder cast a swift return, though his manner was a trifle wooden. "I value your sentiment, William; I do. Your presence here was totally unexpected. You just took me by surprise is all."

Piddlin' pixies! I wonder if... Raine shot the remainder of her thought to her sister of the moon.

There was an awkward pause until Maggie came to the rescue. "William, you seem familiar with how the theatrical phrase 'Break a leg' came about. Are you?"

"No," the sullen student replied, in a tone that said he didn't care.

"Though there's no definite answer as to the etymology of the phrase, it's believed it sprang from the fact that when actors bow or curtsey during curtain calls, they bend, *break*, the leg line ... hence, 'Break a leg!' Anyway, never wish anyone Good Luck before a show. That's bad luck. Very, very bad." Maggie laughed her crystal laugh. "Theatre people are second only to horse-race enthusiasts when it comes to superstition."

"Oooh yes, I'm well aware of the superstitions and eccentricities of theatre people," William said, visibly softening his tone and manner. "Look, I have somewhere to be, so I'd better get going. So long, Dad." He started away, turning after a moment to steal a final look at his father before shaking his head and hurrying off.

When the young man exited, Raine turned to Dr. Lear, more than curious as to how he would respond. "With all due respect, Rex, weren't you too hard on him?"

The theatre director did not waver when he looked the Sister in the eyes to respond, "You don't really know William. I, however, have no illusions about my son. For one thing, he's coldly analytical ... like his mother. It's why he's a math major," he snorted.

The curtain rose, and the mise-en-scène evoked a sense of impending tragedy, for both Raine and Maggie– beyond Shakespeare's poignant story line.

Calm down, Raine sped to Maggie, who was positioned across the stage in the wing opposite. *We took care of the problem. We're simply letting our imaginations get the better of us, applying art to life, so to speak. Wherever there is human nature, there is drama.*

True, Maggie returned the thought, *but that drama is not always where you think it is.*

During the course of the play, the pair found their prompting to be helpful several times to the various actors. At intermission, as they did during the play itself, they made it a point to keep a weather eye on the vial.

Aisling made her way backstage during the entr'acte to whisper to Raine and Maggie, "Beau's on a farm call, but Ian and I are out front with Thaddeus, and the chief's in the parking lot, in an unmarked car with one of his juniors, should we need them. I have my phone on vibrate, if you need us. We're keeping watch out there." She grasped a hand of each cousin, "*You're not alone.*"

"Let's hope we get through this play without any sort of mishap," Maggie whispered in return. "I'm tingling with nerves."

"Aisling, would you mind asking Fitz to wait for us after the play ends? We have something significant to give him, and I don't want to pull it out of my bag now for anyone to see," Raine breathed into the blonde with the wand's ear.

"Sure thing," the senior Sister replied.

When the bell sounded for the curtain to rise, Raine and Maggie were back, scripts in hand, at their prompting posts as the story of the eternal star-crossed lovers played on.

Dr. Lear appeared to be on the proverbial pins and needles, but all things considered, it was anticipated, and his cast and crew understood. In advance of the first act, then again at intermission, he issued a few last-minute directives, tensely wishing his cast well before slipping out front to watch the performance and, like all directors, to sweat it out, alone.

Maggie caught Raine's eye and sent out, into the ethers, this ardent plea: *If you're out and about this night, theatre ghosts of Addison McKenzie Auditorium, I know you're said to be guardians of the performers here and patrons of their work– so please, I implore you, help us to guard these students well.*

After the male lead spoke the line "Here's to my love!" uneasiness stirred in their minds, as the Sisters watched the actor swallow the "poison" to recite, with staggered breath, "O true apothecary … the drugs are quick. Thus … with a kiss … I die!"

Raine struggled to suppress the fear, *Either this kid's a great actor, or that was **cyanide** and not tea!*

Whilst the gasping Romeo breathed his last, Raine and Maggie were both grappling with the alarming sensation that they could *well* be watching the student-actor die! The feeling was almost unnerving, and both Sisters thought that curtain couldn't come quickly enough.

When Juliet awakened from her strong sleeping potion to discover her lover dead, thenceforth grasping the vial to utter the famous lines, "… drunk all, and left no friendly drop to help me after? I will kiss thy lips, hapy [sic] some poison yet doth hang on them …" again that frisson of fear skipped along the Sisters' spines with the chill of a thousand winters.

Goddess, Maggie shuddered involuntarily, *why do we feel this way? We headed off another killing. **We did.*** With anxious eyes, she whooshed a silent dispatch to Raine: *I pray nothing has gone amiss!*

*It couldn't have. We did everything we needed to do. I know what we're feeling. We're thinking of what **could have happened**.*

Maggie and Raine both stared fixedly at the ill-fated lovers, as they lay, still as death, on the stage, and beseeched God and Goddess that nothing had gone wrong.

No way could the killer have snuck something past us. No way, Raine retold herself and Maggie.

Several minutes of what seemed like an eternity later, the Sisters were never so impatient to hear the final lines of a play delivered: "For never was a story of more woe than this of Juliet and her Romeo."

Curtain!

Speedily then, to the sound of applause and the Sisters' fervent relief, did the "deceased" Romeo and Juliet leap to their feet and rush to the wings, with others of the cast, so the curtain call could roll out in the proper order.

It just occurred to me, a calmed Maggie pitched to Raine, *that the final scene of this tragedy unfolds in the dark of night. Romeo and Juliet's love flourished at night, making the lovers' end in darkness all the more tragic.*

Swept up in the magick of the moment, Raine jetted back, *Ooooh, but I think Shakespeare suggested a spiritual light round the couple in a wedding feast **beyond** death.*

When, at the last, the leads, singularly, stepped out onto the stage to thunderous applause, the cast joined hands and bowed, and the curtain closed again.

The students playing Romeo and Juliet played their roles to perfection, Raine zapped to Maggie, who, in the wing opposite, tossed her sister of the moon a brisk, wide-eyed nod.

***Chillingly** so!*

For several seconds, the ovation thundered on, resulting in the final curtain call; whilst Raine and Maggie beheld the director, backstage from the audience, lethargically sinking into the nearest chair, to blow out his breath in what was an almost audible sigh.

"See, Dr. Lear," the actor playing Romeo expressed, laying a hand on the director's slumped shoulder, "everything went swimmingly! Now, how do you feel?"

Staring straight ahead, the fit-to-drop professor murmured, "As well as might be expected."

Chapter Thirteen

Stumbling into Tara's kitchen, Raine poured herself a cup of the strong Irish breakfast tea that Maggie had brewed. The redheaded Sister was sipping from one of the eggshell-thin cups they favored for tea, looking up at her sister of the moon with eyes still heavy with sleep.

"Another Saturday morning when I just couldn't stay in bed," the Goth gal groaned, lowering herself into the chair across from Maggie.

"The reason is because we both keenly feel that something dark and sinister is again about to transpire," the redheaded Sister began. "But where and when?" She picked up her cup to take a swallow of the restorative beverage. Neither Sister liked to taint their tea with sugar, milk, or anything else. They preferred not to alter the taste of the good teas they usually ordered from abroad. "We've got to consult our crystal oracle again today."

"We do. Let's ring Aisling and ask her to come over straightaway. My guess is she's getting the same signal we are." Raine picked up her smart phone and rang the blonde with the wand, who answered on the second ring. "Can you come to Tara first thing this morning?" she asked without preamble.

"I was just about to ring you. Yes, I'll be there shortly. Prepare Athena for another session!"

Less than an hour later, the McDonough witches were seated before their crystal ball, whilst Maggie chanted: "Athena, as we go into a trance/ Bestow on us the magick glance/ Take us forward in time today/ Reveal the future come what may/ Who will Annabel's killer target next?/ Show us, Athena– who be hexed!/ Take us forward for us to learn/ The who, where, and when/ For that, dear oracle, we now return!"

As the colossal crystal ball's powerful energy commenced to flow, the seated, robed Sisters, accompanied by their poppet and the Merlin cats, visualized their vibratory heights intensifying to harmonize with it, henceforth crafting their sought-after connection.

Presently, the Sisters began to feel the powerful magick swirling around them, simultaneous with the smoky mists churning within the crystal's cavernous core.

"We've made our connection," Maggie whispered. "Remain calm and keep your focus. Athena is answering our plea."

"Calm and centered," crooned Cara. "Steady on now … steady on …"

The ball's mists cleared swifter than ever before, as an image swam to life; and for the second time in a matter of days, the Sisters recognized the location– the wooded jogging trails behind Haleigh College. There were several wooded areas about the Hamlet; but through the winter-bare tangle of trees, they could clearly see Old Main's highest turret. They readily recognized the people in the scene as well.

Though all three Sisters kept a tight rein on their emotions, the image blurred, faded and vanished– and they knew Athena's magickal movie had ended.

"Oh, no!" Raine blurted. "We got the where and the who, but we don't know *when!*"

Suddenly, the ball's silvery-grey mists rose, whipped in ministorm, and cleared, producing a beloved face.

"You must get to the college fast!" Grantie Merry exclaimed from the crystal's inner depths.

Then as rapidly as she had appeared– Grantie vanished.

Aisling sprang to her feet. "You two follow the proper steps to conclude our ritual, but be quick! The Goddess will understand and approve our haste, and I'll ring the chief to meet us on the jogging paths behind the college."

After trying all of Chief Fitzpatrick's numbers, Aisling left a message for him to meet them at the location Athena revealed to them.

"He told me he was going to Judge Reardon's house today to get the warrant. I don't want to disrupt that; this killer's bent on–" Aisling cut herself short. "We must leave now! We'll handle the situation ourselves."

In a flash, the Sisters were exiting Tara. Maggie was just about to lock the front door, when Raine shouted, "Wait, I'll only be a sec!"

"Where're you going?" Aisling called impatiently after her. Not getting an answer, the blonde Sister yelled, "Hurry! I'll start the car. *HURRY!!*"

A few moments later, Raine dashed out the door with the bow and arrows she used to light the bonfires at their *Samhain* and

Beltane fests. "You never know!" she bellowed in reply to their startled looks, as she bounded into the backseat. "Let's roll!"

"Park here!" Maggie's hand shot out to point in excited voice, prodding Aisling to screech the black Escalade to an abrupt halt at the converted McKenzie stable that housed most of Haleigh's faculty offices.

"Here, we're close to the jogging trails," Raine put in, swiftly shucking her seat belt, "'n close to creating waterloo for the murderer."

The Sisters sprang from the SUV to head flat out for the wooded paths.

"Quickly and as quietly as we can," Aisling whispered the instant they stepped onto the trail access, a thickly wooded area.

Carrying her bow and arrows, Raine took the lead. "This way."

They hadn't gone far when they spied, secreted behind a stately pine and armed with a bow and arrows of his own– *the killer.* By the grace of the great Goddess, thus far anyway, he hadn't seen them. Rather, he seemed to be in some sort of trance.

"Vengeance is in my heart, death in my hand ... blood and revenge are hammering in my head," he muttered darkly, the wrathful quote reaching the Sisters' sharp ears.

"Off the trail," Aisling whispered, giving her cousins a shove, "and into those pines, there."

Scarcely did they move, when along a curve of the path came a runner– the jogger Athena had shown them earlier. Peering through the dark pines toward the killer, the Sisters saw that he was in shooting stance, his bow poised to let fly an arrow.

Without a word, Raine took her stance to nock the arrow and make ready.

Neither did Aisling hesitate, her resolve breathing the words into her sister of the moon's ear, "Can you take him?"

Without verbal reply, her feet shoulder-width apart, the Goth gal looked down the arrow to align it with the target. Expertly releasing the projectile to hit the hostile archer in the shoulder, she caused him to cry out, though his injury was a mere flesh wound.

From this point everything unrolled in *rapid* succession: The shriek paused the jogger on the footpath, who looked promptly round to spot his attacker, who simultaneously whirled to see who'd shot him. Discovering the Sisters, the killer raised his readied bow with an incensed growl, setting another run of actions into fast forward. A demonic expression morphed his face to one the magickal trio no longer recognized as he took direct aim at Raine, who hadn't time to fix another arrow into her bow.

For a critical moment, time stood still, whilst everything stood out in sharp detail, and all three Sisters were vulnerable.

As the fiend drew back the bow string, the blaze of his predator's gaze sliding down the arrow to the raven-haired Sister, she kept stance, coolly nocking *her* arrow.

Just as the archer was about to relax his grasp on the string, the jogger's strong pair of arms seized him from behind in a vise-like grip, sending the arrow whizzing through the air with a loud hissssssssssssssssss– missing Raine by a mere two inches.

"Hold him, Longbough!" a familiar stentorian voice shouted from the trail behind the Sisters, who couldn't help but be startled. Rushing forward with one of his junior officers, the chief commanded, "Dr. Rex Lear, you're under arrest for the murder of Professor Annabel Lee and for several attempted murders! Read him his rights."

That evening, the chief rang Aisling. "I've been in law enforcement for many years, and *never* have I seen anything like what I experienced today. I've seen this sort of thing in the movies and on TV, but never in person. Our alleged killer will be undergoing a psych-eval, and it looks to me that what we've got here is a split or dual personality. In the language of psychology– *schizophrenia.*"

A session with their Sleuthing Set had brought the Sisters together at the Goodwin home. Raine and Maggie were standing next to Aisling, who pulled them into a private corner of the living room, whilst the others were seated at table in the adjacent dining area.

"I took the liberty of telling the psychiatric examiner that you'd be willing to meet with him at a time he deems fit," Fitzpatrick informed. "Since you … well, Raine and Maggie knew and worked with Lear for several years."

"Of course," the threesome replied nearly in sync.

"These psychological cases are the devil!" There was a pause before Fitz spoke again, his voice, once more, taking on an astonished tone. "Speaking of the Devil, I wish you could've seen him … *Lear*, I mean. It was–" He stopped dead, grasping for expression, then finally gave up. "I don't think I *have* a word to describe it. His face, his voice, his manner, all completely different from his own, his original– or whatever the proper word is– personality. And I'll tell you something else– and you know I'm not one for exaggeration– ***it was spine-chilling!***"

At the Goodwin dining-room table, over a pickup supper of roasted sweet potato corn chowder with crusty bread, the Sleuthing Set was yearning to be brought up-to-date. Raine had swooped by Sal-San-Tries for the savory soup. Thaddeus supplied the artisan bread purchased from a local monastery in the nearby Laurel Highlands. Aisling stopped by The Gypsy Tearoom for a beautiful assortment of Eva's desserts, and Beau contributed the wine, whilst Hugh and Betty did the serving.

"So there's no doubt now– Dr. Lear poisoned Professor Annabel Lee, in addition to attempting to poison his protégée, Trixie Fox, as well as the student actors playing Romeo and Juliet in his own play," Aisling announced.

"My God, and he was the crazed campus archer too! Why? What in Heaven's name was his motive?" Betty probed. She buttered a crusty heel of the bread and crunched a bite, her widened eyes on the McDonoughs.

"You tell them, Raine," Aisling said, looking to that sister of the moon. "You're the best storyteller."

"The short answer is *revenge*," Raine declared setting her soupspoon across the top of her bowl and pushing her empty plate away. "But this is a long and somewhat complicated tale."

She took a quick sip of her wine, but took her time with the story, relating it in her precise fashion for her listeners. "I'll begin with what we learned from Ron Moon, the owner and barkeep at The Man In The Moon pub. During all the mayhem, Maggie and I happened to think how much bartenders, barbers and beauticians are like psychiatrists. You know what I'm saying. Patrons unload their troubles on those people, vent when frequenting their establishments, so we decided to ask Moon if anyone connected to Haleigh College had ever cried in their beer to him about anything that might help us in our investigation. He thought for a moment, and then lit up like the proverbial Christmas tree, sharing with us what Dr. Lear spilled to him one evening when he'd had too much to drink.

"Lear's grandfather, Major Tristan Lear, a fighter pilot, was stationed in England with the Mighty Eighth Army Air Force during World War II. There, he fell in love with Gillian Shipton, an English girl of Scottish extraction. Gillian came from a long line of witches, *famous* witches, in fact, though the girl herself only dabbled in the Craft. The way Lear told the tale, Tristan and Gillian were ill-fated lovers, whose story rivals Romeo and Juliet's."

Raine took another sip of wine, continuing. "It seems during their love affair, Gillian happened to mention that she was descended from a line of witches that reached back to medieval times. She told her lover that if he were ever to forsake her, she would curse all the male descendants in his family, beginning with him, a bane that destined them never to find true love ... that they would never be happy in love."

"A good, old-fashioned family curse, eh?" Hugh expressed, looking up from his soup. "And an interesting one at that."

The Goth gal tilted her head to counter, "Maggie, Aisling, and I all feel that she could *not* have uttered those words if true love existed between her and Tristan, and we believe she *did* truly *love* him, as he loved her. We do *not* feel there was ever a curse on the men of Dr. Lear's family, not cast by a witch anyway. However, we all know what bad press witches have always gotten, and we all know, too, that a prophecy or curse **self**-fulfilled is **nonetheless** fulfilled."

"So you're saying that the men, starting with Tristan, in Lear's family **believed** there was a curse on them, and thus they **manifested** the bane with each generation, right?" Betty asked.

"*Touché!*" Raine replied. "That's exactly what *we believe* happened, but we're getting ahead of ourselves. "Tristan and Gillian rendezvoused every chance they got, but in wartime, disruptive things happen."

"The grim realities of war," Hugh murmured, pointing a finger at Raine with a wink.

"Yes." Raine picked up where she left off. "There came, in May 1945, after Germany surrendered, a time when Tristan was shipped out to the Pacific theater of war. His orders came down quickly, and he was gone. He wasn't able to keep what would have been his final rendezvous with his love; thus, he never got to say goodbye. Instead, he sent a note to her home, via a buddy."

"Let me guess," Beau interposed, "she never got it. Either Tristan's buddy, for whatever reason, did not deliver the note," he cocked his dark head, "*or* someone in her family destroyed the note, because possibly they didn't want Gillian to marry an American and skip off to America after the war."

"That last is what *we think* might have happened," Raine answered. "At this point, we don't know, though what we *think* is not just guesswork. More like *inspired* guesswork I daresay."

"And afterward," Thaddeus put in, hanging on Beau's last words and stroking his van dyke in a speculative gesture, "when Tristan wrote Gillian, the family kept all the letters from her."

"Again, we don't know, but we feel that's a strong possibility," said Raine.

"More inspired guesswork?" Hugh quizzed. "But you're off to a great start, I'd say."

With a bob of her dark head, Raine proceeded: "Gillian's family consisted of her grandmother and mother, both *powerful* witches. Gillian had alluded to her lover that her granny and mother were worried about the love affair becoming so serious that he would want to whisk her away to America when the war ended. In fact, she never invited Tristan to the Shipton cottage for fear her family might say something to him that would offend. But, we tend to think, rather than wielding their wands, the Shipton women were just exercising maternal protection toward a young and innocent daughter. They didn't want her to be hurt."

Thaddeus raised a hand for the floor. "I seem to recall a popular cliché of World War II England: "The Americans are over-paid, over-fed, over-sexed– and over here!"

"You can't blame Gillian's little village of Freckleton if they harbored such feelings. The folks there were *overwhelmed*. There were over ten thousand Americans stationed at the Warton air depot, right next to that tiny village, where the pre-war population was less than two thousand," Raine informed. "During the war, Freckleton was nicknamed 'Little America.' In addition, a great tragedy occurred there when a B-24 Liberator, out for a routine test flight, was struck by lightning and crashed into the village snack bar and a school, killing sixty-one people, including a whole generation of the village's children. God and Goddess rest them. It was not the pilot's fault. To date, the village has never again experienced such a violent storm.

"Think how difficult the situation was for Freckleton, which, by the bye, became known ever after, as the 'Village That Cried.' They had a lot to deal with– the war with all the fears and sacrifices that go with it, the air disaster in their village and the devastating loss of their children, the flux of Americans. As I said, *a lot to deal with.*"

Raine went on after a pensive moment of silence. "We know Gillian never answered Tristan's letters to war's end and afterward. Well, there was a letter in question, but I'll get to that.

"Dr. Lear told Ron Moon that his grandfather wrote her many letters, finally stopping when he received a short, curt note from Gillian in which she ordered him to stop writing, that she'd fallen in love with someone else and was about to be wed."

Raine looked to Maggie and Aisling, saying, "We do *not* believe Gillian penned that letter. If Tristan had ever seen her handwriting, likely by that point his memory of it was dust. In fact, we don't believe there was *any* truth to that note penned and posted to Tristan in America, *we think*, by her grandmother and mother."

"You mean you have a witchy notion that Gillian not only didn't write the letter but that she wasn't about to be wed either?" Ian tested.

"Correct, that's what we sense. We don't know if Gillian ever married. At this point, we have no idea what became of her."

"Hmmm, I wonder if the grandmother and mother had someone in mind for the girl to marry?" Ian considered. "Used to be a lot of that sort of thing– *arranged* marriages they were called– and they didn't want Tristan's letters getting in the way."

"Don't know," Raine shrugged, adjusting herself in her chair. "What we *do* know is that in 1949, *Tristan* married, a local girl, here in the Hamlet; and they had one child, a son, Dr. Lear's father. Now, Tristan began believing that there was a curse, due to the fact that he and his wife were unhappy in their marriage. Thus began this bane, woefully passed down in the Lear family, embroidered on and growing in proportion from one generation to the next."

"Huh," Betty mused. "Perhaps there's something to that old saying that a really good fighter pilot never does come down out of the clouds."

"Do you know for sure that Tristan's son, who was Rex's father, was *also* unhappy in his marriage?" Beau queried.

"Yes, we know that for sure too," Raine responded sadly. "It all seems a great pity. But to back up a bit, Tristan and his wife stayed together, because that's what folks did back then. Tristan's son, the father of Dr. Rex Lear, and Rex's mother split up shortly after he was born. She abandoned her little family, leaving the infant Rex to be reared by his father.

"We discovered from Jo Nosh, who lived next door to Rex all through their school years, that he sought out his mother when he was in high school, and she rejected him a second time. Jo told us how hurt Rex was when his mother told him he reminded her of his father, weak and worthless. Can you believe it? Those were the cutting words she used to her own son– words, as it turned out, that, burned in Dr. Lear's memory, fueled his mounting disorder into full-blown schizophrenia."

"And wait till you hear this next part," Maggie exclaimed. "Raine, tell them what Jo told us about Longbow and Rex in high school."

"Due to the family curse, Rex was ultra-shy in high school; but there was one girl with whom he tried his best to overcome his fears and his wariness. He finally got up the nerve to ask her to the senior prom. She accepted, and he was thrilled. Rex worked after school to earn the money for a tux rental, a corsage for his date, and cash for the après-prom, did all sorts of chores to earn the right to borrow his father's car for the event. Then, a few days before the prom, the gal telephones him to say she's going with Ken Longbough. She had a crush all along on this handsome jock, you see; and when he asked her, even though she'd accepted Rex's invitation, she jumped at the chance. Jo said Ken Longbough's date had taken sick, and though he knew the girl he asked on the rebound already had a date with Rex, he asked her anyway.

"Needless to say, Rex was devastated. He harbored a hatred of Longbow ever since, because, as Jo told us, Ken Longbough *knew* the girl was Lear's date, but the all's-fair-in-love-and-war concept incited him to ask her regardless. Already the target of teasing, the ultra-sensitive Rex Lear became the victim of a whole new rash of mocking afterward."

Raine suddenly remembered something. "When I proposed a toast at our faculty Valentine tea, Dr. Lear was the only person at our table who didn't oblige my salute to true friendship and true love. Instead, Rex pretended to drop a spoon, which he leaned down to retrieve."

"Tell them what Lear's ex-wife, William's mother, said when you interviewed her," Aisling prompted.

Raine stopped to take a long draft of water, flinging her hand out to Maggie to carry on.

"We never expected to like Rex's ex," Maggie began, "but turns out we did. She's a cultured woman, sincere, with a straightforward, down-to-earth demeanor, who had … *has* little patience for what she referred to as her 'ex's illogical balderdash.' Their son, William, resides with her. Essentially, what she told us was that their marriage was disaster-prone from the start. Every little tiff, any disagreement whatsoever always set Rex to thinking about the curse. I recall her saying, 'What marriage doesn't have its ups and downs? With Rex, it was all bliss or doom, and my ex-husband is *the* prophet of doom.'"

Raine resumed the discussion. "Years after his divorce, when Professor Lee joined the staff at Haleigh, Rex was smitten with her from the get-go. We never saw any evidence that Annabel played him, but *he* must have thought so, because she was so nice to him, but Annabel was jolly nice to everyone. She got engaged to Dr. Whitman during our Valentine Fest and ended up dead. With Trixie Fox … well, there was a cat, or I should say *vixen,* of a different color. She used Rex shamelessly to go after her goals– to gain her master's degree and get herself hired in Haleigh's theatre department; then *she* gets engaged, and *she* nearly ends up dead."

"I see why Lear wanted to punish Professors Longbough and Trixie Fox and even Annabel Lee. I'm saying, I grasp why through his fractured way of thinking; but why on earth the student actors in the *Romeo and Juliet* roles?" Betty questioned.

Raine puckered her brow. "Maggie and I looked into that, and after a confidential discussion with Jo Nosh this morning, we discovered that those students were the son and daughter of two of Dr. Lear's high school classmates who were especially insensitive to him during those fragile teen years. Mind that was a different era than today; and because Rex was a sensitive fellow, *artsy,* a bit showy perhaps, in addition to the fact that he never had a girlfriend, he was teased unmercifully by several of his classmates, who spread rumors about him and taunted him for being gay, complete with name-calling, harassment and bullying. Rex isn't gay, but you see what I'm saying."

"I do," Betty remarked. "That sort of behavior is so nasty. Bullies are such cowards!"

"And when Rex met with his mother," Raine swept on, "*she* was unbelievably cruel, which resulted in his tearful goodbye. His own mother taunted him with the name-calling of his schoolmates. Jo told us the same kids tormented her, calling her names because she was a tomboy and loved sports."

Beau inclined his head, letting out a long, low whistle that caused Hugh's German shepherds, Nero and Wolfe, napping in the warmth of the fireplace, to raise heads from paws and prick their ears.

"No wonder the man snapped," Betty muttered. "Hurts from school days are hurts remembered through life. They leave deep scars."

"When I let myself into Rex's home, I saw an oil painting of a beautiful woman, her back to the viewer, looking over her shoulder with an air that clearly screams, 'Get lost!' You see, *he* believed there was a curse, and *he* re-enforced the whole idea of a curse, every day of his life, every time he looked at that painting, for example. Believed that he would never he happy in love, that he'd never find true love. No damn wonder he experienced one rejection after another, as well as unrequited love, time after time."

"People see each of us as we see ourselves," Aisling stated. She sipped her wine, reflecting on a string of people she and Ian investigated over the years.

"Understand," Maggie thought to interject, "Rex was–" she set her lips in a firm line; "let's be blunt about it, rather a doormat all his life. He never rose to the occasion to defend himself or take his own part; and all his life, he felt unworthy, unloved, abandoned and rejected. The layered, amplified sorrows rendered him increasingly bitter, but he just couldn't help himself.

"Then this other personality began to emerge, the dark side of the Dr. Lear we knew. This emerging personality was full of revenge, and– oh, I shouldn't speak as if I am a trained psychologist, though teachers and professors all have to take courses in psychology. We," she flipped a quick glance to her sisters of the moon, "have our own theory about this, but we'll see what the police, the forensic psych evaluation reveals. In a few days, we'll be talking to Dr. Lear's examiner."

Raine paused to peer eagerly at Hugh, who appeared to be ruminating over something. "Hugh, you've been in your old clam shell tonight."

"Why my clam shell?" he guffawed, looking up with sudden attention.

"Because when you're going over something in that sleuthhound mind of yours, you retreat from the world," the Goth gal replied. "I daresay, you can be quite *mysterious* yourself at times."

"That name, the name of the English … *Scottish* girl's family. *Shipton*. Research it. I know I've heard the name before. From history maybe."

"I'm thinking the same thing," Thaddeus commented. "When someone asks, 'What's in a name?' I sit up and take notice."

"We *have* researched the family name of Tristan Lear's World War II lover," Maggie responded. "The Shiptons are a family of powerful English and Scottish witches, the stories about them reaching back centuries. Concisely stated, they're *super*-witches. Raine, tell everyone what we uncovered about them during the World War II era."

"Ah yes, Operation Cone of Power," the Goth gal crooned, setting her wine glass on the table and gearing up for the telling of another good story. "Always room for a compelling chronicle that can transport people to a different time and place. And all the best stories have witches in them." She rubbed her hands together. "OK, remember the Disney film *Bedknobs and Broomsticks*?" Not waiting for a response, Raine hastened on, "In the movie, a witch seeks and subsequently casts a spell useful to the defense of Britain during WWII. Though it's a children's tale, the story holds a lot of truth.

"During the dark days of the war, Germany– *with its formidable war machine*– never invaded England. *Think about that.* If they had– and as professors of history, Maggie, Thad, and I can tell you, there are a lot of *ifs* in history– world domination would, arguably, have been within Hitler's grasp. What stopped this invasion? I know we're getting off subject here, but bear with me, and I'll connect the dots for you. Besides, this Cone of Power account is so damn stimulating."

"Oh, we know you're leading up to something worth waiting for!" Betty exclaimed.

Raine picked up her wine goblet for Hugh to refill it. "The general consensus among historians is that in order to invade England, Hitler would've had to gain air superiority, and that was denied him as a result of the Battle of Britain. Through the summer and fall of 1940, German and British air forces clashed in the skies over the UK, and despite months of targeting Britain's aerodromes, military bases, and civilian population, the determined, beleaguered pilots of the RAF– *Bless them!*– zapped Germany's objective for air superiority. Britain's decisive victory saved the country from invasion and possible German occupation. But there was an *additional* force at work there– *a different kind of air force*. A *simultaneous* fight that I call the *Magickal* Battle of Britain.

"As the Luftwaffe rumbled overhead, a cabal of Britain's witches– Bless them too!– organized intent and visualization to seed ideas in the *unified* mind of the British people, visions to invoke angelic and ancestor protection to uphold British morale under fire. Remember the museum sequence from *Bedknobs and Broomsticks* with the British knights in armor on the move?

"As one of the leaders of the British witches, Dion Fortune, taught, 'What is sown will grow.' She believed that Hitler and his Reich were using dark forces allied in opposition to Britain, hence her conjuring of *angelic* protection. But this wise woman did not stop there. As the war raged on, she orchestrated an extraordinary feat of magick, securing the aid of several prominent witches of the era, including Aleister Crowley, though a controversial figure to this day; Gerald Gardner; and the Shipton witches.

"This powerful circle of witches invoked ancient spirits pledged to Britain's defense, like King Arthur and his Knights of the Round Table, Merlin, St. Michael, and St. George.

"According to several reports, the night Hitler was to launch the invasion of Britain, Operation Sea Lion, the powerful cabal of witches met secretly in an ancient forest, ironically named New Forest, in southern England, and possibly, in addition, on the Cliffs of Dover to raise, via ceremonial magick– a great Cone of Power to stop Nazi invasion.

"Skyclad under the moon, the gathering of witches began to dance in a spiraling pattern around the circle, continuously intensifying the conjured energies to the communal ecstatic state necessary for their purpose. As they danced in that misty wood, they hurled their chants at the effigy of Hitler they'd faced toward Berlin, echoing the magick their ancestors used in the sixteenth century against the Armada and, in the nineteenth, against Napoleon Bonaparte.

"That cold, damp Lammas Eve ritual of 1940, their raised Cone of Power was directed at Hitler's mind– 'You cannot cross the sea … you cannot cross the sea … *you cannot cross the sea!*'– sending out powerful magick, just as their great-grandmothers and great-grandfathers had done to Boney and their more remote ancestors, in 1588, to the Spanish Armada.

"Again, I say bless those British witches, for they paid a *high* price. Most of them suffered from chronic health problems thereafter. For instance, two contracted pneumonia, passing over to the Summerland that year, and Crowley died two years before the war's end. *But their magick worked. It worked!*

"No less than twice during the war, Hitler planned to invade England, but Operation Sea Lion never took place." Raine tilted her dark head, reflecting, "I remember someone asking me the pointed question at a history seminar several years ago, 'Do you really think that report is true?' I turned the question on its head, answering, 'I think it would have been extremely *un*likely that something along those lines would *not* have happened.'"

Raine sighed. "What I just related to you is about the power of witches to channel energies and create a Cone of Power that rises from them like a huge witch's hat, the spell shooting out the apex in an explosion of directed energy to the target– hence, the power of witches to do something that is nearly impossible. And to borrow a quote from Walt Disney, 'It's kind of fun to do the impossible,'" the Goth gal grinned.

"Where there's a witch, there's a way," Aisling murmured. "Speaking of a witch's hat, it acts as a focal point that directs … *funnels* cosmic energies and wisdom to the wearer."

"Absolutely!" Raine exclaimed, "like the Great Pyramids, or Native American teepees."

"In any case, Dr. Lear's grandfather, stationed in England during the war, had an intense love affair with one of the Shipton witches, sooooo," Ian deduced, "she and her family could *well* have put a curse on all the male descendants of the Lear family. Piece of cake after what they did to stop Hitler."

"Could well have, yes," Maggie replied. "*Indeed* yes, but we do *not* think they did."

"And we intend to prove it to save Dr. Lear's son, William, along with future Lear descendants from the fate of unrequited, unhappy love, and withal, Goddess forbid, schizophrenia and murder," Raine interjected. "Right now, it's just a feeling we have," she tossed a glance at her sisters of the moon, "but we intend to prove there was no curse on the males of the Lear line."

"And you intend to prove it, using your Time-Key," Beau stated quietly.

"Most assuredly we do," Raine's jaw hardened, and she answered with more than a touch of determination carrying on her deep voice. "Granny told us we would *need* to make use of the Key to save an innocent from the fate of his fathers. The full moon is three days hence, and that's when we'll take off for World War II England. Needless to say, it's the only way. Things *have* been linking up, but the connections are still far from clear."

Maggie turned to face her other half, her emerald eyes sparkling with fun. "Thaddeus, do you wish to accompany us again?"

"Need you ask?" the professor responded, lifting his wineglass as if in a toast. He threw Beau a quick look that could almost have passed for a nod of conspiracy.

Unaware of the gesture, Maggie laughed her sexy laugh, resting a hand on her lover's muscular thigh.

Raine, in contrast, had snagged the silent signal that passed between Beau and Thaddeus. *There he goes again,* she told herself. *Something is brewing ... gathering force between those two, but what?*

In the prevailing time, Maggie was talking. "Raine and I are going to the village tomorrow to Enchantments costume shop for our 1940s togs. We'll get yours too, darlin'," she said to Thaddeus.

"By now, you're aware that we've done a good bit of research on both the Shiptons and the Lears, so all that's left for us to do is to get our Forties' attire, agree on where our portal will be for this time-trek," Raine deliberated aloud, "and consult Athena for the best date ... best *landing* date. We always stage our takeoffs the night of the full moon."

"It's occurred to me," Hugh began, "that you should get your costumes on early, the night of departure, and head over to The Man In The Moon pub, where the atmosphere and the music will provide you with the 'juice' you'll need behind your intent to time-travel to World War II England. While you're there, talk to Ron Moon about

Warton, the Base Air Depot where Major Tristan Lear was stationed. You said Moon's father was stationed there, too, during the war. I know you, know you'll do more study on Warton and the surrounding area before you take off; but right before you do, talking to Moon about Warton, hearing his father's reminiscences, soaking up the atmosphere of his WWII-era English pub, and listening to the period music he plays in there will be just the ticket– pun intended– you'll need."

"Wiz-zard!" Raine grinned. "Oh, but we can't take off from The Man In The Moon. We set forth on our time-travels at midnight. The Moon's a popular place; it'll be busy."

"Of course you *can't* take off from the pub," Hugh said; "but after you get revved up there, go to Haleigh's Wood and … **do it**."

"Ye——s," Raine, Maggie, and Aisling meditated as one, looking to one another to trade thoughts, "yes, the woods are timeless."

"Moreover *protective*," the pragmatic blonde with the wand added. "We must have a care to safeguard the Time-Key."

"OK, so we soak up the atmosphere at the Moon, drive home to Tara and take off from our woods when the full moon's high in the midnight sky," Raine rhymed, sitting back to again sip her wine. "She reached for a cherry tart, a catlike smile on her lips. "Thanks, Hugh."

"It's settled then?" Maggie bade, looking to Aisling. "We must save William and all future Lear men from what we believe is a *self-fulfilled but nonetheless destructive* bane."

"Yes," Aisling confirmed. "I totally agree."

"Even if you find out that your theory is true, that there never was a witches' curse on the men in Dr. Lear's family, how do you prove it to William," Beau asked, "without jeopardizing the Key?"

Raine, Maggie, and Aisling pondered this for a protracted moment of suspense, with Raine answering, "We don't know the answer to that yet, but–"

The Sisters looked to one another, concluding in perfect sync–

"**Where there's a witch– there's a way!**"

Chapter Fourteen

That same evening, in Tara's sacred attic space, the Sisters were again seeking the answer to an important question from Athena. They knew they'd be taking off for World War II England at midnight during the full moon, three days hence, but they needed to uncover the best date for their landing, so they could program their Time-Key.

Now, seated before their crystal ball, Maggie's chanting was bringing forth the familiar mists. Before the trilogy of Sisters could say "Blessed be," they were looking at an American flyer– tall, dark, and dashing as any leading man in the cinema.

The golden oak leaves on his brown well-pressed uniform with its belted tunic, commonly referred to in WWII issue as the "Pinks and Greens," identified him as a major, and the blue insignia patch on his left shoulder proudly displayed the gold-winged eight of the Mighty Eighth Army Air Force.

In contrast, his cap was the brown crush hat seen in so many WWII films, with brown leather visor that matched the glossy shoes. The battered hat was steeped in tradition, a tradition started by the Eighth Army Air Force's flying personnel as a mark that separated the fledging from the battle hardened of twenty-five or more combat missions. Though the crush hat was not exactly regulation, it was tolerated for those who earned the right to wear it.

The mustached flyer was sitting in what appeared to be a café or pub. As the Sisters watched, he ground out his cigarette to pick up a newspaper from the table. It was then they took note of the date, 19 May 1945.

The fact that they did not *expect* to see anything else, likely brought forth the subsequent scenes in such rapid succession, gratitude and serenity their catalysts.

A woman, who looked to be in her twenties, was approaching the table, bringing the flyer instantly to his feet. Shapely, with dark, medium-length hair parted in the middle and coiffed in a Forties' style, the lady's complexion was "Snow-White" fair, her lips rouged with a rich shade of red.

Wow, thought Raine, *Gillian's a dead ringer for Hedy Lamarr, a popular actress of the era. Those cheekbones are to die for!*

The striking young woman sported the dress uniform of a nurse in the British Red Cross, the dark-blue color deepening her eyes to violet. Beneath, she wore a crisp, white shirt with a neat tie that matched the blue of the tunic and skirt. The uniform's cap, with its gold insignia, was beaked, flattering to her heart-shaped face. A dark-blue shoulder bag was draped over her arm; and in typical English style, she toted an umbrella.

Settling into the chair the major pulled out for her, she removed her white gloves, her eyes following him, as he took his seat opposite her.

"It's been nearly a week." He reached across the table to take her hand. "I've missed you."

"I've missed you more." She pulled her hand away as the waitress took their order for tea and scones.

"No one should look that good in a uniform," he teased. "And no one should have that color of eyes. It's distracting."

Lowering her gaze, a pink flush rose to her cheeks as a slight smile curved the ruby lips.

"And quite captivating."

"I've seen evidence of that." Modesty forbade her to say more; but leaning forward, she voiced in a whisper, "Surely you'll be discharged before too long, now that the Jerrys have thrown in the towel." The Sisters could sense the lady's subtle yet seductive perfume, a heady mélange of white jasmine, myrrh, and night musk.

And something else, Maggie thought. *A woodsy, sweet scent ... amber perhaps.*

Major Lear dallied, looking away to fold and set aside his newspaper, seemingly waiting for a loud burst of laugher to subside from a nearby table occupied by a mix of local girls and American GIs. In the background, the popular music of Vera Lynn played softly, the song "There'll Always Be An England."

After a projected pause, he said, "Since your father is deceased, I think I should do the proper thing and speak to your mother and grandmother. I'd like to tell them of my intentions and ask for your hand. That's how we do things back home in Pennsylvania.

"You'll love my little village. Haleigh's Hamlet is a beautiful place with a surplus of charm and a heap of history. It's in the Pittsburgh area, so I can take you to concerts and symphonies, to plays and all the things we'll both enjoy in the city. Nighttime Pittsburgh from Mount Washington is a magickal spot. Why, even the steel mills are beautiful at night, with the sky above a fiery drama! I can't wait to show you everything and introduce you to my family. They're going to fall in love with you immediately, just as I did." He studied her for a stretched-out moment, reaching for her hand to bring it to his lips, whilst he gazed into her eyes. "I fell in love with you the first moment I saw you, and you smiled because you knew it."

Noting the anxiety that made itself visible on her features, he said, holding his voice to a near-whisper, "Gillian, do I detect a note of apprehension?"

"A note?" She lowered her eyes. "More like a whole symphony."

"Sweetheart, don't you *want* your family's blessing? You and I have talked time and again of marriage, but isn't it only right that I finally meet your family and speak with them about our plans for the future?" His eyes dropped to the hand he held between his own. "Why don't you ever wear the ring?"

Gillian gave a long sigh, leaning closer. "I told you before, I *can't* wear it. Not yet. I'm afraid Mum and Gran won't like the fact that you and I are *making* plans. Plans that will result in my going off to America, and ... oh, Tris, they are so set in their ways," she raised one dark brow, "*the Old Ways* I told you about." Squeezing his fingers, she murmured, "And if that were not enough, for the past few years, Gran and Mum have been right sickly."

The Sisters sensed she wanted to say more about why and how her grandmother and mother succumbed to ill health, but she chose not to. Instead, she said softly, "I saw a shooting star last night, and I made a wish."

"What was your wish, milady?" he asked with anticipation in his eyes. "Tell me."

"Oh, it won't come true if I tell!" she exclaimed with a half-smile.

The waitress brought their tea, and the Sisters could see that the lovers continued holding hands and talking, their heads close together.

"No one should look as enchanting as you; it's not quite fair," he pronounced, "to us mortals."

At that, the image suddenly vanished, wiped away by Athena's eddying mists, as a new scene took form within the crystal: There, the lovers were abed, the sheet covering them, Gillian with her head resting on Tristan's chest.

"I love you to distraction," he whispered, kissing her forehead, as she gazed up at him with eyes soft and misty with love. He was looking at her the way all women want to be looked at by the man they love. "You're all I think about."

"I know, darling, it's how I feel too." A moment later, her eyes kindled, and her face took on a naughty mien, her speech an effected accent. "Awlreet, ducky, if iver y' decide y're tired iv me, if iver ya leave me, I'll be castin' a spell on you and all th' blokes in yer kin, so that none iv yer lot will iver find true love. An' tha knows I can!"

"Tired of you! How could I grow tired of *you*, Gillian? You have bewitched me body and soul. *I love you!*" He pulled her to him to hug her close, then tilted her chin to search her face. "You've no idea how my heart races when I look at you. How it aches for you when–" Of a sudden, he inclined his head, asking, "You wouldn't really do that, would you … put a curse on me?" Though his voice sounded light, the question in his eyes was far from it.

"You frightful idiot," she laughed merrily, reaching out to tenderly touch his face. "I was only teasing. I could never hurt you." Something veiled the brightness in those violet eyes then, for her voice took on a bit of tartness when she added, "And I hope you never hurt me."

The scene vanished to be replaced by an image of the front of a pub. The Plough. Promptly did Athena whisk the watching Sisters inside, where, seated alone at a small table in the rear, that appeared to be the same corner from an earlier scene, they saw Gillian. The young woman seemed to be fretting over the fact that she was alone, for she kept checking the lapel watch pinned to her dark-blue uniform for the time, her face registering what could have been either anxiety or discontent.

Again, the scene in the globe was effaced by Athena's swirling grey mists to produce a further image within the crystal depths.

Seated at his military desk, Major Lear was dashing off a note. Picking it up, he quickly read aloud from the single sheet of paper: "My darling, I cannot meet you today. Orders just came down. I'm being deployed immediately to the Pacific theater. I can say no more. I'll write you as soon as I can. Please wait for me. This war can't go on much longer. I love you with all my heart and soul, and I can't wait to spend the rest of my life with you! Your Tristan."

The Sisters watched the major seal the note in an envelope and scrawl Gillian's name on the outside. Then picking up his gear, he hurried to a waiting jeep, en route pausing a fellow officer. "Tom, can you take this note to the Shipton cottage on Kirkham Road, just outside of town? I don't want to entrust this to anyone else." He waited as a large cargo plane roared overhead. "It's very important, will you do it as soon as you get off duty?"

"Sure, that'll be at fifteen hundred." He checked his watch. "It's twenty till now."

"Thanks, Tom! Do I have your word about the note?"

"Of course. Good luck, Tris, give 'em hell!" he shouted over the noise, as a "deuce and a half" lumbered passed.

The two shook hands; and picking up his gear again, the major hastened off, to disappear in the smoky mists that wiped the ball clean.

Athena's magickal movie had ended.

After a quiet moment, which the Sisters needed to pull themselves back to the present, Aisling asked her sisters of the moon, "Did you see the date on the note Tristan penned to Gillian?"

"Yes," Raine and Maggie replied in sync, concluding, "May 23, 1945."

"*That's the date with which we program our Time-Key*," Raine nearly shouted. "And we know we must be there before three in the afternoon. Jolly good, what!"

"Do you have a spot picked out for your landing?" the practical blonde with the wand queried.

Raine and Maggie nodded to one another, with the raven-haired Sister answering, "We do. On the heels of further research, we've decided on Kirk's Wood rather than the historic Quaker Wood, which is a tidy step, to use the British turn of phrase, about a half-hour hike at a good clip. But wiz–zard," she exclaimed. "Kirk's Wood is right off Kirkham Road, where, we've just learned, the Shipton cottage was located. Mighty fine blessing, this!"

Pulling a folded sheet of paper from the pocket of her ritual robe, Raine said, "According to this old map of Freckleton I printed off, the pub known as The Plough is within walking distance of Kirkham Road." A few seconds later, she reasoned to herself aloud, "Gillian must not have told Tristan that the Shiptons were part of the secret cabal of witches that raised the Cone of Power to stop invasion."

"Of course she didn't tell him, or anyone. A spell loses power when talked about," Aisling replied. "You know that."

Raine gave a brisk nod of agreement. "We did hear her say her granny and mum held to the Old Ways, so she must have told him, at least alluded to the larger truth that they were witches; and I got a strong sense that he'd heard **all** the local talk and stories about the Shipton witches."

Maggie looked to Aisling, as both responded, "We read *that* in his eyes."

"*And*," Raine quickly interjected, "it was evident in the question he put to Gillian, asking if she would really put a curse on him! Oh yes, we can be assured Tristan heard all the local scuttlebutt about the Shipton witches, or he wouldn't have reacted as he did to her messing with him … her *teasing*."

"Our investigation revealed that the Shiptons were grey witches," Maggie averred.

"We know grey witches walk in the balance of light and dark," Raine stated. "They believe that a witch who cannot curse, cannot heal, that nature is neutral and balanced."

"Hmm," Aisling considered, "some would argue that magick in itself is a neutral energy or force."

"I see a grey witch as a middle-ground witch who recognizes her own human quirks and flaws and is willing to take a few steps more to imposing her will on the world around her. And sometimes," the Goth gal executed with one of her perfect, single eyebrow arches, "a step or two more to forcing her will over other people."

"Are we talking about grey witches, per se, or are we talking about Dr. Raine McDonough?" asked Aisling and Maggie with a twinkle in their emerald eyes.

Raine laughed too, surprisingly with good-natured aplomb, for she did so hate to be teased. "Everyone has the right to defend themselves. Granny taught us that; and you said it yourself, Aisling, magick in itself is dualistic. You can't have light without the dark. All magick is neutral. *Intention* defines it. And you know what? The Goddess knows what's in each of our hearts. But don't let's get into Craft 101 discussion here. Things are falling into place for us. Now, all we have to do is lay hands on our Forties' togs, and *that* we can take care of on the morrow at Enchantments."

"Divine Mother, Mother Divine,
Show me the way; give me a sign!"
~ The Sleuth Sisters

Chapter Fifteen

The raven-haired Sister ran her eyes down the roll of items they needed to take with them on their upcoming time-trek, reading aloud: "Appropriate 1940s attire that we'll rent from Enchantments costume shop downtown. I rang them an hour ago with a list of what we need for another of our phantom, fancy-dress dinner parties that Enchantments' owner, Lindsey Taylor, believes we host; and she replied that she thought she had everything I mentioned in stock. So after classes tomorrow, we'll stop and pick up the order." Raine laid a finger to her lips. "You know, we really *should* throw those fancy-dress dinner parties. It would be great fun. Lindsey always fits us out so nicely. Just think: For the Edwardian era, costumes *à la Downton Abbey;* the gay flapper outfits of the roaring Twenties; the fab fashions of the Forties and Fifties; the hippie, boho getups of the Sixties and Seventies!"

"Enchantments is open on Sundays now?" Maggie cut in, her teacup paused before her mouth.

Raine shook her head. "No, no. I simply left a message, thinking she'd get it in the morning; then tomorrow afternoon, you see, she'd have everything *ready* for us to try on. Lindsey must check her messages even on Sunday, because she rang up about a half-hour ago."

"I thought I heard your phone sound." Maggie lowered herself into a chair at the kitchen table to relax with her sister of the moon for tea and cranberry-orange scones from The Gypsy Tearoom.

It was late Sunday morning, and the Sisters, still in their bathrobes, were enjoying a comfy respite.

"To recommence our time-trek list," Raine went on, reading from the paper she held: "A vial of Granny's powerful healing potion, just in case; a compass because you never know; money appropriate to the time and place we'll be visiting; replicated press cards, since we've determined that our best bet would be to pose as American journalists; a limited few grooming items and toiletries; of course our talismans, plus an additional piece, each, of our enchanted jewelry that will specifically aid us in this mission, but nothing ostentatious. I've decided to take our shapeshifting locket, and I've fitted it out with the photographs we'll need. I'll tell you about that in a few. Now, let me see … where was I? Oh, and last but not least, our travel *BOS*," she confirmed, referring to their pocket-size, leather-bound *Book of Shadows* that contained the ancient chant that would transport them through the Tunnel of Time– and get them back home again.

"Good thing Thaddeus has a pretty good coin collection," Maggie remarked, peering out the window to the snow-blanketed woods and fields below. It had snowed, off and on, through the night and morning, and now the landscape glittered like diamonds in the late-morning sunshine. "That man never ceases to amaze me. In more ways than one," the redheaded Sister murmured, the full lips curving in the secret smile that was hers alone. "He's already replicated the press cards we'll need. Did a credible job on them too. The fact that we'll be posing as journalists, garnering impressions and stories from the locals, will give us our chance to sit and talk to Gillian. As witches and empaths, we'll be able to size her up, I should think, in jig-time."

"Right. As empaths, we don't just listen to words, we listen to the *use* of words, tone, and body movements. We watch the eyes, subtle facial expressions; and we interpret silences. We hear everything people *don't* put into words. Like Granny taught us, 'Silence isn't empty. It's full of answers.'" Maggie set her cup down in its saucer. "To recap: Athena provided us with the date we needed; and we decided we're going to program our Time-Key to land at our woodsy destination at 1:45 in the afternoon. Better we should get there early than miss Tristan's courier. We've got to see if that officer named Tom delivered Tristan's note to the Shipton cottage; and if he did, what transpired there afterward."

"Oh, just think, Mags," Raine visualized, "World War II England … I'm rarin' to go. Let's absorb as much as we can. Time-trekking is *enlightening*, so useful to us as witches, as sleuths, and goes without saying what it does for us as history profs. I mean, talk about broadening the educational experience with travel!"

"We'd be wise to get the information we need and get back home as fast as we can," Maggie interposed, stretching catlike as she was prone to do. "As good as our replicated press cards look, we won't have *proper* identification, and we sure don't want to be tossed into the brig there at Warton as spies."

Raine pursed her lips, giving a yielding shrug. "You're right, of course. Nevertheless, I don't think we'll ever tire of time-traveling.

Each trek is thrilling and unique in its own right. Each possesses its own personality, with its own mood, vibes and *ambience*."

Maggie smiled affectionately at her enthusiastic cousin. Though it sometimes worried her, she loved Raine's untamed zest for life. "You know, this is the final week of our Valentine Fest. The Student Union has raised a goodly sum for Old Main's restoration by now. I think they might even surpass their goal."

"Hmmm?" Raine said, having caught only a portion of Maggie's words, whilst coming back to reality from her mind-travel. "I don't think they've reached their goal, but they're getting there, and they've still got this whole week to raise money. The Valentine's Dance, moved from the fourteenth, is this Saturday, and that's the concluding event. I hope to the great Goddess we have everything sorted out by then, so we can kick back and enjoy the final night of festivities."

"Darlin'," Maggie crooned, "I have a feeling by then, we won't have to worry about a blessed thing. We'll have it *all* sorted out." She sipped her tea for a moment in silence. "I wonder when the chief will want us to speak with Dr. Lear's psychiatric examiner?"

"Soon, I should think." Now it was Raine's turn to ruminate over their present state of affairs. "Maggie," she began after a long pause, "I really believe Rex will be found *in*competent to stand trial."

The reflective redhead caught her cousin's eye. "I feel the same way."

The next afternoon, after they'd completed their college duties, Raine swung Maggie's vintage, green Land Rover into a parking space on the town square. Stepping out of the vehicle, she stood for several poignant moments, regarding the Hamlet's snow-capped gazebo to reflect on a moonlit walk she'd taken with Beau years before in the Valentine-decorated streets of their Hamlet, when they were both in their teens, dreams spinning silver pathways over the glistening snow.

Ah, she mused, *does any girl ever forget the excitement of that colossal, ornate Valentine signed in masculine scrawl 'Guess who?' And later ... oh, enchanted winter moon shining down on two bent heads, over mittened hands, the wrapping paper crackling as I pulled the ribbon away, and there it was– the delicate locket set with tiny, glittering what-might-be-diamonds! Whoever forgets first love and the first real Valentine?*

Raine breathed in the crisp, sharp air. *At twilight, the February sun leaves a pink glow on the landscape like a Valentine message of love for watchers. Then night comes, sudden and soon, and it's impossible to mark the moment when day ends. It's like the sweeping of ebony wings across the sky– the brief warmth of the sun is gone; and the air crackles with cold. Oh, but there's something comforting in the deep heart of winter,* she told herself.

Maggie stood regarding her sister of the moon. *She's thinking of Beau and their first Valentine's. I remember mine.* The corners of her glossy red lips lifted slightly. *A silver filigree ring with a heart-shaped, blood-red stone in a tiny, black velvet box tied with crimson ribbon. The boy was my first real beau. He was blond, and his name was Finn. I still have that ring. Years ago, I put it on my charm bracelet for luck. Blessings upon you, Finn, wherever you are!*

Released from her fantasy, Raine said, "Mags, someday, on a nice frosty, snowy day such as this, I'm going to settle down before our hearth fire, in Granny's rocker, with a stack of favorite books *and* those I've always wanted to read but never had time to crack."

Maggie smiled again as a new memory wavered across her mind. "Well, Thaddeus says that a well-balanced life is a book in one hand and a cup of good tea or wine in the other."

"*Someday*," Raine envisaged, "I plan on being completely unplugged. I'll rid of clocks and live by the rising sun, wear wild flowers in my hair and dance barefoot on the dewy morning grass. Worship the moon skyclad and walk totally off the beaten path. Oh *yeah*, I'll live full-out on my own terms, fall in love with everyone I meet, and collect oodles of stories to tell!"

"You do most of that *now*." She sipped her tea, saying after a moment, "Within each of us there's a stillness and a sanctuary to which we can retreat anytime to be who we really are. When *you* become a crone," Maggie warned after another weighty moment passed, "they're never going to say, 'What a sweet old lady!' They're gonna say, as we do for Grantie, 'What on earth is she up to now?'"

"You bet!" Raine snapped her fingers. "Oh, I just happened to think– we've got to pop into the feed and grain store for a big bag of that wild bird seed before we head home."

Maggie chortled. "They're not what *I'd* call wild. If they were any tamer, they'd live in the house. And that goes for your buddy the squirrel too. However, I strongly suggest you do that thing you do and tell him, under *no* circumstances, is he to find his rodent way into the attic."

"Ah, don't get your knickers in a twist. I've already told Nibbles that. Do you remember, years ago, how Granny drove a squirrel out of the attic with bagpipe music? Rodents hate the skirl of the pipes."

"Remind me to put a CD of the Great Highland *war* pipes on, then, when we get home. I mean it, Raine, *no squirrels in the house!"*

Inside Enchantments costume shop on the Hamlet's charming town square, Raine and Maggie walked briskly to the counter and rang the bell for assistance.

In a twinkle, the owner and manager, Lindsey Taylor, emerged from behind the calico curtain that separated the shop from the storage and alterations area.

Securing a threaded sewing needle to the bodice of her corduroy jumper, she greeted the Sisters with her ready smile, "Good-afternoon, ladies. I have everything you asked for ready in shopping bags. Hang on, and let me get them. Be right back." The attractive brunette slipped through the opening in the drape, behind which the Sisters could hear the rustle of paper.

In no time at all, Lindsey reappeared, carrying three filled shopping bags that she set on the counter between herself and the waiting Sisters.

"Here we go," she said, pulling the requested items from the brown paper sacks to hold each up for Raine and Maggie's approval. "Let's start with the ladies' things. We'll save the gentleman's for last, like we always do.

"For each of you, a Forties'-style suit– emerald for Raine and amethyst for Maggie. Raine's is nipped in at the waist and requires no belt, and Maggie's has an attached belt in the same fabric as the jacket. As you can see, the tunic jackets are longer than suit jackets today, the skirts straight-line. Very slenderizing," she stated. Her eyes scanned the Sisters. "Not that you two need concern yourselves with that. However, you know what they say, 'You can never be too thin or too rich,'" she kidded. "I know you wear lots of vintage jewelry, so I suggest you each pin a nice, big brooch to your suit-jacket lapels.

"As I'm certain you are aware," Lindsey rolled on, "nylons were hard to get during the World War II era, but here's a simulated pair for each of you. Note that they have seams, so be sure to get them on straight. I don't rent undergarments, of course, but you'll need the proper garter belt or corselette," she cut off, cocking her dark head. "I somehow think you two have those."

Raine and Maggie traded quick looks. "We do," they chimed.

Lindsey didn't look at all surprised, since the Sisters often sported vintage clothing. "If you would happen to ladder … *run* these– which, by the way, I have to sell you; the nylons aren't rented– just do what the ladies of that era did when they were without nylons. They applied makeup to their legs and drew the seams on with eyebrow pencil. What do you think of the shoes?" she grinned, pushing forward both pair of thick-heeled pumps adorned with leather bows.

"Oh, the darling things!" Maggie exclaimed.

"Good job, Lindsey," Raine proclaimed, reaching for her pair and checking the size. "Good job."

"The dark-green, round-toed pumps will look great with your emerald suit, Raine; and Maggie, these open-toe, sling-back, faux alligator pumps will be perfect for you."

"They *are* perfect," the redheaded Sister acknowledged. "The dark-brown color's good."

"That reminds me. For each of you, a purse to match your shoes," Lindsey said, producing those items from the bags. "These are cross-body purses that were in vogue then … and now. My mother used to say, 'If you've got something in your closet you love but that's out of fashion, hold on to it. It'll make a comeback, sure as shootin'.'"

Raine zoomed the telepathic thought to Maggie: *Those cross-body purses will be ideal for traveling through the blustery Tunnel of Time.*

"Now for the hats." Lindsey opened two of the three hat boxes the Sisters noticed on the counter when they came in. "Aren't these sweet?"

The dark-green one she handed to Raine. The deep-amethyst with antique rose trim went to Maggie.

"Again, perfect," the Sisters confirmed.

Raine's green hat sported a long, full beak and medium-high crown that "… is meant to be worn a *wee* bit to one side," the Goth gal was saying as she tried it on before the counter mirror. "It'll hide my modern coiffure, and the style suits my face."

Maggie's hat was a sexy little affair. Smaller and sleeker than Raine's, it resembled an Edwardian riding hat that dipped over the center of the forehead.

"We'd better try on our suits," the redhead remarked.

"Do that. I want to make sure everything fits you," Lindsey said. "Oh, before you scoot off, let me ask, though I think I've seen you wearing them, do you both have classic, belted trench coats in neutral colors?"

"Yes," the Sisters chorused.

"Raine's is black, and mine's grey," Maggie answered.

"If you should step out in these outfits, consistent with the era, either a swing coat or a trench coat would be good over those suits," the proprietress mentioned.

Trench coats will do nicely, Maggie conveyed to Raine. *It'll be May where we're going, but English springs are typically damp.*

"Actually, I *have* a couple of nice, vintage Forties' suits," Maggie stated, "but it's so much fun to try something different," she winked.

"C'mon, let's *try* these things on!" Raine enthused, pushing Maggie toward the dressing rooms.

Some twenty minutes later, the Sisters returned to the counter in their street clothes, the rented garments over their arms.

"Everything fits perfectly," Maggie smiled. "Like they were *tailor-made* for us– T-a-y-l-o-r! Now, may we see the gentleman's attire, please?"

"For Dr. Weatherby," Lindsey Taylor began, "a three-piece, tweed Forties' suit and an argyle tie. I assume he has a white shirt and brown socks of his own he can wear."

"No problem, those." Maggie examined the tweeds. "Very nice."

"I didn't know if he would have oxford shoes, so I put a pair, in the size you asked for in the past, with his other things. Brown oxfords are what he needs to complete his costume. Oh, and," opening the third hat box resting on the counter, she lifted out a brown fedora, "this hat, of course."

"Of course," Maggie echoed, rocketing Raine the thought: *He could wear the Indiana Jones hat I got him; but it's been through so many adventures with us, I'd hate for it to get lost ... so far away from home. You know how absent-minded my professor can be.*

"Looks like we're all set," Raine put in with characteristic excitement.

En route to the Land Rover, the raven-haired Sister remarked to Maggie, "Full moon's tomorrow. Aisling will pick us up before we collect Thad. From his house, we'll head to The Man In The Moon, then later, into the woods for takeoff."

"Roger that," Maggie returned with her crystal laugh.

***

The following evening, nigh on to ten, when the Sisters three and Thaddeus entered The Man In The Moon, there were patrons at the bar, and several tables were occupied; but the magickal party was lucky– or it just might have been the result of witchy programing– to find a table in the very back, in a nice quiet corner.

Raine, Maggie, and Dr. Weatherby were all sporting their Forties' attire, including their trench coats and hats. In contrast, Aisling was dressed in what Raine referred to as the blonde with the wand's "uniform"– body-hugging, black jeans and turtleneck sweater; high black boots; and black leather jacket.

Glenn Miller's snappy 1941 hit, "Chattanooga Choo Choo," welcomed them, as they settled into their seats at their selected table.

Swiftly scanning the place, Raine whispered to her cohorts, "No one seems to even notice that we're dressed like we are."

"It's dimly lit in here. We won't draw any attention," Thaddeus said, setting his fedora next to him on the table.

"Oh good, Ron Moon's seen us, and he's coming over," Maggie remarked. "We'll ask him to join us, if he can."

"Evening, folks," the pub owner hailed with a broad smile. His glance was marked by questioning curiosity. "You're in the swing of things tonight. That's swell," he exclaimed, spouting Forties' slang, which he enjoyed doing in the Moon's period setting.

You know what, Sisters? Raine zipped to Maggie and Aisling, after glancing round again. *No one ever seems alarmed by anything the Sleuth Sisters wear, say, or do. We've got that going for us.*

"Ron," Raine commented to their host, "I love the music in here. The big bands of the Forties' era have a great sound, don't they?"

"They sure do," he answered. "You'll really appreciate the Glenn Miller album you're hearing now. *The Very Best Of Glenn Miller.*"

"Can you join us for a few minutes, Ron? We were hoping you could share some of your father's reminisces from Warton, the base air depot where he was stationed in England," Thaddeus asked.

Casting an eye over the customer situation, Moon responded with a grin, "Sure, I can take a needed break." He pulled an extra chair from a table nearby to sit between Raine and Maggie, who scooted over to make room.

A waitress took the drink orders, after which Dr. Weatherby probed, "Just tell us whatever you recall from your father's accounts. As history professors, we're frequently looking for recollections suitable for our classrooms."

Fittingly, Glenn Miller's "In The Mood" began playing in the background. The Sisters made eye contact with the thought: *Good omen!*

"Well now, let me think." Moon leaned back in his chair, pursing his lips and gazing up at the ceiling. "One story just popped into mind. My dad was a master-sergeant, and so was his best buddy at Warton. That fella's name was Paddy Ryan. He hailed from Alabama, and he was tough as nails. Before the war, Paddy thought about becoming a boxer. He didn't, but he was a champion scrapper all the same. Anyhoo, one night, he and Dad were on leave in the village. As they walked down the street, Paddy happened to spy a sign in a window of one of the pubs that read: 'No dogs or soldiers allowed.'"

"'You know, Johnny, we're goin' t' have-ta go in there for a drink, don't you?' he says to my father in his Southern drawl. 'No we don't. That's not a good idea,' Dad answers. 'Ah didn't say it was a good idea. Ah said we're gonna have-ta go in there for a drink. *One* drink.'

"To cut a long story short, the two pals went inside, and you guessed it, a fight ensued. Now, my dad was not a big guy, and there were some pretty big blokes in there, so he started inching back against a wall, with Paddy catching sight of him and yelling as the donnybrook and all hell broke loose, 'Keep your back agin the wall, Johnny boy, I'll keep th' bastids away from you!'" Ron chuckled, remembering his father's face when he narrated the tale. "Paddy did a pretty good job of it too … until the MPs arrived on the scene."

"Christmas stories … yeah," Ron said wistfully, "lots of those. I know my dad always got misty eyed when he heard Bing Crosby's rendition of 'White Christmas.' He said it reminded him of the war Christmases in England, of being so far away from family. But the brass came up with a solution.

"With British soldiers away in Europe, war-hit English families received urgent pleas to open their homes to American GIs ... you know, to share their customs and Christmas celebrations with them. Since the Americans brought gifts of extra rations– like nylons, cigarettes, chocolate, fruit juice, coffee, sugar, evaporated milk, bacon, and such– the invitations *poured* out. There was another reason too. An empty chair or two at celebrations or evenings at the dinner table brought sadness and yearning to English families, especially at Christmas. With those chairs filled, hope was revived and worries pushed to the back of the mind ... for a bit.

"On the other side of the coin, posters all around the bases urged GIs to," he raised his hands to draw invisible quote marks, "'spend Christmas at home with a British family.' Y' see, Uncle Sam wanted to promote better goodwill between the English people and their US colleagues. American GIs found the British sense of humor, as well as their customs and traditions ... quite a few things, I guess, different from ours and hard to figure out, at first anyway.

"Just as American soldiers in England worried that their wives and girlfriends at home would be faithful, so did British soldiers in Europe worry about their loved ones left behind. The situation was, at the outset, somewhat– maybe even *more* than a little– *tense*. But my father said once the Americans worked and fought alongside the British, they developed affection and respect for their new-found buddies. Dad recalled one Tommy slapping him on the back to say that the Americans were a 'ver-ry nice set of fellows indeed!'"

Ron reminisced for a private moment. "Several things come to mind ... like my father telling me, from what he observed, that most Americans and most British tried their best to bridge the gaps and get along like the allies we are. I know my dad was invited, not just for Christmas, but for Sunday dinners, too, at an English family's home in nearby Preston. Their last name was Hart, and he dearly loved them. Ernie and Olive Hart," he bobbed his head as the names floated to memory. "Dad said they treated him like a son. I know they stayed in touch for years by exchanging Christmas cards and letters. There was even talk of visits after the war, but things happen in life, you know what I'm saying, to get in the way of plans– work, kids, economic and health issues– that prevented travel back and forth. Nevertheless, the remembrances and the friendship endured and were forever cherished.

"Another thing," Ron spoke suddenly as a memory struck him, "the Americans at the air depots, such as Warton, invited the village children for Christmas celebrations each year of the war. One of the fellas would dress up like Father Christmas and hand out toys, games, and chocolate bars."

Ron nodded as an image of his dad rose again to the movie screen of his mind. He smiled with the memory. "Dad said the Christmas dinners with the Hart family were almost like being at home for Sunday suppers. There were new things to discover all the time over there, like those English Christmas crackers at the holiday dinner." He interrupted himself, thinking that the Sisters and Thaddeus might not know to what he referred. "Those brightly wrapped cardboard tubes with twists at each end that pop with a *bang* when two people pull them apart. And Boxing Day, the day after Christmas. *Boxing* refers to Christmas boxes, presents, traditionally given on that day to the poor, or gifts distributed by employers to their employees.

"Oh yes, those slang expressions that meant something so different from what they sounded like!" Ron gave a reflective nod. "Dad returned home from the war with a liking and a respect for the English people, especially for their strong patriotism and their determination to, as they called it, 'muddle through.'"

"Tell us more," Raine urged. "We can stay a bit longer."

"We're enjoying *and* learning from your accounts, Ron," Thaddeus remarked, "and we very much appreciate your taking the time to share them with us."

"When we spoke of the Freckleton disaster earlier, we eventually went on to something else, and I didn't get to tell you that, like so many of the guys stationed at Warton, my father was part of the recovery at what they called the 'infants' wing,' of the school hit by the downed bomber. Those poor little children! You likely know more about that tragedy of war than I do, because Dad only talked about it once, and then he didn't say much, though I remember it well. It was the first time I ever saw my father cry …"

In the background, the Andrew Sisters' "Don't Sit Under The Apple Tree" gave way to the sisters belting out their iconic jump-blues classic, "Boogie Woogie Bugle Boy Of Company B."

"What about instructions to American GIs from their COs, with the DOs and DON'Ts? Do you recall your father telling you anything about that?" Maggie asked, sipping her ginger ale. The time-travelers weren't indulging in anything alcoholic before their takeoff.

Ron pondered the question, responding after a brief pause, "Y-yeah, in fact, he said the boys received a booklet– entitled *For American Servicemen in Britain,* or somethin' like that– meant to teach English customs in a hurry. The booklet warned not to criticize their hosts, and *never* the King or Queen! I recollect my dad saying that one of the things the booklet underscored was this: If you came from an Irish-American family, and you thought of the British as persecutors of the Irish, or if you thought of the British as enemy Redcoats we fought for our Independence, this was *no* time to fight old wars.

"The Americans arrived in England with their stomachs full, as well as their pockets. I remember Dad telling me another thing emphasized in the servicemen's guide was this: The British very much dislike bluster and bragging." He tilted his head, squinting his eyes. "*To swank,* I think, is the Brit turn of phrase for swaggering. You see, the American soldiers received higher pay than the British, so the booklet and the AAF brass strongly advised against throwing money around paydays, to show off. They counseled keeping in mind, at all times, that the British had been at war since '39.

"It was drummed into the Americans, too, that the British are reserved, so if they don't strike up a conversation on a bus, train, or wherever, it's not because they're unfriendly, but that they don't wish to appear meddling or rude."

"We Yanks, on the other hand …"

In the background, the old jukebox issued forth the soft strains of Vera Lynn's English mega-hit "There'll Be Blue Birds Over The White Cliffs Of Dover."

Ron snapped his fingers at a new flashback. "I recall my dad saying something else too– the Americans shouldn't be misled by the British tendency to be soft-spoken and polite, even formal. The Brits are plenty tough. Thousands of men, women, and children were injured and dead from bombings, yet their morale was unbreakable. Unshakable. England's a nation with guts."

"I'll drink to that," Thaddeus said, raising his glass to polish off his ginger ale.

"Hear, hear!" answered Ron, touching his glass to the professor's and the Sisters', who echoed the toast.

Moon set his glass on the table. "Just happened to think: The *American Servicemen in Britain* booklet concluded with the phrase that while in England the Americans' motto should be 'It's always impolite to criticize your hosts; *it is militarily stupid to criticize your allies.*' Ha!" he smiled in a deprecating fashion. "I'd wager Georgy and Monty never read that little book."

"I'm not a betting man, but that's one wager I wouldn't hesitate to make," the head of Haleigh College's history department chortled. "I've mentioned the rivalry between Patton and Montgomery in my classroom. However, there existed other World War II rivalries among the Allies, that, in my opinion, made more of an impact, such as the one between Monty and Eisenhower over strategy and the competition between Patton and O'Connor over aggressiveness." Dr. Weatherby stroked his beard whilst thinking aloud, "… how much history contributes to our understanding of ourselves."

Raine was thinking out loud too. "I suppose it was only natural there were some things the Americans did that irritated the English, and some things the British did that put American noses out of joint. It's the way with any alliance or friendship. Sometimes even small things can rub the wrong way. For instance, Mags and I love one another dearly, but we sometimes get on each other's nerves."

"Nooooo," laughed Maggie, sending Raine a wink. "I tell my classes that the British, who'd been holding off the Germans singlehandedly for over two years, greeted the Americans with a mixture of relief, curiosity, and worry," she informed.

"Well, I think British mothers and fathers worried about their daughters, just the way *any* parents would in a war-time situation," Ron pointed out.

And that's the concern that'll most concern us, the Sisters messaged to one another telepathically.

It was then, after checking her watch, that Aisling announced, "We really should be going. *It's time.*"

"A spell in rhyme works every time."
~ Every witch who ever cast a spell

Chapter Sixteen

When the Magickal trio and Dr. Weatherby pulled into Tara's driveway, Raine dashed inside for their poppet, whilst Aisling, Maggie and Thaddeus headed for the tree line behind the house.

The property bordered a section of Haleigh's Wood, where they'd decided their portal would be for this time-trek. It was still about forty-five minutes till the stroke of midnight and the witching hour, the most auspicious time for utilizing their Time-Key.

The Sisters knew that turning points– "the betwixt 'n between"– like midnight, the time between day and night; the meeting-point of shore and sea; or the turning of one season or year into the next were *magickal* transitional cusps. Even doorways were magickal portals to the *Other Side.*

The little party waited but a few moments for Raine, who hastened down the back yard to rejoin them, cradling Cara to the bosom of her trench coat. Both she and Maggie had pulled on rubber booties in the car, over their Forties' shoes, after they'd left The Man In The Moon Pub. Snow covered the ground, and though it was not deep, it was wet and icy slick.

At the tree line, Raine paused to look up at the moon, but it had slid behind some clouds, denying her a glance.

On this night of the Snow Moon, it was only partly cloudy but biting cold, as the Sisters and Thaddeus struck a well-used path into the trees. The woods were extremely dark, but both Aisling and Raine used the flashlights, the blonde with the wand had pulled from the large canvas tote she carried, to guide their steps on the narrow trail. At one point, Maggie stopped to take in a breath of air, with Raine following suit.

The Sisters loved the smell of the freshly fallen snow, as well as the scent of the tall pines. It was centering. Scent evokes memories, and the earthy forest redolence of decaying leaves harked the redheaded Sister back to autumn, when last they'd time-traveled, and to Robert Frost's misty words: *The woods are lovely, dark and deep, but I have promises to keep, and miles to go before I sleep– and miles to go before I sleep.*

Night noises permeated the otherwise quiet. In the distance, a coyote barked and howled a startling feral call. As she listened, an owl hooted.

Winter's the best time to hear owls, and February's the month coyotes mate, Raine thought, as she lifted her face to the sky to again check the moon. It was something she did before every time-trek. The large golden orb was just gliding out of cloud cover, and to the Sister's relief, it was not ringed or splashed with red.

I'm grateful there's no blood on the moon. A halo around the moon is a sign of disruption of some sort. And when it's a double ring, all tangled and snarled, anything can happen. Trouble. And trouble is like love ... it comes unannounced and takes charge before you even have a chance to think. She clasped her hands in an ecstasy of respite, releasing her usual full-moon petition: *Oh hail, fair moon, leader of night! Protect me and mine until it is light!*

Deciding to abandon the path, the party plunged through the brush. When they'd trailed far enough into the forest to feel comfortable using their Time-Key, the raven-haired Sister opened their last-minute checklist to full-sheet and, in the ray from Aisling's flashlight, began reading aloud. "Pepper spray, just in case. I happened to think of it this morning, so added a small canister to the things we're taking with us. With our magickal powers and Thaddeus' black-belt karate, we'll be safe enough. However, we must keep in mind, at all times, that we can't do anything that will change the course of history."

"Pepper spray," Maggie answered, her hand slipping into the cross-body purse she wore over her grey trench coat. "Check!"

"Our small, travel *Book of Shadows*," Raine reminded.

Maggie's fingers stretched inside her purse, searching. "Got it!"

Raine's eyes returned to the list, over which Aisling adjusted her beam of light, for it was darker than Hades within the timber where they were standing. "An ampoule of Granny's healing potion."

The redheaded Sister held up the glowing purple vial. "I would never forget this."

Raine gave a short nod, continuing, "A few can't-do-without toiletries."

"Right," she and Maggie reacted in unison, with the latter laughing, "Girls will be girls in any era."

Dr. Weatherby thumped a hand to his chest. "Got my toothbrush." Under his trench coat, in his suit's inner pocket, he had tucked his only carry-on. "Just in case we're forced to stay overnight."

"Darlin,'" Maggie said, addressing Thaddeus, "are you wearing your contacts?"

"Yes," he replied. "And *yes* to the warning on your lips to keep my eyes tightly shut when we take off, so the wind in the squally Time Tunnel won't dry and irritate my eyes. Getting so we think as one, luv."

"Right-O!" Maggie rejoined, endeavoring to get into British mode.

"Aisling," Raine began, "you'll be happy to know that Maggie and I finally remembered to purchase a thermos for Eva's calming brew, Tea-Time-Will-Tell."

"I get how much Eva Novak's special brew relaxes you enough to make your journey through the Tunnel of Time bearable," the blonde with the wand answered, "so I tucked a thermos of it in my bag, whether or no."

Without further ado, Aisling lifted a lantern from the satchel she carried, which was jammed with the things they would need to prepare the time-travelers for takeoff. The lamp burned fairly bright, and the senior Sister hadn't wanted anyone to spy it through the leaf-bare winter trees en route to their chosen spot. Now, in the relative safety of a cluster of pines, she was more comfortable lighting the thick candle inside. Hanging the lantern from a sturdy branch, she said, "With the great Goddess' help and protection, let us embark on our quest."

Setting the big canvas carryall down on the ground, she opened it wide to extract the thermos, then rummaged briefly through the contents to locate and draw out four collapsible plastic cups.

"Galloping gargoyles!" Raine exclaimed. "Maggie and I forgot cups. Glad you're always thinking, Sister. You're the practical one of us."

"We've enough tea for two cups each this time," Maggie remarked, tilting her red head with its spiffy Forties' hat. "You know something? That might do the trick!"

"To what specifically are you referring, Mags?" Raine asked, though she thought she already knew the answer.

"To hitting on just the right formula for passing through the blustery Tunnel of Time without discomfort." Maggie lit up with inspiration. "We drink two cups of Eva's calming tea laced with a single drop– as we did last time-trek– of Granny's Easy Breezy Flying Potion."

"I still think, after having a go with one drop last time, we should try *two* this trip," Raine goaded, "one drop in each of the two cups of Eva's tea."

"Overkill," Maggie argued. "Raine, darlin', you know you've a tendency to *overdo*. Let's hold to one drop this trek, increasing the tea to two cups since we have double the amount of tea with us tonight. If we find that's not sufficient, we can add that second drop of Easy Breezy next trek."

"I agree," Aisling concurred, sending Raine a cautioning regard. "Granny's flying potion is powerful stuff."

"So are the energies in the Time Tunnel!" the Goth gal retorted. "But have it your way." Her voice, however, lacked persuasion.

After pouring the Tea-Time-Will-Tell special brew for the time-travelers and herself, Aisling said, "So we're adding a single drop of Granny's flying potion to everyone's tea but mine … agreed?"

The Sisters exchanged looks. Raine still didn't give the impression of being exactly in accord, but, to her credit, she gave an acquiescing nod.

From the carryall where the Sisters had secured her, Cara shoved a small, glowing vial of Granny's silvery flying potion toward Aisling's extending fingers.

"If my vote counts, I believe a single drop in our first cup will do the trick," Thaddeus voiced.

"All right then, it's decided." When Aisling went to return the vial to the satchel, Cara snatched it from her hand and deposited it safely into the depths of the carryall.

"Sure 'n I hope ye haven't forgotten me?" the feisty poppet asked in a tone that let the group know she was most definitely *not* to be forgotten.

Aisling's feline McDonough eyes kindled. "We could never forget you, Cara." She dove into the bag to produce a flask and a child's cup. "I remembered the good Irish whiskey you favor, my little friend." She poured a small amount of tea into the tiny cup, to which she added a drop of the exquisite Jameson Redbreast 21, after which she handed it to the poppet.

"T'ank ye kindly, lass." The doll lifted the cup to sniff the contents, breathing in the oaky aroma, the action stimulating a quiver. "*Uisce beatha*. Aye, 'tis good– a drop iv th' Irish t' hail yer passage. *Lovely*."

After handing Raine, Maggie, and Thaddeus each a filled vessel of tea laced with flying potion, the blonde with the wand smiled. "As last time, I think this calls for a special cheering cup. Thaddeus, would you do the honors?"

Dr. Weatherby cocked his head and raised a finger in a wordless plea for "Give me a moment," then he gave the dry little cough with which he sometimes prefaced significant remarks. "May the great Goddess keep us safe, and may we achieve a smooth homecoming, armed with the information we need." With that, he raised his cup. "To the full success of our mission! *And*," once o'er he held up a finger, asking for another moment, "let us drink a tribute to the Mighty Eighth Army Air Force and the British RAF, some of whom we may have the honor of meeting."

"Blessed be!" the Sisters and Cara enthused together.

"Here's to our brave flyboys," Raine sang out, "Yanks and Tommys alike!"

"Hear, hear!" the group chorused anew.

The poppet– that is, the ancient spirit who occupied her little rag body– breathed in the wonder of her drink, again giving a wee shiver. "Hear … hiccup … hear!"

Everyone drank, presently draining their second cup, as thoughts turned to their work at hand.

In the glow from the lantern, three pairs of McDonough eyes sparkled and became very green, as senior-Sister Aisling gazed lovingly on the time-trekkers, sending them a special, secret, blessing of her own making for safe travel.

"Before takeoff, let's go over some important data," Maggie said, breaking the transitory silence. "As we've, for lack of a better expression, *role-played* on previous trips, Thaddeus and I are a married couple, Maggie and Thaddeus Weatherby. And as on prior treks, Raine is my sister. Raine will be using her real name, and we all hail from the Pittsburgh area of Pennsylvania, where we work for a significant newspaper, the *Pittsburgh Post-Gazette*, that has sent us on assignment to garner British wartime experiences as well as British impressions of their American colleagues.

"We know the history of our county, state, and country well," the redheaded Sister went on, "so we should have no difficulty answering questions related to the past, should any be put to us. Raine, Thaddeus and I have concocted a likely story as to why we are in the vicinity of Freckleton, due to the air disaster that occurred

there the previous year, as well as the adjacent base air depot of
Warton– 'Little America,' with its ten thousand Americans."

"As you said yourselves, you sure as hell don't want to be tossed
into Warton's brig as spies. You have your replicated press passes,
but you'll have no *proper* identification, and that worries me, so the
fewer people you actually engage in conversation, the better,"
Aisling advised pointedly. "Just get what you need and get back as
quickly as you can."

"That's our standard MO," Raine murmured, hurriedly checking
her face in the compact-mirror she pulled from her pocket. It was
the trusty, lion-faced compact that had belonged to the lionhearted
Granny McDonough. The enchanted item had become a good-luck
charm to the Sisters, providing an extra measure of the magickal mix
of protection, assurance and conviction they carried with them on
each of their time-treks.

Raine and Maggie were both wearing Forties'-style makeup–
crimson matt lipstick and natural-looking base with a hint of rouge
on the apple of the cheeks, jet-black mascara and darkened brows
achieved with a light touch of eyebrow pencil. Raine had nixed her
signature ebony nail polish. Both she and Maggie were sporting
crimson-red nails to match their lips. The makeup of the Forties was
classic and sophisticated; but, the Sisters discovered, easy to
recreate. Basically, the face of the Forties was natural, the "painted-
on" look of the Twenties and Thirties gone the way of history.

"As we have with each time-trek," Aisling reminded, "we'll cast
the same magickal spell to deal with the era's speech."

After momentarily conferring with Raine and Maggie on the
ritual they would be performing, the senior Sister continued, "Within
our secret chant, we'll weave a spell that will *witch* your tongue and
ears. In other words, your speech will be heard by everyone you
encounter as dialect familiar to them; though, since you'll be posing
as American journalists, you'll keep your American accents. The
speech enchantment will work the other way round too. *Everything*
spoken to you and everything you hear will *translate* to your modern
ears like modern American dialogue, slang, and patterns of speech.

"As I tell you before each takeoff, the enchantment is not
perfect," Aisling recapitulated. "Some words and phrases may flee
the charm, but the spell *will* work. Since, this trek, you're not
pretending to be one of those you'll be encountering, you can simply
ask the speaker to clarify his or her words– as you would ask a

Britisher to explain an unclear phrase today." She gave a long sigh. "I think that just about covers it."

"Except for Cara," Maggie said, indicating their poppet, who, extraordinarily quiet, was taking everything in. Cara rarely missed anything.

"Of course, you'll leave her here with me," Aisling instructed.

"Of course," Maggie agreed. "She's here because, as before, she wants to see us off and wish us well."

"*Och!*" the doll squawked, chucking her pet Gaelic cry at them in quick frustration, her little arms, with her gaze, reaching for the stars. "Sure 'n haven't I tole ya time and o'er not t' talk 'bout me as if I ain't right here wit ya!" She ducked her yarn-covered head, and her reedy little voice assumed a note of affection. "I'm obliged t' be here f'r yer leave-takin', so's I kin deliver you a message. Godspeed, me darlin's, 'n Goddess bless! And here's th' blessin' ye're waitin' f'r from yer granny." She'd brought her wee mitt-hands to her mouth to blow a dramatic kiss, flinging her arms out as far as she could from her rag-stuffed body. "Muuuu–waaaaaaaaaa!"

From the bewitched poppet's smeared, crooked little mouth came a rush of crystalline faerie dust, all silver and gold and shimmering, that wafted to the time-trekkers to settle over them, brightening and polishing their auras to a Divine brilliance with an ultra-strong Light of Protection. The farewell kiss had become a pre-takeoff tradition that the Sisters set great store by, for they could *feel* Granny McDonough's presence infusing them with power.

Now, along with Thaddeus, the Sisters thanked the little doll.
It was time.

Fumbling in her satchel, Aisling extracted her black ritual robe, slipping it on over her street clothes, and because it was so bone-chilling damp and cold, even over her leather jacket, after which her penetrating gaze swept the time-travelers, "Are we ready?"

"More than ready!" Dr. Weatherby almost shouted, so eager was he to begin their passage. He lifted his arms to make certain his brown fedora was secure on his head. Then, unbeknownst to the others, he whispered powerful words of his own crafting.

"Sisters," Aisling commanded, "Thaddeus, let us spiritually and mentally prepare ourselves for your journey. If all goes as well as your preceding time-travels, you'll be back in a literal flash, with no actual lapse in time, for we are scientifically mindful, as well as

spiritually aware, that the past, present, and future are simultaneous."
She glanced at the moon– directly overhead. "Let us proceed."

As Aisling delved into her carryall for her magickal tools, Raine caught her breath with a slight gasp. A sensation of extraordinary excitement, like a bolt of electricity shot from the bow of an impish spirit, skittered along her spine. She experienced similar feelings before each time-trek, but never as intense as this night. Smiling softly to herself, she knew *why* this trek would be extra-special.

Rooted to the spot where she stood, Maggie was listening intently. She thought she heard voices in the wind– women's voices. Was that chanting she caught?

She cocked her head, hardly daring to breathe– attending the far-off voices to sway her again. But now only the chill wind whispered, whistling past her ears in an almost teasing, baiting manner. She turned to regard Raine, who–

Also stood with tilted head, listening and waiting. For a fleeting moment, she thought she heard the ardent plea, from a distant place in time and space: *Make right a wrong! Make right **our** wrong!*

Did you hear that, Mags? Raine tele-communicated with quickened breath.

*I did. Great Goddess! Does this mean the Shipton witches **did** put a curse on the men in the Lear family?*

Oblivious of the exchange between Raine and Maggie, or the faraway words carried on the wind, Dr. Weatherby's vivid blue eyes reflected the exhilaration he was striving to contain within his own bubbling essence.

Aisling, too, was unmindful of the thought-trading going on between her sisters of the moon. Watching Thaddeus, she was entertaining a musing of her own: *He always reminds me of a trailblazer, explorer, or pioneer setting off to discover a whole new world. And Maggie's right about him– he never ceases to surprise.*

"Sisters! Dr. Weatherby!" she called, waving her hand before the time-travelers in an effort to bring them all out of their reveries. "Our chant will incorporate all the particulars. The date you've chosen to visit is Wednesday, 23 May 1945.

"Though it is midnight now, we'll program for you to reach the woods off Kirkham Road at 1:45 in the afternoon, just outside the village of Freckleton, so you'll have sufficient time to accomplish what you need to do. Since where you're going, it will be springtime, the woods where you'll land will be leafy but not near dark enough for good cover. You'll have to be extra careful."

Aisling cleared her throat. "I strongly advise you stage your return in the dark of night from the woods. If everything goes smoothly, when you do reenter your own time, as I said and we all know from experience, not one minute will have passed from your departure. I'll be right here, waiting for you."

"Aye, an' I'll be here a-waitin' too. B'tweenwhiles, I'll keep Aisling company." Cara emitted a mischievous giggle. "Witches aire niver too old t' play wit dolls. *Slán agat*," she lifted a wee mitt to snap off a salute. "*Slán go fóill. Tabhair aire.* Safe journey, and *stay* safe, me darlin's!"

Turning toward Dr. Weatherby, Maggie addressed him with the old-fashioned schoolmarm ring of authority she used when instructing her college students. "I know we've gone over this at the onset of each of our time-treks, and at this point in our relationship, I feel I hardly need to; but nonetheless, I'm going to say this *again*. When we arrive, you must not interfere with our plan, our intent. Simply put, we will be witnesses to history, and that is all. We must not, any of us, *in any way,* alter history or do anything to jeopardize our Time-Key."

"*Believe me*, I understand … *verily*," Dr. Weatherby assured.

In keeping with her practice, the raven-haired Sister was bracing herself for the Time Tunnel's bluster. She had decided to wear her coal-black, faux chignon, low at the nape of the neck, in a classic style. It looked very smart and believable under her brimmed green hat. Now, she wanted to make certain both were firmly fixed to her head. The long bobby pins in the back and sides of her Forties' bonnet were for extra security in the windy tunnel through which they must pass. Once at their destination, she planned on removing them.

Taking her cue from Raine, Maggie did likewise, preparing herself for takeoff. She, too, planned on removing the long bobby pins from the back and sides of her hat, to be content with hatpin only, once they were through the Time Tunnel. Both Sisters removed the rubber booties that covered their cute Forties' shoes.

Raine and Maggie, inspired by Lindsey Taylor's fashion advice at Enchantments costume shop, had each pinned a big, bold brooch to their suit lapels. Both brooches were crescent moons set with sparkling rhinestones, and each was cast with spells for physical and mental strength, aura recharge, clarity, and staying in lunar sync.

"Talismans at the ready!" Aisling commanded. Reaching under the bodice of her ritual robe, the leggy blonde pulled her gem-encrusted amulet free from its resting place beneath the black jacket and sweater she was wearing. She lifted the heavy silver chain over her long, silky hair. The talisman's center-stone sapphire and scatter of tiny jewels glittered and flared energy in a beam of moonlight that streamed through the winter web of tree cover.

Thus impelled, Raine and Maggie removed their amulets from around their necks. In addition, each wore a medieval ring of great significance and strong arcane energies. Hundreds of years old, worn and dulled by Time, the rings' brass shafts bore faded secret symbols etched into the sides of the mounts that individually held a large blue moonstone. Already, the ancient rings were beginning to emit a shared bluish luster, a glow that looked particularly eerie in the lantern-lit, shadowy gloom of nighttime Haleigh's Wood.

Under Dr. Weatherby's watchful eyes, the Sleuth Sisters held out and fit together the three necklaces bequeathed to them years before by Granny McDonough, whose influential presence her magickal granddaughters sensed more keenly with each passing moment. In each pair of Sisterly hands, the powerful talismans actually warmed the skin as they verily hummed with energy.

"Thaddeus and fellow sisters of the moon," Maggie enunciated in her mellifluous voice, "for the archaic definition of the word *talisman*, we must hark back to ancient times. Before it was known as a magickal symbol, *talisman* carried a far older meaning. From the Greek word *telesma,* meaning 'complete,' a talisman, in olden times, was any object that completed another– *and made it whole.* I say this to remind and assure us, here present this night, under this arboreal cathedral of the great Goddess– of the majestic Power of Three." Taking her beloved by the arm, she said, "Move in close, darlin', betwixt Raine and me."

The full moon, sliding from beneath a cloud, whence it had briefly cached itself– as if waiting for just the right moment to make its debut– flashed a timely and quite dazzling blaze of light off the fitted talismanic pieces, as the Sleuth Sisters united their voices to invoke in perfect harmony, "With the Power of Three, we shall craft and be granted our plea! With the Power of Three, so mote it be! With the Power of Three, so blessed be!"

Holding her antique heirloom out to her cousins, Aisling said, "I don't need to remind you that Merry Fay is my reason for not accompanying you. I dare not risk being permanently separated from my child. However, take this with you again. You *must* maintain, as much as possible, the sacred and supreme Power of Three," she asserted.

Raine and Maggie hugged Aisling for a long, loving moment, as memories of all they'd accomplished together came flooding back to them.

In the moon-drenched wood, it was a moment of supreme empowerment.

Then Maggie, the middle Sister, slipped the senior Sister's amulet around her neck, together with her own. Raine put her talisman back on, as Aisling rummaged inside the canvas bag she carried over her arm for the container of sea salt, a fire-starter, and a bundle of white sage, handed to her by Cara. Snuggled cozily inside the carryall, the poppet sporadically snuck a sniffling snort of her favorite Irish whiskey from the flask Aisling thought to bring.

With the salt, the senior Sister drew a circle around the soon-to-be-traveling people, whom, together with her daughter and husband, she loved most in all the world. Flicking on the fire-starter, she lit the sage-bundle that she secured inside a small Pyrex bowl drawn from the satchel. In an instant, the air around them filled with the sweet, pungent aroma of the good smoking essence.

Walking a circle with the smudge deosil– clockwise– the blonde Sister cleansed the area of negativity. "Negative energy, you may not stay! We release you; be on your way! From here on out, we banish thee; these our words– so mote it be!"

Finally, Aisling nodded to her sisters of the moon, as the powerful trinity chanted a strong incantation of protection, ending with the petition, "God-Goddess between us and all harm!"

As one, the Sisters continued to chant: "Wind spirit! Fire in all its brightness! The sea in all its deepness! Earth, rocks, in all their firmness! All these elements we now place, by God-Goddess' almighty strength and grace, between ourselves and the powers of darkness! So mote it be! Blessed be!"

In the glow of the tree-hung lantern, and with careful expression, the Sisters and Thaddeus intoned aloud the ancient Gaelic words, the arcane phrases Raine and Maggie had, over the years, so diligently ferreted out, the secret text neatly handwritten across their small

Book of Shadow's final pages– the ordaining language that programmed and powered their sacred travel through time.

The Time-Key.

Since the ancient chant was in Old Irish, in order to get it *letter-perfect*, it was best for the Sisters to *read* the words from their *Book of Shadows,* though the chant had almost imbedded itself, by this point, into their collective memories. After his first spell-trek with Maggie and Raine, Thaddeus's eidetic mind had snagged and stored the Time-Key, a fact that saved their lives on one, especially problematic, occasion in the past.

Their unified voices rising with each line in crescendo, the Sisters closed the current segment of their ritual with the words, "To honor the Olde Ones in deed and name, let Love and Light be our guides again. These eight words the Witches' Rede fulfill– 'And harm ye none; do what ye will.' Now we say this spell is cast, bestow anew the Secret we ask! **Energize the Time-Key!** So mote it be! Blessed be!"

In perfect stillness did they wait.

Not a sound broached the winter silence. The night, at some point, had become totally hushed, the woods quieting even of night creatures and wind, the moon casting murky shadows through the lacy canopy of leaf-bare, snow-glistening boughs to the frozen ground, as the surrounding woods seemed to *breathe* a message that was just beyond hearing.

The Sisters and Dr. Weatherby knew from past experiences not to panic, and so they used the interval to further center themselves, drawing in their breaths and breathing out slowly, sustaining the placid mood bestowed on them by the special brew tea of their cherished Gypsy friend, Eva Novak.

And as it had been with their previous time-treks, it was as though Father Time waited whilst something momentous– suspended by the wise, old Chronos on a coiled thread– were about to unfurl within the established circle.

"The silence has become loud," Dr. Weatherby whispered after what felt like a long wait.

"Let us restate the passage," Aisling wisely proposed. "You have made your choice, and now you must focus. You've woven your intent within the ancient chant. You *will* arrive at your programmed destination. Put aside– each of you– any and all doubts, fears, and," fixing Thaddeus with her piercing McDonough gaze, "*impatience.*

- 294 -

The magick cannot be rushed. Witches know we must learn not to rush most things. When the time's right, wishes, desires, will come to pass." The blonde Sister took a moment to breathe deeply. "Free yourselves from all negativity– and simply allow the Great Secret to happen. For happen it will. Give yourselves up to it."

Once more, the Sisters and Thaddeus chanted the ancient evocation, arms raised in calling forth. Prompted by Aisling, they added at the last: **"Now is the time! This is the hour! Ours is the magick! Ours is the power!"**

Having repeated the afterword *thrice*, the Sisters' ancient talismans, resting against their skins, radiated with heat– and the super Power of Three– as the conjured energies sparked, swished and swirled around them like something very much alive.

They could feel those energies in a growing cone of power– *a huge witch's hat, ghostly and omnipotent*– beginning steadily to rise above their heads. It was the way of strong magick, and thus it did not frighten the trio of witches or their colleague the least bit.

For a fleeting moment, both Raine and Maggie thought they detected something filmy white and vapory above the shadowy tangle of tree limbs and soaring pines silhouetted against the moonlit sky.

The vapor, or clouds, or whatever it was, was shaped like a witch riding her besom!

Could it be the spirit of one of the Shipton witches? A **symbol**, *perhaps, of the Shipton witches?* they asked themselves, zipping the brainwave to each other.

They listened intently. *Were those the witches' elusive words– smothered and carried eerily away upon the reawakened wind?*

Though they strained to hear, they could not make out what the lost words were attempting to convey to them; and then, in the tradition of ghosts, the vaporous form vanished.

Raine and Maggie waited in sharp anticipation, but there was nothing– only the wind whispering through the trees and, beyond, the surrounding woods and textured darkness.

"Ah!" Thaddeus suddenly exclaimed, a glimmer of a smile flitting over his features to spark his flame-blue eyes in the dazzle from the lantern. He could actually *feel* the magick rising.

Like the tingle of a mounting storm on the horizon, they all sensed it.

Then, in the bat of an eye, it came, softly at first, then louder, an electrical crackling sound, as gleaming flashes and orbs of white light zigged and zagged above and around the human circle, turning the tree-shrouded scene increasingly eerie.

Magick crackled in the very air they breathed, as their established cone of power rose higher and higher!

Closing her eyes, Raine could actually see the silvery gold cone of energy that was rising in a huge witch's hat above their heads.

Slipping in and out of cloud cover all evening, the elusive moon slid free of its veil, choosing once again to show itself brilliantly at a significant moment. When Aisling took a step back, outside the circle of time-travelers, the moonlight shimmered in her long, blonde hair as it blew out behind her in the stiff breeze. A terrific gust of bone-chilling wind rushed across the area, whipping the trees and shrubbery wildly with creaking, sharp sounds as the branches rubbed together. Just beyond their circle, a hefty bough came crashing down.

Tonight, the wind's an angry witch, Raine sent to Maggie, who answered–

*Or a **determined** one.*

*Let's **use** its power to cleanse ourselves. Visualize the wind passing through us, carrying away any lingering negativity.*

*It's **empowering**!*

Otherworldly in its timbre, the gale bore on its breath the enchanted flutes of the mysterious race of people from Ireland's ancient past, the mystical *Tuatha De Danann*, from whom the Sisters had gained the coveted Time-Key.

From its supporting tree branch, the lantern was swinging precariously from side to side, causing the thick candle therein to flicker wildly. The mesmerizing music grew louder as the squall whistled and moaned a siren's song of its own.

A heartbeat later, when the mystic wind blew the sputtering flame out, Maggie grasped her professor's arm, gripping hard. "Steady on now; we know what's coming!" she called over the din, as the ghostly gale tore at her grey trench coat, the collar of which she'd raised against the chill.

As always, the Sisters were moved by Dr. Weatherby's impressive show of courage. Standing strong between Raine and Maggie, his upturned face calm and serene, he closed his eyes. "Let it happen!" he shouted, pushing his hat tighter on his head.

Those ordaining words barely left Thaddeus' mouth when, in a burst of light, a bevy of ethereal faces, skeletal figures, and vaporish human forms appeared in the rising mists, their gaunt arms widening imploringly, their mouths opening in what looked to be silent screams. As the strange beings zeroed in on the time-travelers, they caught snatches of the Time-Key chant.

A millisecond more and another burst of bright light! The figures' claw-like hands snaked tightly round the time-trekker's ankles, heaving Raine, Maggie, and Thaddeus, with supernatural strength, toward the vortex of a pitch-black tunnel– a twister of helical wind that threatened to pull them into its infinite void with the force of a gigantic vacuum.

So strong was this gale, howling and whirling with accelerated ferocity, that the copse of pines and the entire encircling woods seemed to strain and shriek, whilst the branches of a large shrub caught at Aisling's long hair and clutched at her flowing black robe.

Not wanting to be separated, Raine, Maggie and Thaddeus held fast to one another, strengthening their power and protection with the intense love they shared, the action setting off a tempest of magickal sparks.

Simultaneously, just outside the circle and their established Doorway of Time, the senior Sleuth Sister disentangled herself from the clutching brushwood to thrust her arms skyward, her blonde locks blowing violently about her upturned face, and her black robe billowing out from her body, as the frosty wind spun her chant round the time-travelers– faster and faster and faster!

Steely and resolute, Aisling's confidence never failed to infuse pluck and purpose into Maggie and Raine. Breaking free of their embrace, Raine and Maggie promptly locked hands with Dr. Weatherby; and for a magickal moment, the time-trekkers were limned in silver– each a nimbus of light that overlapped, one to the other, with stunning brilliance.

"Together wherever we go!" they shouted.

Knowing that "three's a charm" and the love vibration the strongest emanation of all, the "chrononauts" raised their joined arms, the three of them keeping cadence with the chant of the wraithlike figures– to repeat the last line of the arcane passage for the third time.

A thick, vaporous cloud was rising from the depths of the frozen February ground– that started quivering and rumbling beneath their feet– even as the air around them continued to swish and swirl like the mightiest of whirlpools. A jagged streak of lightning cracked the sky behind them, as a great tree shivered and splintered from the impact, and a tremendous roll of thunder assaulted their ears with a mighty **RO—————————AR!**

Maggie squeezed Thaddeus' hand. "It's happening!" she called out, determined to stay calm.

"Take heart!" Raine shouted. "We'll soon be on our way!"

A sudden ear-shattering clap of lightning momentarily transformed the dark woods to brightest noon. A crash of thunder and–

Suddenly, in the vortex' hellish battle with Time, the churning atmosphere opened with a violent suction. Raine, Maggie, and Dr. Weatherby felt as if they were being swept down a giant drain! Rapidly then did the Tunnel wholly swallow them, as Aisling disappeared from their view in a brilliant burst of blue-white light, her voice rebounding after them–

"Bles————————sed Beeeeeeeeeeeeeeeeeeeeeeeeeeeeeeee!"

Quicker than any one of them could answer "Blessed be," the time-travelers were forcibly hauled deeper and deeper– into the long, black Tunnel of Time.

Above the blustering din, Maggie's voice echoed through the dark corridor, **"Hold tight to one another! Can't chance being separrr——atedddddddd!"**

"Where e'er we go," Raine's words rumbled down the mysterious passageway– **"we gooooo togeth——— errrrrrrrrrrrrrrrrrrrrrrrrrrr!!"**

"It's OK to follow a different path as long as you follow your heart."
~ Dr. Maggie McDonough, PhD

Chapter Seventeen

With a loud swish and a flash of light, the time-travelers found themselves in a sun-and-shadow splashed grove of rowan trees.

"Oooh," Maggie moaned, holding on to Thaddeus for support, "I'm rather disappointed in our brew, for I feel a little shaky, not much, but a bit."

"So am I ... *a bit*," Raine restated.

"But would you look at us," Dr. Weatherby whispered with excitement edging his voice. "We've landed on our feet! This is a first for us. A first! And my queasiness is minor compared to our earlier flights."

Maggie and Raine gaped at one another, remarking to Thaddeus in sync, "Nausea's almost past, and you're right– we landed on our feet!"

"Of course, I'm right," the professor retorted with the air of a conjurer.

"Wiz-zard," Raine exclaimed. "And do you see?" She pointed to the grove of trees where they touched down. "Rowan, the tree of power– tree of the Goddess."

A large cargo plane flew over, having taken off from somewhere nearby.

Dr. Weatherby's intense blue gaze followed it for a thoughtful moment. "Let's sit down on that fallen tree and get our bearings," he suggested, escorting the Sisters the couple of feet to the log, where they all sat. "I'm thinking Raine was correct all along. Next time we try *two* drops of your granny's Easy Breezy Flying Potion, and we indulge, as we did this trip, in two cups of Eva's calming tea, one drop of Easy Breezy per cup. That was *no* accident that Aisling and you both brought tea to our takeoff. We all know there are no accidents in life. Twists of Fate, yes. Everything happens for a reason."

"So next time-trek, we should have the perfect brew for our battle with the blustery Tunnel of Time," Raine said, rubbing her hands together and grinning in that pleased way she did when proven right. Those times, her face was so kittenish, it made Maggie smile.

Glancing around, Thaddeus was satisfied no one saw them drop "out of nowhere." He reached for his fedora. It was firmly on his head. He plunged a hand into his pocket for the coins he chose to bring. They were there.

"Stay right where you are," he cautioned, raising his voice over the noise of a second plane flying over. "I'm going to have a quick look around. I'll be back directly."

The Sisters, too, were checking that everything on their persons was intact, beginning with their treasured talismans. Relieved that the heirloom amulets were still resting against their bosoms, they each began a hasty tidy-up.

Taking out Granny's lion compact, Raine neatened her hair and green, brimmed hat, removing all the long bobby pins but one and depositing the others into her purse. She repaired her lipstick and smoothed a few stray wisps of ebony hair into place, making certain her low chignon was neat and secure at the nape of her neck. She also made sure Granny's large crescent-moon brooch was fastened firmly to her suit lapel.

Maggie was busy tending to the same small tasks. "Though it's May– I *hope* we've arrived here in May … 23 May 1945– it's damp and chilly. Glad for our trench coats."

"Oh, I'm sure Thad will let us know if we've hit our mark when he returns," Raine replied. She took a long draft of air, releasing it to say, "Yep, we've definitely time-traveled. I can always tell by the air. And those planes that flew over were WWII cargo planes. No doubt about it. Douglas C-47 Skytrains, standard AAF transports."

All the while, Thaddeus was out of sight, scouting the area and making certain they had, indeed, landed in the wood off Kirkham Road near the village of Freckleton, Lancashire, England.

Presently rejoining the ladies, he announced, "The road's just through these trees. And take heart, I asked a passing fellow on a bicycle if this is *Kirkham* Road. It is. I checked the date with him, also asking for the time, so we can set our watches. Everything's good. It's 2:20, so we've time enough to get to the Shipton cottage to await Tristan's buddy and fellow officer, Tom, who'll be delivering that note to the girl … that is, *if* he delivers the note, which we'll soon find out. It was a sticky wicket checking the year and not coming off as daft, but with some clever conversation, I soon ascertained that we've struck our target date of 23 May 1945."

Maggie dropped her crimson matt lipstick into her bag. "Did you ask for directions to the Shipton place, darlin'?"

He kissed her cheek. "You know I did. It's not far, about a quarter mile yonder," he pointed, "just off Kirkham Road. However, I suggest we get over there now. I'd hate to come this far, be this close, then miss, if you get my drift."

"Hold on to your knickers," Raine nearly shouted. "While we're still in these trees, I want to propose *my* plan."

Some minutes later, when the time-travelers emerged from their tree cover, only two of them were in human form, and both Maggie and Thaddeus had fastened their press cards to the lapels of their trench coats, or "macs," as the British referred to raincoats.

Raine had shapeshifted to the Glamour, the image, of Black Jade, conjured from the photograph she'd tucked into Grantie Merry's locket, opposite a photo of herself. The transformed Raine looked exactly like Black Jade except for the eye color, which had not shifted to Jade's pumpkin hue but remained the vivid McDonough green.

"I'm glad you thought to bring the shapeshifting tool, Sister," Maggie said, running her hand over the black cat's lush fur. She was carrying the "cat," as they made their way to the Shipton cottage. "If the courier delivers the note to the Shipton home, we might not be able to creep up close enough to a window to hear and see what will transpire inside. Since it's May here, it won't be dark till much later."

"Raine can easily leap up on a windowsill to hear and see everything," Thaddeus said. "There," he pointed, "that should be the cottage we're looking for."

The little party paused on the road to cast their eyes over the thatched-roof, vine-covered storybook abode. After several moments, Thaddeus repeated Maggie's remark, "Yes, it's a good thing you thought to bring that locket, Raine."

The glossy black "cat" with the glittery green eyes turned to regard the professor with a single, concurrent "Meow."

Dr. Weatherby checked his watch. "The courier Tom, if he keeps his word to Tristan, should be coming along in about ten minutes. Let's duck into those trees over there to watch for him."

Within the leafy hideaway, Thaddeus and Maggie sat again on a log, Maggie holding Raine, in black-cat guise, on her lap.

"I'll be worried about Raine," Maggie said, holding her voice to a whisper. "I think I glimpsed other cats about the cottage, and–"

"Now, now, practice what you preach. Never dwell on what you don't want to happen. Worrying is like praying for what you don't want, right? No need to fret about our Raine," Dr. Weatherby cut in, "not on *that* score. She'll handle herself … and exceptionally well. Mark my words."

The "cat" gave a low growl.

"All the same, I shall worry," declared Maggie uneasily. "I have an anxious feeling about this that I can't put my finger on."

Thaddeus stroked his beard in a meditative gesture. "We'll move in closer to the cottage at the right moment and crouch down low in the brush."

Several minutes slipped by, with Maggie becoming more and more apprehensive. Suddenly, an open-topped jeep came into view, bumping along Kirkham Road toward the Shipton cottage.

"There's a military vehicle driving up now," the redheaded Sister whispered needlessly. "Looks to be an American officer in it."

Like a bat out of hell, Raine-cat dove from Maggie's lap to dart for the small home, where she effortlessly leaped upon a windowsill.

Two other cats, a yellow tabby and a straggly grey, appeared out of nowhere to give the newcomer a loud feline warning that this was their territory. As Maggie and Thaddeus watched, Raine-cat rose on hind legs, puffing out to three times her size, one black paw extending for a strike, as her little ears flattened. Her McDonough eyes flashed green fire in an answering warning, accompanied by a protracted growl that was followed by a sharp, sibilant hiss-sssssss. Without another sound, the other two cats backed down to slink away.

"Told you," Thaddeus chortled to a visibly relieved Maggie. "Those cats know a contender when they encounter one."

"*I* should've known," the redheaded Sister conceded in her silky voice, "Raine and Black Jade, Mars-ruled both, are like Tasmanian devils when their fur is ruffled."

A few seconds passed, after which Maggie whispered, "The driver looks to be the officer named Tom we saw in our crystal ball." Her eyes remained loyally on Raine-cat, who leaped down, only to spring up onto a second windowsill.

"Let's make our way through the trees," Thaddeus urged, taking Maggie's arm and guiding her along. Ducking down low, they inched in closer to the cottage, crouching to peer through the brush.

The pair watched as the officer stepped lightly from the jeep to rap firmly upon the arched door. In a moment, his knocking was answered by what looked to be a crone, with long, white hair, wearing a black dress and shawl. She was bent over a gnarled wood cane, on which she appeared to lean heavily.

The officer removed his hat and, holding fast to the sealed envelope, announced, "I have a message from Major Tristan Lear for Miss Gillian Shipton. This is her residence, is it not?"

"Aye, 'tis," a younger woman confirmed, who came suddenly into view in the open doorway. She, too, wore all black. Though younger than the crone, she was not youthful. Her long, dark hair, which she wore in a loose bun, was heavily frosted with grey; and both Shiptons looked wan and somewhat feeble.

"Is Miss Gillian *here?*" the officer queried.

"No, but we'll see that she gets this," the crone retorted, snappishly snatching the envelope from Tom's hand. "Thank ye." Without another word, she firmly shut the door, latching it.

The officer turned, strode back to the jeep and drove off, down Kirkham, in the direction of the village of Freckleton.

Maggie and Thaddeus inched as close as they dared to the cottage, whilst Raine-cat, curled up in a tight ball on the windowsill, attentively eavesdropped and observed the two witches inside.

The elder handed Tristan's missive to her daughter. "You read it, for your eyes are better than me own."

With a brusque nod, the younger carried the letter to sit before the hearth fire and peruse it by the glow of the crackling flames. "'My darling, I cannot meet you today,'" she began, reading aloud. "'Orders just came down. I'm being deployed immediately to the Pacific theater. I can say no more. I'll write you as soon as I can. Please wait for me. This war can't go on much longer. I love you with all my heart and soul, and I can't wait to spend the rest of my life with you! Your Tristan.'"

In a trice, the crone nicked the missive from her daughter's hand and, hastily tearing it to shreds, flung the bits of paper into the fire. Grabbing hold of the poker, she stoked the flames, watching with satisfied expression, as they hungrily devoured the evidence. "These dashin' Yank pilots! 'Tis all ver-ry well in war– the damn fancy, th' right strong courage an' all. But he'll be no good t' our Gill in peacetime; I kin tell ya that. Like as not barely able t' support 'er."

Raine-cat noted how the grey-haired witch's eyes enlarged when her mother ripped the missive from her hand.

"Do y' think that was wise?" she shrieked. "Burnin' that th'r note?"

"I cudn't ver-ry well toss it in the dustbin, now cud I? I had to destroy it."

"Gillian has the gift of sight. *She'll know.*"

"She won't," the crone replied with fervor. "This ole besom," she thumped a hand to her breast, "ailin' though I be, still wields th' power! We'll cast a spell to prevent her from findin' out, and we'll niver tell a soul– *neither of us.* We take this to our graves. Do you understand? *To our graves!*" The woman struggled for breath as a violent spell of coughing overtook her. "*Och,* I'm right knackered." She eased herself to a chair before the comfort of the hearth, as the younger handed her a steaming beaker of something to drink, along with more of her misgiving.

"She'll find out, and then she'll *despise* us."

"Rubbish! Yer heid's full o' mince." The crone clutched the mug, holding it firmly between her claw-like hands, for both the relief of its warmth and the potency of the herbal brew it contained. "Gillian niver dabbles in th' Craft."

"I didn't say she dabbles. I said she'll find out. She has the gift!"

"It cud be *donkey's years* afore she iver finds out, and b' then, she'll likely have bairns of 'er own. *Then* she'll know what 'tis to be a mum, and she'll twig what we done f'r 'er."

"I'm askin' meself *why* we're doin' this. *Is* it f'r her? Aire we really doin' this t' protect her or jus' selfish-like f'r us?"

"What's th' difference?" Noting the look on the other's face, the crone expounded, "For her, f'r th' three of us ... what's the bloody difference? 'Tis the right thing. She's the last keeper of our clan's ancient secrets, th' last of our line! Our Gill has a legacy t' folla an' a bloody heap iv lear-rnin' f'r t' do it! We need her *here* with us," she wheezed, overtaken once again by a fit of coughing, after which she drank deeply from the cup, leaning back in the chair with an exhalation that sounded like the moan of a cold winter's wind.

"*The right thing,*" the younger repeated. "Bosh, even a stopped clock is right twice a day!" She moved to the hearth to stare momentarily into the fire. Without turning to face her mother, she put words to her fear. "He said in his letter he was goin' t' write."

"And so he will ... f'r a while." The words came out in jerky gasps. "You're th' one what walks for th' post ivery day. We'll burn his letters like we done this day. He'll stop soon enough, and everything will be tickety-boo. Th' man won't keep on writin' iffin she don't answer. Men have th'r pride."

"Aye." The grey-haired witch continued to gaze into the leaping flames at the hearth. "I hope we're doin' the right thing. 'Tis not always the easiest path t' take, but I fear we might only succeed in drivin' her away, and—"

The crone cut in, "*Och*, will ya cease talkin' bollocks! What we're doin' is *preventin'* her goin'! Remember, we tell no one what we're up t'. Enough of this mindless prattle! Let us make a pact, a covenant betwixt th' two of us. Thence we shall cast a spell to keep this from Gillian. She's left her work at hospital b' now and is in the village, lookin' right bonny an' waitin' f'r him. Whin he doesn't meet her, she'll come home earlier th'n usual, and that cud be anny time now."

The witches were making ready to spell cast when the white-haired crone's arm shot out to point to the window where Raine-cat was watching and listening to their exchange. "Cor blimey, 'tis Little Minx! She's come home. Wait on our spell, whilst you quick grab 'er and bring her inside so she don't run off again t' spread herself round the neighborhood, th' little tart!" At that, a new paroxysm of coughing overtook her, bringing her daughter to her side.

Seeing her chance, Raine-cat leaped to the ground and dashed off, fast as her little paws could carry her, to the adjacent woods where she immediately came upon Maggie and Thaddeus, who'd swiftly adjourned from the bushes back to their log to sit and wait. Quick as an arrow, the feline Raine scurried up a stout tree to flatten herself on a sturdy limb. There, she held on, claws clinging to tree bark, hardly daring to breathe. She figured it to be at least another twenty minutes before her shapeshifting spell ended and she would return to her normal self.

If the Shiptons get their hands on me, while I'm still in cat mode, Goddess only knows what their spell will do!

Bursting from the cottage, the grey-haired witch caught a glimpse of the black cat vanishing into the wood. A couple of minutes later, when she entered the trees, halted breathless from the physical exertion, she was momentarily taken aback to stumble upon Maggie and Thaddeus.

"What in th' name of the great Hecate aire you two doin' in me woods?" she voiced in a wheezing but nonetheless demanding tone. "And who might ye be?"

"We might be lost," Dr. Weatherby quipped. "We were looking for a shortcut to the village of Freckleton; and since we've been walking upwards of an hour, we thought we'd take a breather on this log. We mean you no harm. We're journalists," he thought to add, indicating the press cards fastened to the lapels of their trench coats. Are you all right?"

In silent plea, the Shipton witch raised a hand. The other hand rested against an accommodating tree for support. "Just need t' git back me wind is all. Yanks, ain't ya?"

"We are," Maggie answered, feeling the power of the witch's mystical stare. "Here to garner British wartime experiences, as well as impressions of your American colleagues for the newspaper for which we work back home. You look to be a woman of mature judgement. May we know your name," the Sister asked, feigning innocence, "and what it is you think of the Americans you've encountered?"

The woman thought for only an instant, replying, "Me name's me own business. As f'r the Americans, like anny, the Yanks aire a mixed lot, th' ones I've met annyroad. I'll tell ya flat out, I'm grateful f'r th'r help, but too many of 'im's been fillin' 'r lady folks' heads with fantastical ideas; and the young girls, especially, want nothin' more than to rush headlong off to America."

"We appreciate your honesty," Thaddeus remarked, "and we thank you for it."

Suddenly remembering that Raine's shapeshifting spell would not last much longer, Maggie posed the quick question, "Can you tell us the best way to get to Freckleton?"

"Jus' folla that road," the witch pointed, "straight inta th' village." She cocked her grey head, eyeing the pair with her intense regard. "Ain't seen a black cat come dartin' in here, 'ave-ya?"

"Noo," Thaddeus hedged with pretended thought.

"But we did hear a rustling noise, in the brush, a few minutes ago. Over there," Maggie pointed to an area in the distance, sensing Raine's predicament even stronger.

Just did the Shipton sister totter off, when the Goth gal felt herself begin to reverse shapeshift. As fast as she could, she started down the tree, leaping at the last into Thaddeus' lap– at the express moment when the Shipton witch swung round to gape at them.

When Raine pounced, she was already back to normal, and the impact bowled Thaddeus and Maggie over, in a backward flop, off their log, the three of them tumbling to the forest floor in a heap.

Moving through the scrub vegetation and trees, the witch made haste back to the time-travelers. "I say," she began, again breathless, eyeing the strangers anew– and with more than mere curiosity, "what do y' think yer're up t'? A bit o' slap 'n tickle? I'm old, but I ain't blind. I saw a black cat leap from that tree! Where did it go, and where did *you* come from?" she let fly at Raine. "You weren't here a moment ago!"

The raven-haired Sister sprang to her feet. "I'm with them," she said with a jerk of her head toward the sprawled Maggie and Thaddeus, as she commenced to brush forest debris from her trench coat. "I'd gone up to the road to see if I could hail us a ride into the village. When I rushed back here to my companions, I tripped on a tree root and fell forward, knocking us all to the ground." She turned her pointed gaze on Maggie and Thaddeus. "Sorry about that. Clumsy of me."

By this crux, Dr. Weatherby and Maggie, both on their feet now, began swiping leaves and forest fragments from their coats.

"I believe, madam, I caught sight of the cat you're looking for," Thaddeus remarked, adjusting his fedora, retrieved from the ground, on his head at the proper angle. "It took off like a streak," he pointed, "*that way.*"

The Shipton witch scowled, muttering, "Drat that cat! I'll put a spell on her when next I grab hold of 'er!" For a moment, she stared in the direction Dr. Weatherby had gestured; then fixing her eyes again on the time-travelers, she informed, "Ain't bleedin' likely you'll hitch a ride, lass. Only Yanks and Tommys from the air depot pass on this road … and tractors, though most o' them 'r up for the duration. Farmers been hitchin' plows to horses th' past years. Now that the bloody Jerrys done thrown down, petrol might not be s' hard to lay hands on, but that time's not yet." Something out of the blue seemed to strike the witch's memory, for she suddenly turned and hastened off, back toward the cottage, calling over her shoulder, "If y' see me cat, bring th' little devil to our door, eh? Iffen y' kin lay hands on *her!*"

As soon as the Shipton woman was out of earshot, it was Maggie and Thaddeus' turn to pounce on Raine, saying, "What did you hear and see?"

"Let's hoof it fast as we can into Freckleton," she dodged. "We want to catch Gillian alone at The Plough pub and inn, where Athena showed us she'll be waiting, so we can talk with her and ferret out how *she* feels. I'll share what I learned as we walk. We mustn't dally!"

***

By the time they reached the village, Raine told Maggie and Thaddeus everything she'd seen and heard at the Shipton cottage. Now, pointing to an odd-shaped, red-brick building with white trim, she urged, "There's The Plough. Let's hurry inside."

Pausing a moment in the doorway, to let their eyes adjust to the dim lighting, the time-travelers quickly located Gillian sitting, unaccompanied, in the rear of the restaurant area of the inn, at a corner table. She appeared fretful, for she checked the watch pinned to the lapel of her dark-blue uniform twice in the short span of time since the visitors entered; and her worried demeanor told the tale.

I say we flaunt custom, Raine shot to Maggie.

Without hesitation, the trio approached her table, and Raine took the liberty–

"Excuse me," she began. "May we have a few moments of your time?"

Gillian responded with bemused countenance. "Have we met before?"

"No," Thaddeus answered, hat in hand. "Do forgive us. I realize it's not customary to approach someone to whom one hasn't been properly introduced, especially at a table in a public house; but we're journalists, newly arrived from America, on special assignment. And I'm certain you'll concede that exceptions are made in wartime. May we join you? We promise not to take up much of your time."

Indecision flickered in her violet eyes, then the young woman indicated the empty chairs at her table, "Come and sit cozy here by the fire. It's quite nippy out there today. You may, of course, join me for a short while. I'm expecting someone," she glanced again at

- 310 -

her watch, "who's rather late. What may I help you with?" she asked, her gaze traveling from the press cards fastened to their trench coats to their faces, as the Americans lowered themselves into chairs.

Once names were exchanged all round, Dr. Weatherby cleared his throat. "We were sent here by the Pittsburgh ... the *American* newspaper we work for. Long story short, we're here to harvest impressions from the British people of their war experiences and their thoughts of the Americans they've encountered."

"Your Red Cross uniform tells us you're a nurse, so you've worked alongside American Red Cross. What was it like working with Americans? We don't want to put words in your mouth. Just talk to us; tell us what's in your mind and heart," Maggie concluded, reaching out to pat Gillian's hand, "in your own words."

"All we ask is that you speak frankly," Raine added.

"Oh, I do *that,*" Gillian stated with merry measure. "Sometimes to a fault." She reflected for a private moment. "I started working in hospital early on. It will be four years autumn next. I've been happy to do my part. We all serve– we women too– in one auxiliary 'r other. You know the song, 'There'll Always Be An England!' It's gratifying work, but too often sad. Too many times I've told young men, horribly wounded young chaps, that they are going to be all right. I tell them that because I want it to be true, just the way *they* want it to be true; but too often, far too often, I know... and *they* know it's not true." Gillian sighed. "I've written so many letters home for those brave lads ... letters sealed in my memory forever, as they dictated their feelings to me ... in words that broke my heart."

Tears misted her beautiful eyes. "Sorry. But you don't want to hear sad tales, do you? Not today. The bloody Jerrys have surrendered, and we all need to celebrate that, now don't we?" she smiled.

"We do indeed," Maggie replied, encouraged by their subject's reaction.

"What was it like working alongside the American Red Cross," Thaddeus queried. He had thought, in his journalistic role, to tuck a small notepad and pencil into the inner pocket of his mac, and he was jotting down phrases.

"Jolly good, actually," Gillian answered without pause. "We both have our own way of doing things, our own way of speaking; but when it comes right down to it, we were both after the same end– to defeat Jerry. And that we have!"

"Right!" the Sisters responded in sync. "That we have!"

"I like the Americans. I think, for the most part, most of us do, though for my opinion, they, or rather a number of them an-nyway, do seem, at times, a tad–" she searched her mind then stopped. "What is the proper word?" she asked with tilt of her dark head.

"Brash?" Maggie supplied.

"Precisely." Gillian blushed becomingly. "I hope that wasn't rude of me. Please don't be offended, but you asked me to be frank."

"We did, and we appreciate your honesty," Thaddeus remarked, looking up from his notes. "We Americans *are* a bold lot," he grinned. "Now, may we be so brash as to join you for tea?"

Again, she restlessly checked her watch. "That would be lovely. Tea it is." She caught the eye of the waitress, picking up her empty cup and tilting it sideways. "One of my Yank friends at hospital said it tastes like boiled water," she laughed. "*'Tis* boiled water I told her."

Once the waitress brought their tea, Gillian murmured quietly, "I don't think my American is coming. Something must have deterred him."

"You're keeping company with an American stationed at Warton?" Raine probed, feigning innocence.

"Yes," Gillian acknowledged, seeming to light up. "We've been stepping out for some time now. Met quite by accident; we did. Right here, in fact, where I was having a spot of tea, but I don't really believe in coincidences. Happenstances?" She shrugged. "I believe in Fate. We both feel we were destined to meet."

Everyone seemed to go into a sudden pensive mood, as four teacups were raised to lips.

After a moment, Maggie said softly, "You seem to be really and truly in love."

"*Utterly.* I love him to distraction," the young woman revealed with the passion that burned in her heart. "I have from the moment I met him, and I always will." Again, her violet eyes became liquid. "I've heard talk round about that some of the chaps at Warton will be shipped out to the Pacific to fight the Japanese. It's all the worry, and I'm chilled to the bone that Tristan will be among those going, because he's an ace pilot, you see." Her eyes and her voice dropped. "If he doesn't meet me today, if I never see him again, I know it won't be because of any choice or decision *he* made. I have dreaded this day for weeks now, and–" she choked back the gathering tears, "Sorry."

There was a comforting murmur from Maggie, as she squeezed Gillian's hand. *I like her*, she conveyed to Raine. *She's not only charming, she's refreshingly natural.*

"I know my Tristan wouldn't leave me, not on his own he wouldn't, but I sense that he's already been *sent* away." She dabbed her nose and eyes delicately with the napkin she held in one hand. "I've suffered a beastly feeling about this for days. The last time we were together, and he turned and walked away, I stood there for the longest time, looking after him as a frightful wave of loss, of loneliness swept over me. The strangest sensation speared my heart that he was walking out of my life forever." Her eyes took on a faraway look. "I stared after him, fixing everything in my mind … the way he smiles; the way he moves; the deep, smooth sound of his voice–" she stopped abruptly. "I'm dreadfully troubled over– *forgive me*. I don't know why I'm telling *you* all this, perfect strangers, though you don't seem like strangers. I suppose it's because I can't tell my gran or my mum. Got m' reasons for that," she mumbled. "Oh, no one knows the torment I've been through of late."

Maggie and Raine felt their hearts go out to the poor girl, with Maggie rocketing the thought to Raine: *Her gran and mum aside, she's telling us because she senses we're empaths. It's apparent she's gifted with the sight.*

Gillian smoothed her gloves out on her knee with a nervous gesture, the small act an attempt at composure. Then, upsetting her poise still further, she pled with suddenly widened eyes, "Please don't print this in your newspaper. I'd be devastated if you did. Newspapers are often so sensational in their accounts … oh please don't! It's too personal. Promise me!"

"We promise you we will not print anything you tell us about your beloved," the Sisters answered, whilst Maggie reached again for the distraught girl's hand.

For a second time Gillian stirred uneasily.

"We do promise," Thaddeus echoed, sending her an avuncular beam. "And you can take us at our word."

"You can," the Sisters reiterated.

"I daresay," Raine reasoned, "if you feel that strongly about your American– and I can tell you've a head on your shoulders– then he must be worthy of your love, and your love must be real."

"It is real," the English girl replied in a teary whisper.

Gillian locked eyes with Maggie, who was still holding her hand, and the two smiled at each other in mutual accord. "Thank you." She turned her head slightly to take in Thaddeus and Raine. "You're very kind. Pur-rfect bricks, all of you. I hope Tris finds a way to get a message to me," she said after a moment of collecting herself.

"Oh, I'd wager he'll try his best to do that," Dr. Weatherby stated compassionately, "but as well you know, in war, even the simplest things can go haywire."

"You just hold on to your memories. Keep your Tristan in your heart," Maggie voiced softly, giving Gillian's hand a pat. "And try your best to be of good courage."

Gillian's face revealed sadness as a reminiscence accosted her, accompanied by a pang of compunction. "I remember the last time we were together, I teased him about witching him with a spell, a curse on him and his lot, if ever he abandoned me." Her violet eyes again went misty with their faraway look, and she shook her head with the memory, the picture of flushed misery. "I shouldn't have done that. My conscience has been pricking me, and I'm *bleedin'* sorry for it," she confessed with obvious sincerity. "Tris, understand, is of a *serious* turn of mind, and he took my jest as– If I could take back anything, it would be *that!* Ah, no good crying over spilt milk, but I *do* cry. I have been all day. I believe he thought I was serious! But the truth is I could never hurt Tristan, and I know he would never hurt me. If for whatever reason, I never see him again," she closed her eyes, as a tear ran down her cheek, unchecked, "I will never stop loving him. *Never*," she finished in so soft a voice that the time-travelers almost didn't hear.

Nearly two hours breezed by with pleasant conversation, during which the Sisters and Thaddeus were forming a definite opinion about Miss Gillian Shipton.

When, for the hundredth time, the anxious young woman checked her watch, her face clouded with disappointment, and her voice sounded as dead as a graveyard. "I know Tristan's not coming. *I just know.* Oh, Tris," she murmured in barely audible utterance, her gaze dropping, "wherever you are, *please* look after yourself."

She turned moist eyes toward the Americans. "I really should be going now. My gran and my mum are not well, you see, and I don't like to worry them." Struggling to keep her emotions in check, Gillian stood. "Thank you for the tea and company. Both were soothing to my soul." She looked inquiringly at the Sisters, and a flash of womanly understanding passed between them before she made known in her whispery voice, "Talking to you was like a relaxing bath and warm blanket after coming in from a cold drencher."

Raine and Maggie embraced Gillian in turn, and Dr. Weatherby, in a somewhat courtly fashion, kissed her hand. It was an act of homage and not a mere theatrical courtesy. "Godspeed," he pronounced.

And Goddess bless! "We wish you well, dear girl," the Sisters declared with sincerity.

Maggie couldn't help herself. She sent a silent benediction forward to cloak Gillian: *One day, darlin', someone is going to hug you so tight, all of your broken pieces will fit back together.*

"Best of British! In case you need a translation," Gillian smiled, "best of British luck to you." She started away, then turned to decree with a show of spirit, "I hope our two countries will continue to have a close and special alliance."

Dr. Weatherby's brilliant blue eyes kindled. "I have an … *insightful* feeling," he disclosed, "that will always be so."

So mote it be! The Sisters ordained in their minds and hearts. *So mote it be!*

The Sisters and Dr. Weatherby waited till Gillian exited the pub to formulate their next plan.

"Look, we're here; we might as well make the most of this. I say we wait till dark to Time-Key home from the woods where we landed," Thaddeus suggested. "Until then, why don't we see if we can gather some local sentiments about the Shipton witches."

"I agree," Raine replied without trepidation.

"So do I," Maggie chimed. She leaned in toward her two companions to whisper, "So what's your verdict?"

"She did *not* curse her lover or his descendants. That's my opinion." Thaddeus drained his teacup, setting it down. "What's yours?" he eyed the Sisters for their estimation.

They looked to one another, reciting in union, "*Not guilty.*"

"Beyond a shadow of a doubt," Raine amended. "I don't know about you, but I could go for a bite of pub grub. For a change of scenery, let's visit another pub, get ourselves something to eat and chat up a few locals about the Shipton witches. Once we return home, we can hash this all out, and then consult Athena. What say you?"

"Sounds good to me," Thaddeus answered. "Food's supposed to be good here, but if you feel like stretching your legs after sitting all this time, we could visit The Coach and Horses. It's a bit of a tramp, but not too far. When I visited the gents, I heard a couple chaps mention it."

"Let's go," Maggie approved, rising from her chair.

When the threesome arrived at the impressive white building with black trim, it started to rain, the first drops splattering down on them as they ducked inside. They never thought to bring umbrellas. Spying a nice table before a cheery fire, they quickly headed for it, happy for the warmth.

Glancing round, Maggie said, "It seems all cozy and homey, as England ought to be."

"It's as England *is*. If we want a drink, I'll go to the bar to order," Thaddeus proposed. "Remember, no waiter service in English pubs for alcoholic beverages. "That will give me a good chance to chat up a few of the locals. The order-at-the-bar rule promotes social interaction. So," he said, rubbing his hands together, "what will it be?" He threw off his mac, that held his press card, draping the wet raincoat across the back of his chair before the fire.

"I'll have a half bitter." Raine slipped out of her damp trench coat, placing it over her chair to dry.

"Same for me," said Maggie. She was reluctant to remove her coat due to the chill, but opted to follow Raine's example, inching her chair closer to the crackling flames. "I'm like a cat. When the weather's cool and damp, I gravitate toward the warmth and coziness of a nice fire. Mmmm, feels good."

At the bar, Thaddeus waited his turn, according to British custom, catching the eye of the publican, money in hand. As he waited, he opened conversation with the elderly chap standing next to him, who was fixing to light a pipe. "Nice soft weather we're having today. Kind of peaceful, the rain."

"Aye, 'tis." The man puffed in contented silence, his faded blue eyes skimming the American in a curious but friendly manner, as the pleasant, sweet-smelling aroma of the tobacco permeated the air.

The landlord sent Dr. Weatherby a nod, and he, in turn, gave his order.

"We'll be leaving tomorrow," Thaddeus jerked his head in the direction of his table, "and my wife's been wanting to visit the local soothsayers before we embark for home. I presume you've lived here a long time. Can you tell me anything about them? I know their name is Shipton, and they have a cottage out on Kirkham, but I was wondering if perhaps you knew anything you'd be willing to share with me. I'm Thaddeus, by the way."

The rather shaky-looking fellow pulled steadily on his pipe, and for a few moments, the professor thought he would not respond to the query. The publican, in the meantime, set the drinks on the bar. Dr. Weatherby paid him, hastening to the table with the half bitters for Raine and Maggie. Then returning to the bar, he casually sipped his pint.

"Whin me old lady 'n me waire young," the elderly gentleman began, of a sudden and in a quiet voice, "and our babby took sick, at Death's door she was, my Lizzy went to the older witch, askin' f'r help, f'r no help was forthcomin' from the doc I can tell ya. *He* tole us our little lass wud b' gone b' mornin'. The Shipton witch made a poultice f'r our Margaret, and by mornin' her fever broke. She saved our Margaret's life, so she did."

"Yes," Thaddeus nodded with somber face and complete understanding, "I've heard tell of such things."

"Whin our Peg had mornin' ills, whin she was carryin' our babby," the publican remarked, "the Shiptons made a special pillow f'r her t' sleep with. Stuffed with herbs it was. Bested her sickness. Land sakes, we waire both grateful; I can tell y' that."

A tall, lanky woman, who came up to the bar, added, "I had trouble sleepin' nights … aaah, y' get old, an' everythin' starts t' go, even a good night's rest. Annyroad, I bidden the Shiptons f'r help, an' they made *me* a pillow too. Th' thing's stuffed with herbs all right. Smells right funny. I don't know what herbs or charms, nor do I care. All's I know is that I settle down to slumber like a babby with it. *Sweet, sound sleep.*" The woman mused a self-contained moment. "An' me dreams 'r sweetened too, so they are."

Thaddeus smiled his gratitude to the lady, asking, "May I get your drink?" Then turning to the elderly fella, he indicated his emptied pint, "Will you have another?" He then caught again the publican's eye, "And one for yourself, landlord?" His manner continued polite without being effusive.

The recipients of Dr. Weatherby's gratitude raised their glasses a tad with subtle nods of thanks.

"You have needs t' mend, have ya?" the old man asked.

"No, not really," Thaddeus slickly sidestepped having to fabricate a story with no substance. "Call it curiosity. My wife and her sister are interested in having their fortunes read. What you've told me has given me satisfaction that the Shiptons are good people. Seems they help a lot of folks."

"Oh, they do that," the publican replied. "Them Shiptons wud help just 'bout annyone. But them 'uns aire no one t' mess with."

"That's puttin' it mildly," stated the man of advanced years, taking the pipe from his mouth. "Folks round here run to 'em with the'r problems, but they fear th'm too."

"Why do you say that?" the professor queried.

"I've heard tell they–" he cut off sharply, glancing slyly round. "*I've heard tell.* Like I said, them 'uns aire t' be feared, bent 'n sickly though th' ole besoms be, if they's pushed." He lifted his bushy grey brows, replaced the pipe to his mouth, and resumed puffing.

"If you don't mind," Thaddeus pressed gently, "what have you heard?"

The old gentleman momentarily removed his pipe from between his teeth, raising his brows with widened eyes. "Th'r be stories!" He cocked his grey head slightly. "Gawd blimey, man, with folks like th' Shiptons, suffice t' say th'r always be stories."

When Thaddeus returned to the table, he glanced out the window to see black clouds swirling about overhead. "Getting dark out there, not so much from the hour as the cloud cover, and the wind's picking up. Publican said the storm'll miss us except for a drizzle, but," he warned, scanning the sky, "doesn't *look* like it will pass over. The locals call that type of fog out there *sea smoke*. Happens when cold air moves over warmer water. It could start bucketing down any second." He turned to the Sisters. "Sorry I took so long at the bar, but I succeeded in collecting some information for us. I believe, once we hotfoot it back there, the woods will be dark enough for our purpose," he said, referring to their use of the Time-Key. "Things have been falling into place so well that I think we should go while the gettin's good. No use tempting Fate. We can eat when we get home, if you like. I thought about it, and I don't suppose it's a good idea to fly, like we fly, on full stomachs."

"Very wise of you to think of that," the Sisters responded, gathering their purses and gloves.

"The short drinks won't hurt us," the professor remarked, "for we know from experience that returning to our own time is a much easier ride."

"Right," Maggie replied, standing and snatching up her mac, which was nice and dry from the fire.

"You can share your information with us as we retrace our steps to Kirk's Wood," Raine concurred, hastily pulling on her own trench coat. "I can't wait to hear what you've gleaned. Let's make tracks. If a storm's brewing, we want to beat it!"

No sooner had the Sisters and Dr. Weatherby reached Kirk's Wood, when they heard the sound of a vehicle come to a screeching stop on Kirkham Road, just as they stepped into the tree cover. In the still of the descending mist and murk, a loud shot rang out, sounding like a cannon in the otherwise silence.

"Halt, or we'll shoot!" ordered a booming voice from the direction of the road.

Freezing, the time-travelers heard the distinct sound of running feet.

Great Goddess' nightgown! I hope we haven't walked into a trap! thought Raine.

Trap?! What sort of a trap? Maggie returned.

"**Halt!!**" bellowed the second warning shout.

Two more earsplitting shots pierced the darkness, the bullets whizzing precariously close to where the "chrononauts" were stopped dead in their tracks, with Maggie smothering a little cry at the back of her throat.

Without hesitation, Thaddeus grabbed the Sisters, yanking them behind a large Scots pine and covering them with his body, his hands over each of their mouths, as they shrank into the shadows to avoid detection. "Shhhhhhh," he warned.

I hope our black and grey togs are good camouflage, Maggie thought, hardly daring to breathe.

Fired by fear, the accelerated running feet grew closer, as a man in the uniform of an American flyer dashed past– within a foot of them– in an attempt to escape his pursuers– two uniformed MPs with their guns at the ready; and there was no telling what would happen to the Sisters and Thaddeus if the military police spotted *them.*

"Through there!" the first MP shouted, pointing the way, his flashlight cutting the darkness, as they streaked by– too close for comfort.

Scarcely daring to breathe and tensely flattening themselves against the giant pine to become as inconspicuous as possible in their hiding place, the Sisters and Thaddeus listened intently to hear the sounds of a scuffle.

"Take his weapon and put the cuffs on him!" one of the MPs yelled.

"March!"

As the footfalls on the forest floor returned closer, the MP holding the flashlight stopped. "Wait," he said, skimming his beam over an area mere inches whence the time-trekkers stood pressed against the tall pine. "I think I heard something over there."

"A forest critter," answered the MP clutching the flyer. "Let's go, we got the two-legged critter we were after."

For several precarious moments, the former lagged behind, scanning the brush with his light.

"C'mon! I need that damn light over here!" called the other, his spiky insistence putting a swift end to the sylvan search.

In the misty moonlight, Raine, Maggie and Thaddeus watched the military police parade their prisoner out of the trees, alongside the Shipton cottage and to the road, where the jeep awaited.

"Get that pinched bicycle strapped to the hood," one of them ordered. "We're goin' right by the pub. We'll return it to its owner." Within moments, the jeep sped off.

In a window of the dimly lit cottage, the glow from the hearth fire behind them, three faces beheld the scene for a brief few seconds before reclosing the blackout drape.

Inside, Gillian leaned her head against the wall to give a faint but long sigh of relief. *For a moment, I thought it might be Tristan. I'm relieved it wasn't. Tristan, wherever you are, stay safe, my darling,* she prayed.

Gillian wasn't the only one to release bated breath.

"Whew!" the Sisters gasped.

"I thought I'd given our position away when that first shot startled me," Maggie sighed.

"That was a close call," Dr. Weatherby whispered, "and not just due to the flying lead. I didn't want the challenge of talking to MPs without proper papers. Let's stay put for a few seconds, just in case the Shipton ladies feel like investigating their wood. Then we'll Time-Key home."

"Good idea," Maggie breathed. "No use to court disaster."

"Hmmm," Raine cautioned, "it's as though these trees have eyes. Makes me think the Shiptons cast a protective spell over these woods."

After several quiet moments passed without incident, a trio of very grateful people, who were never afraid to take a leap of faith, made their way deeper into the woodsy haven, where they paused to center themselves. The wind had fallen, and the moon was shining peacefully through the lacework of branches above. In the distance, their ears picked up a faint rumbling.

"From the sound of that distant thunder, the publican was right. The storm seems to have blown out to sea," Thaddeus remarked.

Wiz–zard, Raine thought, we*'ve escaped the MPs **and** the storm.*

Maggie, meanwhile, was reaching into her purse to extract their small, travel *Book of Shadows.* Opening the grimoire to the ribboned final pages, Raine, Maggie and Thaddeus clasped hands tightly to begin then the ancient Gaelic invocation, *the magickal Key that would unlock the door of Time–*

And take them home once again.

"I have crossed oceans of time to find you."
~ Soul-Mates, Olde Souls, Empaths, and Starseeds

Chapter Eighteen

The following day, Raine and Maggie were correcting papers in their shared turret office of Old Main when a soft rap sounded at the door.

"It opens," the raven-haired Sister called out, continuing to mark the college blue book she was perusing.

"Dr. Whitman!" Maggie exclaimed, shoving her reading glasses to her head. "Come in and sit down. We've been meaning to stop by your office to check on you. How are you, dear man?"

Despite his usual elegant appearance, Barron Whitman looked drained, as if he hadn't been getting enough rest. "I'm taking one day at a time. I've discovered that old adage really is the best way to deal with life's challenges." He took hold of a chair that was resting against the wall and drew it forward so that he faced the twin desks of the McDonoughs when he sat.

"We heard the scuttlebutt that you'll be leaving to go back to Boston. We hope it isn't true," Raine let slip, setting her pen down on the desk to pause in her work.

"It *is* scuttlebutt. I *am* going back to Boston but only for our upcoming spring break. As well you can imagine, I've issues to work out with my mother. She's getting on in years, and those issues cannot be put off any longer."

The Sisters swapped glances, remarking, "We're happy you'll be staying with us."

Whitman looked down at his shoes, seeming to study them, and the Sisters sensed immediately that he was out of his comfort zone. "I stopped in to thank you for solving Annabel's murder. It's a start to closure, and that means a great deal to me."

Raine sent the thought to Maggie. *He's relieved his mother had nothing to do with Annabel's death. He was actually worried that she might have some connection to it.*

Yes, the whole ordeal has been ultra-trying for him.

"Dr. Whitman," Maggie voiced, "you don't have to thank us. We could not have sat idly by and not offered our assistance to the police."

"It's what we do," Raine rejoined. "We just did what we always do."

"Barron," Maggie spoke gently, opting to call their colleague by his first name, "we hope you keep in mind that your mother made what we've come to see as a valiant effort to save Annabel."

"My poor Annabel," Barron whispered. He said nothing further, and the Sisters could clearly sense that it was uncomfortable for him to be so open about his feelings.

God and Goddess grant her peace, the Sisters thought in silent prayer. "Rest in peace, Annabel," they said aloud. "You will remain in our hearts and memories as the dear, sweet soul you were in life."

"The reality," Maggie stated softly, "is that you will grieve forever. You don't *get over* the loss of a loved one. You learn to live with it. You will *heal*, however, and you will rebuild yourself around the loss. You *will* be whole again, but you'll never be the same, nor *should* you be the same."

"Nor would you *want* to," the Sisters concluded together.

"I can't help recall how Annabel looked at you with unconcealed adoration," Raine remembered, "the day she announced your engagement."

"I adored *her*," Barron murmured wistfully. Then, in the next moment, he seemed to explode. "This whole business has been astonishingly incredible. If one of my students had written a story including all of what's transpired on this campus in the past several days, I would have told him or her it lacked believability, that it was far-fetched. I suppose 'Truth *is* stranger than fiction.'" Dr. Whitman seemed to retreat into himself, climbing, hand over hand, out of his contemplation after a long, private moment. "What do you think will happen to Dr. Lear?"

"We can't answer that," said Maggie. "We don't know."

Barron raised his brows. "There's a lot of chit-chat going around."

"It's only natural that there should be chit-chat, given the circumstances," Maggie replied evenly.

"The college is conducting interviews, as we speak, to hire a new head of the drama department, and all we know for sure," Raine added, "is that Rex is being evaluated by a psychiatric examiner to determine if he is competent enough to stand trial."

"You don't think he is, do you?" Then after a beat, "Good Lord, you don't see any chance of his getting off?!" Dr. Whitman thundered.

"I seriously doubt he'll walk," Raine interjected.

Dr. Whitman rose from his chair in preparation to leave, muttering as an afterthought and with unusual flurry, "Diabolical, what he did!" Some of Barron's carefully repressed anger carried on his voice, and bitterness gave emphasis to his words. "So cleverly planned." He struck a clenched hand into his palm. "There's nothing more amazing than the extraordinary sanity of the insane! But again I ask: What do *you* think will happen to Lear? Will he be found incompetent to stand trial … locked away in an institution for the criminally insane, or will he be made to stand trial and face a jury for what he did?" He caught himself. "I'm sorry. Forgive my insistence. It's– I need to know that it's only a matter of time until justice is served. I need an answer to the question of that murderer's fate!"

The Sisters seized each other's brainwave, with Raine answering, "I expect we'll *all* know the answer to that in a few days."

They had never before seen the composed, self-assured Dr. Whitman come undone, and somehow, it rattled them too.

Before driving home from the campus, the Sisters stopped by Dean Savant's office, as per his request earlier that afternoon.

When Raine and Maggie entered the office, he gestured to two chairs positioned across from his desk. "Please, have a seat. This won't take long."

Scarcely did the Sisters sit down, when the dean continued.

"I called you in here to let you know that I've expelled Liza Berk, Sylvia Blair, and Tiffany Browne from this institution."

"It was the right thing to do, Dean," Maggie and Raine said at once.

"And we admire you for it," they added after reading each other's thought.

"I want to thank you again for letting me know that Liza Berk was expelled from the prep school she attended, as well as one other college before coming here the second semester of her freshman year. When her parents came in to see me, I pretended *I* had uncovered that information from my own fact-finding and that I could not divulge my sources; though I would never have found the info, since there was no existing record of any of it. Her father's money expunged any record of both incidents on condition she would leave those schools. As for the other two girls, they had no prior black marks on their school histories until they took up with

Liza here at Haleigh. Then, the rebukes and reprimands quickly tallied up against them. Such foolish girls!" The Dean inclined his head, his eyes narrowing, "How *did* you discover Liza's hidden track record?"

The Sisters looked again to one another, with Raine shooting the thought to Maggie, *Good thing you had those visions of Liza in her former schools, Sister. And thank the great Goddess that Aisling and Ian were able to ferret out two retired school secretaries who were willing to talk.*

"We can't tell you how we unveiled what we did," Raine stated firmly, "but we knew if you pretended to be cognizant of the fact that she'd had trouble in her former schools, and you named those schools, with the corresponding dates, Liza's parents would back off. Suffice to say we weren't at all shocked to learn any of the nasty things we dug up about Miss Berk."

"Very nasty," Maggie echoed in a quiet voice. "A more ill-bred girl we cannot ever recall encountering on this campus. Always seemed to have a puffed-up sense of her own importance, that one."

"In fact," Raine picked up where she'd left off, "we experienced a profound feeling she'd been tossed out of other schools before she came here, *way* before we even began our scrutiny of her."

"She's languishing in jail as we speak," the dean pronounced with satisfaction. "Thanks to the information you supplied to the police, namely getting Professor Lee's elderly neighbor to open up about what she witnessed and informing the police about Berk's near attack on you."

Again the Sisters snagged the McDonough vibrations speeding through the room.

"Wait a minute! Her parents' lawyers haven't gotten her out on bail?" they exclaimed, slightly stunned by the dean's reply.

"We were figuring Berk would be out on home arrest or something," Maggie remarked in a tone of surprise. "Well now, that's good. Very, very good."

"When her parents came in to see me, we had a long talk; and believe it or not, after I hit them with the ammunition you provided me, they admitted that their daughter had been expelled twice before, and they decided to let her stew in her own juices." Dean Savant pursed his mouth. "Let's hope it teaches her a lesson, though it's late in her life to begin that kind of lesson."

"Our granny used to say, 'Better late than never,'" the Sisters chorused.

En route to Maggie's Land Rover, Raine's phone sounded with the music of Rowena of the Glen.

"Dr. McDonough," the Goth gal's deep voice rumbled into her phone. "*It's Fitz*," she shot to Maggie.

"Raine, sorry for the last-minute notice, but can you and Maggie meet me at county lockup? I've telephoned Aisling, and she's agreed to come. I want the three of you to speak with Rex Lear's psychiatric examiner."

"When?"

"Now, if you can make it. Aisling's on her way. I'll meet you downstairs at the main entrance."

"You got it, Chief!" Raine answered. "We're just now leaving the campus, so it should take us about twenty minutes to get over there."

"Consequently," Dr. Frenic was explicating, "declared 'incompetent to stand trial' is *not* a free pass. A finding of incompetence merely signals a hiatus in the criminal proceedings. In the majority of cases, a mentally ill defendant deemed incompetent receives treatment until he is considered 'restored to competence.' If, later on, the determination is made that Dr. Lear will not be restored to competence, then commitment proceedings will be initiated."

"That's what we thought," Aisling, the former police detective, replied.

The Sisters were seated with Chief Fitzpatrick in an alcove of an examination room at the Braddock County Prison in Unionville, where Dr. Rex Lear was being held.

"Raine, Maggie, since you worked with Lear for several years, please share with Dr. Frenic whatever you can from your own recollections and observations," the chief requested, sitting back in his chair. "I've already briefed the doc on the Sleuth Sisters, though I didn't have to. He's fully aware of who you are."

Aisling sent Raine a nod, and the raven-haired Sister plunged into everything they'd ferreted out about Rex Lear with her usual zest for direct action, being careful to protect their Time-Key.

"I daresay Dr. Lear was a respected figure on campus, so when first we brought to light clues that *he* was Professor Lee's murderer, I hardly need cite we were shaken. He was hardworking, a perfectionist, in fact; and he mentored several of his students who went on to study at prestigious drama schools, like Carnegie Mellon in Pittsburgh and the famed Actors Studio in New York City. Dr. Lear was liked by both faculty and students. He was somewhat eccentric and a tad chichi, but we all thought it perfectly suited the head of our college's theatre and drama department.

"In preceding weeks, Aisling, Maggie, and I have dug deeply into his history and his problems. To understand what made Rex Lear, to use theatrical metaphor, drop through the trapdoors of depression and schizophrenia, we had to take our search back to his grandfather, Tristan Lear, who served our country as a fighter pilot during World War II. Tristan was stationed at Warton Base Air Depot, in Lancashire, England. There, he met and fell in love with an English nurse of Scottish extraction, Gillian Shipton. The two were very much in love, but were separated when, in May 1945, Tristan was suddenly shipped out to the Pacific Theater.

"Stay with me here," she said, "this all has a direct bearing on Rex Lear's actions."

Raine poured out everything they knew about Gillian and Tristan, closing, "He never got to bid his love even a hurried farewell. Rather he sent, by way of a fellow officer, a note to Miss Shipton."

The Goth gal shared, too, everything they'd gathered about the Shipton witches, as well as everything they knew about Tristan's destroyed note and the subsequent letters. "We cannot break a covenant to tell you how we know about that segment of the Lear story, but Chief Fitzpatrick can vouch for our integrity. What I have related to you is absolutely true. Every word of it."

"So what you're saying is that Dr. Rex Lear believed that his grandfather and all his male descendants were cursed with the misery of rejected love, unrequited love … *unhappiness* in love," Dr. Frenic remarked when Raine paused in her account.

"We're not saying that curses do *not* exist, for we've dealt with such occult phenomenon in a couple of past cases, but within the Lear family … *no*. There was never any curse heaped on the males in the Lear family. *However*," Raine said, "and this is a *significant* however, a prophecy or curse *self*-fulfilled is nonetheless *fulfilled*."

The psychiatric examiner gave a nod. "I most certainly agree. The mind is a powerful force. It can enslave or empower us … plunge us into the depths of misery or take us to the heights of ecstasy."

"Dr. Lear believed in the existence of a curse because his grandfather Tristan made an unhappy marriage, as did his son, who became Rex Lear's father. And we can tell you that Rex suffered one failed love affair after another, including a bad marriage."

"Tell the doctor what we gleaned from Rex's ex-wife and from his childhood friend," Maggie prompted.

Raine obliged on both counts, concluding, "Rex Lear's ex-wife told us that their marriage was doomed from the start. Rex was always a sensitive person, *ultra*-sensitive, whose feelings were easily hurt. In addition, he never acquired any real self-esteem. Other than the applause from audiences after his plays, Rex told us once he got no genuine affection from anyone; hence, we figure that's why he went into the field he did– *for the applause.* After following our line of investigation, we believe that was why he became such a perfectionist in his craft– the applause meant the *world* to him. And our soundings confirmed what he'd told us, that he never received any real affection from anyone, including his own mother."

The Goth gal let everybody in on what they'd uncovered about Rex's mother, how she'd abandoned him as a baby, and how, after he did reconnect with her when he was in high school, she was terribly hurtful and caustic, her second rejection leaving him even more scarred and ever more vulnerable.

Raine went on to recount, in further detail, Rex's high-school rejection by his date for the senior prom, a girl Rex was crazy about, which resulted in enhanced torment from the high-school bullies. "Dr. Lear's hatred for Ken Longbough intensified over the years; thus, Rex attempted to get back at his old nemesis, whom he knew abhorred anything that smacked of Valentine's, by making it appear that Longbow was the one shooting those wounding arrows on campus.

"Maggie had a flash vision of Dr. Lear spying a few of the arrows Professor Longbough uses in his archery classes on the floor in a corner of the gym, when the vendors were in there," Raine revealed. "On pretense of tying his shoe, Rex picked them up and hid them in his umbrella. He would have murdered Longbow, if we hadn't stopped him. I'm certain the chief has filled you in on that.

"Finally, after years of abstaining from dating, for fear of getting hurt, Rex fell head over heels for Professor Annabel Lee. When she was so sweet to him in return– Annabel was sweet and kind to everyone– he believed, for a short while, that she reciprocated his feelings. We discovered she attended a couple of campus lectures with Rex over the past year, even theatre in the round at St. Vincent College in nearby Latrobe. To Annabel, those were not dates, but something one does with a friend, fellow and colleague.

"Then, to the surprise of the entire staff at Haleigh College, Annabel gets engaged during our campus Valentine Fest, and you know the rest of that story. I think you behaviorists call that last straw that triggers a break and causes someone to snap, a 'stressor.' Well," Raine tilted her dark head, "we reckoned– *dead* reckoning as it turned out– that inadvertently Annabel was Rex's stressor."

"We figured, too, that the reason Rex probably tried to murder his protégée, Miss Fox, was because he very likely knew *she* was playing him. Dr. Lear's an intelligent man, and Trixie Fox was *obvious*. By that juncture, his dark side had emerged to the point of rationalized revenge, fueling his disorder to full-blown schizophrenia," Maggie put in, having sensed that Raine needed to take some water. "We believe that Trixie Fox symbolized *all* the women who'd ever used and abused Rex, for she was *so* obvious about what she was doing.

"When," Maggie continued, "Dr. Lear attempted to poison the principals in his *Romeo and Juliet* production, we're thinking he believed Providence placed them in his path *for* the express purpose of, again, *sheer revenge*. The female and male stars of the play were the children of two of the bullies, the *worst* bullies in fact, who'd tormented him in high school. The girl playing Juliet was an understudy who stepped into the role at nearly the last minute; and, to Rex, that was destiny and a *sign*– a sign to act."

The chief set a small bottle of water before the raven-haired Sister, who, thanking him, immediately took a long swallow.

"We are all like the moon," Aisling declared during the brief lull. "We all have a light and dark side; but most of us, most of the time, keep ourselves balanced. We learn to deal with the challenges life sends us, and when we do, we become tougher."

"Rex was such a *sensitive* individual," Raine went on, "with so many emotional scars, including the belief that he and his son were the victims of a curse, that his dark side began to emerge, stronger and stronger, to *deal* with the hurts that his own psyche could not handle, until, in our humble opinion, the dark side took over. The former Rex could never stick up for himself, could never muster enough self-confidence. And no amount of campus respect, no amount of acclaim and applause was enough– again our opinion– to balance the void of love in his life, the love he determined the curse denied him."

Raine took another sip from the water bottle. "Then there's that startling painting in Lear's house of a woman, turning her back and looking disdainfully over her shoulder. Every time he looked at that image, he was re-enforcing the idea of a curse that forbade him happiness in love."

"If I might interject something here," Maggie entreated. "My cousins and I have been patrons and participants in our community theatre for some years now, and it occurred to me, after something Raine once mentioned about thinking in terms of theatre, that Dr. Lear may have gotten into an unhealthy habit of looking at things from point of view of a stage set, rather than from the point of view of reality … Shakespearean deception, revenge, accusations of betrayal, and all that."

"*Good point*. In fact, the last thing out of Rex's mouth before he took aim at Professor Longbough was a Shakespearean quote of revenge," Raine confirmed.

Dr. Frenic, who had been nodding his head with deliberate, intermittent bobs, spoke then. "Penetrating insights into our patient, ladies … and into life," he enunciated just as deliberately. "Thank you. I'm appreciative of your observations, and, quite frankly, I'm impressed– you're fully on target with your deductions."

Like all gifted witches, the Sisters could gaze into the dark hidden corners of the human psyche just as the full moon can light up the darkness of the night.

"We hope we've been of some help," the Sisters returned humbly.

Fitzpatrick stirred. "Your masterly deductions and, may I say, your discretion, have been an enormous help to my office– *again*."

"By the way," the examiner added unexpectedly, "Rex Lear's son, William, was here today to visit his father. He didn't stay long. The boy flew out of here like the Devil himself was hot on his heels, before, I'm sorry to say, I was able to speak with him. I wonder if that young man, too, will go on believing in this ridiculous curse?"

"We are going to do everything in our power to make certain that does not happen," the magickal three answered in perfect sync. "Everything in our power."

"Actually, we've already made that our top priority," Maggie commented.

"Dr. Frenic, before we go, may we see Rex?" Raine asked boldly.

When the Sisters approached the holding cell where Rex Lear was sitting on his bunk, they were staggered by his changed appearance. In fact, he didn't even look like the same person. His boyish face had hardened, and the eyes that peered out at them were windows to a dark soul.

"**You!**" he yelled, his face morphing even darker. "Why are *you* here? Haven't you done enough to foil my plans?"

"Rex, we were trying to stop you from harming anyone else, from digging yourself deeper into–"

"Always the good Samaritans, aren't you?" he snapped at Raine, cutting her off. "What about the people who hurt *me?* They *deserved* what I planned for them. And they would have gotten their due punishments, if not for **you**! **Get out!**" he bellowed, jumping to his feet, which quickly brought the guard to the cell door.

"Calm down!"

To the Sisters, the uniformed officer said, "You'd better go now."

"Goodbye, Rex," uttered Maggie and Raine sadly.

"When you're feeling better one day," the Goth gal put in, "there are things we'd like to reveal to you."

Ignoring the guard's second warning, the prisoner burst forth to seize and rattle the bars with the low visceral growl of a wild animal, his convulsed psychosis spinning out of control. "**I'll have my revenge, I tell you!**" he roared. "**Revenge for all I have suffered!**"

Time screeched to a halt when Raine and Maggie looked into Rex Lear's eyes– *and beheld madness*, his icy glare freezing them to the marrow. It was as though an archfiend were masquerading as their former friend.

In rasping speech and oblivious of the interceding guard, Lear revealed, "Didn't you wonder why I allowed you to prompt the night of the play? You're so clever. Didn't you *wonder* about that? I had *earned* the ultimate *triumph* of getting away with murder right under the meddling noses of the celebrated Sleuth Sisters!" With the gleaming eyes of a maniac, he snarled in a voice they did not recognize, a voice so chilling it held them spellbound. *"But you* ***stole*** *that from me.* ***I should have started with you!"***

Great Goddess! Maggie exclaimed in sudden, released thought to her sister of the moon, completely unaware that she was backing up in horror. *It's as if he's possessed. His face is demonic!*

He isn't possessed, Mags. We'd ***know*** *if he were, and we could help him. Schizophrenia we cannot vanquish. We must leave it to the experts.*

Possessed, as *they* were, with mingled emotions, the Sisters left the area in glum silence.

And for the remainder of their lives, they would shudder with the remembrance.

"I assure you we'll do our best to help him," the psychiatric examiner told them, when he saw their faces. "For now, it's best you stay away. I'll be in touch with Chief Fitzpatrick, and he'll keep you informed of our progress."

The Sisters accepted the dictum. For now, there was nothing else they could do. When, at last, they took leave of the Gothic, grey-stone building, that was the imposing Braddock County Prison, they stood for some minutes in the parking lot, talking.

"I'm not sure what we could have said to Rex," Maggie admitted, her eyes lingering on the poetic Bridge of Sighs that connected the Braddock County Courthouse with the county prison, through which Dr. Lear and all those prisoners since 1892 were escorted to lockup. *That rusticated archway holds* ***layered*** *energies,* she told herself, remembering the heaviness she'd experienced crossing it. *I could hardly breathe.* "All I know," she said aloud, "is we weren't prepared for what we encountered. He's not the same person we knew and worked with."

"That's exactly right," Aisling stated firmly, "he is *not* the same person. Granny always said that the heart of another is a dark forest, always, no matter how close it has been to one's own. Don't beat yourselves up over matters. We acted as quickly as we could. We always do."

"Now we have to concentrate on helping William. We can't let him go down the same dark path," Raine reminded. "I propose we go home and consult Athena for whatever she wants us to know at this point. Aisling, can you follow us home?"

The blonde with the wand checked her watch. "I know Ian is ready to put supper on the table, and I don't want to miss having dinner with my hubby and Merry Fay. Tell you what; I'll meet you at Tara afterward … say between eight and eight-thirty, and we'll get after it."

"You're on," Raine replied. "In the meantime, Maggie and I will go home and eat that great chicken fettuccine alfredo that Hannah prepared for us yesterday. It's even better reheated."

En route home in the gloaming of that eventful day, they passed by the big, rambling house where William's girlfriend, Jill Holroyd, lived. Glancing over at the Victorian residence, Raine, behind the wheel of Maggie's Land Rover, murmured, "Isn't that William's sweetheart in the driveway?" She slowed the car practically to a standstill. "Looks like she's crying."

"Stop, and let's find out what's wrong," Maggie urged.

Flipping on the turn signal, Raine pulled over to the curb and parked. Exiting the vehicle, the Sisters hurried up the drive to Jill's blue Chevy, where they stopped before the young woman, who was attempting to hide her tears, though her eyes were swollen and reddened from weeping.

"What's wrong, Jill?" Maggie inquired softly. "Are you all right?"

"Oh, Doctors McDonough, I am *far* from all right," she choked, anguish rising in a lump at the back of her throat. "William has broken up with me, and I just can't get my head around it." The girl began sobbing into the tissue she put to her face. "Why would he do that? Why? Why?"

"May we go inside," Raine asked, for both she and Maggie could see the girl was badly shaken. "It's cold out here, and perhaps we can brew you a nice cup of tea." The Sister's keen eyes caught a glimpse of the figure of a woman half-hidden behind a window-curtain in the house next door. "Besides, it's never wise to let your neighbors in on all your secrets," she said in a half-joking tone with a jerk of her head toward the neighbor's window. "We think we know why William has done this. C'mon, let's go inside. No sense standing out here, shivering."

"My parents are in Florida, so I'm here alone. I'm glad I don't have to explain my tears to them." A sob caught in her throat. "Somehow, though, I don't expect I'll mind talking to you," she said, unlocking the front door after fumbling with her bag. "Please, come in. Shall we go to the kitchen first and brew that tea? It's warm and cozy in there," she indicated with a welcoming gesture.

The Sisters followed Jill down the hall into a well-appointed kitchen, where she invited them to sit while she made the tea.

"*You* sit, darlin', and I'll brew the tea," Maggie said, taking over the task the girl had tensely begun.

Jill sank, sobbing and shaky, into a chair next to Raine at table. "You say you think you know *why* William has broken up with me?" She brushed a wisp of her black hair back from her face.

"Tell us first what exactly happened," Maggie said, setting cups, in saucers, on the counter.

Jill sighed, endeavoring to pull herself together. "William never was one for commitment. More than once, he hinted that it was because of some *craziness* in his family. That's the word he used, but for God's sake, I never took it *literally*. We've dated all through college, and as you know, we're both seniors now. However, I really can't say we're going together, because, as I said," she swept on in her torrent, "he always refused to make a real commitment. I mean, he hedged and shillyshallied whenever I mentioned it, which wasn't that often. I was so afraid of scaring him off. Then, just about an hour ago, he rang me on my cell and broke up with me. Just like that! No explanation to amount to anything, just a 'We can't see each other anymore.'" She started to cry again.

"Did you ask him why?" Raine questioned.

"Of course I did," she swiped her eyes and nose, "but he couldn't tell me, or wouldn't. All I got from him was that it wasn't anything to do with me, or so he said. He told me it was everything to do with him, with the craziness in his family that he always refused to discuss." She stood and pulled a silver tray from a cupboard. "I'm being a terrible hostess to two of my all-time favorite teachers."

"Nonsense, we can see that you're stressed, and we want to help," Maggie returned, resuming the tea preparation.

"I know he's upset, *terribly* upset, and understandably, about his father." Jill flopped down into a chair, coughed and blew her nose. "It was such a shock." Her eyes met those of the Sisters'. "Hit both of us like a ton of bricks, and it's put a great strain on William. I suppose that's what he meant by the craziness in his family. Does he think insanity *runs* in his family; is that it? Is that what he meant? I couldn't get him to talk … oh, what's the use? What's the use?"

She lapsed into more weeping, while the Sisters waited for her to calm.

"I know William's father must've had some sort of breakdown to do what they say he did, but insanity in the *whole* Lear family?!" Jill shook her head. "Why, William is the sanest, most … well-balanced person I know! Or thought I knew."

"Tea's ready," Maggie said in her quiet voice, filling the cups, and then adding two teaspoons of sugar to Jill's at the young lady's request. "Our granny always said," she smiled, "'Where's there's tea, there's Hope.'"

"Granny liked to say, too, that Hope stands for '**H**old **O**n, **P**ain Ends,'" Raine put in with a smile.

"Come," Jill stood, setting her cup on the silver tray and attempting a thin smile of her own. "Let's take our tea into the living room now. Dr. McDonough," she looked to Maggie, "will you be so kind to carry the tray? I don't trust myself. I seem to be shaking all over."

When they entered the parlor, Jill snapped on a couple of lamps, bathing the old-fashioned, tastefully furnished space in warm, golden light. Persian rugs adorned the dark hardwood floors. The walls were paneled in a pale-blue damask, the furniture antique rosewood with the rich glow of fine wine. A Degas of ballet dancers hung over the ornately carved mantlepiece, and tall potted ferns embellished the corners.

Setting the tray on the pink marble coffee table, Maggie's attention was immediately captured by the Degas, which whisked her back in time to a sunny, April afternoon in Paris. She had been a teen then, strolling with her parents past an art gallery, when she espied, in the window, a bold pastel by Edgar Degas. She looked harder at the print over the fireplace. It was the same scene, and she remembered how she'd felt when Degas' ballet dancers threw her imagination into a whole new gear. In that pivotal moment, within the quick movement of a danseuse's whirling pirouette, she arrived in the exciting realm of the Great French Impressionists. Then and now, she drew in her breath. The effect the Degas had on her was *dizzying,* for that was the defined moment in time when she adopted painting as her avocation.

Funny I should think on that now. I must take my sketchbook to Montana on our spring break, she told herself anxiously. *Why am I feeling uneasy?* In another dizzying moment, via one of her flash visions, she knew the sketchbook would come in handy, and again she drew in her breath. *I won't dwell on this now; I'll get overload. Goes to show, however, everything happens for a reason!*

"Please," Jill was saying, "make yourselves at home." She moved to one end of a dark-blue brocade couch where she sat.

Released from daydream, Maggie took a seat on the couch as well. Raine lowered herself into a recliner across from them, before a wall covered with framed family photographs. On impulse, she stood and, sipping her tea, began to peruse the pictures. "Yours is a beautiful family, Jill," she commented, determined to inject a little balm into the prevailing situation. "Ooooh, who's this little chap on the pony?"

"That's my father when he was a boy," their hostess replied in an absent sort of way.

Raine continued to view the family images, quietly sipping her tea.

In the interim, Jill resumed pressing Maggie. "Do you think that's what William meant by the craziness in his family? Does he think insanity runs in his family, and he's afraid to make a commitment to me?"

"Ordinarily, I would say find a man who ruins your lipstick, darlin', not your mascara; but, Jill, please don't give up on William," the redheaded Sister urged, leaning forward to pat the girl's hand. "You're right. He *is* considerably upset about his father, and he's likely self-conscious and ashamed about the turn of events. It's *had* to have taken a great toll. Nonetheless, *don't give up on him.* Magick happens when we don't give up, even though we might want to. The universe always falls in love with a stubborn heart. *Trust* us. You do trust us, don't you?"

For answer, Jill again burst into tears, until, finally, with a nod, she whispered, "*Yes.* Yes, I trust you."

Maggie kept wanting to reach out and comfort the young woman with a hug, but the thought occurred to her that it might be best to let her cry it all out first. "If you have faith in us," the redheaded Sister went on, "then give us a chance to talk to William. We *will* be talking with him, and though we can't promise anything, we would wager that, after we sit down with him, he'll be calling on you to get back together."

Still standing before the wall of photographs, Raine asked, "Are these," she indicated a wedding photo, "your parents?"

Swiping her eyes with the tissue and giving a little hiccup with a shaky sigh, Jill replied, "Yes."

"You look like your mother," Raine said, putting forth aimless questions and remarks in an attempt to take the girl's mind off her woes. "Drink your tea, dear."

Jill took a swallow from her cup. "Ummm, it's good," she said contentedly. "Mother says I look like my great-grandmother. That one's of her," she pointed to a vintage photo in a silver frame. "She was a nurse in Pittsburgh. My family's *from* Pittsburgh; it's where I grew up. We've only lived in Haleigh's Hamlet for five or six years. After my father opened one of his hardware stores here, my mother fell in love with the Hamlet, and we sold our Pittsburgh house." To Maggie, she redirected, "Do you really think so? Think he'll want to get back together?"

"I think he will, after we talk to him, get him settled down, so to speak." The Sister smiled, tilting her redhead, "I'll just bet he comes over here, hat in hand, and asks you to the Valentine Fest Dance, which, by the bye, is tomorrow night. How time flies! Raine, did you hear us? The Valentine Fest ends tomorrow night with the dance."

"Yes," the distracted Sister answered, "I heard." To Jill, who was sipping her tea and looking much calmer, she said, "Who's this?"

Jill's dark-blue eyes rested on the photograph Raine was indicating. "Oh, that's Uncle Mortimer, isn't he a hoot? That was taken at a New Year's Eve party here in this house. He was dressed as Father Time."

The Sisters spent several more minutes chatting with Jill, trying to cheer and reassure her that William would come round, once they had a chance to reason with him; and they promised they would speak with him first thing on the morrow.

"We'll ring him tonight to arrange a meeting in the morning," Maggie said, rising.

"We want *you* to be available for that meeting too," Raine said unexpectedly, causing Maggie to shoot her a searching look.

"Yes," Raine said, accepting Jill's hug, "you be available tomorrow, say from nine in the morning on. "I believe you should be a part of our discussion with William."

"Thank you," Jill said, embracing Maggie, who had opened her arms to her. "You've both been very kind."

When the Sisters were back inside the Land Rover, Maggie voiced the question that was pressing on her mind. "I know you've some sort of plan for getting them back together. I can almost hear the wheels turning."

Raine glanced at her watch, then started the car and pulled out onto the road. In the glow from the street lamp, her green eyes sparkled. "I'll tell you all about it en route home. It's getting late. Before we know it, Aisling will be at our door. We've work to do tonight, and we best get to it ... right after Hannah's reheated chicken fettuccini."

"We all have our own life to pursue,
Our own kind of dream to be weaving,
And we all have the power to make wishes come true,
As long as we keep believing."
~ Louisa May Alcott

Chapter Nineteen

By the time Aisling arrived at Tara, Raine and Maggie had already prepared Athena for the scrying session in their sacred attic space.

As per their custom when scrying, the Sisters were seated in a semi-circle facing Athena, behind which a Himalayan salt lamp, recently added by Maggie, provided a soft glow in addition to a cleansed, tranquil environment.

Straightaway, the redheaded Sister began a comfortable breathing pattern, allowing all the stress and negative energies to flow completely out of her body as she exhaled. At once, her two sisters of the moon followed suit, breathing deeply: *Healing energies in ... negative energies out.*

"Healing energies in ... negative energies out," Cara repeated, as she, too, slipped effortlessly into the meditation.

There was a peaceful silence as the magickal trio, with their poppet, applied themselves to their quest.

Several more moments slid by, after which Maggie began to chant softly, "Athena, as we go into a trance/ Bestow on us the magick glance/ Take us back in time today/ Reveal what happened come what may/ Back to Freckleton, England, post war/ Show us Gillian Shipton; open the door / For secrets to be unlocked/ Within the hours of the clock/ That you have chosen for us to learn/ ***The facts!/*** For ***that***, we now return!"

Henceforward, the seated, black-robed Sisters pictured in their minds' eye their vibrations mounting to harmonize with the antique sphere, as the colossal crystal ball's powerful energy began to swell, coursing through them and around them. *The magick was working– just as it should.*

"Remember, expectation is *not* helpful," Maggie gently reminded. "We know from experience, we must vanquish any and all anticipations and probabilities. We will see what Athena wants us to see– nothing more, nothing less."

Though the Sisters were becoming more comfortable with Athena, it was ever so much more challenging, this particular session, to keep from becoming antsy.

Thrice Maggie chanted their plea.

"Now, let us allow our minds to become as clear as the crystal. *Relax* and gaze, with peace and love, into the ball's mysterious crystal cave."

"Calm and centered," Cara sang softly. "Ca–lm and centered."

Maintaining their gazes on their crystal oracle, the McDonough witches virtually beamed magick, and within the mystical amethyst orb, the familiar ghostly grey mist made its appearance. It was sudden like– Maggie's movement of hands, the chime of the downstairs clock, Raine and Aisling's subtle smiles– and, in a *poof*, the magick was there!

"Our connection with Athena has been crafted," Maggie drawled. "The door is opening. Let Athena's mists draw us in."

"Off we go …" warbled Cara quietly.

The lit lamp behind the huge purple ball illuminated the moving mists therein. Sluggishly did the haze stir at the start, then faster, then little by little again, before the crystal began to clear.

"Wait for it … we can never rush the magick. Eeee–asy does it. We are afloat," Maggie droned, the hum of her voice matching the heartening purrrrrr of the Merlin cats at their feet.

As the ball's mists cleared, the redheaded Sister, careful not to raise her voice, cautioned melodiously, "We might see and hear what we do not foresee. We realize this is so, but Athena knows best what we need to know," she rhymed smoothly.

Maggie drew in another breath, releasing it as she easily held her focus. She was breathing as one with Athena– breathing as one with the all-inclusive globe of Universe– breathing as one with the stream of Time– past, present, and future. "Do not try and make sense of anything till everything has faded away, for attempting to sort out will only break our spell and bond with Athena this blessed day. Simply *allow* the scenes, one into the next, to *flow*."

"*Calm and centered as we go*," Cara trilled.

The Sisters were discovering that each session with their crystal oracle was easier than the last, just as Grantie Merry promised.

Meanwhile, inside the crystal ball, there emerged a daytime image of a small, stone post office, where a lone woman, in wool jumper and skirt, was sorting mail. Of a sudden, the image showed Gillian Shipton entering the building. She was sporting a long, hooded, dark-purple cape, and except for the civilian clothing, she appeared virtually the same, though there was a melancholy in the violet eyes the Sisters hadn't previously perceived.

"Morning, Gillian," the postmistress greeted, handing her a small bundle of mail. "I'm sorry 'bout yer mum. Suppose it's lonely f'r you now that yer mum and yer gran are both gone."

"Thank you, Kate. Yes, it is rather. I've been thinking about going to live with my cousin in America. She's invited me several times."

As the Sisters watched, they noted the calendar on the wall. *February 1950.*

Inside Athena's crystal depths, the postmistress was watching too, watching Gillian as she looked with discontent through her mail.

"You still think about yer American, don't you?"

Gillian nodded; then, with a sad little smile, turned to take her leave.

For a shamefaced moment, a quiver of uncertainty flustered the woman who, for so many years had charge of the small post office. Her countenance mirroring guilt, she called after the retreating Gillian, "Wait! Forgive me, Gill, but I was terrified to tell you whilst yer gran and mum were alive. I knew they never gave you his letters. I could tell *that* every time I'd see yer face somewhere here in the village."

Gillian froze. "Letters?" she asked, spinning round to lock eyes. "What are you saying, Kate? Do you mean to tell me that Tristan *wrote* to me?!" she shrieked with dazed expression.

Kate reflected for a weighty moment. "Many times. Canny remember straight off f'r how long he wrote, but I know he penned many a letter, wrote f'r months 'n months, so he did." Her face went scarlet when she delivered the ensuing tidings, "And yer mum," she swallowed, reluctant but determined to form the words, "yer mum posted a letter to *him*. After that, he never wrote again."

Gillian stood as if transfixed, and the Sisters saw two tiny spots of red tint her high, blanched cheekbones.

"Cor blimey, Gill, you've gone as white as a bloody gannet!" Kate stared, reaching out, "Do you want to sit down?"

When the stunned Gillian shook her head, the postmistress burst suddenly into speech.

"I culdn't tell you, Gill. I jus' cudn't! F'rgive me, I was afraid, afeared they'd put a spell on me 'n mine! You know what they were!" Kate clapped a hand to her mouth, as if she'd suddenly said too much. "How they cud be, i-i-if they thought someone went again' th'm!" she sputtered in conclusion.

Gillian gave a start at the remarks, but words failed the muddled young woman. In a fog, she turned and walked unsteadily out of the post office, her thoughts and emotions in turmoil.

Outside, she leaned against the small building's stone wall, breathing hard as if she had run a long way. Closing her eyes for a timeless time, she managed to conjure, in her mind's eye, a vivid image of a soulful Tristan.

A few moments later, floating upward through a confusion of dreams and memory, she surfaced like a person who'd been close to drowning. "I must get hold of myself. This confirms what I always believed," she murmured, as she started with purpose on foot for her cottage, "my Tristan did not forsake me. Now, I'll no longer call my longing a dream. By the lasting love I bear in my heart, *it's a plan*."

Striving to contain excitement, the Sisters were grateful to have their suspicions verified by their crystal guide. It felt good. Reining in their emotions, they hoped the magickal movie had not ended, as the huge amethyst ball filled anew with the accustomed smoky mists.

Abracadabra and a second image began taking shape inside the crystal. This time, the Sisters were looking at Gillian on board ship, at the rail, staring out at a choppy, grey sea that looked deep and cold and hungry. She was bundled up against what they sensed was a stinging, salty wind, but the look on her face revealed determination.

As Athena's swirling mists effaced the scene in her crystal depths, Maggie's soft voice helped keep the Sisters centered and focused. "*Relax.* Athena will show us what she wants us to know."

"Re—lax," parroted their poppet. "Steady on now. *There be more ...*"

Sure as the great Goddess' crown, yet another image was taking form within the ball. Slower to manifest this time, though emerging clearer and clearer, arose the familiar reflection of Haleigh Hamlet's quaint little park by the river. The Sisters recognized it immediately, and by the blossoms on the trees, they deduced it was spring.

Standing off to the side, behind a towering oak, was Gillian Shipton! Through the foliage, she was intently staring at something—or someone. At first, the Sisters could not detect what or whom, until the mists completely dissipated, and they saw—

Seated on one of the park benches, Tristan with a petite brunette woman holding a baby.

Raine sucked in her breath. *Tristan, his wife and their son.*

There was no doubt about it– but still the Sisters wondered …

Within the crystal ball, tears streamed down Gillian's face, as she leaned against the stout trunk of the tree for support, resting her forehead against the bark to weep quietly. "Oh, Mum, Gran, you had *no* right," she whispered. *"You've torn out my heart!"*

After several poignant moments, the forlorn woman drew herself up to wipe her eyes with a handkerchief she pulled from her purse. There she stood, perfectly still, with eyes closed. Thenceforth, after a final fleeting look, she turned and, squaring her shoulders, walked briskly away.

Before the Sisters could let out their held-in breaths, the vision was gone, expunged by Athena's effacing grey mists– to swirl the globe crystal clear. The Sisters knew now, for certain, that Athena's magickal movie had ended.

"Gillian came here, to Haleigh's Hamlet," Raine stated with verve, once they thanked for the information they received. "I told you that was a World-War II photograph of her in her blue nurse's uniform that I saw on Jill's wall. She must have come to Pittsburgh and settled there. Sisters, it's time to do further investigation of our own. Let's conclude our scrying ritual in the proper manner, and then get down to our computer. I'll bet you that Gillian … Ellis Island! Yes, that's it! There would be a record of her entering our country. Immigrants came through Ellis until 1954."

"You two go on downstairs and get started, and I'll finish smudging Athena," Aisling offered. "Then I really must get back home to my hubby and daughter."

"Thanks, Sister. We promise to ring you later!" Raine and Maggie chorused, as they hurried from the attic to Tara's tower room where they did their paperwork.

This was a charming room. From floor to ceiling, bookshelves encircled the high, round chamber, where the tall windows were crisscrossed with ecru lace curtains. The carpet and walls were an intense hunter green, and the woodwork, as throughout the manse, was a dark and enduring English oak.

Raine perused the text on the computer screen. "It's what we thought. Gillian's sponsor was her cousin, who had come to America before the war and who resided in Pittsburgh. Now, let's connect the dots.

"We know, from Athena, that Tristan told Gillian the name of his hometown here in Pennsylvania, and he mentioned that it was in the Pittsburgh area. Gillian's obit tells us she began working as a nurse at Pittsburgh's Mercy Hospital shortly after she landed here, became a citizen straightaway too and later, in 1957, married a successful, Pittsburgh businessman, Niall Atkins, to whom she bore one child, a daughter she named Elizabeth. Gillian passed away at her daughter's home in 1989." The Goth gal printed off the pages and sat back in the padded leather office chair, thinking, one leg crossed over the other, the raised foot jiggling with eager energy.

Maggie was deliberating too. "Gillian must not have passed her sad tale down in her family," she said, brushing a finger across the big Herkimer Diamond– the talisman of researchers– they kept on the claw-footed law table that held their computer, fax machine, and printer.

"Perhaps she *did* tell her tale, but I'd wager she refrained from divulging Tristan's name. Gillian was the type of woman who would never have wanted to cause a problem for him. She would *not* have wanted to come between him and his wife and child," Raine mused aloud.

Maggie gave an emphatic nod. "That's very astute, and I couldn't agree more. Little did she know how miserable was his what-can't-be-cured-must-be-endured marriage. And though William knows Tristan's tale, he wouldn't have realized that Jill was a descendant of his great-grandfather's lost love, due to the simple fact that on the female end of things, the surnames would have changed down the line. You know, I am just now realizing how much Gillian and Jill resemble one another, and how much William looks like Tristan. If William had a mustache, he'd be the spittin' image of his great-grandfather. And Jill's ebony hair, alabaster skin, and violet eyes … why, except for the modern hairdo, it's Gillian all over again."

"Great Merlin's staff! Jill and William have no idea," Raine stated quietly, "*no idea* they are direct descendants of the ill-starred lovers with whom this sad saga sorely started!"

"They have no idea *yet*, but they will tomorrow; and *tomorrow*, the story will take a whole new direction," Maggie smiled. "We're going to tell them, just as we told Emerald, that they have the power, at the moment of revelation, to say, 'This is not how the story's going to end.'"

"Right," Raine replied by chucking Maggie an appreciative glance. "We'll tell them that *life* is their story … hopefully, the rest of their *life together*. They must write well and edit often."

"And we'll put the pen in their hands!" the Sisters exclaimed in sync.

***

"So you're telling me there never was a curse on the men in the Lear family?" William uttered in disbelief, clambering out of the soft, deep chair to his feet. He crossed the short distance to the bay window, staring out at the snow-glistening trees for several moments, wistful.

The Sisters had telephoned him the evening before to ask to visit him at his home, where they were now seated in the living room. His mother was out, due to a dentist appointment and needed shopping, and thus Raine and Maggie were happy for the chance to speak with the frazzled young man alone. They started from the beginning, informing him of everything but the time-travel and their sessions with Athena.

The shimmer of the Sisters' words prompting him to seek further confirmation, William turned brusquely from the window, his analytic mind taking over. "But how do you **know** all this? You've told me how you discovered some of it, but not all; and frankly, with all due respect, I–"

Maggie interposed with a soothing authority. "Attributable to a covenant we've made, we cannot share all our sources with you. Through years of teachings, training, and intuition, we guard our secrets well. Suffice it to say we have to, but I think you know our reputation. Over the years, we've worked with not only our local police, but with authorities from other areas, including the FBI and even Interpol. I believe you know, too, that you can trust us. We would never tell you anything that wasn't true. That would be breaking an even *greater* covenant with ourselves and the Divine."

"William, if we thought for one moment," Raine cut in, "that a curse really did exist, we'd help you to vanquish it. We would *never* tell you that one did not exist if it did. On the contrary, we'd be planning straightaway to rid you of such a bane; and trust me, we've dealt with curses."

"Your poor father was tortured by the belief that a menacing curse hovered over the males in his family, yes; but, William, he wrestled with so many torments that it finally became too much for him. Did he ever tell you about his mother?" Maggie asked kindly.

"Only that she left him and his father when Dad was a baby." William ruminated over the situation in gloomy silence, sinking into a chair facing the Sisters, who were seated, opposite, on the couch.

Raine recounted everything they had ascertained about Dr. Lear, after which the magickal pair could tell William was deeply affected, for again the young man rose and wandered to the window, where he stood, staring out for a protracted time, finally turning to face the Sisters.

"Dad never told me all that. He was forever in the clouds. You know what I'm saying– never in the moment. And I never knew … realized how much he was hurting … all tangled up in conflicting affections. I guess he went through a lot."

The Sisters sensed he was thinking about his own tortured relationship with his father, for his eyes became moist with unshed tears– tears that likely had been held back for years.

"On the other hand, please don't reverse the blame onto your mom for your parents' failed marriage," Maggie thought to mention. "As your mother told us, with Rex's belief that a curse existed, their marriage was doomed right out of the gate."

"We don't want to see *you* throw away happiness with both hands," Raine imparted with conviction.

"We do *not* want you to suffer and be tortured over something that simply doesn't exist!" Maggie put in with vehemence.

"Look," William began, running his fingers through his dark hair, "I don't mean to dispute or doubt what you've told me, but you can't deny that one Lear male after another had a bad marriage. One after another was unlucky in love. **You can't deny that!**"

"We aren't attempting to deny it. William," Raine said patiently, "a prophecy or curse *self*-fulfilled is nonetheless *fulfilled*. Do you know what I mean by that?"

"What you believe becomes your world, William," Maggie expounded in her gentle way. "What you think about, you bring about. That's a *law*– the Law of Attraction. We call it the Great Secret. It's a *powerful* thing, the mind. It can create, *manifest*, what you program. Especially if one *dwells* upon whatever it is, and especially if *emotion* fuels those thoughts."

Raine tagged on the additional consideration, "Never say anything about yourself you don't want to come true. The universe responds to what we believe about ourselves. I AM," she enhanced, "are two of the most powerful words *in* the universe, because what you put after them shapes your reality."

"That's right!" Maggie jumped back in with both feet. *"What we think, we become. What we feel, we attract, and what we imagine, we create."*

"Y-yes, I suppose I believe that," William replied somewhat noncommittedly. After several more moments of silence, however, he added, "It does all seem to fit together to make sense."

"OK, now we're getting somewhere! You're using your head, putting the grey cells to work for you," Raine interrupted, bringing her hands together with a jolting clap. "Education is not so much the learning of facts as it is the training of the mind to *think.*"

"In all honesty, my mother and I have spoken of the things you mentioned many times," William set forth, "and my pastor has told me pretty much the same things; but I always believed they were telling me what they did just to make me feel better about," he hesitated as though slightly embarrassed, groping for the words to express the residue of his thought, "well, about who I am." This last told the Sisters he harbored resentment toward his father.

"In philosophy class, we've discussed this stuff more than once, and–" the young fellow stopped abruptly, fixing the Sisters with an intense look before venturing to make his request. "Look," he began, raking his hair with his fingers, "I'm only going to put this question to you once. What you tell me, I'll accept, because I do trust you both. Are you holding anything back? Have you told me the *absolute* truth about everything?"

"We would not come here, to your home, and tell you anything *but* the absolute truth, William," the Sisters answered in nearly the same words, their McDonough eyes burning with candor.

Raine looked to Maggie and twinkled, after which the latter, who was virtually trembling with excitement, sent her sister of the moon a tiny nod.

"Now, William, there *is* one more piece of information we came here today to tell you," Raine began, noting that the handsome young gentleman's face took on a receptive air. With delight, then, she revealed that he and Jill were direct descendants of the star-crossed lovers, Tristan Lear and Gillian Shipton.

"You two even look like your great-grandparents," Maggie said, pulling from her bag images of both to hand to William, who stared hard at them with an unreadable appearance.

"I'd say that's a sign right *there*," Raine flung out a hand to the pictures, "that you two are destined to be together."

The Sisters were touched to see William's eyes brim over. "Wow, this is a powerful lot to take in! No family curse. No evil ... *unhappy*, at least, destiny. The nightmare of our lovelorn family chronicle is over, and now you tell me Jill and I–" His face, which had momentarily brightened, suddenly fell. "Oh God, I'm such a fool! I've made a *terrible* mistake," he confessed, spilling out that he'd broken up with Jill the day before. "And after she's been so good to me, trying her best to help me through what happened with my dad!"

"As I tell my students, making mistakes is far preferable to faking perfections," Raine replied evenly. The Sisters said nothing else; they just waited whilst the young man finished pouring out what he'd said to Jill. Confession, they knew, was good for the soul.

Finally, Maggie spoke. "William, it's time for you to be *happy*, past time, and no one can steal your *happy* unless you give them the keys. Just let things *flow* ... it's said that the love we hold back is the only pain that follows us in the hereafter."

The Sisters' inundated student stirred with a groan, again running shaking fingers through his hair in what they recognized as a nervous habit. "I wasn't very nice about how I broke it off. In fact, I was downright *cold*. I acted that way, so she'd accept that it was *over*. I'd gladly eat humble pie, the *whole* pie, if only–" Tears welled in his eyes as they sought those of the Sisters'. "I'm an ass. A prize ass! I've made a *disgusting* mess of things. I doubt she'll ever speak to me again, let alone want to get back together."

"Oh, I don't know about that," Maggie said, turning toward Raine, as her Mona Lisa smile curved her full, crimson lips.

"Why don't you ask her?" Raine grinned reassuringly. "She's right down the street in the Will-O'-The-Wisp Tearoom– *waiting for you*."

"Oh, and you might re-invite her to the Valentine Fest Dance tonight on campus." Maggie smiled broadly. "Why, I think this is just about the most romantic story we've ever encountered! Rivals any faerie tale I've ever heard or read." *Goes to show– nothing wrong with a little benevolent interfering.*

With a heaping spoonful of witchcraft stirred into the brew.
Raine twittered with laughter, so pleased was she to witness the
change that came over William. He was in that moment a different
man. The lightness was now actually visible, and it cleared what had
been a heavy atmosphere like a good smudging. "Love and laughter
will do the trick every time. *Romeo and Juliet* with a happy
ending!"

"Don't you mean a happily-ever-after ending?" Maggie trilled
her silvery laugh, for when she turned toward William, he'd already
snatched up his coat– and was bolting out the door.

"No one is too old for faerie tales."
~ Dr. Thaddeus Weatherby, PhD

Chapter Twenty

That night at the Valentine Fest Dance, the gymnasium, void of vendors, was vibrant with symbols of love. On the stage, a local disc jockey was playing vintage love songs from a variety of eras, whilst the decorations of hearts and cupids lent a festive ambiance to the otherwise sportive setting. A giant poster depicting a fundraising thermometer proudly displayed the fact that the energetic Student Union's month-long Valentine Fest exceeded their projected goal of $100,000 toward the restoration of Old Main.

"Vendor sales, the Valentine faculty tea, this dance, combined with donations from alumni and local businesses and topped with the grants Haleigh's been awarded have made the Valentine venture a *huge* success," Raine stated with pride.

"It was a good thing we made up large batches of our potions and perfume when we did," Maggie remarked. "Sold out completely. Our Hannah did a great job hawking. In fact, she's proven herself, with her homespun wisdom, to be a clever salesperson. *Bless her.*"

Raine and Beau decided at nearly the last minute to attend dressed as Scarlett and Rhett. When Beau grasped the Sister's hand to waltz her across the dance floor, the couple reaped a number of approving glances.

His costume included a black cutaway over snug, dove-grey pants and matching vest with attached dickey and cravat. Reminiscent of a dashing riverboat gambler, the brimmed, flat-crowned hat was also dove-grey. Beau's ebony hair and mustache, together with his rakish grin, made him the perfect Rhett Butler.

Raine's frock, over its hooped underskirt, was a head-turning replica of Scarlett O'Hara's unforgettable, green velvet portière gown. The famous gold drapery-cord belt sashed her small waist, and Scarlett's matching plumed cap sassily topped her head. To complete the look, Enchantments costume shop supplied a Scarlett wig with the outfit.

Whilst the raven-haired Sister and her Beau glided round the floor to Bette Midler's "Wind Beneath My Wings," her tip-tilted green eyes rivaled Scarlett's as she delighted in the song that, years before, they had christened *their* song.

The merry movement of Granny's earbobs at her ears, Raine declared in her husky voice, "Beau, Grantie says you'll never find a better dance partner than your own spirit, but I so love dancing with you."

As throughout the fest, ticket holders to the dance were encouraged to sport fancy dress of romantic figures from either history or fiction; and glancing round, it was evident to the Sisters and their partners that most of the attendees had indulged in this whim of fantasy.

Creative impulse incited Maggie and Thaddeus to come as the Irish hero, Brian Boru, and his fiery redheaded queen, Gormlaith. This Sister's medieval gown was also green, an exquisite gossamer creation of spider webbing that looked as if it would dissolve at the touch of a hand. Emeralds kissed her ears; and at her throat rested the emerald, over a thousand years old, that had once belonged to Boru's goddess-like queen. Thaddeus acquired the museum piece a decade before at a famous auction house, presenting it to Maggie a couple of years ago, after he'd commissioned the ancient green stone be surrounded by tiny, glittering mine diamonds and set into the point of a twenty-two karat yellow-gold circlet.

Thaddeus's knee-length tunic was a heavy, whiskey-hued affair trimmed in faux fur and sashed with a wide sword-belt. Tights and high boots sheathed his muscular legs; and he carried a replica, round medieval shield with claymore sword, both of which he left at their table, whilst he and Maggie took a spin round the dance floor.

"Ah, never underestimate the healing, feel-good power of music, dance, wilderness, the ocean, or moon and stars. I always feel so free when I'm dancing. What're you grinning about?" Raine asked Beau, as magick flared between them and they whirled to the romantic music, her gold earrings catching a beam of light from a wall sconce.

"I was thinking of Gladys Washington," he replied, pausing, *à la* Rhett, to push his hat further back on his head. "I called her into the clinic today on pretense that I wanted her to give a young cat owner a bit of advice. I told you she always had the oldest cats in Braddock County. All but a couple lived to be twenty, and those were healthy to the end. Anyway, I presented her with the little black kitten I rescued the other night along the road into town. It was crying, alone, wet, hungry, and scared. I took it back to the clinic for shots, a warm flea bath, good food, and vitamins. It's a male, and Gladys has already named him Ace.

"I told her you and Maggie would take excellent care of her kitty, should she pass away before him, but to make certain to state in her will that she bequeaths the cat to you. Apart from her arthritis, the old gal seems in good health. By the way, it was her birthday today. I had *no* idea of that when I gifted her the kitten. I took it as a good sign."

"How old is Mrs. Washington? Did she say?" Raine asked.

"Eighty-five," Beau answered. "She said she planned on hiring the neighbor boy to help her with the heavy kitty litter. She was devastated the last time I saw her, when her Angel Baby passed away, but *today*, she was like a new person. She might be elderly, but she's sharp.

"She told me that after each of her cats passed over, she beseeched the Divine to let her hear from the departed feline within three days, three being the most sacred number, as well you know. She said she always got an answer, loud and clear. She mentioned that it was either a line of dialogue from the TV, words spoken by a friend, or a line from an opened book. Whichever it was, the response had, to use her word, a *glimmer* to it. You know what I'm trying to say– the answer *stood out* each time.

"Gladys is a very spiritual person. Truthfully, I'd go so far as to call her a *mystic*. The third day after Angel Baby crossed the Rainbow Bridge, she said she was just getting on her computer, to visit her Facebook page, when this popup occurred with the image of an elderly woman sitting on a bench, crying, and next to her the ghostly image of a cat. The words in the caption descended over her like a benediction: 'I stood by your bed last night. I came to have a peep. I could see that you were crying; you found it hard to sleep. I mewed to you softly, as you brushed away a tear, "It's me. I haven't left you. I'm well; I'm fine– *I'm here!*"'"

Raine's feline eyes shimmered. "When we pass over, there's a trilogy of questions put to each of us humans: 'What love did you learn? What love did you give? What love do you bring home with you?' We were gifted that a few years ago by a brilliant sister of the moon, High Priestess Kelly, at the Blue Rose Coven Seminar out in Washington state. We never forgot that very special sister or her wise words."

Beau kissed her forehead, as again his teeth flashed in that lazy Rhett Butler smile. "Speaking of love, have you given any more thought to my proposal, my *literal* proposal?"

Raine regarded him through the thick veil of her lashes *à la* Scarlett. "I have, and my answer is *yes*, but don't get too excited. It's actually the same answer I gave you in Salem, at Emerald's handfasting– *yes but not yet, not now*."

A low guttural sound issued from his throat.

"Oooh, Beau, you must admit that you've at least gotten a *yes* out of me, as long as it's a traditional Celtic handfasting, and not a muggle wedding. And as long as we live at Tara, and that you understand and accept that, at this moment in time, I'm not yet ready for … *the big* step. Not yet."

Beau knit his brow. "I don't see a problem with living at Tara. Look, I would never come between you and your sisters of the moon, nor would I interfere with what you do. I know you have a destiny to fulfill. I've come to accept that, as I'm certain, over time, you've noted."

She looked deeply into his eyes, thinking, *Years ago, as a very young girl, I programmed what I wanted in a soul mate. I ordained a man with a Celtic warrior spirit, hot blue eyes, strong healing hands, and a poet's heart. My wish **has** come true with Beau.*

"Granny once told us that we each have two eyes, two hands and two feet, but only one heart. So it's up to us to find the twin heart of our soul mate. I have no doubt, Beau, that you're my soul mate, and I do admit," Raine acquiesced aloud, reaching up to gently sweep an errant lock of ebony hair from his forehead, "you've been a lot more accepting of what I do, but I'm simply not ready to take the ultimate step. I promise one day we'll handfast in a beautiful ceremony of our own making; but for now, I want to leave things like they are between us." She smiled sweetly, intensifying the dimple in her cheek to imitate Scarlett, "I won't think about this now. I'll go crazy if I do! I'll think about it tomorrow. Tonight, I just want to dance and dance and have a good time!"

The inspirational Carole King's "Will You Still Love Me Tomorrow?" from the artist's *Tapestry* album began playing, as Beau executed a waltz underarm turn, pulling her firmly back to him to caution–

"Don't wait too long, Raine." Something in the ring of his words captured her attention. And she was very conscious– that was *all* he said.

"My Maggie," Thaddeus began, as he often did when he had something significant to say to her, "I must put the question to you again, the question with which I have not plagued you for some time now. Have you considered my proposal for a handfasting within the next few months?"

"Two weeks. It's only been two weeks since you last asked me. Thaddeus," she pronounced softly, "I told myself after my divorce that I would never marry again, and I shan't, not in what Raine refers to as a muggle ceremony. However, coming as I have, to love you more than I have ever loved anyone in my life, I have decided to answer you as I did in Salem, with a *yes ... which is actually a promise.* I promised you then, and I promise you now that I will consent to a handfasting, a Celtic handfasting; but, as I am certain Raine is conveying to Beau as we speak– *just not yet.*"

"I am well aware of the fact that you, Raine and Aisling have a very tight bond, and I know how you feel about your home, Tara. I would never attempt to take away your home or your time with your sisters of the moon. I would never attempt to impose my name on you, or take away your identity in any way. Therefore, allow me to set forth the rest of my proposal. We could live part of the time at Tara and part time at our mountain retreat; and later, when you, Raine, and Aisling inherit the Salem cottage, you and I could spend part of the time there too. I'm thinking we could sell my house. We won't need it, for I would like for us to travel as well."

He gave her a speculative glance before continuing. "You know," he began, "I was contemplating retiring from teaching before you and I became a couple. I would doubtless have taken an early retirement for the express purpose of travel. Then, when we began our relationship, and we started time-traveling–" he paused to collect his thoughts, smiling magnanimously. "I daresay, time-travel must be magickally rendering me more youthful, because I don't think I want to retire just now. Or is it you, Maggie? Are *you* the reason I feel so much more vibrant and alive?"

She chose not to answer with words, opting rather to nuzzle closer to him, as they spun breezily round the dance floor.

The professor laughed softly, kissing her forehead. "Being madly in love lends one a remarkably *ageless* feeling, I think. Let's make a pact to love, laugh, and live each day to the fullest because each day is the oldest we've been and the youngest we'll ever be again."

"I do love you madly," Maggie cooed. "Not for your looks, your gifts, or anything else superficial, but because you sing a song only *I* can hear."

When the music ended, the couples returned to their table to sit and chat, while the disc jockey took a short break. It was during this interval that the Sisters noticed William and Jill entering the gymnasium. Spying the Sisters, they waved and started forward.

"They make a strikingly handsome couple," Maggie stated, a pleased smile manifesting on her face.

"Yes," Raine perceived, "truly healthy, happy, and very much alive."

As William and Jill approached, Raine and Maggie were both struck by the resemblance the pair bore to their ancestors, especially in their fancy dress. William was wearing the World-War II uniform of an American flyer, complete with brown leather jacket and brown, beaked crush hat. He sported a mustache, courtesy of Enchantments, and the look on his face told them he was a changed person. Jill's dark-blue uniform and Forties coiffure harmonized with the one Gillian was wearing in the photograph on her great-granddaughter's living-room wall.

"We wanted to tell you again how much we appreciate what you did for us," William proclaimed with warm sincerity.

"It does our hearts good to see you so happy ... *together*," the Sisters replied.

"You've been given a great gift, not by us," Maggie revealed, "but by whatever you call the Divine, an opportunity to put an end to, though a nothingness, nonetheless a *darkness* that would have gone on for generations."

Jill smiled. "I think your ... *magick* had something to do with it."

"Oh, it's *magick* all right! Everything is magickal when you see it with the heart," Raine put in. "There's nothing more powerful than the *Love* vibration, and you two hold the *power* to set into motion a whole new tradition for the Lear family."

"I've asked Jill to marry me," William announced suddenly and with the beam of high spirits.

"And I said *yes*," the young woman declared with visible joy. "We told my parents and William's mother, and here's the plan. We're going to live in the third-floor apartment of my home. It was once a maid's quarters. A couple of years ago, my parents remodeled it to lodge whomever they hire as house-sitter-caretaker when they travel.

"Now then," Jill bubbled with the expectation of their plan, "after graduation this spring, while William's going straight through for his doctorate, I'll be working full time as a counselor at the high school. When William begins his career, I can go back to college and get *my* doctorate. We'll be a great help to one another. My parents spend part of each year in Florida, so for those months, we'll have the whole place to ourselves. They're relieved that the house won't be left empty while they're gone each year, and they won't have to worry about hiring a caretaker. It was tough finding a live-in they could really count on. Something always seemed to happen to necessitate hiring someone new."

A thought popped into Jill's head, her face lighting up with excitement as her violet-blue eyes danced. "I asked my mom about my great-grandmother Gillian, and she told me that Granny Gillian *had* talked about her lost love. You know, told her story in the family, but you were correct in your assumption that she never divulged her American flyer's name."

"Show them the ring," William urged.

Jill held out her left hand to display the antique engagement ring crafted in the shape of a crowned heart holding two prominent stones, a garnet and a white sapphire. The heart was surrounded by tiny white sapphires, and white sapphires graced the crown.

"I was saving the best of the tale for last," the blushing girl giggled. "You're never going to believe this, but when I spoke with my parents on the phone about William and me, Mother told me to go to what she referred to as her 'Treasure Box,' that she kept cached away in her bedroom, inside her granny's old trunk. She said I'd find a smaller box inside, an ancient-looking, very ornate, wooden ring box. You should see it! It's tall but small enough to fit in the palm of my hand, the sort of box that Romeo might have used to present a ring to his Juliet. I'm *amazed* that Mother knew exactly where she'd stashed the ring. She's forever putting things away in what she calls a 'safe place.' The place is usually so safe she can never find the items again.

"Anyway," Jill rushed on, "inside that unique little box was the ring Granny Gillian received from her American flyer, who purchased it for her in England during the war. Mother said Granny Gill had never worn it for fear *her* mother and grandmother would learn of the seriousness of the relationship with her American. Even so, Mother told me the ring was passed down in her family, but that she never wore it either. She was afraid she'd lose the keepsake, for it was big on her, and she didn't want to have the gold cut. It's 9 karat rose gold, dating to the 1890s. The 9k hallmark is very English, and the old rose gold has such a lovely pink glow. It fits *my* finger perfectly."

The Sisters caught each other's winged vibes.

"Hmmm," Raine mused, studying the love token. "Tristan probably purchased Gillian's ring in an antique shop, and I'd wager the shop keeper told him the story about it." She turned her gaze on Jill. "Do you know what this is?"

The young lady appeared to be totally in the dark, spurring the Sisters to shed light on the subject.

"It's a 'Witch's Heart'!" Raine and Maggie responded in sync.

"The folklore of the crowned Witch's Heart reaches back to the seventeenth century or earlier," Raine explained. "But the tradition of giving a beloved a crowned heart, a Witch's Heart, really became popular during the Georgian era, roughly from the mid-1700 to the mid-1800s. The Witch's Heart came to mean that the wearer had *bewitched* the giver. The two stones together signify commitment, the crown loyalty. White sapphire is said to bestow a marriage with abundant happiness; and garnet is the stone of physical love, of strong and intense feelings– *passion and desire*."

"At the risk of sounding fanciful, it's the perfect engagement ring for you," Maggie sighed. "Think about it. Truth be told, it's the *highest degree* of perfect. The purification of love. This ring was symbolic of your granny Gillian's *secret*, her wistful, bittersweet secret; and now, the Witch's Heart has finally given up that secret, its destined power, to the pair of you. It's just sooo romantic!"

"I don't want William to have to spring for an engagement ring when he needs every cent of his money to go toward his doctorate, and I agree– *this ring is perfect*. In fact, I *feel* as though it were destined for me," Jill stated, looking up at William with love in her eyes.

"One day," he said, returning the love, "I'll buy you a big diamond."

"*No!*" Jill replied with vehemence. "I appreciate your sentiment, darling; but this ring, Granny Gillian's Witch's Heart, will continually bring us an abundance of blessings. I sense her watching over us. No, I won't *ever* want to replace it with another."

William gave a brisk nod. *"Destiny,"* he murmured almost to himself. "I have to agree."

The Sisters acknowledged this with a solemn bob of their heads and with Maggie concluding, "Your Witch's Heart will forever be a symbol of enchantment, mystery, and romance."

"We'll show you how to keep your ring cleansed and charged," Raine offered. "Oh, and William, I have something for you. You will need to cleanse your home, for your sake and your mom's, not from any ole curse, just from negative energies, mostly fears." The Goth gal pulled a bundle of white sage and a small folded sheet of paper from her purse. "It's a cleansing chant: Cleanse this space, remove the past," she read. "I've found my happiness at long last. Fill this space with joy and love; send Your blessings from above!"

The Sisters chatted for a bit with Jill and William about smudging, sun cleansing and moon charging, after which–

William went on with his news, "Like Jill's parents, my mother's happy about our decision. Of course, it helped that *you* both," he gestured toward Raine and Maggie, "spoke with her yesterday and with Jill's parents over the phone. So it seems like everything is falling into place. It's a *good* feeling," the gallant young man declared with a smile that was clearly Tristan's.

Maggie sent Raine a subtle wink.

"Yes," Raine replied, "when you find your peace, everything falls into place. We're so pleased and happy for you."

William shook his head. "How could I have ever felt cursed, when this beautiful, *amazing* woman loves me? Yet it was only yesterday when I thought everything in my life was falling apart."

Looking up at him, Jill clutched his arm, "So did I."

Maggie smiled. "Sometimes when things are falling apart, they may actually be falling into place."

"Every time you're tempted to react in the same old way, in a negative manner, ask yourself if you want to be a prisoner of the past or a pioneer of the future. Always remember that *your life's what your thoughts make it*." Raine gave a little titter. "Easy really, all y' have to do is keep the Faith; hang on to Hope– and Love will do the rest."

"You're such great teachers," Jill enthused.

"The heart's our first great teacher," the Sisters replied.

"And it's not meant to be a dustbin for life's worries. It's a golden vessel for collecting all the sweet moments of life. *Be happy!*" Maggie laughed, picking up Jill's hand to squeeze it. "That is, first and foremost, what the Divine, whatever you call the Divine Source, wants for each of us."

The disc jockey returned to his post to spin Celine Dion's "My Heart Will Go On."

"Oooh, I love that song," Jill stated softly, snuggling closer to the man she so loved.

Yes, the perfect song for this perfect ending, Maggie imparted to Raine. "We can't always choose the music life plays for us, but we can choose how we dance to it; and I think it's time you ask your lady to dance," the redheaded Sister said aloud to William, placing Jill's hand in his.

Raine nodded, sending the thought to her sister of the moon: *Ah yes, music is what feelings sound like.*

Maggie smiled in silence, *So endeth another adventure ... or should I say* **quest***?*

Both, the Goth gal tele-cast in reply. *And I'm more than ready for our next adventure!*

***

After the dance, when Raine, Beau, Maggie, and Thaddeus entered The Man In The Moon pub for a nightcap, Aisling and Ian were there, holding a table. When the pair spotted them, Aisling stood and beckoned them over. This time, several people did turn to stare at the costume-sporting foursome whilst they made their way to their favorite table in the back.

"I guess people do gawk at the Sleuth Sisters when the costumes are as far-removed from modern life as these are," Raine whispered to Maggie, when they were pulling off their warm capes.

"Raine," Ian exclaimed, "you look exactly like Scarlett O'Hara."

"Fiddle-dee-dee," she laughed. "I declare, suh, how you do run on!"

"So how did things go at the dance?" Aisling queried.

"As Time Goes By" began playing in the background, Raine and Maggie shared with Aisling and Ian the news about William and Jill, concluding, "Once again, I'm happy to borrow a quote from the Bard, 'All's well that ends well.'"

"Hi-di-ho, folks!" Ron Moon greeted *à la* the Forties' flair, as he approached the table. "I couldn't help but notice you when you came in. You gals always look stunning," he smiled at the Sisters. "But tonight ... well, all I can say is 'Wow!' Mind if I join you for a few moments?"

"Please!" the Sisters and their other halves cried in unanimous expression, after which the ladies thanked their friend for the compliment.

"Let me get your order first," Ron said, commencing to do so. "On a night as frosty as this, I prescribe brandy and soda."

"Brandy and soda all round," Thaddeus said. "Nothing like brandy for warming body *and* soul."

In a short while, Moon returned with their drinks, setting them atop the table. "On the house. After all you do for our town, the least I can do is stand you a drink." Then, to a comeback of thanks, he copped a chair from the next table, to sit between Maggie and Aisling with a drink of his own.

"I am amazed, again and again, by your uncanny ability to unearth hidden facts and solve the most tangled mysteries. Fitzpatrick is a good chief of police, but he's lucky to have you. The Hamlet is lucky to have you!"

"Thank you, Ron," the Sisters chimed, with Aisling remarking, "We had plenty of help."

"You're too kind," Maggie directed to Moon, along with her most charming smile.

"And you're too modest," Ron declared, thinking back on the succession of cases the Sisters solved over the years. "Not to gush, but you girls have a nose for detection, a real *talent* for sensing evil and iniquity, *and* it takes a great deal of courage to do what you do."

"I daresay, we do have a nose for sleuthing, but some villains and criminals have a real talent for hiding their wickedness," Raine stated.

"Right," Ian interjected, "and that's where the courage comes in."

"I read in the paper that Dr. Lear was declared incompetent to stand trial," Moon commented. "What will happen to him?"

"He'll receive treatment, including meds, and if he's eventually found competent to stand trial for Professor Lee's murder, he will, as well as for several attempted murders. If not, then he'll be committed," Aisling revealed in a flat tone. "Either way, he'll be confined for a long time, quite likely for the remainder of his life."

"What a *shocker* when I first learned the news! You could've knocked me over with a feather. My wife said she could almost hear my jaw drop," Ron yammered uncharacteristically, after which he took a sip of his ale. "*Dr. Rex Lear*," he shook his head in disbelief. "I would *never* have thought. I mean, he always was a markedly peculiar man, as I told you, even strange at times; but he never seemed like a fella who could do what he did. In fact, he came across as someone who wouldn't hurt a fly. And he was so gifted. Damn shame he went afoul."

"He *is* gifted," Maggie put in. "And yes, it is a shame. Dr. Lear was a textbook example of a tortured soul. There's always a satisfaction in getting our man when solving a crime, but in this case," she issued a sigh, "it feels different, though the sadness is tempered by the good that has come–"

"You know," Raine interposed with what she often referred to as snips of history, "I was just thinking that even a war cloud has a silver lining." When the others sent her questioning looks, she gave explanation. "To mention but two consolations: Plastic surgery was a result of all the horrific facial injuries suffered during World War I; and psychiatry came into its own after World War II."

The lively talk at the table led round once again to Dr. Lear.

Looking to the Sisters, Moon verbalized after a brief lull in the conversation, "I just hope the sins of the father won't be visited upon the son."

Raine and Maggie responded in unison, shaking their heads decisively, "No, William is most definitely on the right path."

"We've spoken with him at length about his father, and we're certain that William has begun to forgive him," Maggie said. "Forgiveness is an attribute of the strong, not the weak. When you forgive, you heal, and when you let go, you grow."

Ron spoke with a tinge of sadness. "True, but I'm wondering if maybe this little Hamlet of ours is not the idyllic place we all imagined."

"Oh, with all due respect," Aisling rejoined, glancing over at her detective husband, "human nature is pretty much the same everywhere. It's just more difficult to observe it closely in a place like Pittsburgh, or in *any* city; that's all."

There was a short silent interlude as everyone digested what Aisling said.

"I reckon, when you consider all the wickedness we're deluged with in the news, our Hamlet is a relatively safe ... and peaceful place," Moon decided. "As idyllic as can be in the world in which we live today."

"By the way, Ron," the blonde with the wand voiced with sudden recall as "That Old Black Magic" drifted over to them from the vintage jukebox, "the information *you* shared with us started us down the path of discovery '... like a leaf caught in the tide,'" she quipped from the song's lyrics.

"*You*," his eyes lighted on the Sisters, "are very *powerful* women, but I'm glad I could help." Moon took a swallow of his ale. "Speaking of help, I was happy to find out today that the Student Union met their goal toward the restoration of Old Main. Most of us businessmen and women in the Hamlet participated. Will the renovation begin any time soon, do you think?"

"It's supposed to commence during spring break and follow through the summer," Thaddeus answered. "The college wants most of it done by fall."

"I also read in the paper that Liza Berk's in jail. Undoubtedly a bitter pill to swallow. In my opinion, it's where she belongs. A more odious creature I've yet to encounter," Ron reacted to the Sisters' nods. "I had to toss her out of here more than once."

"*Odious* is a good word for Berk," Raine put in under her breath.

"Succinct, Ron. Quite so. She's thrived on hurting others; that's for certain," Maggie concurred. "Let's hope she's learned her lesson, though I have my doubts she ever will."

"I, too, will be knocked for six," Raine said with a nod of assent, "if the girl ever cleans up her act. Some people are just plain mean and controlling, and that's all there is to it."

"Her parents created that monster," Thaddeus blurted, "but according to the Hamlet grapevine, they are *through* cleaning up her messes. So perhaps there's hope for the kid yet. It's going to take some doing. She's got the air and ego of a tyrant, though I strongly suspect that under the bluster of that obnoxious bully facade, the superiority conduct is really an *inferiority* complex. *All bullies are insecure.* Miss Berk doesn't really like or respect herself. Hence, she has no respect or empathy for others."

The conversation continued, as the big-band sounds played on the jukebox, and laughter and happy chatter filled the air.

At one point in the evening, Maggie, Aisling, and Raine left the table to visit the Ladies'. On their way back, they were astonished to see Trixie Fox sitting in Maggie's vacated chair and cozily chatting up Thaddeus with her familiar cajoling routine. The redheaded Sister stopped dead in her tracks when Trixie extended a hand to stroke the professor's bearded face.

No scruples whatsoever, appraised the magickal trio as one united energy force.

Removing the vixen's hand from his cheek, Dr. Weatherby stated tightly, "I think *not*."

When Trixie stood and turned to go, she found herself face-to-face with the redheaded Sister, who asked in her usual soft timbre, "Why, Miss Fox, you seem positively *down in the dumps* today!" *Jeu de mots intended*, she thought with a strange smile on her face.

"I'm having difficulty finding someone else to mentor me." Some nuance in their manner made Trixie tilt her head and look sharply at the Sisters, who were fixing her with their witchy McDonough stares. "The new theatre director turned me down flat, and I have a sneaking suspicion *you* had something to do with his decision. Y' know, a couple centuries ago, you three would've been burned at the stake. At this instant, I suppose," and her glare was smoldering, "you're about to gloat with something like 'Karma's a bitch,' right?"

Maggie gave a little chortle, trading a sideways glance with her sisters of the moon before replying, "On the contrary, my dear. Karma's only a bitch– *if you are*."

"How about another round?" Thaddeus suggested, standing. "Come on, Beau, we'll go to the bar and get everyone a refill. And," the professor posed to Ron Moon, "one for yourself, landlord?"

"Thank you," he replied. "You know that's how they do it in real English pubs," he remarked to Maggie.

"Right-O," she rejoined. The Sister's eye caught sight of a tin beer sign on the wall. "'Beer is proof that God loves us and wants us to be happy,'" she read aloud. "Ben Franklin is the Founding Father who continually winks at us."

"Franklin said that?" Moon asked, surprised.

"In a letter to a friend," Maggie responded with a nod, "Ben used wine rather than beer, but the notion was his."

When Thaddeus and Beau returned, each carrying a tray with the drinks, along with fish and chips for the table, everyone cheered.

"Sea salt and vinegar for the fish and chips," Beau said, setting the condiments in the center of the table, so all could reach.

"Best fish and chips this side of the pond," Ian declared.

"Everyone," Moon said, clinking his pint with his fork and standing, "I propose a toast. He lifted his glass. "To the Sleuth Sisters for all the good work they do and for saving the day again!"

The Sisters were touched when the entire pub rose to their feet, and a bevy of faces lit up with admiration. "Hear! Hear! To the Sleuth Sisters!" the house shouted with heartfelt jubilance.

Modesty and a flood of sudden emotion forbade response, as an old English toast, that seemed verily appropriate to the Valentine mood, leaped to memory. Raising their glasses, the Sisters shouted out in cheerful accord–

"'Rose-lipt maidens and lightfoot lads!'"

Over an hour later, the Sisters and their party exited The Man In The Moon pub, calling "Good-night" to Ron Moon and the others inside. They no sooner stepped out the door when a bright shooting star burst across the night sky, leaving in its wake a trail of silvery stardust that, mirrored in Moon Lake ringed with its tall pines, was replete with enchantment.

"Look!" Raine called out, pointing upward, her face reflecting awe.

Beau, Thaddeus, and Ian all paused to gaze skyward, each reacting in his own way.

There, below the brilliance of the shooting star, was the same cloud formation the Goth gal and Maggie had seen the night they'd time-traveled, just before their Time-Key hurled them through the blustery tunnel.

"Granny always said, 'Never stop looking up!'" Aisling exclaimed. "It's a sign. You know the old Celtic legends about a shooting star, Sisters."

"Yes," Raine and Maggie effused.

"A shooting star is a sign that it's an auspicious time to make a wish; or that a witch has passed over to the Summerland; or–"

Raine joined in Maggie's recitation at the last with, "… that a wish has been *granted* to a witch."

"Oh, not just any wish," Aisling amended, "but a very *significant* wish. And, in this instance, not just any witch."

"I feel the flicker of a *knowing*," Raine stated with conviction and certainty. "That cloud formation," she pointed, "is symbolic of the Shipton witches, and that includes Gillian. *They are pleased and happy about what we did.*"

"Gillian's gran and mum *are satisfied that their secret has been unveiled and their wrong righted,*" the McDonoughs recited in harmony, with each other and a universe that did not outshine the galaxies contained within the spirits of those very special Sisters.

"Witch by birth or witch by choice, we all must listen to our inner voice. Though our paths be many, we all are one– one love, one life when day is done!" they chanted.

As they stood looking up, with stellar brilliance in their eyes and auras shimmering, a second shooting star raced beyond that captivating dome of glittering night to re-kindle the witchy cloud creation.

Aisling aimed a finger aloft, quoting o'er their granny, "'Waste not, want not.' Let's make our own wish."

The Sisters quickly switched thoughts, releasing their unified desire into the ethers.

"Starlight, star bright, shooting stars we see tonight/ We wish we may/ We wish we might/ Have the wish we wish this night!"

"Look, there goes another one!" Raine nearly shouted. "*Three's a charm.*" She was grinning like a contented Chessy cat.

"Our wish will be granted," the magickal trio chorused in delight.

"You bet it will," Aisling murmured softly. "It's already happening."

And again, their shared mystic twinkle rivaled the stars.

"Blessed be!" the Sisters called to the great Goddess, whose powerful love flamed– in each witch's heart.

"Blessed be!" Thaddeus, Beau and Ian echoed in Love and Light– And all that was Merry and Bright.

~ Epilogue ~

Raine rang off and set her phone down on the kitchen counter. "We're all prepped, and it's all systems go! Cousin Sean has taken care of our ranch accommodations, so we'll simply reimburse him when we get there. Our plane reservations are done too. On Eva Novak's recommendation, I rang up her niece, Beth Addams, who recently opened a travel agency here in the Hamlet. Nice girl, much like Eva in looks, voice, and personality. I told Beth we'd be certain to use her service again.

"Anyroad, we fly out of PIT to Billings, Montana, changing planes at Denver. Sean will pick us up at Billings Logan International. I've already given him the date and flight info. From the airport, he'll drive us southwest to New Moon Ranch, which is on Rock Creek, at the edge of Yellowstone National Park. The ranch is about a thirty-minute drive from Sean's remote log cabin." She poured herself and Maggie a second cup of tea. "Folks out West, in places like Montana, Wyoming ... the Dakotas don't seem to mind driving long distances from one place to the next. Used to it, I suppose."

"You're right about that," Maggie remarked. "They keep their gas tanks filled. It's a *long* stretch between gas stations out there."

The Sisters were enjoying a late, leisurely breakfast, a well-earned weekend respite from obligations and commitments.

"I'm looking forward to this excursion at spring break for a number of reasons," Maggie replied, taking a sip of tea. "It'll be wonderful to visit Sean, and this'll be the first time since our salad days that you, Aisling, and I will be vacationing together, *just the three of us*."

"Hmmm, New Moon Ranch is going to end up a *memorable* experience; I *feel* it." Raine rested her chin in her palms, elbows on the table. "I'm trying to remember what Cousin Sean told us about it, Mags. Let me think; so much has happened since then." After a few moments, she rattled on, "He said we'd love his friends' ranch, because, for one thing, though it's a guest ranch, it's not a golf-course-type dude spread, but a *working* ranch. Much better, that, for appeal and atmosphere."

"For certain," Maggie agreed. "If memory serves, he told us the owner, Nigel Hawkes, is a retired British colonel from out in East

Africa, and that Nigel met his wife, Marjorie, a native of Montana, when she was on a camera safari in Kenya several years ago."

"Yep, and remember, too, he said there's always an interesting mix of guests at the ranch which leads to lively conversation at the cocktail hour and mealtimes. Sean mentioned that we'd especially enjoy the colonel's 'yarn-spinnin',' as he called it. Nigel's family settled in Kenya back in the 1800s, so the colonel's got a passel o' stories to tell from the African bush." Raine sipped her tea, lost in thought. "I wonder what the mystery will be on our next adventure?"

"Mystery?" Maggie's eyes widened. "I don't recall Sean touching on a mystery."

"Of course, there'll be a mystery! I can't imagine a vacation without some sort of thrills, chills … and secrets to unearth. When I talked with him on the phone this morning, he said his friend Nigel's repertoire of stories included a very mysterious enigma … or did he say more than one?" Raine tilted her ebony head as if listening for an unseen collaborator to clarify it for her.

Like a bolt from the blue, their poppet, Cara, manifested on the kitchen counter. "Raine's spot-on. Mysteries folla you wh'river ya go. A new one falls inta yer laps whin ye're settin' still b'twixt 'n between, which ain't iver too long iv a spell, 'n ya know what I mean. Ye're *mystery magnets*, you aire. F'r sar-tain, they'll be a mystery! And I'm tinkin' like you– gonna be at least two."

"As I was about to say," Raine went on, blowing the ragdoll a kiss, "the area we'll be visiting is Crow country, so we'll likely chance encounter more than a few Crow Indians, at least I *hope* we do, because there are some pretty mystical, unexplainable stories that have survived throughout the ages in their culture."

"Yes, yes indeed. I recall that our parents did a field study on Crow land some years ago," Maggie murmured. "They uncovered some pretty scary things, if I remember correctly. Or perhaps the stories frightened us because, at that time, we were so young."

Raine drained her cup, setting it down firmly in the saucer to counter in her low husky voice, "Nooo, Mags, the stories *were* scary. 'Come-into-my-parlor-said-the-spider-to-the-fly' scary. But oh, so fascinating. Remember the creepy physical remains in the Smithsonian that our fathers spoke of?"

The flash vision that struck the redheaded Sister at Jill's home, when she decided to take her sketchbook on this trip, came crashing back to jolt her now. In her mind's eye, she peered over her own shoulder at the drawing the vision showed her sketching. "Like I said– *scary*."

"Bwahahahahahahahahaha!" Raine guffawed with sudden outburst. Leaning back in the kitchen chair, she locked her hands behind her head. "I can't wait to get there! It's been a while since we've been out West. I so loved accompanying our parents on field studies to the Great Plains, the Rocky Mountains, the national parks–" she broke off, whooping, "Magpie, I have a feeling that our spring break will be sated with mystery *and* magick!"

"I think you're right," Maggie laughed. "Both sometimes pop up in strange … er, that is *unexpected* places. Oh, and let's be sure to remind Aisling to bring the powerful astral projection ring that Grantie Merry bequeathed us. My keen witch's intuition is telling me we'll need to make use of it this trip."

"I'll bring the shapeshifter locket too," Raine commented. "I believe we'll need it as well."

"*Och!*" Cara screeched. "Whilst ye're makin' yer list, y'd best put *me* on it. Y' need t' take me wit ya."

"And *why* should we do that?" Maggie asked with genuine concern and curiosity.

"Tink about it," the crafty poppet demanded. "You can't take Athena on the plane. She's too big and heavy … and breakable. But *I*, contrariwise, am small and feather weight." She seemed to be smiling her curled-up crooked smile. "Trust me, darlin's, ye're gonna need me whaire ye're goin'."

The Sisters faced one another to utter in sync: "She has a point."

"You can make the journey in the side pocket of my purse," Maggie replied.

"Me favorite way t' travel," Cara responded in snappy salute. "*In style*."

"Raine," Maggie said, "don't let me forget to pack my sketchbook, along with a small box of drawing pencils. I want to capture a scene to translate to oils when we get home. My art's such an important part of me, and lately, I've had no time for it. Mysteries aside, this *is* to be a vacation, after all." She decided, for now anyway, to keep the scary sketching vision to herself.

At that moment, Black Jack and Black Jade came strolling into the kitchen, side by side.

"They're telling you something," Maggie said, looking to Raine. "I can't read them like you do, so tell me what they're saying."

As Maggie lifted Jade, Raine scooped Jack into her arms, gazing deeply into his pumpkin-hued eyes.

"He's telling us that Black Jade and Panthèra will watch over our Tara while we're away," the Goth gal said. *Why only Jade and Panthèra?* she asked her familiar, citing but two of the trio of Merlin cats. *Are you planning on a vacation too, Jack?*

She hugged the Watcher close to "Raine" a cascade of kisses upon his velvet face. "I love you, Jack! Your heart and my heart are very, very old friends. I cherish all our kitties ... *you and Black Jade especially,*" she whispered. "I'm putting *you* in charge whilst Maggie and I are out West. Hannah and her hubby Jim will be staying here while we're gone. Hannah'll be spring cleaning, and Jim'll be doing needed maintenance around the place, as well as caring for you and the horses. Beau will stop over periodically to check on you guys. *Please* be on your best behavior. Again, I'm counting on you."

As was his habit, Black Jack licked the tip of her nose, sending her the communication: *You're not listening, Raine! You will need to take **me** on this trip. Remember, Thaddeus won't be with you, and–*

At that moment, Tara's loud antique doorbell sounded, causing Maggie to roll her emerald eyes, "One of these days!"

Raine set Jack down and dashed for the entrance, calling in her wake, "Postman must have a package for us."

The raven-haired Sister beat a rapid retreat to the kitchen, where she set the mail on the counter to open the single parcel delivered "To the McDonoughs of Tara."

"Had to sign for it. It's from Grantie!" she exclaimed. This Sister was always as excited as a child when a parcel arrived at Tara. Impatiently, she tore the wrappings off to expose a square box covered with gold glittery paper. "Grantie usually sends packages for the three of us to Tara, knowing that, weekends, Aisling and Ian are often away from the house." After peeling off the clear tape and removing the lid, she lifted out a clear quartz sphere, about the size of a baseball. "Oh, Mags, look!"

"There's a note inside," Maggie said, opening the little card to read it aloud. "'You girls should have a *portable* crystal ball, just as you have a portable *Book of Shadows*. I sense you'll need it. Treat this oracle the same way you treat Athena. Begin by christening it with a name. As always, use it wisely and enjoy it in good health– mind, body, and spirit. PS: Don't pack the crystal ball in your luggage. One of you tuck it into your purse with Cara.'"

Shaking her head in wonder, Raine declared, her expression awed, "Grantie Merry's a marvel, isn't she? How did she know we'd be taking Cara?"

The Sisters' words prompted their poppet to throw her wee mitt-hands in the air and shake her yarn-covered head at the express moment Grantie's face appeared in the crystal ball Raine was holding.

"You'll need to take Black Jack with you too, dear girls. **Oh, don't look so surprised!**" With that, she disappeared in a swirl of silvery mist.

Told you! You'll need to shapeshift me to Sean before we board the plane, Jack tele-communicated to Raine. *No way am I traveling in a freezing cargo hold in my cat carrier, and what difference it from a moving jail cell? Nooooo way!*

Calm yourself, the Goth gal conveyed to her Watcher, *I wouldn't do that, especially since we have to change planes. Rest assured you'll travel, out West and back, as Cousin Sean.* Aloud she murmured, "Maybe you should be in human form the whole trip. Aww, I'll figure it out."

The wily look on her familiar's face paused her when she snatched his thought–

*Hmmmmm, Montana… didn't I hear on the telly that it's called "Big Sky Country"? Sounds like a place where I can let my natural feline curiosity run wild. And the call of the wild is callin' to **me**.*

There'll be none of your shenanigans, mister! The Sister's brainwave broke over Black Jack like a tsunami, causing his pumpkin eyes to open wide. *You just remember that you're going along as my … **our** personal assistant.*

"Now," said Raine after a brief recovery, "let's think. What do we name our mini-ball?" She thought for a moment, when suddenly her face lit up. "Listening to oldies must've triggered this, or maybe it was Beau telling me Gladys Washington's cat tale; don't rightly know for sure," she rambled, as she was sometimes prone to do.

"Well, for Goddess sake, what is it?" Maggie pressed.

"Angel Baby!" the Goth gal said in a burst of enthusiasm. "What say you to that?"

"Most appropriate. I *love* it. We'll ring Aisling and pass it by her, and if she likes it too, we're good to go," Maggie answered heartily.

"She'll like it," Cara put in with certitude, and though the Sisters couldn't be sure, the voice sounded a lot like Grantie's.

When they exchanged looks, the poppet flung her little mitt-hands upward again. "*I know tings!*"

Later that morning, their travel plans tweaked, Raine and Maggie were washing up the breakfast things, when they began to chant softly.

"Still around the corner a new road doth wait. Just around the corner– ***another secret gate!***"

~About the Author~

Ceane O'Hanlon-Lincoln was born at the witching hour of midnight during an April thunderstorm, and she has led a somewhat stormy, rather *whirlwind* existence ever since.

A native of southwestern Pennsylvania, Ceane (SHAWN-ee or Shawn) taught high school French until 1985. Already engaged in commercial writing, she immediately began pursuing a career writing both fiction and history.

In the tradition of a great Irish *seanchaí* (storyteller), O'Hanlon-Lincoln has been called by many a "state-of-the-heart" writer.

In 1987, at Robert Redford's Sundance Institute, two of her screenplays made the "top twenty-five," chosen from thousands of nationwide entries. In 1994, she optioned one of those scripts to Kevin Costner; the other screenplay she reworked and adapted, in 2014, to the first of her spellbinding *Sleuth Sisters Mysteries*, **The Witches' Time-Key**, conceived years ago during a sojourn in Ireland. As Ceane stood on the sacred Hill of Tara, the wind whispered ancient voices– ancient secrets. *O'Hanlon-Lincoln never forgot that ever so mystical experience.*

Fire Burn and Cauldron Bubble is the savvy Sleuth Sisters' second super adventure, **The Witch's Silent Scream** the sexy third. **Which Witch is Which?** is the witchin' fourth whodunit, **Which-Way** the spine-tingling fifth, **The Witch Tree** the haunting sixth, and **The Witch's Secret** the scintillating seventh *Sleuth Sisters Mystery*.

Watch for *Careful What You Witch For*– book eight in the bewitching series– coming soon!

Ceane crafts each of her *Sleuth Sisters Mysteries* to stand alone, though for the most surprises, it is always nice to read a series in order.

A prolific writer, Ceane has also had a poem published in *Great Poems of Our Time.* Winner of the Editor's Choice Award, "The Man Who Holds the Reins" appears in the fore of her short-story collection *Autumn Song*– the ultimate witchy-woman read!

William Colvin, a retired Pennsylvania theatre and English teacher, said of her *Autumn Song*: "The tales rank with those of Rod Serling and the great O. Henry. O'Hanlon-Lincoln is a *master* storyteller."

Robert Matzen, writer/ producer of Paladin Films, said of *Autumn Song*: "I like the flow of the words, almost like song lyrics. *Very evocative.*"

World-renowned singer/ actress Shirley Jones has lauded Ceane with these words: "She is an old friend whose literary work has distinguished her greatly."

In February 2004, O'Hanlon-Lincoln won the prestigious *Athena*, an award presented to professional "women of spirit" on local, national and international levels. The marble, bronze and crystal *Athena* sculpture symbolizes "career excellence and the light that emanates from the recipient."

Soon after the debut of the premier volume of her Pennsylvania history series, *County Chronicles,* the talented author won a Citation/ Special Recognition Award from the Pennsylvania House of Representatives, followed by a Special Recognition Award from the Senate of Pennsylvania. She has since won *both* awards a *third* time for *County Chronicles*– the series.

In 2014, Ceane O'Hanlon-Lincoln was ceremoniously inducted into her historic Pennsylvania hometown's Hall of Fame.

Ceane shares Tara, her 1907 Victorian home, with her beloved husband Phillip and their champion Bombay cats, Panthèra, and Black Jade and Black Jack O'Lantern.

In addition to creating her own line of jewelry, which she calls Enchanted Elements, her hobbies include travel, nature walks, theatre, film, antiques, and reading "… everything I can on Pennsylvania, American, and Celtic history, legend and lore.

Moreover – I *love* a good mystery! Historians, in essence, are detectives– we're always connecting the dots!"

~~~

~ A message to her readers from
Mistress of Mystery and Magick–
Ceane O'Hanlon-Lincoln ~

"There's a little witch in every woman."

"I write because writing is, to me, like the Craft itself– *empowering*. Writing, as the Craft, is *creation*. When I take up a pen or sit at my computer, I am a goddess, a deity wielding that pen like a faerie godmother waves a wand.

"Via will, clever word-choice and placement, I can arrange symbols and characters to invoke a whole circuitous route of emotions, images, ideas, arm-chair travel– and, yes indeed, even time-travel. A writer can create– *magick*.

"I am often asked where I get my inspiration. The answer is 'From everything and everyone around me.' I love to travel, discover new places, and meet new people, and I have never been shy about talking to people I don't know. I love to talk, so over the years, I've had to train myself to be a good listener. One cannot learn anything new, talking.

"People also ask me if there is any truth to my stories about the Sleuth Sisters. To me, they are very real, though each is my own creation, and since I have always drawn from life when I write, I would have to say that there is a measure of truth in each of their essences– and in each of their witchy adventures."

How much, though, like the author herself– *shall remain a mystery.*

~ ~ ~

A Magick Wand Production

**"Thoughts are magick wands powerful enough
to make anything happen– anything we choose!"**

Thank you for reading Ceane O'Hanlon-Lincoln's
Sleuth Sisters Mysteries.
If you enjoy Ceane's books, help spread the word about them!

**The author invites you to visit her on Facebook,
on her personal page
and on her *Sleuth Sisters Mysteries* page.**

**May your life be replete with—
*magick!***

"The most beautiful experience we can have is the *mysterious*. It is the fundamental emotion that stands at the cradle of true art and true science."
~ Albert Einstein

Sometimes we all need a little– ***magick.***

Believe!

Printed in Great Britain
by Amazon